HIS DOLL

His Doll
Copyright © 2023 by Rainelyn

Rainelyn asserts the moral right to be identified as the author of this work.

All rights reserved. This is a work of fiction. Names, characters, places, events and incidents either are the product of the author's imagination or are used fictitiously. Any similarities to real persons, living or dead, events or places, is coincidental and not intended by the author.

No portion of this book may be reproduced, or stored in a retrieval system, or transmitted in any form or by any means, electronic, mechanical, photocopying, or otherwise, without express written permission of the publisher.

ISBN: 9798372740716

Cover design by: 3Crows Author Services

Art by: @Ebbarts instagram

First edition: February 2023

HIS DOLL
RAINELYN

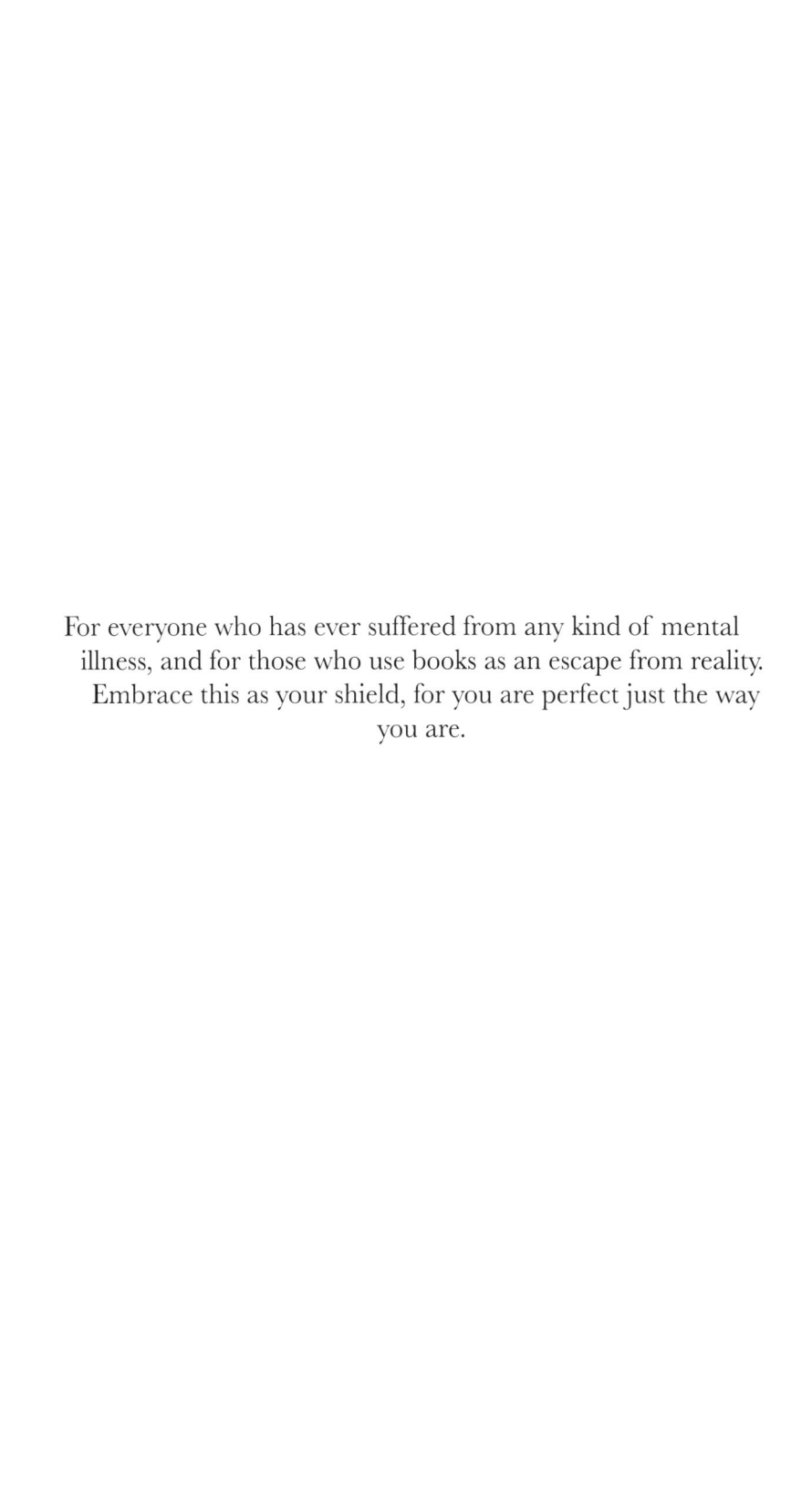

For everyone who has ever suffered from any kind of mental illness, and for those who use books as an escape from reality. Embrace this as your shield, for you are perfect just the way you are.

Spotify Playlist

Author's Note

Countless hours of research were put into this book. This book is a stand-alone and includes subjects that may be triggering for some. If you feel that these topics below negatively affect your mental health, I strongly recommend that you reconsider reading this book.

 This book contains explicit sexual content, scenes with questionable actions, characters with foul language, mentions of graphic violence against adults and minors and trafficking rings. This book also contains scenes of death and torture, as well as mentions of mental illnesses. The mental illnesses and symptoms portrayed in this book are based on my own feelings and those of the characters. You should be aware that everyone feels differently when they are suffering from any kind of mental illness, such as anxiety, depression, post-traumatic stress. The road to recovery is different for every human being, and those mentioned in this book work solely for the characters. If you feel like you may be suffering from any mental illness, I would strongly recommend seeking a professional therapist.

 This book contains characters who do questionable actions and are considered morally gray.

 If you decide to continue reading this book, I sincerely hope you will enjoy it as it is my debut book and closest to my heart.

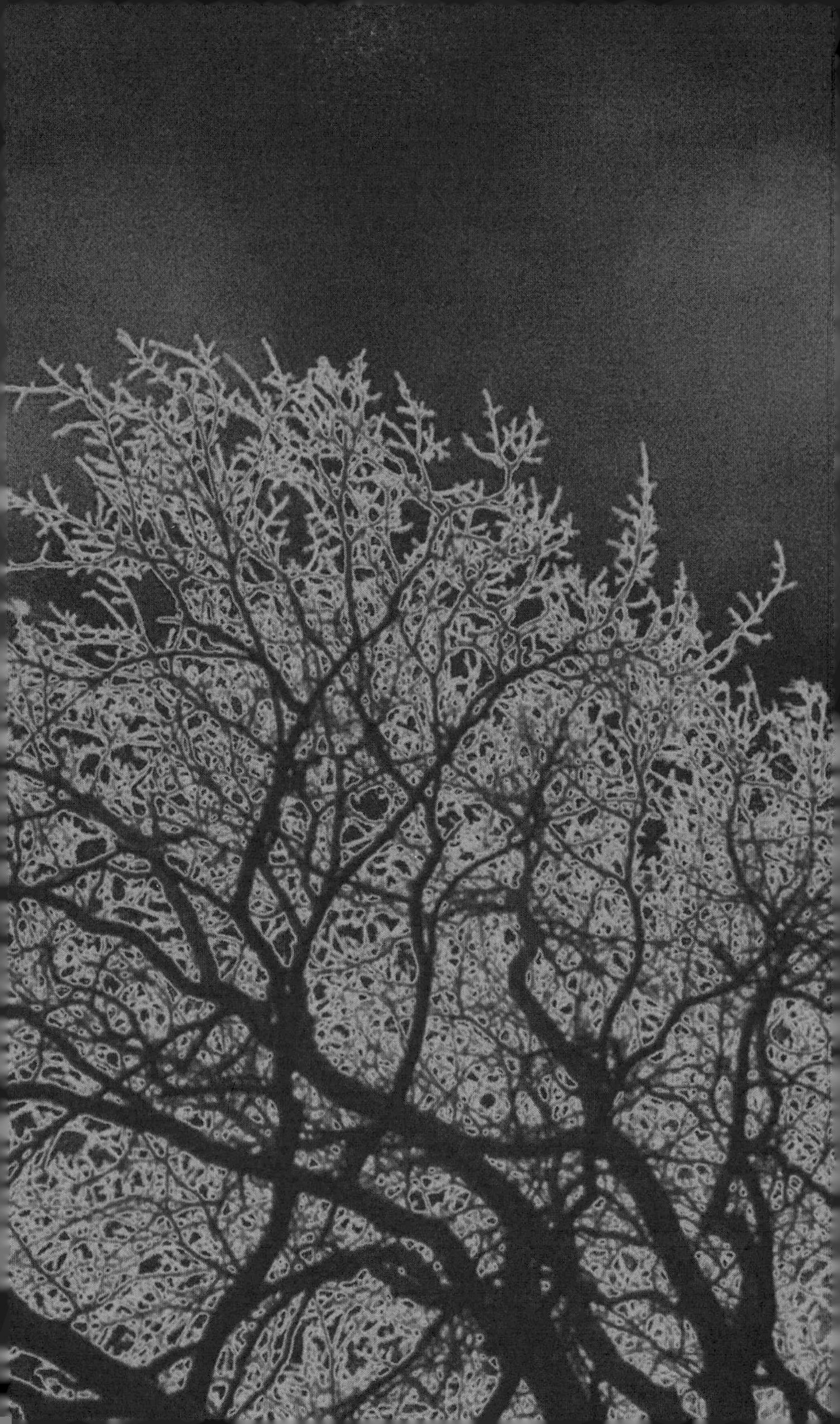

Part One

Once Upon a Time

DARKNESS. A wonderful occurrence, yet something many fear. Every twig snap, every howl of the wind sounded menacing, like a predator coming to hunt its prey, piercing them into ripped flesh.

There was nothing odder than the outside world as the darkness settled over the horizon and the last sun rays kissed the heathland. Nothing was odder than the pink and purple melting into one, becoming their true color under the moonlight, taking the last ounce of daylight with them. A safe haven for many creatures. Yet many feared the unsettling sounds of the wind's howls, the rustles in the bushes as rabbits darted forward, and the trees becoming silhouettes of monstrous things. For these people knew. When the darkness fell, they knew they were easy targets for whoever sought fun and danger. They knew the most terrible things happened during those hours when nobody had the chance to observe what was happening behind closed doors.

In the distance, sirens echoed in a monotonous sound that did not change its pitch, staying the same throughout the city.

A young mother pushed a yellow stroller in front of her figure, the only color visible from afar in the darkness. Avoiding the sirens was easy. They rarely posed any danger to the citizens. They were a normal occurrence in a world built by evil people—murderers, robbers, and kidnappers. The sirens were not to be feared, even if they symbolized that something unnerving had occurred. It wasn't the mother's job to pay attention to the sirens. It was the police's job. Their job was to deal with the evil creatures and make the world a safe place for future generations.

How was her child supposed to live in that cruel world? No, she did not like that thought.

The mother should not have ignored those sirens that chilly night in October when the orange and musky-colored leaves had fallen to the ground.

The leaves left the trees as dead as they had been the year before and the one before that. A natural cycle. They grow and then they die, leaving behind the trees as they fall. Just like humans who grow up and then die when their time has come.

She shouldn't have been as naïve as she had been that night. For what had she been doing in the streets under the shining moonlight when she knew it was not a safe place to stay in the darkest hours? It was not safe for a woman to be alone. There were too many horrific things that had happened in the dark for her to ignore. She was paranoid, turning at every bush rustling and jumping at every sound the night's animals made. Surely her child in the stroller could not defend her if something were to happen.

Apprehensiveness filled her, but she ignored it and picked up her child, despite having knowledge of what could happen.

"Go on, my Rora." The mother urged her daughter as she ran out to the playground, giggling at the excitement of being outside again for the fifth time that week.

The chilly October air blew in the breeze, dragging leaves with it and producing a deafening sound. Coolness spread through her, forcing her to close her jacket. Her eyes were glued to her daughter, observing her as she was swinging on the swing set with a smile that showed her gums. A warmth spread throughout her body, and she realized she couldn't have been happier. Despite her daughter's absent father, she managed to pay the bills on time every month, work a full-time job, and raise the girl who had become her everything.

Rora had never met her father–a mistake, the mother realized. Too many questions were asked about him.

"All my friends have a mother and a father. I only have you," the little girl had exclaimed one time when her mother picked her up at the kindergarten.

They'd had a mother-father day, where everyone brought pictures of their parents. The daughter had brought a picture of her mother and one of her grandmother, causing the other children to look strangely at her.

Children were nosy, always wanting to know everything. They had no boundaries and could throw out any words without knowing the consequences of them.

How could a mother explain to her child that she didn't know who her father was? It had been a one-night stand.

A mistake, she realized once again.

It was stupid of her to be so stubborn to have sex with a random man at a party while being somberly drunk. Despite that, she never regretted her decision to keep the baby during her pregnancy. Rora was her everything.

The mother—being too lost in thought—had not realized the speeding black SUV coming closer to where she was standing. As the car came to a stop near them, its wheels screeched against the asphalt from stopping abruptly, and her little girl was still swinging.

In the blink of an eye, everything had changed.

The sound of sirens grew louder as they drew closer; children screamed inside the SUV, and metal was kicked against its doors. That didn't seem to bother the four men getting out of the car. They drew their guns at her.

Her first instinct had been to shout for her daughter, to tell her to run away as quickly as possible, but the words were stuck in her dry throat. She watched in fear as two of the men came closer to the girl who was still swinging without a care in the world. She did not notice what was going on around her. The mother screamed for her daughter, urging her to run away from there, and begging her to never look back. Everything had blackened the second after her screams, her body thrashing down on the cobblestone. She did not understand why, and for a few seconds, she felt nothing.

Only numbness filled her blank mind, and her soul was shattering.

It wasn't until the pain settled over her—a pain so deep and raw it could rip open her entire flesh—that she truly feared for her life.

In her last moment, she could see her daughter's tears as they streamed down her puffy cheeks. Her attention was drawn to the two men pulling her daughter towards the SUV. She could do nothing, for she felt the pain taking over, ripping her open from the inside out, flames inside her skin burning her alive. She could only watch as her daughter disappeared in the black SUV speeding away from there.

    The sirens came closer by the second. It was too late. The mother's mind clicked into place.

    She should have taken the sirens as a warning.

One Year Later

THE PLACE IN FRONT of her seemed demolished. In the old house, mold covered the walls and the windows were cracked. A musty smell permeated the manor. Her eyes were drawn to the trees swaying in the wind while she was sitting on a bench outside, covering herself with a jacket to keep warm. Autumn was in the air and the leaves were falling from their mothers. A season full of symphony and changes from the warm summer leaves. It was the time of year for crisp autumn leaves, horror movies, and hot mugs of tea in the evening.

At Grimhill Manor, they forbade such traditions as Halloween. They didn't even let the children carve pumpkins. Yet the girl could remember all the times she and her mother had baked cookies for the tradition. The smell of freshly baked bread mixed with the musky-sweet smell of a leaf pile was something glued to her memory. She could remember them being huddled up on the couch, each with hot cocoa in their mugs as they watched movies together. She remembered it as if it were yesterday, and oh, how she wished it were.

When the leaves fell from the trees, they brought back memories of that night.

Her most dreadful night.

The night when they stripped her of her freedom, only to never give it back again. They thrashed her inside a black car with tinted windows—a car with screaming children in the back seats. The mere sight of those children had been terrifying itself. Their clothes were ripped from fighting to get free, their mouths were taped, and their hands were tied behind their backs.

It was a sight she wanted to forget but never would.

As horrible as it sounded, she had been glad she wasn't alone in the mess, for she did not know how she would have survived otherwise. On that horrible night, they had introduced her and the other children to the mysterious manor with its squeaking floors and whispers everywhere she turned.

A moment of silence fell over their surroundings. The wind stopped howling, and the children playing indoors stopped laughing. There was a ringing bell in the distance, the one that indicated it was time for a meeting. Together with the boy beside her, they headed into the house. Silent sentences fell between their gazes on the way, both equally shocked by the ringing. They had forgotten it had already been a month since the last game played out. Theodore took her by the hand and made sure she made it safely into the house. He was the first person to have ever talked to her when she arrived at the manor, and they had been inseparable since. He was the *only* person. Everyone else looked strangely at her, murmuring things about her, spreading rumors, making her

feel like an outcast. They said it was because of the color of her eyes.
    They hated her eyes.
    Theodore loved them.
    Theodore protected her.
    She was lucky to have him.
    "It's time to play hide-and-seek!" called the master of the house from inside. While he spoke, his voice remained steady and calm, attracting everyone's attention.
    "Come on," whispered Theo in her ear as he motioned for her to keep on walking towards the master.
    The house was an eerie place, with creaking wooden floorboards that were heard during those hours of the night when the moon stood highest in the sky. Cobwebs surrounded the roof's all corners, making the house look like it hadn't been cleaned.
    Halfway through the parlor room, the girl sensed something flickering in the corner of her vision. There was a black and white light behind the bookshelf in the left corner. A shiver curled through the hair on her back and spine, her heart pounding at the sight of the mystical thing. As fast as it had appeared, it disappeared again, leaving her with the feeling that she was being watched. The girl remembered the tales that had been told to her when she first arrived. She could still feel her body's fright at the mention of it, still remember the goosebumps, the desperation of wanting to run away as far as possible.
    Many years ago, there was a middle-aged man living in a secluded mansion together with his family. In the deepest forests, far from civilization, they built the mansion.
    Grimhill Manor.

The tale says that the man could see mystical creatures lurking in the darkness of the woods and see shadows in the left corner of the attic. There was even a rumor that he could hear child-like screams at night, and hear the voices of ghosts calling for him to save them. The man did not pay attention to the voices. Someone allegedly placed a curse on the decaying manor. A curse in which children appeared at their doorsteps without a logical explanation, dressed as dolls. He was told by the voices that the only way to save himself and his family was to take care of the children. The tale says that the children eventually turned into real dolls. Many years later, the man's son found his father's body in the dungeons below the house after the man became crazy. Our master claimed the curse to be true once, and the children were all there for one purpose.

To be his dolls.

And no one dared say otherwise.

According to an ancient legend, the man's corpse was still lying there. No one had access to the vault leading into the dungeons. And the rumor would explain why there was a smell of rot and decay outside the vault. It was the smell of rotting meat and had a nauseating effect. To say it was creepy was an understatement, especially for the girl who was only seven years old at that time.

She walked behind the other girls in the manor, towards the left side, dreading to see the flicker once again. They parted ways. Theodore stood behind the boys on the other side of the room. Within minutes, everyone living in the manor had gathered to form those two separate lines. The children who identified as neither girl nor boy, as both, or didn't know what to identify as, were forced to stand in the line the master thought most suitable for them. In that way, the master disrespected many of the children's feelings, which they found unacceptable. No one could do anything about it. Everyone was too afraid.

The newcomers looked around out of curiosity at the room they had never been to before. A black SUV arrived last week with dozens of children. A car exactly like the one who had taken her a year ago. The newcomers were the only ones who weren't aware of the house rules. The children who had been here for months, even years, already stood obediently in their lines as their eyes raised to look at the master. An eerie silence settled over the room, and whispers were heard. The girl wondered if anyone else could hear them, if anyone else could see the flicker of light she had seen earlier, or if she was a lunatic.

Everyone in the left line had their hair tied in two braids on either side of their shoulders. Each girl wore a gray dress. Outsiders would mistake them for being real-life, human-sized dolls.

Like the curse had predicted.

Ancient paintings surrounded them on the parlor room walls. As the girl observed them, she noticed their black and white colors. Her understanding was that those paintings were from a bygone era and that they represented different people who had lived a long time ago. Many of them wore white wigs like those that had been popular over a century ago. Her eyes filled with a great deal of unpleasantness regarding the paintings, making her shudder. The people in the paintings watched her, observed her every move, her every breath. Maybe they were the ones whispering to her, making her aware of every mysterious thing that happened.

It looked like the furniture around them inside the parlor was from the Victorian era. The paper covering the walls was golden with yellow floral patterns.

"The rules are simple," shouted the master for everyone to hear. "You hide. The first ten to be found will receive their long-waited punishment."

The seven-year-old girl turned her attention to him. He was standing in front of the children, explaining the rules. Her heart was drumming in her chest, noisy and desperate to escape the confines of the bones imprisoning it. Fear crawled from her bones to every cell in her body as her ears roared from the blood rushing. The entire parlor room was filled with a mind-numbing silence as everyone listened for further instructions from the master. It was not her first game since coming to the manor, but she feared it would be her last. Being the obedient girl that she was, she followed all the older children's examples of being quiet and standing with a straight posture to appear more sophisticated. Her mother had taught her that as a child.

The man's gaze swept across the room, inspecting all the children to see that everyone was behaving as they should and that no one was breaking any rules. But as his jaw tightened and the look in his eyes darkened, she realized that someone in the room had broken a rule. There was a newcomer boy standing diagonally in front of her in the second row. A boy whom she recognized. She had watched him getting dragged inside the manor, handcuffed, last week. The boy's eyes darted all over the room. It was apparent that he wanted to escape, but what he did not understand was that there was nowhere to escape.

Death was the gateway to freedom.

In his mind, he thought he was whispering, but he was talking loudly as he mumbled to himself.

"God, may God help me," he repeated over and over again. His voice quivered, breaking.

In a matter of seconds, his head shifted from right to left. He spun around in a desperate attempt to find somewhere to run to. The small boy bounced against the children in front and behind, causing them to roll their eyes and mutter in anger. They looked at the boy with frustration, but their facial expressions were void of emotions, just like everyone else's. No one dared to show emotions. He was breathing loudly where he stood. He and all the other boys wore gray suits.

It was too late for the little boy.

The master, who stomped forward from his seat further on, had already spotted him. The little boy's body shook rapidly as he noticed the master's attention on him, the fear in his eyes clear, and he took off to run away.

Within seconds, a gun went off, and the boy's lifeless body fell to the ground. The master smiled contentedly before returning to his place behind the desk as if nothing had happened. As if he hadn't just killed an innocent boy. All the children flinched at the sudden sound of the shot echoing through the walls. Fearing that they would become the next lifeless body, they immediately resumed their positions. The seven-year-old girl fought back the tears that threatened to fall down her cheeks, her eyes stinging from the tears brimming her eyes. From the corner of her eye, she could see the pool of blood forming around the boy's dead body. A light flashed before her eyes, a voice piercing through her ears in agonizing pain before it went silent. No one reacted to the voice. Had they heard it?

Those who surrounded the boy as he was shot were covered in a sticky liquid.

His blood.

After the substance had splattered on them, dark, red splotches stained their faces and gray suits.

It looked like something from a horror movie.

And to them, it was.

Their shoes had too become sticky and been painted red instead of their normal clean white. Their faces said it all. The disgust and terror they felt were overwhelming.

An indescribable feeling filled her body. It was as if a rock were pressing against her chest and squeezing her lungs. Whimpers were heard from a young girl somewhere in the line behind her, though the little girl could do nothing but appear unfazed. It was such a strange sight to see people so uncaring yet so caring. Deep inside, they grieved for the lost life, but on the outside, they had to show no emotions.

Just like real dolls.

As if nothing happened, the master exclaimed, "I'm setting the clock now. You have a few minutes to hide before I seek."

Before the seven-year-old girl realized what was happening, she was the only one left in the room. Her eyes watched all the other children run away in a mass of panic to hide. Some children tripped over furniture, causing them to fall to the side, however their only concern was getting out of the parlor room in time. Not even a second had passed before they were up on their feet again, running for their lives.

A chill crawled up and down the girl's spine, but her legs remained glued to the ground. The fear of what might happen set in, making it impossible for her to run away and hide like everyone else. For a second, her muscles were too paralyzed to function.

"You'd better hide, dear Aurora. Otherwise, you will suffer the punishment that only a loser deserves."

The master appeared in front of her and his hand lifted to stroke her cheek, causing a lump to form in her throat. As the girl closed her eyes, she thought about her beloved mother. The young girl knew her mother wouldn't want her daughter to die from being too afraid to run away. For her mother's sake, she had to run and hide. Using her legs, her muscles seemed to function again, and she fled from the parlor room without knowing where she would end up. Whenever the girl tried to move forward, she had to zigzag around furniture that was overturned everywhere. A little over an hour ago, the room had been tidy, but now it was chaotic and a little boy's lifeless body was lying on the floor, covered in blood.

She had to force herself to swallow the lump in her throat that threatened to break into a scream. She heard children walking above her, in front of her, and behind her, trying to find spaces to hide. Trying to find a hiding place, she stumbled up the stairs to the upper floor. The clock below counted down to the end with loud ticks, and Aurora's heart sank into the pit of her throat as she fumbled to get up.

"One minute left," called a voice that could only belong to the master, and the girl managed to get to her feet.

Then she could see it, the shadow in the far corner of the room. An instinctive feeling inside her urged her to follow the shadow, and so she did. Her breath was loud when she continued to run through the corridor. As she passed several brown wooden doors, a carpet stretched through the long corridor and she followed it. The shadow vanished before her eyes, but there, at the far end, was a ladder, a small hatch poking out from the roof. In the corner of her vision, she could feel the presence of the shadow above her, whispering things to her. Things that made her quickly ascend the ladder and enter the room beyond. Closing the hatch behind her, she breathed in deeply and realized where she was. She found herself inside the notorious attic where the man had seen crazy things. Darkness overtook it. The only source of light came from the cracks in the floorboards. She hoped dearly that she wouldn't see anything that logic couldn't explain. She feared to see the shadow, to feel the presence. Not in the dark, and especially not when her mother wasn't there. It had been several months since she had last seen the woman who gave birth to her, giving her happiness and safety. A pang jolted through her heart at the thought of her absent mother.

First her father, then her mother.

She was slowly losing everyone she ever cared about, and she was terrified of losing Theodore too. He needed to survive the game. Yet she never gave up hope. One day, she would reunite with her mother. That, she would ensure. Only then would she finally find peace and be free.

A sense of coldness spread through the attic as if she had walked into the season of winter where only snow surrounded her. Chills skittered across her skin, leaving her numb. She knew it. Something was keeping her company. The presence felt strong, and it came from the left corner of the attic. The girl wanted to let out a shriek, but she couldn't. Not if she wanted to survive the game. No one was physically in the room with her, and she considered that she might have become crazy. She remembered the legend of the man who had sensed a presence in the left corner of the same attic centuries ago, and the hair on her arms rose.

Despite the presence, there was no threat, only the sense of being watched. It didn't move around, it just stared at her, as if it monitored her. She knew she shouldn't feel scared, but she felt terrified.

After a few seconds, she understood it would not harm her. If it wanted to, it would have already done it. Maybe it kept an eye on her? The questions rose in her mind and she desperately tried to breathe to calm down her nerves. In her ribcage, her heart pounded hard. Her survival depended on not being found first. Ten people ahead of her needed to be found before she could rush out of the hiding space. A terrifying thought pervaded her–she had no way of knowing if the others had been discovered. Would the children scream out of pain? Would they shout for help? Plead in desperate voices?

As the girl was sitting inside the attic in an uncomfortable position, she heard a painful feminine scream of a child. Her body jerked as the scream tore through the silence to her ears, causing her own heart to ache from agony.

She knew they had found someone.

In only a matter of seconds, something happened that was not allowed to happen in a little girl's world. Her tiny ears heard another shot ring out below, and then the screaming of the child died down. She couldn't help the tears of terror that trickled down her cheeks like a waterfall. Wet spots appeared on her gray dress, forming a pattern. Master would not be pleased.

As another shot rang out, she understood that the punishment the master had talked about earlier led to death. Every other game they had played led to death, different games each time, same punishment. With her hand pressed to her mouth, she tried not to scream outright when another shot rang out.

Sensing the presence, calm settled over her. In spite of how strange it seemed, she realized she wasn't alone in that terrible madness.

Having no idea of how long she had been in the attic, she muttered the numbers of each person who had died a sorrowful death.

One shot, two shots, three shots,

... and then, at last, a tenth shot.

The presence disappeared when she opened the hatch as if it only wanted to keep her safe. Descending the ladder, her shaky legs could barely hold her body weight. Waiting downstairs for her was Theodore, who was just as shaken as she was, and she ran into his arms. He embraced her, letting her tears fall down her cheeks, blurring her vision.

He had survived.

She felt nauseated and haunted by her surroundings. Her face turned as pale as a ghost when she saw bloody handprints on the previously unmarred yellow walls. The further they moved from the attic, the more bloody handprints formed on the walls. When she reached the staircase leading downstairs, she let out a heartbreaking cry.

There, at the bottom of the staircase, lay ten bloody, lifeless bodies, each with a shot in their head.

Please help

Save her

Please

My last hope

Dying

Help

Please help

Chapter 1
Him

Present time…

"DEAR ASHER.
You are receiving this letter as I have something extremely important I want you to have knowledge about. I am alive, little brother. You and Mary must have been told I was sent to a reformatory school all those years ago, which is not the truth. Father is not the man you thought he was. He was a man of honor, a man who only cared about his properties and money, and he sold me off to a secluded house far away from society, a place no one knows about except the inner circles. This must sound surreal to you, I know. It came as a shock to me too. That place, it's a place you never want to visit. I do not have much time left. The man and woman who took me away from the manor will be back soon. I am dying, Asher. And I am so sorry for not being able to deliver this letter to you personally. I wish I could, but I live in the States at the moment. This man and woman, they are going to kill me. It has been their goal ever since getting hold of me. They are truly sick in their heads. But, little brother, I have found peace in this refuge. I was never supposed to survive the

manor, and I have accepted my fate. I hope you will too. It will be hard for you, but I do not want you to mourn me, for I was never supposed to survive. Live your life to the fullest, for me.

They are going to kill me, and therefore, this letter is sent in a rush. You need to receive it before I die, for I don't know how to move on in the afterlife if you don't help me. When this letter is sent, I understand that you will do as I ask. Only then can I find peace in life after this. The house I was sold to, it's a hell house. A place where they dress the children and force them to behave like real dolls. It's really creepy. It's a secret organization, one which kidnaps and buys children as if they were toys. You need to put a stop to this trafficking ring, please, little brother. I cannot stand any more children getting hurt.

In the house, there's a girl. Her name is Aurora, and she has the most unique eyes I have ever seen. You will know who she is by looking into her eyes. This girl has been my best friend since arriving at the house. She helped me survive all those years and made the place better. With her there, it wasn't a burning hell house for me anymore. Then I was taken away from her, and the look in her eyes told me that she would not be okay. The house is the devil's house, I can assure you of that. Please save her, Asher. Please save my best friend from all the pain that the house causes her, save her from her traumatic childhood. This is the last thing I wish for on earth, only this. Go to Grimhill Manor and save the girl who saved me. Please save my best friend. Only then will I be able to rest in peace.

Yours sincerely, Theodore."

I gripped the letter harshly in my hands, focusing on breathing properly. My breaths were shallow, rasping, as if they needed to be anointed with oil. I stared at the words on the piece of paper for the millionth time. Many months had passed since I received the letter, and I knew the brother I once had was gone.

The pain in my heart felt too extreme. It carved out a hole in my chest that made the grief flood over. The pain was grueling, a kind of pain that makes you hungry, yet disgusted at the mere thought of food. He was gone, and he had asked for one last wish to be granted. One I needed to fulfill, for him, my brother.

It had taken me months to find the location of the secluded manor. It wasn't a simple job. A place that was deleted from the records. No matter how many times you googled its name, it was nowhere to be found. Every time I tried, my screen turned up with the message, "Your search—Grimhill Manor—did not match any records." It was as if someone had completely hidden the mysterious places, making it nonexistent.

It was existent, though. My brother wouldn't have told me otherwise. After months of research, months of finding the tiniest little number that could lead me to the next step, and months of proving myself worthy, I had finally gained access to the location of the place. They had invited me to a monthly day where many masters came to pick up their dolls. I wasn't proud of the tasks I had to perform to prove myself worthy of them. The worst was the one where I kidnapped a guy who was on the organization's hit-and-run list. They wanted me to slice his throat with a sharp knife in an empty barn, cover up the tracks and run. The darkness had overtaken me that day, filling me in the same way it did the night when I slept on the streets, the night *he* had gone too far with his drinking.

It was worth it. I would kill over and over again if it meant giving my brother peace in the afterlife. No life was more worth than his, and I could bear the pain for his sake. Proving myself to the organization had been worth it, they had given me the location. Although I did not know whether the girl he was talking about was alive, I had to take the chance.

For him.

DAYS LATER

"I WANT HER," STRETCHING out my arm lazily, I gestured toward the tiny girl in the room's corner. There was something about her that drew me in, the posture in which she held, the innocent aura surrounding her. She had been the first one to catch my attention when I first stepped into the manor. Perhaps that was the girl my brother had been talking about. I could not yet see the color of her eyes and hoped dearly that they had a unique color. The color my brother had been talking about in his letter.

"She is the one I am looking for," I repeated the sentence, using a low, dark tone of voice.

The house gave me the chills with its eerie atmosphere. It was too cold in there for it to be counted as a regular temperature. If it was intentional or not, I did not know. On top of the chilling atmosphere, there were children in one corner. A group of them was singing a creepy song, "Come out, come out, wherever you are," as they played a game. Some of them sat up straight, their eyes glued to the walls behind them without seeming to be aware of what was happening around them. How could one be so cruel to take over children's lives like that? Many believed that true evil did not exist, but I knew better. That house was the devil's house itself, and I wish I could erase the smug smile on the old man's face in front of me.

The sight outside of the manor had been something I never wanted to experience again. A shuddering breath escaped from my throat at the memory of the children's bodies laying outside, near a hopscotch area. The blood had been glistening, and I just knew that they had recently been killed. It felt as if someone had ripped my heart from my chest, and to be honest, I wished that someone had.

I needed to play the role correctly if I wanted to stay. Few people were allowed into the manor to collect a real-life doll, and I was one of them who had made it. It disgusted me that I had done such horrible things to deserve that spot, but I would move heaven and earth for my brother.

No one knew my real name here. I went under a fake identity, Kaden Scott. They did background checks on everyone who arrived, needing to know as only the inner circle was allowed inside. Kaden Scott, a butcher who wasn't afraid of getting muddy from blood. Kaden had proved his butchery by killing people without complaining. Those who didn't make it to the inner circle were either too self-absorbed and sloppy with the job, or they were too cowardly to handle the tasks and complained.

The worst thing the organization knew was crybabies.

The only reason why I had come that far with my mission was because of my best friend, Draven. He was a hacker and together we had figured out everything we needed to know. Without Draven that would never have happened, and he knew how much my brother meant to me. He, too, had a girl whom he needed to pick up. His mother's best friend from Bulgaria had lost her daughter before her own husband murdered her. Draven felt inside of him that he needed to save the girl for his mother's sake, but his mother was no longer alive. We both felt the same grief for lost loved ones, and that bond brought us closer.

To find the girl who my brother had been talking about, I needed to play the role of a master wanting a plaything.

There was a flash of intimidation on the old man's face beside me, which prompted a grin to spread across my face. His terrified expression made me feel euphoric. By tilting my head to the right, I made a mental record of every move the girl made. She was sitting at an old, brown wooden table in front of a sofa that seemed rather uncomfortable. Not even cloth surrounded its edges. Essentially, it was a piece of wood carved into a piece of furniture. There were scratch marks that were caused by a cat on the sofa. Of course, that was absurd, since they permitted no animals in that place. I wondered how those had come there, but guessed it was some crazy child who had broken down. Not that I even cared. All I cared about was the rage rising inside my veins, the desperate attempt to get rid of it, and getting the girl my brother begged me to save.

The table in front of the girl had a pile of books on it. Seeing how beaten up and aged they looked, I assumed that they were old and had faced many readers during the years. Many of the covers were peeling and shreds of dust jackets clung to them, and the pages were dog-eared from having been folded to serve as bookmarks for all the many readers it had evidently seen. There was a tendency for bookworms to live inside their fantasy worlds, and they viewed the world from a different perspective.

I only hoped she was the right girl.

My attention was quickly drawn back to her and she was sitting with one leg over the other, furrowing her eyebrows as her eyes scanned the book's pages. The book's world diverted her attention, and she wasn't aware of what was happening around her. While she turned the pages of the book, her hair remained perfectly placed on her shoulders despite the movements of her head. There was a glint of sunshine coming through the curtains that covered those large windows, causing her hair to shimmer in the sun. Her strawberry-blonde hair almost glowed in the natural light, and the red shades in it became highlighted. I glanced at her eyes for a brief moment. They were beautifully graceful, and I knew I had found her.

The sound of her pink, plump lips moving as she hummed a melody soothed my ears. It amazed me how she could focus on reading as well as humming. She was sitting on the sofa with such grace that it made her look sophisticated just because of her posture. The sight of her stirred something deep within me and for a second all my anger subsided, the rage inside my veins calmed, and my organs could finally receive enough oxygen from my blood vessels. I knew I didn't just want her because Theodore begged me to save her.

No, I wanted her for myself.

I needed her to continue living in that hell, to be able to calm the rage inside me, consuming my every thought. She calmed me in ways no one had before, and that terrified me. The girl reading her books–unaware that I was staring at her–would be my downfall.

"But Sir–"

My thoughts were interrupted by Frederick, who stared at me with a fearful gaze.

He was an old man, in his seventies, with wrinkles on his face and prominent veins. Just looking at him disgusted me. What disgusted me even more was the way in which he led the organization, the way he allowed all of these children to be trafficked. I knew what I was about to do eventually would save them as best as I could save them.

All I could do was stare at the beautiful girl who had captured my entire attention. As I examined her body, I realized that the white and gray checkered dress she was wearing perfectly hugged her figure. She adjusted her seat. Her movement was so smooth, yet so doll-like. One could almost think she was a real doll. Such a well-trained one. A smirk spread across my lips in amusement.

"Are you hearing me, Sir?" My gaze shifted back to the man. "Don't misunderstand me right now, by any means. I do not mean any harm. She is the one no one wants. At nineteen, she's too old for people to want her. I can promise you, you will never want her. She is too old to learn to obey another master. Choose another girl, Mr. Scott."

Irritation grew inside me when I listened to Frederick speaking. Did he really think he could tell me what I should do? The way he deliberately provoked me made me click my tongue. With an exaggerated sigh, I forced a fake smile toward the man. *Play your role right.*

"I know what I want." My voice became sharper. "She is the most suitable one."

There was a strange feeling inside of me, an inner voice urging me to take her and claim her as mine. In a nod of approval, the old man beside me smiled awkwardly. My eyes followed him as he walked toward the girl with a stiff posture. When his legs trembled, my mouth curled into a grin, and my body filled with amusement. Seeing him like that, I felt incredible amounts of joy. Tapping my foot, I waited impatiently for the man to deliver the girl. I would have loved to have received her myself, but my mind decided that a stellar first impression would be more important.

I fixated my eyes on the girl's arm, on the way he was gripping it tightly with his own liver-stained hands. I wish I could wipe that ugly smirk off his face as he lifted her from the sofa so forcefully it caused her to yelp. Upon falling and hitting the wooden floor, her book slammed against it with a loud thump. The old man dragging her towards me didn't care about the fact that she was in obvious pain. Anger once again reddened my field of vision as it filled my entire being. Something inside of me fueled up, and all of my previous calmness vanished at seeing the girl my brother cared for so deeply getting inflicted by pain.

I didn't give a shit about the girl. For my brother, however, I would do anything for him. Even in my fucked up state of sense, I knew I couldn't let him down. He wanted her safe, so safe she would be.

My eyes narrowed at the thought of someone else hurting the girl who belonged to me. I could feel my whole body shake with the anger that pumped adrenaline through my blood. It needed to come out somehow. I needed to hurt someone. The urge grew stronger with each passing second. I wanted to kill the old man, watch his life drain from his body through the blood that would pour from his gunshot wound.

Don't hurt her.

It was as if a voice from my subconscious told me–begged me– to obey it. These thoughts, however, became irrational to me, and I stopped listening to them. The annoying presence inside of me told me that everything I did was wrong. The voice told me that I was a monster for being so careless. And maybe I was.

I simply did not care.

The man who grabbed the girl didn't give her a chance to pick the books up so she could bring them. He just forcefully dragged her towards me. Another wave of anger surged inside me, and I became aware that I was on the verge of exploding. He was hurting her. I had promised Theodore that they would never hurt her again. I was ready to kill that fucker.

Grimhill Manor. The creepy, mysterious manor my brother had lived in for years, forced to dress like a doll.

To be Frederick's doll. He who was hurting the person my brother had cared for dearly.

She was a true beauty standing before me, her legs shaking as if she was a deer caught in the headlights. Her eyes met mine, making her neck turn red as she shifted her gaze away from me.

What a shame, I thought.

My body teemed with desire. I wanted to take in the sight of her eyes and treasure them forever in my memory. Our shared gaze lasted for only a fraction of a second. Moments after she looked into my eyes, I felt myself slip away. Something inside of me clicked into place, and my heartache decreased. It was as if someone saw me, the real me, for the first time in years.

In a moment of unconsciousness, she had bitten her lip while staring at me intensely, steel-blue eyes gazing in my direction. She had her eyebrows furrowed as if she was concentrating on something. The moment my eyes landed on her lips, blood filled my cock. Quickly and unnoticed, I adjusted my pants so my hard-on wouldn't be visible. I hadn't fucked a girl in a long while and the bare sight of her made me want to take her right there, on the floor.

The girl was the most beautiful and sexiest person I had ever met. None of the other one-night stands I had were that attractive. And those girls didn't mean shit. I had fucked them hard and ruthlessly, with their consent, of course, only to make the rage inside of me subside. And those girls only sought my attention. They only wanted a good fuck. No one had ever looked at me with such intensity and curiosity as the girl in front of me did.

For a brief second, my eyes fell on her round breasts covered by the dress, and I wondered if my palm would fit around them.

As a child, I believed eyes were like windows into the soul. All I wanted was to absorb every detail of them, to be able to meet and experience the soul she had within. Hers were vivid and bemused. Even though our shared gaze only lasted for a short while, I could see the blue-gray in them. The way they glowed in the lamplight attracted me, but that wasn't the only thing that caught my attention.

There was something special about her eyes.

They had splashes of dark purple. It reminded me of the hue of Morning Glory flowers. *Unique eye color.* After months of searching, I had finally found the girl I was looking for. She wasn't dead; she was very much alive, and she was standing right in front of me.

How I wished that Theodore could sense that moment, that he could know that I hadn't let him down, from wherever he was. I had found the girl, and I would save her.

The moment I stroked her hair, I felt drawn to touch her, drawn to feel her under my fingertips. She calmed the anger inside me, but I did not calm hers. My touch instantly stiffened the girl's body.

"Oh Dolly, don't be so scared." My sentence only made her even more uncomfortable, making me laugh inwardly at her reaction.

'Dolly,' good job at playing the role right, Asher.

The old man grabbed her wrists once again, making her already stiff posture flinch. It was his way of showing me his domination over her, and the rage surged through my veins like flames.

"Why are you so rough on that poor girl, may I ask?" I shifted my attention to the old man, and he gave me the keys to the handcuffs.

My attention focused on him, and he seemed to notice it. His presence fueled the rage within me. "You are afraid," I stated matter-of-factly.

A statement I knew to be true, even if the man would deny it. I knew he wasn't telling the truth when he shook his head, indicating a simple 'no.' It was impossible not to smirk as he looked terrified of me. I would be lying to myself if I said that didn't amuse me. His fear was evident, and I enjoyed it. *What a psychopath.*

In the manor, I noticed the clock keeping track of how long I had been there.

Once again, my gaze fell upon my doll and I asked her, "It's time to leave, don't you think, Dolly?"

Chapter 2
Her, earlier

I T WAS IMPOSSIBLE TO stop rolling around in the sheets. The blanket I had been lying on rustled, making me unable to sleep. The sleeping pills I took had no effect on my eyes, as they did not tire.

"Ugh!" my voice was all that could be heard as I groaned out loud.

How I wished that the human body wouldn't require sleep in order to function. Every single night I experienced nightmares, and every morning I woke up sweaty. Despite the devastating consequences of sleep deprivation, my brain hated to sleep.

On a specific date every month of the year, guests would come to visit. That day of the month, everyone had to prepare, make sure the house was clean, dress up more than we already did, and behave like obedient little dolls to please the master.

Looking up at the clock showing five a.m., I let go of the deep breath I hadn't known I had been holding. The cold floor felt pleasant under my bare feet as I stood out of bed and made my way toward the wardrobe. My eyes scanned the dress as I pulled it over my head, not caring what it looked like.

No one would choose me, anyway. I was too old for someone to want me.

It surprised me how long I had stayed here. Having been a legal adult for one year, I had been sure that they would soon release me from the hell that it was.

I had been wrong.

The only way to be let out of there and into freedom was through being chosen by a new master. Being of legal age would not in itself grant one freedom. Electricity always powered the fence surrounding the manor, making it impossible to escape. In order to ensure that we didn't escape, the staff always watched over us, keeping track of every step we took. Nobody had ever escaped, no one had ever reached beyond the fence that was located several meters behind the house. There had been cases where people had tried but failed miserably. The guards always caught up to them, letting no one leave, and ensuring that they executed the escapees on the spot.

Even children. Murdered in cold blood.

My entire body trembled as I thought of it, and my attention shifted to the bookshelf instead, which covered a huge part of the wall. Grabbing a bunch of my favorite books, I walked out of my room and into the huge parlor room. The interior of the room had changed from when I first arrived as a seven-year-old girl. One thing that remained was the black and white paintings that used to scare me as a child. In one corner of the room was a group of couches, and armchairs lined up around a small—but extremely thick—TV. One that looked as if it had been taken from the past. The TV was the only way for young people to know what was happening in the outside world. There was no internet at the place, and the computer I had hidden in my room did not work. Yet I kept it, for maybe one day I could use it.

Sitting on a chair next to the table, I laid the books out in front of me. I ignored everything around me, focusing solely on the book I had brought. The room started filling with children and young adults as the hours passed. Breakfast was served, games were played, and chit-chat was exchanged.

The books were the only thing occupying my attention.

It surprised me that Frederick hadn't yet ripped the books out from my hands, forcing me to eat breakfast as all the other obedient dolls did. The possibility of him throwing me out lingered in my mind, and I was worried that he had grown tired of me. Although the house had ruined my childhood–ruined my future–it had given me food and a roof to sleep under. Having lived there for as long as I could remember, I didn't know where I would go if he threw me out. I barely knew how to function around other people. As a seven-year-old girl people had made remarks about my appearance, causing me to shut down and refuse any contact with the other children.

Growing up made me realize they were the ones at fault, not the victim of bullies. A few months ago, a new teenager befriended the idiot clan and decided to say something shitty about my mother–a sensitive subject. Being locked in a cellar in the dungeons for forty-eight hours was my punishment for beating him up. It was worth it.

As for the outside world, I didn't know what it looked like. For the past twelve years, my only exposure to it had been through a screen.

The silence surrounding me caught my attention in an instant. Something was amiss, but I continued reading regardless, being too caught up in the intense story.

Then it hit me. A month had passed since the last terrifying game.

As I lifted my gaze, I saw the doll master standing majestically in front of all the girls and boys gathered together in lines; one line for the boys and one line for the girls. My heart was pumping hard inside my chest, to the point where it hurt from the force when I made my way toward them. Days like that terrified me. It was almost impossible for me to predict whether or not I would return to daily life the next morning.

A special day was set aside for the guests to arrive. It struck me how odd that monthly day had fallen. Rarely did the master allow games on the day of a so-called 'fine visit.'

"My dear dolls, please proceed to walk outside and wait for further instructions," his voice echoed off the walls, causing several young people to whisper.

They hugged one another as they frantically tried to get out, afraid that upsetting the master would cause him to become angry. Disobeying his orders never ended well.

The frosty morning chill spread over my bare arms as I stood outside the house, which looked like it might collapse at any moment. A gust of wind whipped through the trees, causing them to sway aggressively next to each other. The sounds they made were creaking, like someone sitting on an old rocking chair. As long as I lived at the manor, I would never be able to forget the feelings that I had and everything that had happened to me. In response to the master's order, the lines were formed, and he emerged shortly thereafter. Standing in front of everyone, dressed in a warm coat and wearing shoes, he surveyed the stairs. A special treatment that only he received. The rest of us were forced to stand in our short-sleeved clothes when the temperature felt negative, and our feet were bare on the wet grass. My eyes wandered to the house, which was menacing and imposing. Somehow, I could imagine the peace and freedom of not surviving the day. I would never have to feel such fear again. Even during the day, the house looked sinister.

"We're going to play a game of hopscotch. As you all already know, the location for the game is marked out further away." His hideous, wrinkled fingers pointed to the area that he meant.

It was clear that he was aging, and that in itself was a relief. Such evil as he did not deserve to live.

All the children stood still and in front of me, I could see a little girl's tears slowly rolling down her cheeks. All I wanted to do was hug her and tell her everything was going to be okay. But I couldn't. And nothing would ever be okay. Any one of us could be dead by the end of the day, and that fact gave me chills. Ice filled my body, freezing every cell and making it impossible for me to breathe as I waited for further instructions.

"My beloved dolls, you can now go to the area." No one dared to say anything else.

The morning light loomed behind the house on the horizon, a promise of a coming day. But it was a promise that would not hold for everyone.

The first person to jump into the hopscotch box was a little boy. He could not be older than six years old. During that period of waiting for the master's approval, his whole body was shaking. The panic was evident in his eyes, but he was too scared to run away. Everyone knew no one would ever succeed.

The master made everyone watch as the boy jumped, but all I wanted to do was curl up in a corner and cry until the angels from heaven came to save me. My eyes were filled with tears as I witnessed the horrific scene.

The boy jumped. His youthful body had not yet learned to keep its balance. When he landed on the asphalt again, his foot twisted and he fell headlong to the ground. A roar of gasps and upset voices was heard from the gathered crowd. The boy's screams were the only thing that filled my ears as he realized his fate in panic. If I could, I would have saved him. But there was nothing either of us could do, and it was devastating.

The master's smile would forever haunt my dreams when he walked up to the boy, happy to kill him as satisfaction roared through him.

True evil.

From his jacket pocket he pulled out a sharp kitchen knife, and the boy's screams echoed in my ears. It was like it was begging me to save him, but the master was fast, despite his age. He would have time to kill all the children before anyone escaped. All hope was lost as he pulled the knife through the child's throat, and tears formed in my eyes and fell at a steady pace. I wanted to scream and my heart felt as though it was going to sink as deeply and terribly as the Titanic did. In no time at all, staff had extricated the boy's dead body from the area and placed it next to the hopscotch box.

During that entire hour, a total of ten young children died, both boys and girls. Their bodies lay dead and bleeding, crimson red paint spreading across the otherwise gray asphalt.

Then it was my turn.

The rush of blood roared in my ears as I jumped into the first box. Twelve years of that game had made me proficient, and I had secretly practiced when no one was watching. To survive that horrible game that claimed the lives of so many children, I had to practice. Most of them were young and still hadn't learned how to maintain their balance. Tears streamed down my cheeks in panic, and my heart was beating so hard it felt like it would break the ribs that protected it. My breathing was uneven as I jumped, and the feeling of everyone staring at me made it even worse. With each jump I took, my heart sank in the belief that the next one would seal my death.

But when I reached the end, I could finally exhale. The smile on the master's lips disgusted me. The look of pride made me want to drive his knife through his heart and stab him a hundred times over. One stab for every child he had ever killed.

The game was over for the month, and everyone had to return to their everyday routines. They wanted us to act as if nothing had happened. But how the hell were we meant to continue living during the day, eating our food, reading books, and laughing together when the master didn't notice, when over ten children had lost their lives?

They would never again wake up, never again see the morning light reflected inside the windows, never again experience the feeling of freedom that the outdoor air gave. They would be out there until some member of the staff had the nerve to move them. A normal funeral wouldn't be held for them, and they wouldn't be respected. The mere thought of it made yesterday's food come up my throat.

Every now and then, I wanted to give up. I was drained. I was tired of living like this without knowing which day I would live or not. Tired of how no one here deserved the fate the master put us through. All I wanted was for all the children here to be free, to return to their families. Hate was an emotion that was too weak to describe what I felt. I felt something worse, something stronger than hate.

    We had to return to our normal routines. With shaky legs, I sat down at one table, trying to push away the memory of the lost children. They didn't deserve that. It was nearly impossible to focus on reading my books when the dead bodies of the children invaded the space behind my eyelids. Many would think that I had become accustomed to seeing the dead bodies of children, considering how many I saw every year here. That was far from the truth. No one could ever get used to a sight that grotesque.

    As the hours flew by, I focused on my books. They were my escape from reality, and for a moment I forgot about the horrible game of the morning. The story fascinated me, and I was oblivious to my surroundings. Having something else to think about made me take advantage of that time while it lasted. I didn't notice the shift in the surrounding atmosphere, nor did I notice how people stopped to stare at something, or how whispers formed.

    I noticed nothing until a hand pulled me up in a tight grip.

    The pain radiated through my body like hundreds of fireballs, and I couldn't understand what was happening to me. One second I was reading, living in my own world. Then another shot of pain rushed through my arm and I realized that someone had grabbed my upper arm. With a grunt and a tightening of my eyes, I cringed. Everyone's eyes were on me as my book hit the floor with a loud thud. My body yanked upward, forcing me to stand on my legs. The old man, with a gray beard, mustache, and bulky glasses which sat far down on the nose, had grabbed my arm. He was the one causing the pain. Frederick pulled me through the room and my eyes looked desperately back to the room, landing on my beloved books. My attempts to break free were desperate.

I had to get my books.

However, Frederick did not care. We stopped walking when we reached the other edge of the parlor. As soon as my gaze caught sight of the shoes and legs in front of me, I raised it.

I would never forget the day I first saw him.

His amber-colored eyes looked into mine with such intensity yet so much warmth beneath the surface, deep down. There was a thick fog of darkness covering his eyes. I could see, however, that there was so much more to him than the façade he had built up. I was transported to a field of daydreams at the slightest scent of his subtle cologne. His woody fragrance made its way into my nostrils, sending a jolt of attraction through me. The mere sight of him gave my body a sense of déjà vu, and at that moment, I felt as if we had always known each other. I had never wished to feel that way about him, but his appearance, his muscular body straining against his clothes, made me unable to stop the sensual feeling from rising inside of me.

That was the day I met the devil for the very first time, the man who was determined to change my entire life. I wish I had anticipated how his influence would turn my life upside down. I knew from the moment I saw him that things would never be the same. For I knew that man had many secrets.

I recognized the look in his eyes from my own.

Those hurt eyes, those eyes that held more pain than words could ever describe. I knew that the man in front of me had his dark demons. They were also in my possession. I could see the

HIS DOLL

rage filling his mind, his nostrils flaring with anger, his fist clenching and unclenching. I was scared for my own life, for I did not know that man, and for the first time in my life, I prayed I wouldn't get out of that hell house.

Chapter 3
Her

MY SPINE TINGLED AS I stood beside the creepy man. He wasn't like anyone else I had ever met. With every passing second, my heart beat faster and faster. He looked at me so intensely, as if he were a predator and I was his prey. Like he wanted to keep me forever, take away my freedom. Like he wanted me.

When he patted my head, my whole body shook with discomfort. He touched me as if I were something extremely precious to him. I didn't want to be something precious to him. Yet I couldn't help but feel drawn to him. There was something so intimidating about him, but also something that filled me with anticipation. That man meant danger. I felt it in every bone. He stood there beside me, his black coat draped around his upper body and his black jeans. A casual outfit, yet somehow sexy. There was something about the way he was standing there, with so much confidence it radiated throughout the room.

I noticed how his chocolate-brown hair contrasted with my hair, a perfect match. His jaw was defined, matching his domineering vibe, which caused something inside of me to tingle. He was the most handsome man I had ever laid my eyes on. *The most beautiful creatures were always the most evil ones. And this creature took me in his embrace, sang to me like a siren, drowned me in his eyes.*

Inside, I prayed he wouldn't choose me as I kept my fingers crossed. Yet there was a tug inside of me, pleading to drag him down with me, pleading to let him devour me. In the twelve years I had been here, no one had ever chosen me.

No one wanted me, not even the devil himself.

And if someone chose me today, I prayed it wouldn't be that man. The man with angel eyes in a devilish body. *Anyone but this one.*

If he took me, I knew it would be the end of me. He was something out of this world, having darkness surrounding him. I had to stay away from him, but the tug inside of me told me not to. Somewhere deep within me, I knew I wanted him and craved for his muscular arms to caress my body.

An eerie vibe settled over him. As if by magic, a tangible, living force that immobilized my brain kept me helpless. My pulse was the only sound I could hear ringing inside my ears. The man in front of me was a man of mystery. A puzzle craving, longing, urging to be solved. With his enigmatic posture, I knew a menacing aura possessed him. And he wanted me to find the key to his heart, solve the puzzle, and set him free. However, I couldn't set someone else free unless I was free myself.

The longer he stood there, staring at me with intensity in his eyes and making me feel like a mouse in a cat's trap, the more I realized I would rather live alone in the streets, or in those terrifying woods.

My throat was dry, begging for the release a water glass would give. It ached and pained me in ways only people in deserts had experienced.

"What did you say, Dolly?" He asked me, his eyebrows lifting in wonder.

As our eyes met, I glanced away, trying to utter something that only reverberated in the thick air. I only succeeded in making myself cough, causing tears to well up in the corner of my eyes.

In the man's presence beside me, I wanted to run to safety, but my feet wouldn't allow me to. His eyes landed on Frederick, the one who was the master of the house. The owner. Frederick Grimhill, whose family the manor had been named after.

"Haven't you given her anything to drink?" In contrast to my expectations, he was furious with Frederick.

I had assumed he would be mad at me for disrespecting him by not being able to answer him. Instead, he was mad at the man beside him.

As Frederick's shoulder stiffened, I witnessed a tremor in his body. It was strange that an old man who enjoyed causing children pain was a coward when standing before a much younger—but extremely handsome—man. Frederick had caused more pain to children than anyone I had ever heard about. A psychopathic man who deserved no remorse. Memories shoved their way into my mind and I forced them away.

"No, uhm, she didn't deserve to drink any water."

I rolled my eyes at his comment. It was annoying to have someone like him around.

"Is that a reason not to give her something to drink? Don't you know water is the main reason we're alive?" The creepy man raised his voice. "Upon arriving here, I expected everything to be in order and for the children to be well cared for. Not in this fucking state!"

I watched as his nostrils flared while he stared at Frederick, who winced like the coward he was.

"I'm sorry, Sir," he replied and lowered his gaze to the floor, avoiding the man's stare.

"Oh dear, an apology will solve nothing." The creepy man's mood changed in the blink of an eye.

He became the soft yet intriguing man he had been a few minutes ago. All anger left his aura, and only calmness remained. As I shifted my weight to the other leg, I glanced down at the floor, attempting to block out everything around me.

The moment I realized the man had grabbed something from his jacket's inner pocket, I heard a scream. During that terrifying experience, a rather young girl screamed. She couldn't have been more than sixteen years old. There was something with her hair, the color of shimmering copper. Her forest green eyes were blank, yet filled with so much dread. In them, I could practically see the way Frederick had taken her childhood, taken her innocence. Like he did mine.

The man held an item in his hand that was black and familiar to me. Something Frederick used every single month. Every single month when he killed the ones who defied him, and the ones who lost his games. The man was holding a revolver and pointed it at Frederick's forehead. In the corner of his eyes, a tear formed at the sight of the gun pointing at him. The same look of pure terror I had seen in children when they realized they wouldn't live to see another day.

In an instant, a chorus of screams emerged throughout the parlor room. Everyone had stopped dead in their tracks, realizing what was happening in front of their eyes. They were too innocent to see that, some only five years old. My heart broke for them, and for my inner child, who had suffered that kind of terror for twelve years.

Twelve years of this nightmare.

My childhood was stripped away from me, my freedom made into nothingness, and my innocent eyes were lost forever.

The screams pierced my ears, and the young girl had fallen down to the floor in shock. Broken chairs lay underneath her body as her arm bled from the force of it crashing into her, scraping her skin. I wanted to run to her, hold her in my arms, and comfort her. She reminded me so much of my sixteen-year-old self.

So lost, so confused, so broken.

When Frederick realized the gun was pointed at him, he began to weep. In an instant, a chorus of screams emerged. The girl had stopped crying, her eyes filling with numbness and something else. Acceptance. She understood Frederick would die, and she accepted it like she accepted her faith.

"Please, don't do this." His voice broke as his eyes frantically searched for a way out.

The action reminded me of the time when I was seven when the newcomer had been shot as he had tried to escape. The memory caused a lump to form in my throat and in my stomach. I never wanted to be reminded of that again.

"Beg," the man commanded in a low, raspy voice as he stared at Frederick with a stern look.

"W-What?"

"Beg, for your life," a grin smeared across the man's lips, and a shiver spread down my spine. He was enjoying the moment. He loved the way he had made Frederick terrified. What a horrible person.

"P-Please, don't kill me," Frederick whispered. "I beg you!" He lowered his gaze to the floor, and I watched as his throat gulped.

The man's smirk grew wider and a deep, rough chuckle escaped his throat. I couldn't move a muscle in my body. If I wanted to save Frederick's life, I wouldn't be able to without getting shot myself. And for a split second, I remembered the reason Frederick shouldn't be saved, for he had never saved me. He had never shown me mercy.

He was the reason for all my pain.

"Aurora, my dear girl," called a voice from across the room. My gaze met his, and I stood up. At a ninety-degree downward bend, I bowed to my master and looked down at the ground. No one was allowed to look him in the eye unless he demanded it.

"Come here," the master instructed and with a pounding heart, I followed his order. We walked through a corridor, down some stairs, and reached the dungeons. The dungeons from the tales. Panic rose to the surface, and I wanted to scream my lungs out.

'Not here, not here!'

But all I did was stare at the locked door. Inside was the room where the staff and guards brought disobedient dolls. Those who broke the rules and deserved—according to the master—to die. What were we doing here? Inside my chest, it felt as if someone was clawing at my heart.

"There is someone I want you to see in here," said the master before pulling the keys from his pocket and unlocking the door to the forbidden room.

My head was lightheaded as my heart beat hard inside my ribs. What were we doing here? The master loomed large in front of me as I stepped into the room. I had expected to be locked up here for something I did, but what I didn't expect to see was a little boy sitting on a chair, strapped down. His mouth was sealed with silver tape, and his wrists were tied behind the chair with a strong rope. The sweat on his forehead was clinging to his hair, his eyes were wild with desperation and anguish. I recognized the boy in front of me in an instant. My face paled.

"This is the guy who touched you without your permission?" asked the master with a firm tone.

In a state of confusion, I turned around to look at his dark gaze. Frantically, I shook my head, trying to answer his question and tell him that wasn't the case at all. But no words came out of my mouth. Because of my shock, I couldn't utter a syllable. The boy looked at me with desperation in his eyes, begging me to help him and I wished I could, but the fear that gripped me paralyzed my body. The master seemed to interpret my silence as a yes, and he pulled a knife from one of his pockets as he made his way toward the bound boy.

"No!" I yelled, and his shocked gaze turned to me.

"I wanted to hold his hand, Master. Forgive me, forgive me. It wasn't his fault, it was mine! He comforted me and I grabbed his hand. We held each other's hands because I initiated it. I was sad, and he comforted me. Please, Master," I cried out, trying to explain what had happened, begging him. I knew what waited.

The master's gaze showed nothing but darkness. He was getting mad at hearing my truth, and nothing I said would make him believe me.

"He touched you, Aurora, and for that, he will be punished. You are my girl. Do you understand that? MINE! No one else's," he shouted and tears formed in my eyes.

Before I knew it, there was a heartbreaking scream and the boy whose hand I had been holding for comfort the day before was gone. Frederick had murdered him in cold blood with a knife, just because someone other than him had touched me. Tears streamed down my cheeks and emptiness deadened my emotions. I never wanted to live again.

Every muscle in my body had become tense, and I stood motionless next to the man. I reluctantly tried to erase that memory from my mind. The memory from when I was sixteen years old. All my eardrums could hear were the screams and cries of the children as they ran over each other, trying to reach their rooms or the outside doors, which were locked. As I stood in the middle of the chaos, surrounded by chairs and tables scattered everywhere, I felt like I was stuck in a time freeze. The moment I heard the trigger being pulled, tears pooled in my eyes and my body swayed back and forth in pure despair. The sound sent a brusque bolt of shock right through me.

Frederick's lifeless body did not even have a second to spare before it fell into the pool of blood forming around his dead body. As I looked at him, I saw the hole in his head caused by the bullet. The creepy man laughed as he turned toward me. I did not dare to move a single muscle, not that I could have with them being so tense. Looking down at the body of the man he had just killed, he put the revolver inside his inner pocket.

"He was an asshole, wasn't he?" the man asked, amusement ringing in his voice.

Despite my inability to comprehend what had just transpired, I tentatively nodded my head.

"Meet me outside in five minutes. Go and pack your stuff," he said before he disappeared through the doors. As if nothing important had happened.

Without being able to think any further, I ran upstairs to my room. There was a squeaking sound as I walked through the house. It was so old that it was almost uninhabitable. After getting into my room, I packed my suitcase with my clothes. From under my bed, I grabbed the computer hidden under my mattress. A few years ago, I had stolen one of the many laptops Frederick stored in his office, in case I would ever need it. There was no internet connection that far away from town. I couldn't search for anything, nor could I contact anyone. But I kept it, just in case. I knew I was Frederick's most prized possession. The girl who had been here longer than anyone else, the most obedient girl. He trusted me enough to let me inside his office, yet he loved to hurt me. Loved to torture me, loved to see me suffer.

Taking a deep breath, my gaze swept around the room. I would never see that room again, and somehow, that thought pained me. It had been my safe place for twelve years. When I entered the hallway outside, I looked at the hatch on the roof. It led to the attic where I had hidden as a young girl, scared of getting caught. That place had been my safe spot during all the games. The place where I always hid. It was my place, and no one knew it existed.

On my way out of the house, I stopped by the table I had been sitting at earlier. Bending down, I grabbed hold of my books and put them inside the bag. A metallic smell filled the room, like a rusty smell frosting away. My mouth dropped open with a gasp as I realized the source of the disgusting smell. My eyes glimpsed the lifeless man whom I had known for twelve whole years. His body was slowly losing all its blood, and was already becoming pale. The sight of him imprinted itself on my memory, a horrible yet beautiful sight.

He was dead. He would no longer hurt me.

Much to my horror, I saw the unpleasant man outside the manor on the phone with someone. In an attempt to eavesdrop, I crept closer to him without making a sound.

"Yes, they are safe in the house," his voice filled the outside world.

Who was safe? The children? Who was he talking to?

"What do you mean, you can't make this case a priority? They are children!" He screamed the last sentence with frustration, causing my body to jerk.

Was he talking about the children at Grimhill Manor?

With each step closer, I acquired a better view of him. While he talked on the phone, his body language was stiff and I noticed his free hand was tightly clenched.

"I expect you to make an appearance tonight. Someone shot a man here, he was the leader of this organization." A moment of silence followed as the person on the other side of the line spoke. "It doesn't matter how I know this information. Look up Frederick Grimhill, he was the leader of the Grimhill trafficking ring."

A gasp released from my throat at his words. "Thank you, officer."

He had called the police? Would the children here finally be free? Would I?

No, I certainly would not. The excitement inside of me dropped to the lowest level when his eyes met mine, and his presence was strong as he walked toward me. He grabbed my wrist and stormed out of the manor. A flicker of light filled the corner of my vision, a sensation telling me something I couldn't quite understand. The flicker lasted longer than usual, lingering around until I had walked out of the gates of the manor. Low whispers in the wind, far away behind me. There were more voices than usual. Silence penetrated my ears when we came to the pavement outside. I heard the whispers bid me farewell, and a feeling of uneasiness filled my body at the amount of whispering at once.

It had been my home for as long as I could remember.

The rain poured down outside, the clouds drenching us in their tears, making it nearly impossible to keep my eyes open. Deep down, I knew I should have been more scared.

He had killed another man.

While stumbling forward on the pavement, trying to figure out where to put my feet, all I could perceive was numbness. My entire life, I had been a prisoner, never once tasting freedom. Getting out of there did not feel like a relief, rather I felt nothing. In theory, I should have been relieved, but I was not.

A dead man had been lying in front of my feet.

I took another step and swallowed hard. A man I had known forever. I should have felt devastated to lose someone, traumatized from seeing someone die in front of me, seeing his gaze as he took his last breath. I felt nothing. No sympathy, no guilt, nothing.

"My doll, don't cover your eyes. I want to see them and stare into them forever."

The man laughed again like a fucking fool, and his emotional state changed as fast as lightning. He sure as hell was showing psychopath traits. We approached his car, and I noticed its tinted windows. It would be impossible for anyone to save me if something happened.

A chill spread through my body, making the hair on my arms rise. I stepped into the car before the man—whose name I could not recall—opened the passenger door. A warm sensation spread throughout my body as his hands brushed against mine, making my heart race. The moment he buckled his seatbelt and stared into my eyes, a sense of calm swept through him. His eyes were filled with desire.

Fuck, did he want me?

When his skin stopped brushing against mine, the thought quickly dissolved from my mind. He jumped into the car in the driver's seat and smiled awkwardly at me. With a loud hum, the car started, and he drove away from the place I had called home for all those years. I would have been lying to myself if I hadn't admitted I was terrified. At that moment, my body trembled at the mere idea of what he might do to me. Leaving the place that provided me with a roof to sleep under was nerve-wracking.

The drizzle on the window caught my attention, and in front of me, I saw an abandoned road emerge in the middle of the dark forest. A dark green forest surrounded the car on both sides. In some way, it was beautiful and charming. All the leaves that belonged to the trees were still hanging from the branches. Not a single one had fallen to the ground. The dense growth of the forest made it impossible to see into it. There was nothing too visible in the forest except trees and bushes. Gravel from the bumpy and uneven road flew off the tires as we drove forward at full speed. The moon appeared behind the clouds after a long drive in the car, glinting small signs of vileness against the dark night sky. Its light cast over the road, lighting up the gloomy night. Deep inside the forests, shrieks came from outside, far away, as rain pounded on the windows of the car. Shadows crept behind the trees, the night seeming unnaturally dark as if someone had drained it of all the light.

As he hummed a tune, the man tapped the steering wheel, filling in the silence and preventing the awful noises from outside. Every muscle in my body tightened when listening to the melody.

How did he know about that melody?

Cold sweat rolled down my forehead as I felt my heart race. That melody was a signature of my mother, who I hadn't seen for years. I was the only one who still remembered the tune she used to sing to me every night before tucking me into bed. How could he know about *my* melody?

Paranoia filled my entire body.

His eyes were glued to the road and eventually, a small paved road came into view as we pulled up onto it. In the distance, we saw a beautiful, yet old house. From one glance at the house, I could tell that it wasn't his style of choice. He seemed like a man who liked horror. I couldn't help but wonder if he had a girlfriend or wife, for that matter. A sting of jealousy filled my body, but I quickly shook it off. Why did the thought of him having a girl bother me?

My panic rose as I noticed how isolated the manor was. It was similar to Grimhill. That wasn't what I had wished for. I wanted to be free from these architectural monsters, from manors with eerie atmospheres and their mysterious essences. Dense and large trees surrounded the huge, mysterious manor, making me wonder who else lived there other than him. Surely, he couldn't be the only person living in such a huge estate. The grass around the house had dried out as the season had changed to late summer. Candlelight came from inside the manor when the dark clouds rolled closer, covering the moon and taking its life with it.

In front of me stood the huge building. A spacious gate led into the yard, through a cramped and short tunnel. There was a connection between the gate and the rest of the house. We were too far away for me to see behind the gate. Rain pattered on the car windows, making it even more difficult to see out of them. The exterior walls of the house were painted gray, and the lights outside on the patio dimly illuminated the architecture of the building. The house's vertical proportions and external buttressing gave the manor an even more sinister aspect. Its pointed arches created a sturdy look.

 The car's engine stopped, and the man pulled the handbrake. He exited the car, walked over to my side, and with a swift movement, opened the car door for me. I stared at him without daring to touch him. At that moment, I realized how fast his calmness had turned hostile as his angry eyes fixed on me. Quickly grabbing his hand, I stepped out of the car. The rain poured down on me, drenching my clothes, and the grass smelled fresh from the nourishment of the rain.

 "My doll, this is your new home," he said when we reached the front door.

 "It's beautiful," I forced myself to reply, swallowing away the anxiety that wanted to explode inside of me. It was indeed beautiful, with a decaying softness to its edges. Once upon a time, it had been magnificent.

 As the bitterly cold wind blasted into my face, it howled and whistled as if it were sending me a warning. The front door creaked open before we entered the hall, as if swept by an unseen shadow. Heart pounding from the weird encounter, my gaze shifted to the hall. An open place with a stone floor. In front of us was a staircase leading to the upper floor, with two pointed arches forming an opening in front. To our left were several other pointing arches, replacing the doors found in ordinary houses. A long corridor stretched into the distance. The ceilings inside the hallway was vaulted and supported the building from its weight and force.

The unpleasant man grabbed my jacket and helped me take my shoes off. Before his hand came up to cover my eyes, I glimpsed two antique gargoyles placed between two openings. My body froze and I tried to focus on breathing normally. Meanwhile, he covered my eyes and led me up the stairs. The hinges of a door creaked when he removed his hand from my eyes.

Taking a look around the room, I scanned it and noted what it looked like. A bed with a checkered bedspread, pillows, and sheets adorned the old-fashioned room. Next to the bed was a stick chair leaning against the wall. A desk stood beside the chair, and when my eyes fell upon it, I noticed dust covering its surface.

Among the things that caught my attention was a doll on the desk. As I examined the doll, I found that there was a layer of dust covering her, too. Her brown hair was curly, and she wore an elegant white hat. Her dress featured beige and gray. The pattern was plaid, and it had a white collar added to it. Grabbing her tiny hand, I thought about how lovely the doll was.

"Isn't she perfect, Dolly?" His voice sent a sensation of discomfort throughout my body. Despite his calm voice, I knew he was anything but calm.

In order to avoid a bad outcome, it was imperative that I responded to the man. If not, things could turn out badly. While trying to keep my voice from trembling, I could only say, "Yes."

As he patted his hands like a young child, he laughed. "I know! Her name is Mary." He smiled like a child who had just been given candy from his mother after a tiring day.

"I-it's a very charming name." My voice sounded more like a whisper.

I put the doll back on the desk and met the man's gaze. It appeared as if something that was not okay had affected him. His face displayed an expression of extreme seriousness.

Oh no.

Despite his unpleasant voice, I tried not to be intimidated by him as he spoke.

"Let me tell you the rules, Aurora." He gave me an intense, long look, and I returned it by staring back at him. "You're not allowed to leave the room at any time." He paused and continued, "When I say something to you, you will obey." His eyebrows raised, and he stared deep into my eyes, into my soul.

As I remained as still as possible, sweat poured down my body. In an effort to remove sweat from my palms, I wiped them on my dress.

"You know what happens if you disobey, don't you, my doll?" I nodded uncertainly, having no idea what would happen. "You'll have to figure out the rest of the rules for yourself."

That wasn't fair! My mind raced. What if I acted improperly even if I believed it to be okay behavior? What if I was to break the rules without knowing I had broken them? That was not fair. How could he do that to me?

"Sleep, get used to your room and I will see you tomorrow morning," the man exclaimed before exiting the room.

I lay down in bed. Normally, I would have had a thousand thoughts swirling around inside my head, but at that moment my mind was blank, and no thoughts or worries arose. It was only a matter of time before everything that had happened would catch up with me, but only emptiness filled me. An emptiness inside me that grew bigger the heavier my eyelids became, and then I fell asleep from exhaustion.

A younger girl's giggles filled my ears, waking me from my peaceful sleep. Chills spread over my body like a constant cold. The temperature dropped dramatically. Children's laughter echoed through the walls, and behind the eyelid of my left eye, a flicker appeared. The feeling was so strong that I felt as if whatever was there wanted me to be aware of it. It was the same kind of feeling I had constantly experienced at Grimhill Manor, where every corner was haunted by all the children who had been murdered in cold blood over the generations.

I needed to pull the covers over me as the temperature became even lower, and my eyes fluttered open. There was a presence on the left side of the room, not something I could see, but rather something I could feel in every bone of my body. In my soul.

"W-watch out f-for the m-man," the girl shivered in my ears.

"Who are you?" Fear took over every nook and cranny of my body. I would never get used to that feeling.

"Mary."

My face turned pale, as though I'd seen a ghost. Ironically. When my eyes scanned the room, I noticed the doll I received from the creepy man was placed next to me on my left.

"H-he i-is f-filled with d-darkness."

A skin-prickling breeze skimmed over my face before it disappeared, leaving me utterly anguished, with the giggles fading away further from the walls.

When I woke up, my lungs were struggling for air. The discomfort remained, and as I looked around the room, I saw Mary on the left side of my room.

She had been on my right side when I fell asleep.

Panicked, I tried to tell myself it was just a dream. But the dream had felt so real.

As the man entered the room again the next day, I discovered he had something horrible in store for me. The dream had been true. Mary had warned me about him.

"Now I think you're ready, Dolly," he said while entering the room.

I looked at him with a confused expression on my face. He examined his fingers.

"Let's play a game!" He exclaimed.

My lack of game skills would ensure the game wouldn't end well for me. It was a wonder I survived Grimhill Manor, and it was mainly because I had been Frederick's favorite doll. While breathing became increasingly difficult, my heart pumped faster and faster. Anxiety forced its way to the surface.

"I'm about to tell you about a place in the house, and you're going to find it in just one try. If you enter the wrong room, a punishment will wait for you. You'll get a reward if you go to the right room." I nodded my head while taking a deep breath.

"Isn't it a wonderful game, my doll?" He emphasized the word 'wonderful' as he spoke.

A smile spread across his face, and his hands started clapping in excitement. Seeing him act like a child only made my heart thump faster.

"Let the game begin, Dolly."

Chapter 4
Her

"Hmm, we will start off easy. Find the kitchen," the creepy man exclaimed.

The moment my feet took the first step out of the room, I tried to swallow away my fear. My gaze fixed on the hallway outside of the bedroom as I surveyed my surroundings. The manor was oddly quiet, and on one side of the corridor hung torches. The light danced in the shadows like a nightmarish ball, causing goosebumps to spread over my arms and down to my legs. I walked through the hallway, unsure of which way to go. My throat was filled with saliva as I swallowed a loud gulp, realizing there was only one chance to win the round.

A common theme I had noticed when reading novels was that the kitchen was always located on the first floor, whether they were romance novels or fantasy novels. The kitchen at Grimhill Manor was tucked away in one wing, but still occupied the first floor. If I had luck on my side, it would be on the first floor here, too. That was what I had to strive for.

Grabbing the railing for support, I descended the stairs with slowed steps. Footsteps behind me indicated that the man was following behind and watching my every move. An unnerving feeling settled over me. It was only us two in the hallway, his breathing light and mine heavy and rough, as I panted from the terror suffocating me. There was something about him I couldn't put my finger on. He had a certain vibe revolving around him. With every step he took, he showed confidence glowing out of him as if he were the stars in the night sky. That man wore his arrogance on his sleeve, proudly displaying it to everyone who dared look his way.

The nightmare resurfaced as I remembered Mary warning me about a man. My blood ran cold, froze to ice as if it was a glacier. The dream had sure as hell caught me off guard. Surely the man she referred to was *that* man, he who walked behind me and made my nerves twitch until I didn't know how to act. Or maybe, Mary in my dream hadn't referred to anyone, maybe it was just that; a nightmare.

When I reached the first floor, my hand let go of the railing supporting my body. Had I not been wearing socks, the cold stone floor would have frozen my body in place. Taking a deep breath, I looked up at the manor's vaulted ceilings that had scared me when I first saw them. Besides the amazing architecture of the house, I was even more intrigued by its interior design.

From a lighted candle that hung on one wall, shadows were formed around one of the gargoyles that occupied the floor. It spread an uneasy feeling through me, for it felt as if the gargoyle was staring at me with its observing eyes. Or maybe it was the man behind me; his gaze burned a hole in the dress I wore, pushed its way through my back, and went straight to my heart.

Despite having my back to him, I felt his gaze on me. He was waiting for me to make a choice, to continue playing his sick game.

My eyes lingered on the gargoyle for a second too long as I debated whether to turn right or left. I knew I had only one chance, and walking in the wrong direction would cause immediate punishment. When I took a step to the right, my heart raced up to my throat as if trying to escape. A long corridor stretched ahead, with several candles suspended as the only source of light. While searching for a door that led to the kitchen, I felt myself shrinking away. When I finally had contemplated on which one, I gently pushed it open. A creaking sound accompanied the opening of the door, as if the wind had swung a rusty gate shut.

Please let this be the kitchen.

I was captivated by my surroundings, but for a very different reason than what I sought. In the room, there was only one couch. Dust filled its layers and the air inside felt stuffy, making it harder to breathe through my lungs. The room had a wood-like wallpaper, but other than that, it was a dull space.

Definitely not the kitchen.

A sudden outburst of laughter awakened me. "Oh, dear. This is the wrong room."

Upon turning around to meet his eyes, a smirk was etched across his lips and his eyes were gleaming.

My eyes dropped to watch his lips, which were moist with saliva, making them even more kissable. A sudden pull made me want to taste them, feel them on mine, to know how he felt against me. My gaze swept across his face before he could notice me staring at his lips, a silent heat brushing against my cheeks.

"You lost," he said in an obvious tone.

Deep down, I wanted to roll my eyes at him, but I chose not to act on my impulse. He made me fear the consequences of disobeying him.

"Stay here, Dolly. Don't touch anything."

Without his voice in my head, I could only concentrate on my heartbeat. Minutes felt like years before the closing of a door broke my trance. He had left the room, and that was my cue to conduct a brief scan around the room. Without making a sound, I took a step closer to the window and its rusty pink curtains hanging from the ceiling.

Outside the window was a beautiful garden. Lots of flowers were planted in rows, well organized and tended to. It was an appealing and colorful place, with a small pond in the middle. It was like something taken out of a fairy tale, I had seen nothing like it before. The view from my room at Grimhill Manor had been a rotten wall opposite. Even if I could have had a view of nature, everything would still be decaying and dried up.

The windows had no handles but were locked with a keyhole, which meant there was no chance for me to escape.

Fuck.

All I ever wanted was to be free, and seeing them locked without a handle made the hope fade.

Until that day, my only goal was to meet my mother again. She was the only person I had ever loved and cared for. The hope of one day reuniting with her remained in my heart every single day. One of the main reasons I fought was because of that. I could have ended it years ago at Grimhill Manor, but didn't. If there was even a slight chance of me meeting her again, I didn't want to waste it by ending my life.

Not knowing when the man would return, I chose to sweep my gaze around the room again. The more I thought about what was coming to me once he returned, the more desperate I became. It was hard to ignore the cursing wave of despair floating inside of me.

Among the belongings in the room was a doll lying in one corner. It was a matter of seconds before he would come back, and that thought in itself made my nerves tickle with fear, but also something else. It was a feeling I didn't want to feel, almost like anticipation. While he stared at me, my body felt drawn to the intensity of his eyes, like he was holding me in his arms, as if he was consuming me.

When I walked closer to the doll, I worked to avoid squeaking the floorboards. An instance such as that would draw his attention.

The doll's hair seemed disheveled and one of her eyes was missing, yet she was still an eye-catching sight.

A beauty draped in darkness.

The crack on her right cheek was one of the things that made her so unique.

I found her to be one of the most beautiful dolls I had ever seen. A doll like that would have horrified the children at Grimhill Manor. They always pointed out one's flaws, but they couldn't see the beauty in the broken. In the accumulated dust and dirt, the doll's previous white dress had turned a darker shade.

"What are you doing?" The voice from behind startled me, making me almost drop the doll from my grip.

He was scaring me all the time. I held the doll closer to me, wanting to warm her in my embrace as if she was a real baby.

"Put. It. Down," I watched as he grit his teeth and his narrow squint conveyed a deep meaning.

After putting the doll on the floor, I looked into her eyes. It was as if she was begging me not to put her down again, judging by the look on her face. As if she knew she would rot if she remained on the dirty floor. The whispers in the walls far away seemed to come from her, despite the fact that I knew she couldn't beg me. A feminine voice whispering nonsense.

Impossible.

She wasn't real. I couldn't help but feel the worry gnawing inside me, the deep sense of uneasiness held me rigid.

A feeling of being stabbed in the stomach filled me as I walked toward him. There was a part of me that wanted to run away from here and never return. It was impossible for me to see what the man was holding with his hands behind his back.

He pointed to the object in his hands and said, "You deserve this punishment."

Scissors.

My body froze in its place.

Scissors? Why the fuck was he holding scissors?

I stared at it for a moment, his eyes piercing into me before my hands grabbed the object without my consent. While my conscience refused to grab it, I felt as if my movements were controlled by him.

"My dear, be a good doll for me and cut yourself."

My eyes widened. There was no fucking way.

Coldness spread over my body like the time of the ice age. My hands stopped listening to all the rational thoughts inside my brain.

Why am I obeying this man?

"Please, no," I choked out, but it was too late.

An intense strike of pain caused me to scream, my lungs not getting enough air, my chest constricting. When I pushed the scissors into my thigh, the flesh ripped from my body. A cascade of tears flowed down my cheeks as I watched blood seeping out of the wound, down my leg, and then landing on the floor. A sense of helplessness came over me. My hands were out of control.

It was impossible for me to see through the pain clouding my eyes. My screaming was the only sound I heard as the man just stood there. He did nothing, just stared at me falling apart. And then everything went silent. Blood still dripped down my leg as the scissors fell to the ground beside me.

"You deserved this. I'm so sorry." His eyes filled with guilt for a brief moment.

That warmth behind his dull eyes was visible. He was more himself than he had been a few seconds ago. Something was up with that man. If it was pure craziness, I did not know. It was as if his shell contained clouds and mist, making it impossible to get through to him. The only way was to let him do what he had to.

A second later, his eyes returned to the icy, dull ones. "It's not over yet," he continued.

His eyes were no longer filled with guilt. Fury sought its way up to my surface. If looks could kill, I would have the man lying on the floor, screaming out his lungs until he died the most painful death. Gosh, I fucking hated him.

He told me without emotion, "Find the bathroom where the lights are off."

A grunt of pain escaped my throat when I tried to leave the room. My thigh was still bleeding, and he did nothing. No amount of pain could make that worse. My legs led me to the staircase, and I used the railing to drag my body to the floor above. When I put my weight on the leg with the cut, I widened my eyes and winced from the pain.

In case the light was emanating through the cracks in the doors, I took help from the wall and looked under each one. Every door I walked past had lights seeping out from under it, except for one. A sigh of relief escaped my lips. My attention drew to the other door, which was also dark.

You're kidding me.

Curiosity drove me to open one door. It was a bedroom. I heard the man behind me clapping his hands again and laughing.

"I have to say, you suck at this game, Dolly."

While a coldness spread throughout every corner of my then frozen body, I nodded my head, admitting that I had never been good at playing games. My survival at Grimhill Manor had been a miracle, but I had learned my way of surviving them.

A smile was displayed on his face. "Let's see what your punishment will be." He looked as if he was contemplating my punishment. "Oh, I know," he exclaimed. "I know you hate small places since Frederick told me."

I almost choked on my saliva when he said those words.

Would he confine me to a small room? Small spaces had never scared me. What I feared was to feel like I couldn't breathe.

"This is the perfect punishment for a naughty little girl like you, Dolly."

He grabbed my wrist and dragged me into a room on the first floor. My thigh ached when I walked behind him, and when he opened the door, I saw a coffin. My eyes widened and I asked myself how he could have a coffin.

"Dolly, come here," he said in a dark voice, a smirk spreading across his face. "My friend dared me to buy a coffin, thought me to be a coward who wouldn't dare to do it, but here we are. It serves a better purpose now."

I walked toward him in slow motion as he reached out his hand, prompting me to take it. He instructed me to lie down as he opened the coffin. Despite him telling me to follow his instructions, I shook with fear. It was as if my legs were whimpering, wanting to give up their weight.

When he spoke, he smiled with a sad expression on his lips. "Don't think I want to hurt you, Dolly, but it is your punishment."

In farewell, he closed the coffin and waved his hand.

My surroundings became pitch black. There were footsteps outside, fading away, and a door that opened and closed.

He was gone.

Fear gripped my heart. Fear of not being able to breathe. All I could hear was the sound of my breathing. Hyperventilation almost overtook me. My chest felt tight as my heart pounded against it. The air filled my lungs as I attempted to take deep breaths, but it did not work. My knees kept knocking together from the trembling of my body. The only way I could breathe was by taking deep breaths, but even so, it was difficult. Panic filled my body. I shouted and banged my hands on the lid of the coffin. It was my attempt to catch the man's attention so he could allow me to leave. Trying to breathe became more difficult as I cried and howled. After I caught my breath, I began screaming again like a maniac, unable to control my feelings.

After a while, I sensed activity outside the coffin, a door opening. I wasn't sure how long I had been in there, and it took a while for me to hear whoever was outside after I had stopped screaming. Even in my desperate attempts to hear anything, I couldn't. When laughter interrupted me outside the coffin, every nerve in my body froze, and my lips glued together in a seal.

He had joined me.

"P-please let me out!" I was knocking on the coffin, begging for freedom. His laughter increased in volume.

"P-please!" I tried to catch my breath. It was as if I had run a marathon.

"I—I can't breathe!" Before speaking up, I paused. "I beg you!"

The man had stopped laughing. "Oh Dolly, I'm not finished yet."

The salty taste of my tears lingered on my lips as I swallowed them. "Please!" I begged with desperation.

"A few more minutes, Dolly."

It was the most torturous experience of my life. The small space made my head feel lightheaded, and I banged on the coffin in a constant rhythm. The coffin swung open and exposed the man, smirking down at me.

"Welcome outside, Dolly," he said in his dark and raspy voice.

My lungs could breathe again and relaxation spread throughout my body. Standing up, I breathed in and out while holding my hand to my chest.

The man said, "Let's continue," with such coldness in his voice.

It was his stare that caused my eyes to widen, and I knew I couldn't continue playing that sick game. "Please, I don't want to." I shook my head in desperate pleas.

"Oh Dolly, do you think you have a word in this?" I could sense his mocking tone when he talked to me.

As I shook my head again, I sighed. "Please, no." Tears formed in my eyes.

"It will be easy," the man promised, yet I knew it wouldn't be.

When was it ever easy?

"Find that bathroom. It is very easy, Dolly."

He who stood in front of me was the devil himself. His eyes showed no emotions, no guilt, and especially no remorse. He wanted to see me suffer, and his body filled with enjoyment at that. As I limped over to the door, nervousness filled me. He said it would be easy. I had opened only one door the last time I was in that hallway.

Perhaps the other door would be the bathroom?

As I walked to the end of the hallway, two doors revealed themselves. One of which I had opened before, and one of which I hadn't. Taking a deep breath, I exhaled.

Please let this be the right room.

My heart was pounding faster and faster as I grabbed the handle of the door. When I saw the room that opened up before me, all my worries flew away.

It was the bathroom.

"Well done, Dolly."

The realization that I had succeeded made me sigh with relief.

"I told you it was easy. You are such a genius doll."

When he looked at me, I saw a glint of pride in his dull eyes, and my gaze shifted to the darkness, not believing that I had won.

"Now, do you know what you want?"

As I gained the courage to speak, I nodded my head, taking a deep breath. I whispered in a mumbling voice, "I want to leave this house."

"Because you won. It isn't more than right to give you what you want."

I couldn't believe what I just heard. Was he planning to let me outside? After all these years, could I finally return home? To meet my mother again?

His eyes fixed on the hall as he walked there. Opening the front door, I followed behind him. My lungs filled with fresh, cold air as I breathed in deeply. My wrist was handcuffed within seconds, and the other hand was placed around a pillar supporting the roof. Disappointment filled me as I realized he wouldn't let me out of his sight.

"Y-you said—"

He interrupted me. "You wished for me to let you out, my dear." He looked at me with cold eyes, freezing any warmth left within me. "So I let you out, but now you have to stay handcuffed so you don't run away."

He smiled softly at me. A tightening sensation filled my chest. What if I could never escape? With each passing second, my hopes for freedom continued to crumble

"Be a good doll and stay here. I'm heading inside."

Then he walked off into the house, leaving me all alone in the darkness. Somehow, I felt frightened. I could hear an owl hooting and a wolf howling to get its pack's attention. Several meters away from me, something rustled in the bushes. That sound made me flinch. The reason I felt so tense was a mystery to me. I was desperate to get inside as soon as possible. I felt like I was being punished rather than rewarded. The melody I used to sing at Grimhill Manor echoed in my head as I stomped my foot against the wooden floor. When I fiddled with my fingers to relieve the boredom, my gaze shifted to them. From the bushes, rustling sounds continued when the wind blew against the trees. Whispers came from the forest far away.

It wasn't real. They didn't exist, and no one could save me. Whispers were all around. Yet I didn't know if it was the mystical animals or if it was all in my head. I was too damn paranoid. My entire body tensed, waiting for something to happen.

FOR SOME TIME, I sat handcuffed outside the house. Having been unaware of the time, I guessed that I had been sitting outside for at least forty minutes. The chilly breeze of the late summer night swept over me, making me worry about catching a cold. I had always hated the coldness. If I fell ill, would he be nicer to me?

Sitting out here was much better than being inside. The events of what happened earlier the same day came to the forefront of my mind, and I remembered all the pain he had caused me. I found it somehow peaceful to sit out here, taking in the dark landscape around me. Growing up taught me to embrace the darkness and see its beauty. Something very few could do. Darkness scared me as a child, but not anymore. Grimhill Manor was so full of darkness that I learned to accept it, embrace it, and live with it inside of me. A blackened heart, a broken soul, a shattered memory.

No fear of the dark anymore. The pain had decreased, making me able to relax more. My thoughts wondered when he would go get me. He couldn't be that cruel to leave me out here. The man with a devil's appearance and angel soul deep within. A fallen angel, I would say. There was more to him behind those dull, amber-colored eyes. The way he looked at me had a unique combination of warmth and coldness.

"Are you cold, Dolly?" A soft voice spoke from behind, causing me to flinch at the sudden attention. I shifted my body, so I was facing the owner. *Speaking of the devil.*

"Yes," I whispered, lowering my gaze and looking at my cuffed hand. An icy wind blew over me, causing my hair to ruffle in it and my body to shiver.

"This is your reward. You asked for it." He sat down in front of me and grabbed my hand.

At first, I flinched away, thinking he would hurt me. I couldn't take any more pain, couldn't take anyone fucking touching me. While I knew I was slowly breaking down from the inside, I tried to remain strong.

I really tried.

It was hard when I, my entire life, had felt so lost, with hope being my only saviour. While he had my hand in his, he uncuffed it and I relaxed slightly, still on guard. My walls were too high for me to let go, and I couldn't let anyone come close to me. His warm hand held my trembling, cold one. The human touch felt weird on my skin, so unfamiliar. His hand grabbed mine for a long while, and in my peripheral view, I saw his eyes staring at me.

What was that kind of feeling? And why was he holding my hand after having been so cruel earlier?

Was the devil shedding its facade?

When he looked into my eyes, it felt like a spark of electricity was burning between us. Rather than showing my shyness, I forced myself to look away as a red blush crept up my cheeks. I fantasized about a world where he would hold my hand in his as he made love to me. As he touched every part of my body, seeing everything of me, making me feel ecstasy.

What the fuck are you thinking, Aurora?

By shaking my head, I was able to rid myself of the fantasy that would never, could never, come true.

"You are not too cold, right?" he asked, shocking me.

"No, I'm not," I replied, unable to state otherwise. Even though I felt my teeth clattering.

"Your cut does not look that terrible." He caressed my thigh, near where the cut and dried blood was.

"It wasn't that deep." My voice was only a whisper as I tried to not think about what his touch did to me.

"That is very reassuring," he breathed out through an exhale.

As our eyes met, I could see guilt and something more in his gaze. I didn't recognize that *something* and wondered what it could be. We sat like that in silence as several minutes passed. In an electric touch, I came to my senses, realizing that his hand was still on my thigh and making its way upwards. His fingers danced in circular motions on my skin, as if he was tracing an old and precious painting. As if he was afraid to ruin the painting. That one touch from him, his hand almost burning my thigh, was enough to make my insides clench.

When I felt him starting to stand up, my hand quickly grabbed his wrist before I could perceive my actions. Maybe it was because of that gnawing feeling inside me that my anxiety welled up. I didn't want to be alone again. The mere thought of that scared me more than I wanted to admit.

"Please stay. I'd like some company." I almost begged him, desperate to feel him close to me again.

He was someone I should have feared, someone I needed to be careful around. Yet at that moment, it felt as if it was just a façade he had built. As if he had built a thick wall around his heart. The way he behaved shocked me and gave me mixed signals about how I should feel. One second I hated him for what he had done so far, but the next I softened in his presence. That side of him was somehow caring, and my heart ached for him.

I wanted, for just a moment, to let down my walls. I deserved to be held.

For a second, he stopped caressing my thigh while still resting his hand on it. His eyes darted to mine in quick haste before looking down at my leg again. If I hadn't known better, I might have believed the reddening of his neck was real. My eyes had observed him during those few seconds, and he appeared to have a sense of warmth behind his eyes. At that moment, something was happening to me, a thing my brain could not comprehend, but my body intuitively sensed. It was as if he had let down his walls, allowing me to see who he really was.

The exhaustion reflected over my body, and I drew closer to the man beside me without even noticing. His presence was like an automatic attraction to my body, and that terrified me.

I had never been the one to get attached to anyone, always knowing that everyone eventually left. No one really stuck around, so what was the point in having a friend, a lover, a someone?

Even so, I felt a tug in my heart to be wary of him, yet to trust him.

I was going crazy, completely and utterly crazy.

A shoulder was all I needed at that moment to relieve the fatigue that had taken over my body. The whispers I had heard earlier from inside the woods had silenced in his presence.

In response to my pleas, he gently grasped my head and made me lean against his broad shoulder. His toned muscles tensed beneath the skin on his arms and my eyes landed on his biceps, feeling a tingling sensation inside my stomach. I wondered if he worked out. I was almost certain he did. No one had that kind of well-built body without exercising.

To my surprise, he moved his hand up to caress my hair, scratching my scalp and making me close my eyes in comfort. My lips parted in a deep exhalation.

"No one's ever done that to me before," I whispered, although my voice wasn't very audible in the loud howling of the wind.

"Done what?" He asked as he continued to scratch my scalp in a gentle act. I wondered if he did it mindlessly, or if he did it to soothe my nerves.

"That," I said, and nuzzled closer to him.

Being so close to another man was strange. Even though he had hurt me before with his sick game, something had changed within him. That man differed from the man I had spent most of the day with. That man showed me his true self through his eyes, a thing I was certain no one else but I could see. The warmth in his eyes heated my freezing body, sending a jolt of electricity through me. I would blame that feeling on my prolonged lack of intimacy.

Never before had my body experienced the touch of a man in that way. A man to whom I felt some underlying, non-likable attraction to. Never before had someone caressed me the way he did. The fact that I had felt nothing like that before was a testament to how much I yearned for his touch. Something within me told me the dullness had disappeared from his aura. For now, at least.

"Yeah?" He whispered as his hand stroked the top of my head again.

God, there was something with his voice that made me feel like I was flying. It pierced my ears in a gentle act, filling me with a sense of peace, and giving me something I had never felt. Butterflies.

My eyes felt heavy, the exhaustion from the day pulling me down. While we talked, fatigue gripped my body, and I felt like I would fall asleep on his shoulders. Hours earlier, he had caused me extreme pain, and at that point, I felt safe enough to sleep near him.

What is wrong with you, Aurora?

"You must be in pain."

Before I could respond, he lifted me into his embrace. In bridal style, he carried me up the stairs into the bedroom. The room I would have to call my own, even though I didn't want to.

"While you were outside, I gathered some clothes from your wardrobe for you to put on. Warm clothes, to say. Josephine hung up your clothes in your closet, by the way."

He put me down on the bed, walking over to the pile of clothes. "Do you want me to help you put them on?"

There it was again, that glimpse of guilt covering his gaze, causing a weird feeling inside my stomach. He had felt no remorse earlier, and yet he hadn't apologized for his actions.

"Uhm, no thanks," I said, finding it strange that he would stay with me.

Even though I wanted him to help me, I knew I could not let him do it. I had more self-respect than that.

There was something with him, the way he looked at me. His gaze was always so intense, even when his body language appeared calm. It caused a certain attraction inside of me.

I loved the way he looked at me.

I hated the way he acted toward me.

It was hard not to wonder where the emotionless, bitter man from before had gone.

"Alright then," he walked over to the door, taking one last glance at me. I saw his Adam's apple as he swallowed before speaking, "Sleep well, my dear," and then he closed the door.

"What in the heavens just happened?" I murmured to myself in confusion.

Deciding not to disobey him, scared of him getting into a weird mood again, I changed into a pair of pink sweatpants with a matching hoodie. Finally, something warm was on my skin.

Laying down under the covers, I thought of the gentleman's kindness, his hand caressing the top of my head. I thought about the way he had looked at me with such intensity, and the way he had caressed my thigh before I drifted off to sleep. My lips twitched with a faint smile.

IN MY HAZY VISION, I could see a rather young woman. She opened the curtains that the man had drawn before he left my room the night before. With the dawn chorus drifting in from the closed windows, and the first rays of the sun lighting up my room, I arose to the sounds of birdsong. The night had transformed into morning. Having rubbed my eyes to clear my blurry vision, I examined the woman in front of me.

Her black dress was adorned with a white apron, tied at the waist. Her brown hair was pulled into a high ponytail. No makeup was visible on her face, yet her appearance was stunning. Her skin was almost glowing in the light streaming from the lamp.

"Good morning," the woman waved at me and smiled.

"Morning." My voice was a whisper, unsure if it was okay to speak to her or not.

"Do not worry, you can talk freely with me at the moment. Asher will not hear us as he is downstairs, waiting for you at the dining table." Her eyes widened when she realized what she had said. Her hand flew to her mouth to cover it as a gasp escaped from her throat.

"Ash-Asher?" I asked her, confusion visible in my facial expression.

"Oh no! I am sorry. Sir's name is Asher. Please do not let him know I dared to mention his name." She talked at a rapid pace, as if she had to hurry with her words out of panic.

With her eyebrows furrowed, she looked at me, worried. I gave her a reassuring smile to calm her stiff shoulders.

"I won't. He's already terrifying enough." A shiver ran down my spine as I recalled yesterday's forenoon when he had played with me as if I was his doll.

When he made me cut my own thigh.

Relief was shown on the maid's face when she heard me speak those words. Her shoulders sunk down in relaxation. She closed the door and stood beside the bed.

"He told me to clean this cut as soon as you woke up." From the bag she had placed against the bed leg, she grabbed a first aid kit.

She soaked a gauze pad in something and dabbed the wound that was on my thigh. The stinging pain from the liquid and gauze caused me to wince and hiss. It was a type of pain that branched across my leg like lightning.

"Sorry, this is chlorhexidine," her gaze looked at me in apology.

Despite my wincing, my mouth said, "It's alright," even though it wasn't. It hurt and stung like hell.

Once my wound had been cleaned, she smiled at me again. "I am Josephine, one of Sir's closest maids," she said and held out her hand.

Despite the pain from my wound, a smile spread across my face when I grabbed her hand to shake it. "I am Aurora."

"Such a lovely name!" the maid named Josephine exclaimed, making my cheeks heat from the comment. I wasn't used to compliments.

A question crossed my mind as I spoke to the woman, and I blurted out, "How did he afford this house?"

I had obviously shocked her, yet she composed herself and answered. "He inherited it from his parents. It's been in their family for generations. In addition, he also received a lot of money. He won't ever have to worry about not having enough. Don't tell him I said that. He hates to talk about money."

So that was how he received his money. Interesting.

"Now that I have cleaned the wound, Asher would like to meet you for breakfast in the dining room. He told me he wanted to talk to you about something. If you follow me, I can show you the way."

Josephine helped me out of bed and I used her shoulder for support while we walked down the stairs to the first floor. Although I was still limping forward due to the wound, having Josephine's help made it easier. My heart rate didn't slow down but pounded like a madman. I wondered what he might want to talk to me about. If only he could caress my hair and look after me as gently as he had done the night before.

With nerves taking over my body, I thought *I guess I just have to find out.*

Chapter 5
Her

WE HAD REACHED A double door leading to an area which I presumed was the dining room.

"Okay, here it is. Good luck!" chirped the young maid as she bolted from there, leaving me alone. A knock later, I stood in front of Asher by the door inside the dining room. He held a phone in his hands, the form of which I recognized from my books where the main characters used one. Frederick had used one too on special occasions. Even though Frederick had kept us away from reality, he had still made sure there were classes to attend. We could all read, write, and do math.

The lessons were taught by two teachers who took turns every other day in the room we called the parlor room. The living room was where everything happened.

Asher put down his phone and laid it inside his pocket before he looked up at me.

"Good morning, dear," he said to me as he gave me a heartwarming smile, easing my nerves.

"Good morning," my voice was barely audible through the whisper as nervousness grabbed hold of my insides.

"Come, sit down."

Asher placed his hand on my back as he led me to the table, a move that was so innocent, yet sparked something within me. His touch made me flinch at first, having never allowed a person to hold me, but the way he placed his hand on me made something stir to life. A feeling which outweighed the discomfort. I wanted his hand to slide down my back. I wanted him to hug me and take me into his embrace. The intensity of my thoughts almost made me act on them.

You are sick, Aurora.

But his touch felt so *right*. Even if my dress stopped his hand from coming in contact with my skin, it felt as if it burned through the fabric and touched my skin directly.

With a shuddering breath, I shook away my thoughts and sat down beside Asher. The breakfast laid out in front of us contained one plate with scrambled eggs and one with bacon. Someone had placed two glasses filled with an orange liquid between the plates, and I assumed it was orange juice. A large plate of pancakes lined up next to them, watering my mouth. I couldn't remember the last time I had eaten that kind of 'fancy' breakfast.

Too long.

"Do not be so voracious, dear," Asher chuckled and added, "Be patient."

Two other maids came into the room. I expected to see Josephine, but she was nowhere in sight. We each received a portion of food from the maids. When they left the room again, Asher welcomed me to eat. I cradled a piece of bacon inside my mouth and the taste hit me in an instant. The taste was appetizing and the bacon was crispy on my tongue and sank into my mouth, making me taste it even more. The chance of getting food poisoning never occurred to me and even if he would poison the food, the risk of dying was worth it. The food tasted too good.

A perfect last meal.

"It tastes delicious, doesn't it, my dear?" He took a piece of bread from his plate.

I watched him place the bread inside his mouth after opening his lips. In some way, I felt that the action stirred something within me. As if I longed to have him close to me, longed to feel his lips on mine. The craving to touch him freaked me out, and I forced myself to ignore my feelings.

He wasn't handsome, he wasn't caring, and most importantly, he wasn't someone to fantasize about.

To reply to his earlier question, I nodded my head and enjoyed the food. Meanwhile, he stared at my lips with such danger and I almost didn't notice where his gaze was. Throughout consuming the food, I licked my lips to make sure I savored every bit. If I didn't know better, I would have thought Asher was staring at my lips. He couldn't be. My eyes rolled from the absurd thoughts occupying my mind.

Never had I experienced any sort of sexual attraction towards anyone. I tried to convince myself that my feelings for him were imaginary. I had to ignore those thoughts. They were only dreams I wanted to be true.

When I took another bite, I groaned at how delicious it tasted. The fact that I hadn't eaten for over a day made me enjoy breakfast even more. It was like eating cotton candy, with the food melting on my tongue.

It tasted amazing after not eating for a day. Once again, Asher let out a chuckle.

"We will have visitors today, dear, which means I expect you to behave well," he said before taking another bite of the bacon.

My mouth stopped chewing midway through eating, shock filling my body at his words.

"Don't worry dear, it is a close friend of mine. He will not hurt you nor touch you."

Perhaps I could escape if there was another person coming? Could I finally be free after all the years in captivity?

"He will bring a girl around the same age as you. Will that not be lovely, my dear?" Asher's voice sounded deep, rusty, even.

I looked at him with astonishment in my eyes. The possibility of meeting another girl my age implied they knew where I came from, and my hope and the possibility of escaping decreased.

Shit.

"I can see you have many questions, dear. Only by yourself can you find out the answer."

The corner of his lips curled into a crooked smile. After almost finishing all his food, he sipped orange juice from his glass.

Nodding, I swallowed my food and answered, "Yes, I understand."

I continued eating, even though the fork in my hand felt heavy under his intense gaze. A maid from earlier came into the dining room to remove our empty plates.

"The food tasted delicious, thank you." My voice sounded low as I thanked Asher.

I did not want to seem ungrateful, so despite my discomfort, I had to thank him for the food he had provided me with. He had given me a proper meal, which they didn't give me at Grimhill

Manor. Frederick fed the children as little food as he could. Partly because of his stinginess and his unwillingness to spend an excessive amount of money on children he didn't care about. His main reason was that he believed all children should be as thin as dolls. We were, after all, his dolls.

My stomach dropped to my feet with a strange feeling of saliva forming in my mouth. The nausea made me want to throw up my food.

Frederick.

At once, the memory from two days ago appeared in my mind.

Frederick's lifeless body did not even have a second to spare before it fell into the pool of blood forming around his dead body. As I looked at him, I saw the hole in his head caused by the bullet.

Tears burned in my eyes, but I refused to let Asher see me cry at breakfast. With a disgusting shudder creeping down my body, I swallowed the saliva that had formed in my mouth. It felt like I had repressed the events of that day at Grimhill Manor. The day Asher chose me as his doll. The memory of Frederick's lifeless body with a hole in his head replayed in my head. I fought another wave of nausea when I closed my eyes. I hated Frederick with all that I was, and a certain feeling of relief had filled my body when I watched him die in front of my eyes. Still, the sight of his dead body had been too much for me to bear.

When I opened my eyes, Asher was looking at me strangely. A reaction to my weird behavior. A smile formed on my lips and I shook my head to show him it was nothing. One of his eyebrows rose, but I ignored it and instead focused on what he said next.

"You are free to take a shower. I will show you to the bathroom." Luckily for me, he had forgotten my strange behavior.

My relief grew as he mentioned the word 'shower,' and I responded, "Yes, please."

He stood up from his seat and I followed suit. The corridor we walked through had many paintings lined up on its walls. The candles between the paintings lit up the space and cast shadows. It was as if the shadows held the secrets of the mansion within them. The floorboards we walked on creaked. That, along with the moving shadows on the wall, made chills tingle across my skin. As I strolled down the corridor, I felt a sort of Déjà vu. Shivers found their way into every bone in my body, and I gasped.

"Follow me," a voice whispered in my ear, causing me to wake up in a hurry. The voice lingered in the room, in every cell of my body, refusing to let me be.

"Follow me," the voice hissed in aggression and my feet found the floor in haste.

My white nightgown appeared in the window as a silhouette when I sneaked out of my room, making my way to where the voices came from.

My footsteps were silent as a mouse, my breaths forming clouds ahead. The cold spread faster with each step I took. A long corridor appeared with lights as the only source. Then I heard breathing behind me, panting at the back of my neck as I reached the painting. In a flash, I turned around to check if anyone was nearby. And before me stood Asher.

But it wasn't Asher.

His eyes were black with darkness, his face indistinct in the glow of the lights, and his breathing was too loud to be normal. My heart raced into the pit of my throat as I noticed the blood coming from his hands, his chest, and his shoulders. A scream escaped my mouth. I stared in horror at the man in front of me.

"Help me," he whispered, his lips moving at a too slow pace as the words flew out of him.

"*Help me, Aurora. Help me stop the darkness from taking over. Please,*" tears ran down his cheeks and mixed with the blood in a mahogany-colored liquid. *Frightened, I tried to reach for him, but the darkness encompassed him. Devoured him. And then he was gone, with the blood as the only proof that he was ever there.*

I shuddered, thinking about the nightmare I had dreamt of last night. I wasn't sure if it was a nightmare. It had felt too real to be a dream, yet too surreal to be a reality. Had Asher been bleeding? Had he cried for help? While it wasn't very likely, it felt like it had happened. The manor messed with my head.

When we reached the second floor, he showed me to a bathroom.

"Use that hand towel that's laying in front of the shower to step on to dry your feet." As he pointed to the drawer beside the faucet, he said, "There should be towels in that drawer. And there is shampoo, conditioner, and soap. If you need anything, shout after me."

I nodded my head and closed the bathroom door. Even though the lump in my stomach was still there, the warm shower water softened the nerves and relieved me.

You can do this, Aurora.

I couldn't make it. My nose stung, as it so often did when I was about to cry. I couldn't fight back the tears that threatened to fall. The memory of seeing a dead person was unbearable.

I had seen a man die in front of my feet. A man I had known almost all my life.

My chest constricted, making it harder to breathe, and my naked body slid along the wall downward. I huddled on the floor as my arms wrapped around my legs. Despite my best efforts, I could not breathe normally. It made me want to disappear into nothingness, seeing such despair and hopelessness. Sniffling, all I could do was sit there, huddled down on the floor with tears streaming down my face. They mixed with the water from the shower, cooling my body. I wanted to scream to release the aching pain inside of me, and perhaps I did scream. I couldn't hear it. My blood pumping was the only sound I could hear.

I had seen Frederick die in front of me.

It caused my heart unimaginable pain, yet I knew he had deserved it. That man had tortured me for twelve years and I was grieving him? *What the fuck, Aurora.*

Tears poured down my cheeks. The sight of his body was terrifying, the sight of the blood surrounding it. The smell that his body gave off. *He had died, and it was my fault.*

A scream rippled from my throat at the thought. *It was my fault. Asher had killed Frederick because of me. He was dead because of fucking me.*

My eyes did not even register someone entering the room until the shower curtain disappeared and a male body emerged. Asher's eyes gave off a worried expression, and he held out a towel to me. Sobbing uncontrollably and without energy in my body, I let him wrap the towel around my body while my gaze fixed on a point on the wall. At that moment, I didn't even care if he saw my naked body. I was too numb.

"Shh, you're safe. You're safe," he whispered in my ear.

I couldn't resist feeling that I was safe in his embrace, even if he had hurt me. He picked me up and carried me outside, and I felt the same sense of closeness I experienced the day before. As my eyes met his, it was like the world stopped around me. For the first time in years, I felt secure. My head rested on his shoulder as he carried me to my room, only a towel covered my naked body.

Once we arrived inside my room, he helped me get dressed in a white hoodie and black sweatpants before he sat me down on the bed. I noticed his eyes were looking somewhere other than me, and a red hue appeared on his neck. Seeing me naked embarrassed him.

My face lit up, though I didn't understand why.

Asher put the covers over me to make me feel warm. He then touched my forehead with his palm with a tenderness that could make my heart burst. I had only met the man two days ago.

Why did I even feel safe with him?

The question gnawed at me as he left my room after saying goodbye, with a promise to return when our guests arrived.

Taking in my surroundings, I swept my eyes around the room. My eyes still stung from crying. Even though the room looked too old-fashioned for my taste, and dust accumulated on every surface, I still did not complain. The air wasn't as dusty and sultry as it had been after I'd had breakfast the day before. Josephine must have cleaned the room.

I crawled down under the covers Asher had put over me. The mattress felt as soft as the clouds in heaven, or so I imagined. There was a pile of books beside the bed. Reading one of them, I turned page after page. The heavier my eyelids became, the harder it became to keep them open.

As I reached the part of the book where the main character confessed her feelings for the male character, I closed the book. No matter how much I wanted to continue reading, I couldn't as fatigue clouded my vision and blurred it. Leaning my head against the pillow, I managed to relax, trying to figure out why Asher suddenly acted nice, and if the nightmare was true or not.

Chapter 6
Him, earlier

IT FELT LIKE MY head was going to explode. I sat on a bed with white covers and blankets around me. Sunlight crept through the beige-colored curtains that hung above the windows. Someone was inside the same room as I was, a brown-haired young woman. There was a pounding in my chest and it tightened. Was I in danger? My mind couldn't process my surroundings and I did not recognize the room I was sitting in. The woman in front of me moved the curtains to let in more sunlight. With my hand, I covered my eyes to protect them from the brightness.

"Excuse me?" I asked out loud, confused.

Her curvy body jumped when I spoke out loud. An expression of shock appeared on her face as she turned her head toward me. She cupped her hand over the skin covering her heart, a motion made of surprise. Her black dress and white apron shaped her body to perfection, making me guess she attracted many men. Her skin had some acne on it, but that didn't make her any less pretty, though I didn't find myself the least bit attracted to her. As I pondered my past night's sleep, I wondered if I had ever slept with her. It wouldn't be the first time I had slept with a woman I couldn't remember, although I never fucked them in my bed. I didn't enjoy having strangers in my bedroom, especially when I was having sex with someone. It was either in the guest room or not in the house at all. I did not sleep with women often, but it happened occasionally.

There was an ache in my head, as if someone had hit me with a glass bottle. It made me wonder if I had drunk something yesterday and was hungover or if I'd had another *episode*.

Please tell me I didn't sleep with the woman in the apron.

It was almost like I was begging. When my eyes fell on the windows, I saw a picturesque landscape outside of them. The day outside was pleasant, with the sun shining bright and the grass green.

"I'm sorry Sir, I didn't mean to wake you up." The brunette spoke, her tone feminine and soft.

Two green plants and a pile of books filled a shelf on which she held a feather duster. Her nails were well-manicured. Who was that girl and what was she doing in that room? I felt rather detached from reality, and I remembered nothing from the day before.

"Who are you?" I asked. As I spoke, my voice sounded distant and my head was spinning. The whole situation was stressing me out.

"I am Josephine, your maid," she turned to look at me, her eyes furrowed with surprise.

Memories clicked together like puzzle pieces, becoming one whole.

Right, she is my maid.

Her face filled with sympathy, but she turned around once she realized I had stared at her.

"I came to let you know that breakfast is ready," she spoke again. Her back turned to me as she continued to clean the shelves.

The shelf inside *my* room.

My memory was a blur, and the last thing I could remember was tucking a girl into her bed in one of my rooms after we had sat outside on the porch in the middle of the night. I didn't know how she had come inside the house, nor remember why. Questions were raised in my mind as I thought about what her name was. I couldn't remember anything about her, except the way she looked.

As soon as I stood up from bed, I put on clothes and headed to the dining room. There were so many weird things happening in my life. From gaps in my memory to different episodes where only rage filled my vision.

"We suspect you might be suffering from some kind of mental illness."

That sentence had been playing in my mind for weeks, yet I could not remember where or when I had heard it. Or if it was my imagination. Maybe I was becoming crazy after all.

When I entered the dining room, I found it vacant except for several plates of food that seemed delicious. The creaking hinges of a door prompted me to look up from where I was sitting, and a strawberry blonde-haired girl entered. Her hair faded into a light purple color toward the end. She wore a gray dress, with short sleeves that showed off her sweet and fair skin tone. Her dress was almost floor-length, I realized as she stepped forward, revealing more of it. It looked like it would have been common during the nineteenth century. Dressed in a glamorous outfit, the girl looked stunning.

"Good morning, dear," I rasped out in my morning voice.

A smile played on my lips, but it faded in haste when I noticed how uneasy she seemed to be. As she sat down, not daring to look at me, my heart pounded in my chest. What had I done to her?

Voices played along in my memory, her pleading for me to let her out of something. A feeling of nausea took hold of me as my arms wrapped around my chest. The voices inside my head were screaming, but it wasn't multiple voices, it was one voice.

Hers.

A faint memory flooded into my mind. I recalled her screaming with pain as blood oozed down her one thigh in front of me.

An image of scissors lying in a pool of blood, imprinted on my memory. My chest tightened as if someone was pressing the air out of my lungs.

What had happened to her?

Despite the maids bringing breakfast into my room, I didn't have any appetite. If I had been able to puke, I would have gone straight to the bathroom. Though I unclenched my fists, the image of me torturing her would remain in my mind forever. I realized that the beautiful girl in front of me thought I had caused her to cut her thigh. That it was me who had done that to her. It wasn't me, it couldn't have been me.

What if it was me?

Taking a deep breath, I thought about the possibilities. If it was me, something must have triggered me to black out.

Fuck.

My memories showed me torturing and hurting her, but I could not recall ever doing those things.

While forcing away the memories, I tried to compensate for them by being gentle. She had limped towards the table when she first arrived. Now she was licking her soft pink lips as she looked at the food.

Chuckling, I said, "Do not be so voracious, dear. Be patient," to which she nodded her head.

My eyes couldn't help but scan her body. There was something about her that made me feel drawn to her. Something inside me awoke when my eyes fell upon her. Licking my own lips, I thought of kissing that grope on her neck. Would she enjoy it? Moan for me, wanting more?

No, no, she would not like that. At least not after what I had done. The picture of her looking at me with devastation as blood seeped down her thigh refused to leave my cornea. How she had screamed from the unbearable pain, dropping the scissors in the pool of red liquid.

I had caused her pain, yet I remembered nothing of it.

AFTER CARRYING AURORA TO her room, I made my way through the manor. My heart was aching for her and the vulnerable state she had been in. Her body had been wet from the shower she had taken, and her cheeks were puffy from crying. I remembered the clenching in my stomach at the sight of her. That overwhelming feeling of needing to protect her had filled me. The feeling was so strong, ripping me apart with the need to hold her safely in my arms. And I knew it wasn't only because of Theodore I cared. She had been in a state of mind where all she did was cry, so it was inappropriate to feel that way about her. But for a brief second, when my eyes had landed on her body, heat had filled my cheeks. The girl was out of this world and the mere thought of her excited me.

My heart broke when I thought back to her stiff body, huddled down on the floor. How her salty tears had mixed with the water inside the shower.

As I approached my office, memories started piling up in my mind, my head filled with images of an event.

The car started with a loud hum and I drove away from the place called Grimhill Manor. Beside me was the girl with the unique eye color. The girl Theodore wished me to save. What he didn't know was that I had changed. I wasn't the same guy I was when he last met me. When Mary was still alive. He didn't know about my rages, about the flames burning inside my skin, eating me up alive. He didn't know about the pain I could cause another human, only from getting blinded by a trigger. One that could make me do horrible things. Like killing another man. Why the hell did I allow this girl close to me?

Emotions rose to the surface, and I felt the panic coming through. What had I been thinking? Why the hell was that girl near me? My entire body started trembling and my chest heaved, craving for air. The feeling was so strong, and I hit my chest, trying to get it to fucking breathe. I had to take support from one chair so as not to fall apart. My knees were hitting each other with the trembling of my body as tears glistened behind closed eyelids. *Breathe.*

I needed to get out.

With wobbling legs, I exited the dining room and wandered over to my backyard. As soon as the fresh air hit me, my lungs allowed me to breathe in. The calmness spread over me and I embraced it like a warm blanket, comforting me. The wind blew on my face, and the weather was perfect. My body wasn't trembling anymore, though the after-effect had me panting, and I needed to walk it off. Strolling around the garden, I was unaware of how long I had spent admiring the landscape surrounding the manor. A place near which there was no civilization was the perfect location for the perfect house. The only people I acquainted myself with were my staff, and I was okay with that. I was too afraid of hurting anyone else when I raged.

    Looking out to the horizon, I remembered how my siblings and I used to run away in that exact garden as children. We played hide-and-seek before mother called for dinner. Father didn't allow us to play inside, paranoid that we would break his bottles of bourbon. They were more important than his own flesh and blood. And then, if everything fell apart, he became abusive.

    My father.

    Confronted by my reality made a wave of inability to focus on anything flood over me. *This was where we all used to play together.*

    My eyes fixed on a blade of grass while I sensed myself slipping away from my grip on reality. In my heart, there was a sense of calm and peace. It washed away like a tsunami. A blurred sense of identity filled every inch of my body, making my palms sweat and my heart pound. For one second, I felt myself being in the peaceful garden. The next, I felt darkness cloud my vision, as if I was watching myself in third-person. I didn't feel like myself when the painful memories took over my chest. When it took over my entire heart and headspace. Rage fueled every ounce of me.

    Making me lose control of my body.

Chapter 7
Her

RAIN. Raindrops were all I heard from the window outside, as if the clouds were crying in rivers. They clattered against the glass, and outside the sky was a dark shade of gray. A gloominess spread over the country. The mere sight of the clouds outside made my body freeze, but not just from the weather. Someone else was in the room with me, and suddenly I was so aware of his eyes on me.

He was staring at me. I could feel that even though I didn't know where in the room he was. His eyes glued me to the bed, made ice spread through me and I didn't know how to interpret that feeling.

He stood by my door, one arm casually leaning against the door frame, giving me those eyes only he could muster. My eyes stared at him, watching his every move as he reached over and turned on the lamp. The previously nice, dark light had become sharp and annoying. Groaning out loud, I blinked my eyes open to get used to the bright light from the lamp.

In front of me stood a silhouette, Asher, with his fists clenched and a glare so intense it heated my core. Gray clouds obscured the sun in the sky outside. Realization hit me when I saw how his eyes almost pierced through mine.

I had slept too long.

"How the fuck can you be asleep? Get up!" He yelled at me to get up as fast as possible.

Although I felt pain radiating through my leg because of the wound, I was unable to do anything other than ignore it. Having been sleeping in sweatpants and a hoodie, I changed into a gray dress. Asher stormed out of the room, and I followed him. His steps thumped on the wooden floor as he walked, making my heart race in my throat. His temper caught me off guard, and I knew I needed to keep my cool around him. What was wrong with him? His sudden anger puzzled me since he had been tender earlier. Something was up with him but I didn't know what. His behavior was not what I wanted. I wanted the guy who made my nerves tingle, who made me nervous around him for reasons other than fear for him.

To make my hair look decent, I pulled one hand through it on my way down. In the mirror by the staircase, I caught sight of myself and exhaled.

Would I ever feel like a human again?

Until now, I had always been forced to dress like a doll and appear like one. It was all because of Grimhill Manor. My entire childhood was torn away like a plaster, and made into nothingness. I could still remember the clothes my mother always dressed me in for kindergarten. I was five and loved dresses more than anything. She always let me wear them when I was playing with other kids, even when I was in the sandbox. A mother who loved to see their children happy was the best kind of mother.

I missed her. So fucking much.

Tears stung my eyes as I thought about my mom, causing my nose to itch. All I wanted was to be treated like a normal young woman. It had always been my dream to make it to high school proms, graduate, have my first kiss, get married, have kids, and travel the world. That was something I would never have the opportunity to experience.

Grimhill took that away from me as they took me away from my mother. They had taken everything away from me, stripped me of my freedom, but I would not let that place drag me down. I had to stay strong. I owed that to myself for surviving all these years.

Following Asher, we walked through the hallway with the candles lighting up the space. The lights casted mysterious glows across the room, shadows resembling monsters where we walked. To prevent the wooden floor from being damaged, the wax melted from the heat and was caught by its holder.

There was a clinking sound of footsteps against the floor, but no one spoke a word. Asher was in front of me when we walked under the two pointed arches forming an opening. The hall emerged in my vision, the stone floor cold under my bare feet.

"Hello," said Asher in an enthusiastic voice.

He walked up to one of the two unfamiliar people in the hallway. The two men shared a brotherly hug before Asher stepped up to my side.

The other man wore a white T-shirt, exposing his ripped muscles, and seemed to be around the same age as Asher. The few glances I had caught of Asher while he was wearing T-shirts indicated that he had more defined muscles, more ripped. Probably more sexy. Upon observing our guest, I noticed he was holding two helmets. They appeared to be motorcycle helmets. He casually set them down on the floor before smacking the gum he had in his mouth. Over his white T-shirt, he wore a black leather jacket that matched the rest of his black and white outfit.

    Upon taking off his jacket, I noticed a snake tattoo running along his wrist to the edge of his T-shirt. The snake tangled around flowers and its leaves on the stem, twisting and turning as if it had all the time in the world. A beautiful piece of work that stood for rebirth and power, something I only remembered from one of all my books. Unfortunately, I wasn't able to see any more of the tattoo since his shirt covered his upper arm. A few hair strands were hanging over one of his nut-brown colored eyes, and his hair was jet black.

    The woman—with whom he was holding hands—was a brunette with golden brown hair. No matter how hard I tried to find her hair pretty, it simply wasn't. Those light-bleached pink tips did not fade well into her brown hair. Rather, it made her look chaotic. I watched as her hazel brown eyes took in the hallway and its gothic architecture. Amazement filled her eyes when she looked around, and I silently agreed with her. It was truly beautiful.

    The girl's dress had white sleeves that covered her entire arms all the way to her wrists. Pink and white checkered patterns were incorporated throughout the rest of the dress. A heartbeat that was usually slow raced the moment I saw her. I only knew of one place where girls were forced to wear colored tips in their hair and dresses like that. My gaze lingered on her for an eternity as a sense of trance filled me.

"Hello, you must be Aurora." The man next to the woman had spoken.

I could not help but notice how comforting his voice sounded as he talked. Breaking my gaze, I instead looked at the man as he looked at me. A smile formed on his lips, much more comforting than the smirk Asher wore frequently. Though the man had—like Asher—a tough façade.

"My name is Draven Brax. I'm a friend of Asher's. Our parents knew each other, so we kinda grew up together." He made a pause and shifted his gaze toward the woman beside him. "Her name is Everlee."

Somehow, the name woke a feeling of familiarity inside of me. Had I heard it somewhere else? What if she too was from Grimhill Manor? My lips curled into a soft smile as shock settled inside of me. The entire situation felt weird.

Keeping me as close to him as he could, Asher wrapped his arm around my waist. He was embracing me in a steady hold. A spark of light ignited within me when he touched me, and a heat spread to my cheeks, causing me to moisten my lips because of how dry they had become. My God, I was so aware of him close to me. My heart wished for him to be holding me like that out of love. It wished he somehow cared about me, wanted to hold me close to him, to feel me against him. I knew deep down he held me as a way to prove his ownership of me to the others and my heart crumbled at the thought.

As the atmosphere in the room changed, it turned into an uncomfortable silence and awkwardness spread. A thin layer of emotion engulfed the hall where we stood. I shifted from my right leg to my left while trying to ignore what Asher's hand on my waist was doing to me. The sensation of his hand around me, so close to *that* part, thrummed through me. His hand squeezed lightly on my side, causing me to catch my breath. Disbelief coursed through me at the bare thought of how much affection he had for me. He made my heart thunder, made my core heat in something I could never have, something I shouldn't even want. His gaze remained fixed on my eyes as if they drew him to me like a magnet. There was never a moment when he broke our eye contact. Even as I wiggled to escape, he never looked away.

No, he just held me tighter, affecting my body more with each second.

In a different world, he held me because he wanted me close to him. Though I knew he didn't see me as a person or as a lover, he only saw me as an object.

I was, after all, his doll.

Draven, who stood beside Everlee, glared sternly at her as she bent down, trying to untie her pink high-heels. Putting her foot on the floor again, she leaned forward ninety degrees toward Asher and spoke in a soft tone. That voice was unmistakable. I had heard it before. The sound of her voice was like honey to the bees, so soft it easily calmed my nerves.

"I am truly sorry, Sir, for not waiting for your permission to remove any of my outwear." Her eyelashes blinked several times, showing how much interest she had in him.

It was impossible to miss how she drooled when she saw Asher holding me before she stepped through the door. In an odd way, I felt something I could not put into words. The thought of the two of them together felt like a stab in my heart. Unwanted images played in my mind of his beautiful smile when he looked at her. The imagination disgusted me and made me want to fake a puking sound.

You are not jealous, Aurora.

For all I knew, she could gladly have him. I couldn't stand him, anyway. They would make the perfect couple. Her obedient manners only showed how well she had been raised.

"Do not worry, Miss Everlee. You have the permission to come inside. Draven as well."

Asher led the way to the kitchen on the same floor, and I followed him with Everlee and Draven following behind me. On the kitchen counter, someone had prepared biscuits and juice. The food looked delicious, and my stomach grumbled in hunger.

Asher sat down on one stool along the counter, and I remained close to him. Our two guests made me nervous, and Asher was my only anchor at that moment, even if his vibe caused me to shiver. Everlee stood beside Draven, fiddling with her hands and staring down at the floor. Her body was stiff, almost as if she was one of the gargoyle statues in the hallway. The two men's voices filled the awkward silence inside the kitchen.

"You girls can go up to Aurora's room," Asher stated, squeezing my shoulder and giving me a reassuring smile. It made my heart melt, but I knew it was only a show.

My legs made their way upstairs to my room, trying my hardest not to show that I was limping. We did not need unnecessary questions asked. Coldness covered the hall as I walked up the stairs. It was like a wildfire that spread across the room. A shudder was heard behind me, and I knew the girl was following me. Casting a gaze back to her, I saw how her arms drew over her body as if she was hugging herself. Her lips were dusty pink, and they were quivering from the coldness. My body had become used to the constant temperature drops inside the manor.

Another sense of awkwardness settled over me as I, and the girl behind me, entered my room. I was not used to having conversations with people. Reading books while lying on my bed or a couch and living inside a fantasy world the books built up, was what I did best. I did not know how to hold conversations with other people, especially not someone who looked to be about my age. Never had I had girls talk, a sleepover, or anything like that. After everything I had been through at Grimhill, I never spoke to anyone nor engaged in any conversations. Keeping to myself was what I did to survive, letting no one come close. It was dangerous to let people in, something I couldn't afford. Having friends, someone to care for, only led to heartache. You could lose them at any time, and that pain was nothing I was prepared to feel again.

I didn't want Everlee in here. I wanted to read my books. They were enough company for me to be happy, or as happy as I could be inside the eerie manor. As Everlee closed the door behind us, I spotted the beautiful doll sitting on the desk.

"Wow." Her exclamation made my heart race.

My hands grabbed Mary, not wanting Everlee to lay her eyes on my doll. It dawned on me how possessive I was of her.

"This room is much more pleasant than my room, where Draven lives." Everlee said from behind me.

Taking Mary inside the wardrobe, I closed the doors before she noticed the doll in my arms. "You think?" I spoke before my brain could process it, an awkward smile forming on my lips.

"Yes, it is," she said as she stood there in the doorway, like a freaking rod. It made me nervous.

I had already seated myself on top of the bed. To reduce awkwardness, I patted the bed sheets beside me to let her know she could sit down as well. In a straight posture, she sat down with one leg over the other, a trait she had received from Grimhill Manor, I supposed.

Her hands clasped together, and I watched as she delicately fiddled with them. It was impossible for me to absorb the surrounding atmosphere, no matter how hard I tried. Most of all, I wanted to take out one of my books and start reading, ignoring the fact that I had company. However, Asher would not have approved of that. Thus, I forced myself to sit still like a polite girl on the bed and wait for one of us to break the silence.

In a rigid position, Everlee began wiggling her foot and playing with her fingers.

It was I who broke the silence when I became tired of her awkward behavior. As soon as she had entered my room, I had sensed her nervousness and discomfort.

"Okay, that's enough. I can't sit here and stare at you when you are too nervous to say a single word to me. I can't stand the rigid silence. What's worrying you?"

She couldn't blame me for my random outburst. The vibe in the room was too stiff. All I wanted was for her to stop wiggling her damn foot since her actions caused the entire bed to shake. I wanted to get her to talk to me, which she could well do, given that she was a guest at Asher's house and in my room. She looked at me in apology.

"I'm sorry," she said after a pause before staring straight into my eyes. "Draven is being so harsh towards me. He makes me scared to say or do the wrong things. I don't know how he will act. Even after I came to know him, he never showed me any soft sides. I fear the future and what lies ahead." She talked out her feelings without halting, not taking any time to breathe.

A part of me could identify with what she was telling me. I recognized the feelings of terror for a man in the same house, down the stairs. I thought back to before, how I had recognized her hairstyle and voice, which was difficult to forget. Although I didn't want to jump to conclusions or make her miserable, I felt compelled to ask. "You don't happen to be from a faraway place? Grimhill Manor?"

Her eyes widened as realization struck her. "So that is why I recognized your style of dress," she murmured, more to herself than to me.

"Have you seen me before?"

"Yes, many times, but I was unsure of it until now. I recognized you immediately downstairs." Her sentence made me want to laugh at how ironic it all was, but then reality hit me.

"When did you leave Grimhill Manor?" My eyes landed on the door in front of us as I listened to her talk.

"Two days ago." Her voice was almost not audible, a lump forming in my throat.

"You left after Frederick was killed?" I eagerly awaited her response.

"Yes, the same night."

As my hands clenched together and my lungs dragged in a deep breath, I tugged at my bottom lip. "What happened after Asher killed him?"

A picture that would forever stay in my mind was the one of Frederick lying lifeless on the floor in a puddle of blood. I never wanted to see another human being murdered right in front of my eyes ever again. Taking a deep breath, I managed to calm my tensing nerves.

"Everyone had run away from the parlor room, either into their rooms or to somewhere else on the property. Everyone was too shocked to do anything. When the sun fell over the sky and darkness began to set, we realized he was dead for real. There was no food on the dining table, and no one from the staff was in the house. We gathered everyone in the hallway, while some headed to the parlor room to make sure he was actually dead. The expressions on their faces told us everything. It was not a pretty sight. Everyone made the choice to stay together, although we would leave the property. We packed everything we could find in the cupboards, freezer, and fridge. At the time of our departure, we all had our bags ready to go." Everlee made a pause as she spoke, and I noticed how her hands were trembling.

"After arriving at the enormous gates leading out of Grimhill Manor, we saw several cars arriving on the road. All hell broke loose. People fled in every direction as screams echoed throughout the manor. Despite following most of the stream and running into the woods, I tripped on a root. I could see how everyone ran away from the manor in panic, trying to save themselves. I knew that wouldn't be me when I felt arms close around me. It was Draven who had stumbled across me when he started chasing after the others, and he was fine with having me. He collected me as if I was a doll inside a toy store."

Tears had now fallen down her cheeks, making them puffy. "I watched as some other men had caught a few young ones, but most of them had escaped. I guess that somehow makes the stone in my heart less heavy. Yes, I was caught, but at least most of the children and teenagers had escaped. They will now have the chance to find their families," she said.

A lump had formed at the back of my throat again. Trying not to cry myself, I swallowed it. I had to stay tough.

Some children will find their families again.

Despite the pain, I smiled and imagined what the families would feel when their lost children finally returned home.

"I wish I had that opportunity," I murmured, attempting to push back the tears forming in my eyes' corners.

I refused to get upset over something I had no power in changing.

The thought of all the families finally being able to breathe easier made me happy. Imagining them holding their children again made me think of how relieved they would be. I could not help but fantasize about meeting my mother again. Or the day I had been ripped out of her embrace in that playground many years ago.

Only for her to never see me again.

Chapter 8
Her

THE MINUTES PASSED AS Everlee and I sat on my bed, side by side. We became more and more comfortable with each other's company. In another world, I knew we would have been best friends.

Regardless, there was no such thing as a happy ending in our world.

"I miss my family," I heard Everlee say, fiddling with her fingers even more.

There was a long silence between us, and I could not escape the wonderful scent of her perfume. It was a kind of flower fragrance, floral and fresh, with a delicate undertone of berries. I didn't feel like disrupting the comfortable silence by replying. She needed someone who could make her focus on something else other than the absence of her family, and I was the only person with whom she could confide at that moment.

"Would you like to talk about it?" Afraid of appearing presumptuous or interfering with her private life, I cautiously asked.

"Bulgaria, five years ago," whispered the young woman next to me in a shaky voice. She kept talking before I even realized what she was saying. "In a mall," the broken voice caused my body to stiffen.

I didn't know how to handle another girl who cried. As I tried not to appear too unaffected, I choked out, "Go on."

The scent of her perfume crept through my nostrils and settled like a gentle mist over my room, making it smell like a flower field.

"I had lost track of my father and was wandering around hoping to find him. I looked everywhere, and asked every stranger I saw if they had seen my father, but without success. Then, a couple of older men approached me with the promise of showing me to him. They said they knew where he was and would take me to him. So I followed them out to the garage where a white van was waiting."

Her voice trembled, and she had to take deep breaths to continue speaking. I could predict how the story would end. Stories like that always ended the same. A white van appearing, someone being kidnapped. It was awful how the world could contain so much evil.

"Dad was leaning next to the van, a wide grin playing across his lips. Mom was standing beside him, crying, while two other men held her. For me, it was strange that they were in the same room as each other. I had understood as a child that they no longer loved each other. The men behind me brought me into the van, a rope around my feet and arms. My mother's scream cut through my eardrum, but neither she nor I could do anything. We were both tied up as my father had the most amusing smirk. Before I felt the bang on the back of my head, I saw Dad receive a bundle of money. I glimpsed mom being kicked to the floor repeatedly in the middle of the empty garage."

It had gotten to the point where the girl next to me started crying. Tears flowed down her cheeks at full speed, and all I could do was take her in my arms and hug her.

"It's the fact that I don't even know if my mother is alive that's the most distressing. If she even survived the abuse my dad allowed. And I don't even know where my little brother ended up after that. He wasn't in the garage that night." She wiped away tears with the sleeve of her dress.

Her eyes were bloodshot. It was I who had asked her to tell her story, but I didn't know what to do with someone who was crying. Even at Grimhill, I had occupied my mind with reading. As best as I could, I held the heartbroken woman in my arms and offered her my support. I did not feel like strolling down memory lane, so I pushed down the lump that formed in my throat, needing to force away the memories of my family.

Now is not the time to think about them.

"I am sure they are okay," I blurted out, even though I had a gut feeling inside of me that they weren't.

Most likely, her mother had been shot to death in the middle of the garage in front of her ex-husband's eyes. Not because he seemed to care much. I understood that much from the fact that he sold his daughter off to England.

"Y-you think?" She looked me in the eye, a worried expression on her face, and I didn't have it in me to break her heart more.

She needed the hope, otherwise, she would drown with nothing to live for. I knew the feeling of hopelessness, something I would never wish upon anyone, not even my greatest enemy.

For some, hope was the key to survival. Hope was something people could hold on to, something to be cherished, and something to be looked at when things became tough.

She needed hope.

I needed hope.

Once, my hope of returning home had faded away into nothingness. It was a period in my life where everything had felt pointless. Even so, I refused to give up hope now, determined to one day see my mother again. I lived my life for her sake. She had been my rock as a child, always being there for me whenever I needed it. It was always her priority that I had friends, and that no one would be mean to me because of the color of my eyes. Those eyes which she adored so much. And my grandmother loved them too. She told me I was extraordinary and that the universe made me like that to make finding my soulmate easier. It was us three against the world, living in our small apartment as a happy family.

That was, until Grimhill destroyed everything.

When I thought of not having either of them in my life, my heart clenched. They had provided me with my only safe place. In the absence of my father, my grandmother had taken on the role of a parent, along with my mother. As for having a father, I couldn't give a shit. Rather than some unknown douchebag, my grandmother was what mattered most.

Fuck, how I missed them both.

That familiar feeling returned, like I was stuck in a loop. The stress of it all crashed into me like a shock wave, sweat formed in my palms and I clutched my dress in my fists to stop my hands from shaking.

Think about something else.

Yes, I could not have a panic attack next to the girl whom I barely knew.

Think of Asher.

The person who had such beautiful eyes, I felt like I could drown in them, the person who looked at me with such intensity that it brought a certain feeling to life within me. Asher, the one who hurt me, made me feel everything but nothing at the same time.

Fuck, don't think about him.

It wasn't until my nails started hurting that I noticed how tightly I was gripping the dress. With all the self-control I could muster, I took a deep breath and calmed myself.

As a distraction, I replied to Everlee's question with, "Yes, I do. As strong as you are, I know she is twice as strong."

Another big fat lie, though I had a sisterly instinct inside me to protect the girl from any harm. She was too vulnerable. No longer was I annoyed by her.

Another tear slipped down her cheek, and she wiped it away. "My little brother was three years old when I was shipped off," she spoke in a quivering voice. "He would be eight years old now if he made it. I can't help but think, 'what if he doesn't remember me?' I love him with all my heart, but he probably doesn't even know I exist in this world."

She let another tear fall down her cheek, and my stomach sank.

I'm not even sure he is still alive, Everlee.

Of course, I never said those words out loud, leaving her with the hope that they were still living.

After a long period of comforting silence outside my door, we heard Draven and Asher's voices. Several creaking sounds preceded the door opening. As the two men walked into the room, Everlee and I jumped up to greet them.

"We decided that we wanted this day to be fun and full of excitement. A day to remember."

It was impossible to not notice the grin that spread on Asher's lips. One that sent a shiver down my spine out of fear of what was to come.

"It's a game, you two girls against us men," Draven continued. His eyes pierced through Everlee beside me as if to say, 'don't fuck this up.'

She shifted her body closer to me, her fingertips touching my dress. To be honest, I was as terrified of what that meant as she was. This side of Asher seemed unconcerned about the cut on my thigh, which had not yet healed. The thought of his tenderness when he had held me as I cried the other day gave me a kick in the stomach. This didn't feel like the true him. The warmth behind his eyes had disappeared, replaced by only dullness. It was as if someone else had possessed his body.

"What do you want to play?" I asked, wrapping my arms around myself, feeling the room growing too cold.

"A game of hide-and-seek," Asher said, watching my arms fasten around my body. "Is it not fun? It will be even more fun when we are all together!" he exclaimed and clapped his hands together, laughing like a maniac.

I noticed how uncomfortable Everlee became from his sudden behavior.

The words "that sounds thrilling" slipped out of my mouth without a second thought, hiding my nervosity behind them.

I suspected that Asher would've been even more amused if I seemed scared. When he picked me up at Grimhill Manor, I immediately noticed his pattern of behavior. He fed on fear. At that moment, he fed on Everlee's fear.

"Great! It is a normal hide-and-seek game. You two dolls will hide and we will count to one hundred, then we will come to search for you." Draven pinned down Everlee with his gaze as he spoke, making her gulp.

She seemed far too innocent to be subjected to these kinds of games or punishments. The thought of him referring to us as dolls made me nauseous. *We were viewed as dolls in his eyes.*

"There is one catch, one punishment." Asher was next to pin me down with his gaze. Amusement showed on his face as he knew how bad I was at playing his games. He predicted I would lose.

"Whoever gets caught first gets chained to the bathtub filled with ice-cold water," Asher walked toward me. His hand lifted and stroked my cheek in a gentle act, but I knew it was anything but gentle. His mouth leaned closer to my ear and his breath fanned it when he uttered his next words in a whisper. It spread from the tip of my ear to the base of my neck.

"You will be let out first when you are on the verge of freezing to death."

His voice came out low, almost sadistic, making his words sound more like a threat than a promise. My earlobe was nibbled on by him gently, almost unnoticed, causing me to gasp softly. A few seconds later, he backed away, glistening in the lamplight. Pain was not all that was hidden behind those amber-colored eyes, there was something more.

My heart beat at an uncomfortable pace. The thought of suffering such a torturous punishment made me feel sick to my stomach. I felt like that man wanted me dead, despite showing me a soft side. Not that I cared about what he thought, although it stung my heart. I knew he had a soft side, a side where he cared about me and caressed me in ways no man ever had. I realized it was that soft side that made me want to commit to him on my knees. Behind those dull eyes, there was warmth. I had witnessed it and I wouldn't give up on him.

When my eyes caught Everlee, who was on the verge of crying, I slipped my hand behind her back in an attempt to stop her. Asher wanted to see her cry, and I would not give him that amusement. I couldn't stand hearing one more of his outbursts.

I took a deep breath, said, "Okay, let's do this," and turned to look behind me at Everlee, who was uncertainly nodding her head.

"It will be fine," I whispered to her, without Draven or Asher hearing us.

Because I knew *she* would at least be fine as I didn't plan on causing any pain to the vulnerable girl beside me. My gut feeling told me I had to protect her at all costs.

Chapter 9
Her

"WE WILL START COUNTING now, Dolly," Asher said with a smirk on his lips.

A shivery sensation of fear flew through me when he stared at me, giving me those eyes a hunter would give his prey. Their voices were light with a sense of amusement as both Draven and Asher counted together.

My body shut down from all reactions for a fraction of a second, trying to process everything going on around me. It felt like a bewildered state of neither being asleep nor awake at the same time. It was a state of complete mental absorption.

Their voices buzzed in my ears. I felt the hammering of my heart in my chest as I struggled to fight through the rising panic inside of me. The panic that was clawing at my insides as if it might break out. I hated these games they wanted us to play.

"One, two, three." With each other's voices blending into one, they continued.

Because of my fear, my legs were wobbly, and I could not move my feet at first. It felt like I was struggling to stay afloat.

Since Everlee was counting on me, I knew I had to get out of there as soon as possible. While we both sprinted through the corridor away from the two men playing with us like real-life dolls, I grabbed her hand and yanked her behind me. The sweat was running down her hands, making them clammy. We almost bumped into someone when we ran down the stairs. It all happened so fast that I was forced to halt right where we were and caused Everlee to bump into my back. In front of us stood Josephine, the maid, and my attention drew to her right away.

"Oh, my! Be careful." Her voice was stern, yet concerned, as she looked back at me. Her brows furrowed. She tugged at her lip when she saw the sweat forming on my forehead, and the terrifying look Everlee gave. "Are you two okay?" She asked us both with a look of shock on her face.

While I could not utter a word, my head nodded as a 'yes.'

"What happened?"

With gray eyes that shot me a worried look, she took a deep breath.

As a paranoid feeling overtook me, I glanced around. There was a candle burning that smelled like vanilla and cinnamon, a type of scent I loved. The type that made you feel safe.

I was anything but.

My tongue licked my lower lip. "Hide and seek."

Listening around me, I knew Asher and Draven were about to finish counting. Talking to Josephine below the stairs would allow them to find us right away. She nodded her head with narrowed eyes. With those three words I had uttered, she understood what I was trying to convey.

"It is one of his games, isn't it?" She gave me a doubtful look, as if she couldn't believe Asher had started yet another game.

The lump in my throat reappeared, clawing at my insides as if trying to escape, and I swallowed it down. "Yes."

As she walked away from the staircase, she called us to follow her. Her brows drew together, a crease forming between them, and her stress was clear in the quickening of her breath. My hand still held onto Everlee's as we followed Josephine away from the stairs. Together, all three of us stepped into another room. Josephine walked into it with confidence, showing how much control she had over her surroundings. Showing us how well she knew the house.

Better than I ever would.

The darkness devoured us, making it impossible to see anything. I could vaguely see where I put my feet, the room somber with its silence. The pitch-black atmosphere was impenetrable, giving the room an all too eerie vibe. Terror thundered inside of me when my thoughts wandered to what would happen when they found us.

As Josephine suddenly stopped in the middle of the dark room, I needed to avoid bumping into her body. There was a scratch on the wooden floor we were standing on. Josephine's silhouette caught my eye as she fumbled with something. From the material that touched my leg, I assumed it was some type of rug. She worked fast and without making a sound. The rug had a hatch large enough to fit an adult and its material was the same color as the rest of the floor, which caused them to melt together like camouflage. Josephine motioned with her hand for us to go down into the cramped space. At the open hatch was a ladder that led down under the foundation of the house and under the ground.

"Why are you helping us?" I asked, shocked that she would disobey her employer. The corner of Josephine's lips twitched as she spoke.

"I know Asher, and when he's in these kinds of moods, it's wise to stay out of the way. I don't want you to get hurt and I don't want to give him the amusement of seeing you hurt." She made a pause to look around the room before she spoke again. "But do know he has his good sides, and those are worth gold. Now get down." Her hand motioned for us to go down the ladder, yet I couldn't stop thinking about her last sentence.

His good sides are worth gold.

The further we descended, the cooler the surroundings became. Thanks to a single small light source–a candle I received from Josephine–I could look around. I was the first to descend the stairs. Only a few meters separated us from the space. It was a thousand years ago that stone-hardened walls had been used to construct houses and buildings. Bare stone walls surrounded me in a kind of masonry structure. Soft material covered the floor where my feet landed. Despite the room cooling my bare arms, the carpet stretched across the floor and warmed my feet. Opposed to the house above, the basement was more confined, and the air felt suffocating.

I had difficulty sucking in air, despite maintaining my focus on breathing and on Everlee, who had just hopped down the ladder. After Josephine closed the hatch leading up, the light disappeared completely. When I listened for sounds above us, I only heard footsteps fading away.

The feeling of being able to breathe easier came over me at that moment. We had, after all, finally found a safe place to hide.

A place Asher did not even know existed. It felt as if my heart was slowing down and returning to a normal rhythm.

There was no furniture in the room, and everything was cold and damp. The carpet was the only decor that existed, apart from all the cobwebs I had glimpsed when I'd climbed down. Every corner of the room had them, and I didn't want to think about how many spiders there could've been down there. Everlee's heavy breathing echoed throughout the room as the light dimmed.

"Are you okay?" I whispered to avoid Asher and Draven hearing where we were.

"Yeah." Her voice was too timid for my liking.

Closing my eyes, I took a deep breath and became lost in my own thoughts. Hopefully, none of those two men would find us here. Josephine had earned my trust enough to not lead us to a room where they could find us immediately. If they knew about that room, I didn't imagine they would believe *we* knew about the room. Asher with certainty wouldn't have thought that one of his own staff would betray him.

Moments ticked by, seconds, minutes, hours. I did not know. The silence was all I could hear around me. Everlee was quiet and hadn't uttered a single word since we arrived down there. As goosebumps spread across my body, my hair stood up, and a creepy feeling filled every nook and cranny of me. It sounded like voices were coming from above the room, very close to us. Even though the sounds were faint, they belonged to men. They could only belong to two people, Draven and Asher.

Shit, shit, shit.

My heart beat as it pumped blood through my veins, which rushed to the tips of my fingers. The experience made me acutely aware that I still lived, that I was a breathing human being. The faintest sound of their footsteps above us made the ringing in my ears worse. With my eyes closed, I clasped my hands around my legs and leaned my head on them.

Please, don't find the hatch. Please, please.

I begged in silence as my thigh thumped from the pain of the cut. The cut Asher had caused me when I had played the first of many of his games. Much to my surprise, the faint footsteps and sound of mens' voices above us faded away. As the creaking from the ceiling intensified, it was obvious that they were leaving the room above us.

"That was close." Everlee's quavering voice shocked me. Undoubtedly, she was scared, as it was an overwhelming situation for her.

"Where are you?" I asked, wanting to know exactly where in the room she was so I could crawl over to her.

"I'm here," her whispered voice came from the other side of the room. It was too dark for me to locate my way to her.

"Where is here?"

"Here."

I tried to follow her voice, though the room was too pitch-black for me to make out anything. The darkness devoured us both. Tracing my hand across the carpet in front of me, I avoided further injury to my thigh. Needing to get to Everlee, I crawled.

"I'm trying to get to you, keep on talking."

"I know, I can hear you dragging your body on the carpet."

I continued to crawl my way forward, shifting my body to the right where I had heard her voice seconds ago. A gasp escaped my throat when I felt something bump against me and my heart raced to the top of my throat, making it ready to escape my chest.

"Take it easy, it's only me." Everlee's voice was barely a millimeter away from my ear, her arms grasping my body to move me closer to her. She was holding me against her in an attempt to hug me.

"Everything will be fine," I said, knowing that everything would be fine for her.

It would not be fine for me.

She had her hand on the top of my head in a gentle act, patting my hair with her other hand around me. My head was lying upon her chest, her heart thumping through her ribcage. The sound of her heart calmed down my nerves, knowing that I wasn't alone in playing their sick games. The awkward silence once again crept up to the surface, neither of us uttering a single word. Her breath was the only thing that filled my ears.

"Is this the first game Asher has played with you?" I could hear the hesitation in her voice, carefulness filling it as she was nervous about asking that particular question.

"No. The other day, he played this sick game with me. He would tell me the name of a room, and I had to find that room. I don't know if you noticed, but I have a cut on my thigh which makes me unable to walk properly. This was a punishment for losing the game." My voice was barely audible, only a whisper in the chilly room.

Trying to stay warm, I wrapped my arms around myself. It didn't surprise me when her response to my words was a soft gasp, followed by silence in our surroundings. Letting my arms unwrap around myself, I instead shifted my position, so that I was facing Everlee. She moved closer to me, letting me wrap my arms around her. Rubbing up and down them, I pursued to make her warmer than she had been minutes ago. Her body was no longer trembling against me, her teeth no longer clattering together.

"Thank you," she whispered into my ear, her hot breath fanning against it.

Closing my eyes, I laid my head against her chest once again with Everlee's chin resting upon me. We both needed the rest.

WHEN I OPENED MY eyes again, my neck was stiff from the uncomfortable position, and my butt, too, was hurting. There was nothing particularly dreamy about the rug on which I sat. While we were resting, my ears could hear footsteps and voices from above us. No one had found us so far, nor had anyone noticed the small space we were in. The silence settled over the room like a thick fog. There was nothing else to be heard except Everlee's steady breathing. Having been so terrified of the two men somewhere in the house, I assumed she had finally dozed off. Seeing only blackness around me, my thoughts wandered away from the room.

What if Asher didn't even know that the room even existed? What if I could use that space as a place to escape when things became too much between him and me? That could work as my hideaway.

Unfortunately, the punishment was inevitable, either I or Everlee needed to receive it. I had no plans of letting her get it; she deserved so much better. The same thing applied to me, but I could deal with my own pain. What I couldn't handle was seeing her in pain when I could have prevented her tears. The need to protect her grew stronger with every thought of her hurting. Only one option was available. I had to climb up those steps on the ladder, away from the safe space of our hideaway. I had to bare myself completely to my surroundings, making it possible for Asher and Draven to spot me.

To prevent Everlee from further suffering, it was the only option.

Chapter 10
Her

MY FEET ROSE FROM the ground as I stood up. I was careful not to injure Everlee's head when I removed it from my shoulder. With her eyes closed and breathing steady, it was obvious she was asleep. It was time for me to get up. The tingling and numbness made me sway when my foot finally woke up from its sleeping state. It was chilly in the room, and the hair on my arms stood up.

Shivering, my body approached the steps leading up to the house above us. A blind panic crawled over me, worry gnawed its way inside of me, eating me alive. In no way did I want to be caught, and I definitely didn't want to be punished.

But I had no choice. I needed to save Everlee.

Something had awoken in my mind when she told me her background, sympathy and pity. But there was something more. I could relate to her in ways I hadn't related to anyone before. She was the only person near me who had suffered from the terrible things I had, and we both had survived. I felt connected to her. We both had lost our parents and none of us knew if we would meet them again. I wanted to protect her from the pain one of us would experience from the punishment. Perhaps it was my way of making up for all the guilt I felt toward the Grimhill children I could not save.

It wasn't my fault that the children were murdered. However, somewhere deep inside of me, I blamed myself for not being able to save them. They deserved so much more.

I deserved so much more.

I need to do this. Yet a deep sense of uneasiness held me rigid. It was the only way I could save the girl who I had come to call *my friend*.

A friend, it occurred to me as I tasted the words on my tongue. Strange and unfamiliar, a word I could grow accustomed to using. I hadn't had a friend in many years.

"What are you doing?" Her disembodied, soft voice echoed behind me.

"I'm sorry. I didn't mean to wake you."

My body's rocking kept it from standing still and I continuously shifted my weight from my left leg to my right leg. My arms embraced me in an attempt to warm me up. Whispers came from the walls, murmurs that were barely audible, words I couldn't make out. It wasn't human, that I knew. I drew in a sharp breath. The room was in complete darkness. The whispers silenced just as my heart rate picked up. My younger self would have screamed, but I had grown fond of the whispers.

Was I losing my mind?

"Where are you heading?" Everlee repeated the question, her tone firmer than it had been before.

"Up."

In my ears, I could hear her getting up, the sound of her dress rustling as she moved. A double flip of my heart pounded within me when I touched something warm, and I couldn't tell where she was in the room. Someone grabbed my hand in a firm grip, one that was meant to prevent someone from leaving.

"Do not leave," she said in a hushed tone.

"I have to do this."

"You don't have to do anything! Please don't leave me."

For every word she uttered, the strength of her voice increased. No longer was she whispering, but rather a panicked voice would soon attract attention if she didn't keep the volume at the right level.

"Shhh, please let me go," I begged the frightened girl.

The tight grip she placed on my hand was painful and if she continued to hold onto me with that strength, she would stop my blood flow. With my other hand, I loosened her grip on me and grabbed the ladder. She had no choice but to let go of me as I began climbing. Taking a deep breath, I bit my lower lip with my teeth.

It was now or never.

"Stay here until it's safe to move. Until Asher and Draven find me. Promise me, Everlee. Promise me that." I demanded, taking another deep, shuddering breath.

The more steps I climbed, the easier it became to breathe. The air above the earth was clear and refreshing in contrast to the air below which was suffocating and stifling. My hands groped for the hatch handle as I pressed down to push it up.

My attempt to open the door was interrupted by a whisper coming from behind me. "I promise."

Only a fraction of a second passed as my foot slipped on the metal step, my mind being somewhere else than on holding on to the ladder. A burning sensation spread over my thigh, the fresh wound not so fresh anymore. A loud yelp escaped my throat and my teeth clenched harder.

Fuck, that hurt.

Everything happened so fast, and before I knew it, I was hanging with one leg in the air and my two arms holding on as if my life depended on it. In the unexpected pain, tears rimmed my eyes as my already wounded thigh was scratched up by the old rusty ladder.

"Oh my god! Are you okay?" Everlee's voice came from underneath me.

"Yes," I gritted my teeth.

Despite the pain, I pushed hard to open the hatch, finding it difficult. The carpet blocked my path.

"Let me have a look at your wound."

I ignored her, needing to continue climbing. Otherwise, I would be tempted not to follow through with my plan, and then I would not be able to save her. It struck me how much she cared for me, even if she didn't know me. My chest warmed up at the thought of another person caring about me in the way Everlee did.

Coming to a standstill, I approached the room above. The ticking clock filled the dark room with an eerie atmosphere, even in the dim light. I brushed my hands over my dress to remove the dust that had accumulated. Involuntarily, my feet led me toward the door leading out of the room. My legs felt like slime, clumsy, and at any moment about to come loose from their other parts.

Amidst the nervousness, my entire body shook as my slimy legs put one foot in front of another. The pure thought of what would happen when they found me made the soul inside my shell shake. I didn't know if it would be my last day. The Asher I had come to know could be highly unreliable.

I wish he could show his soft side more often.

I sucked in a deep breath as my feet carried me through the dark room to the door. The silence was stunning, and I could hear my heart pounding hard inside my ribs. With my hands tracing the surrounding objects, I felt the wall in front of me.

A tiny source of light illuminated the room through a narrow crevice, indicating that I had reached the exit door. As I yanked my gaze back from the door, my heart pounded like a madman inside me as I bent forward to open it.

I am doing this for Everlee; I had to remind myself.

As the door opened, the hinge creaked, in critical need of replacement. The kitchen in front of me was the birthplace of many aromas.

"Come here, Rora," shouted grandmother and my short legs ran over to the kitchen in excitement.

"What is it, Ma?"

The old woman chuckled and showed me the ingredients on the counter. Sugar, butter, milk, eggs. All you needed to bake. My body twitched with excitement, causing me to smile.

"We are going to bake your favorite cookies, my child." She exclaimed as my mother entered the room with a disappointed yet playful expression.

"You're spoiling her, mother," my mother said to my grandmother with a clicking of her tongue. But I could spot the faint smile on her lips.

My grandmother kissed the top of my forehead as I exclaimed, "Chocolate chip cookies!"

She smelled like home.

The memory of my grandmother made my chest constrict tighter, making it difficult to breathe. I missed her more than anything. I missed the scent of her, balsamic with a hint of vanilla, and the way it lingered in every room she entered. I missed her smile and how she lit up my entire day just by hugging me. She was one of the strongest people I knew and carried everyone's burdens on her shoulders, yet she never gave up her smile. She always made sure my mother and I were happy, and with her, we were.

Two silhouettes sat on two of the bar stools in front of the wood-colored kitchen island. One more muscular than the other, but both equally handsome. The muscular man turned and his amber-colored eyes met mine as he heard the door echo when it opened. It was impossible to move a muscle as I stared at the creature in front of me for a moment, admiring its beauty and fairness. He was the type of handsome who crawled through your skin, stuck to every bone in your body, and never let go. The kind of handsome that made me wet my lips from how dry they became.

"Such a brave doll." In its dark timbre, the creature spoke directly to me, catching my attention without my consent.

It wasn't a conscious attraction that drew me to him; it was a connection made through my soul. I definitely didn't want to feel that way about him.

Yet, I did.

My heart beat faster than before, but for a completely different reason. The sound of his voice captivated me, and all I could do was stare into his beautifully colored eyes. My lips parted slightly as I took in his beauty, which I had not appreciated before. He was like the creatures in fairy tales. In the same instant, the man in front of me showed hollowness in his gaze as he studied my face. He lowered his eyes to my lips for a moment before lifting them to my eyes again. The area between my legs felt hot and burning.

Was he attracted to me?

Better yet, *was I attracted to him?*

"You have such a kind heart," replied the not-so-muscular man on the other bar stool.

As my gaze shifted from one to the other, and then back, I saw the darkness in his eyes. The man in front of me on one of the bar stools was Asher. Reality came crashing down on me like an airplane crashing into high-rise buildings and I woke up from my trance.

How could I indulge in fantasizing about him?

In only a few seconds, he walked up to me and stroked my head with one hand. Asher peered into my eyes. Moments after his gaze caught mine, I felt as if the stars had collided. A sense of calm filled me, a need so strong it would make me go crazy. It was as if I was experiencing an extreme emotional surge. However, the feeling quickly subsided.

What's wrong with you, Aurora?

Draven stood up from his chair. "You sacrificed yourself for a girl you just met."

Trying to escape the reality that awaited me around the corner, I closed my eyes out of sheer reflex.

"Open your beautiful eyes again, Dolly," the dark voice belonged to Asher. When I opened my eyes, I stared right into his deep gaze.

Shivers spread over me, covering my entire spine and making me regret my decision to close them.

His eyes were so beautiful.

My brain shook as if it didn't agree with my heart on the matter. Draven moved his body out through the kitchen door as Asher grabbed my waist and ran after him. When he touched my body, my brain filled with unwanted thoughts. I wanted his hands on me, wanted him to feel every body part of mine, roam over my body as I roamed over his.

The dark clouds in the sky were visible through the half-opened windows. Nothing but darkness hovered on the horizon and the rain slammed against the windows. As molten as silver, the sky's silver hues swirled in ripples of continuous motion.

The room was too dark to be a bathroom. All the walls, the ceiling, and the floor tiles were black, and it was impossible to ignore them. The bathtub—which normally would have been white—was a shade of dark gray, positioned in one corner of the room.

Upon touching the bathtub, my bare feet cooled down after coming into contact with the cold floor. Water and many ice cubes filled the space where I would soon become exposed to something awful. My curiosity got the best of me, and I dipped my hand into the water to feel how cold it was. Right before my fingertip touched the surface of the water, Asher stopped me. He looked at me with such intensity in his gaze that I immediately yanked my hand away from the water.

"Dolly, save it for later. You'll soon be able to lie down in it."

His arm moved once more around my waist, and he pulled me closer to him and the bathtub. His touch was against my skin and something pulsed in the air between the two of us. A perverse thrill tingled my brain as he both radiated an aura of danger and safety. In his eyes, he spoke all the words his mouth couldn't. His eyes bored into mine in a way that had my core crumbling. His hand against the skin on my stomach made me feel a surge of electricity rush through me, as if a bolt of lightning had hit me. I inhaled a shaky breath. His intense eyes on me made my legs tremble, the heat in my core making me throb in places no one had ever touched me.

For a split second, I noticed the way his head tilted, and smugness fell over his lips. His eyes stayed steady on mine, just looking into them. None of us did anything for seconds, his hand still on my skin. His eyes filled with so much warmth, so many promises I wanted him to fulfill, so much gentleness.

Then his warmth disappeared, and his hand disappeared behind his back. His cold eyes froze any warmth left inside of me, causing me to shiver and regret ever falling into his trap.

His hand motioned for me to enter the bathtub, but he refused to look at me. I had no other choice than to obey him. As soon as the water advanced over my body, my eyes shut. Cold water was the most efficient thief of heat. It stole the heat from my every bone. The water surged around my skin, covering every inch, the weight of it almost enough to topple me over. Slowly but surely, I felt my body giving up, feeling too numb to continue fighting through the pain. I lost sensation, first in my heels, then in the rest of my legs. I felt how the icy water was burning my skin, gradually paralyzing every single muscle.

At first, I couldn't move my legs and arms, but soon, I struggled to breathe too. As my pulse was slowing down, all the sensations in my body vanished, and I sank into unconsciousness.

ASHER

AS AURORA LAY IN the water, completely still, my gaze fell upon her body. The color of her lips was blue and purple, making her look like the epitome of a sleeping beauty. Enjoyment filled every inch of my body as I watched her body unconsciously shiver under the surface of the freezing water. It somehow terrified me, that unknown feeling inside of me. It was as if I couldn't stop myself from getting angry at her, wanting to cause her pain.

Wanting to hurt someone for what they did to my sister.

Nothing good ever came out of revenge, yet it was a great delight to know that you were paid back for all the pain caused. Revenge wasn't something good, yet it fueled many human beings.

It fueled me.

I had no control over my anger or desires of vengeance as darkness filled every corner of my body. Making me unable to stop hurting people.

Deep down, I didn't want to hurt her. She was too precious to be hurt. She deserved so much more. But the darkness, the darkness made me see black. And inside I was screaming from the pain ripping my heart apart.

"Asher, she looks a bit too pale. Maybe we should remove her from the water?"

Draven demanded, rather than asked. I knew he was right, but I wasn't in the right mind to admit it. A presence lurked below the surface of my emotions, telling me what a horrible person I was.

And I was.

Anger rose to the surface when I heard Draven's words. He thought he could tell me what to do? I was the one who could decide whether to take out my Dolly.

I was the only fucking one.

The only thing I knew was that I wanted her to live. Although it was amusing to watch her suffer in unconsciousness, I was not yet ready to let her go. And a punishment was a punishment. Never once in my life had I broken a rule of my own games, and I intended to keep it that way.

"Shut the fuck up, will you?" I yelled out, rolling my shoulders back, and added, "Is she your doll? No, I didn't fucking think so. Mind your own business."

My nostrils flared as I stared at Draven, my jaw clenching in annoyance. Self-control was not something I had any experience with.

"Woah, chill there buddy. Don't let this situation get out of hand."

He was right, of course he was right. If I didn't let her out, she would die from hypothermia. A tugging panic made my chest tighten, a sensation making my soul want to escape its prison.

"Fuck," I cursed under a breath. "Help me, Draven."

Together, we lifted the sleeping beauty out of her bed of roses and placed her gently on the ground. As Draven hurried to fetch towels and blankets to keep her warm, my mind couldn't focus on anything.

I felt as if the room was closing in around me. My body felt as if it would explode if I didn't do something soon. The rage inside my veins flared up, and it made me furious.

What had I done? I felt myself pacing the room, dragging my hand through my tousled hair. Something needed to be done to calm the rising fury inside of me. A roar escaped my lips.

I saw red. My heart pounded harder. Inside, I felt myself burning.

Flames under my skin.

Flames that were going to burn me alive.

Flames that took over every reasonable feeling.

Then my eyes found hers. The presence below my surface took over for a second. The calm took over, washing away the flames under my skin, drowning them. A sense of peace settled over me as I stared at the beautiful human wrapped in a warm blanket.

And then the flames disappeared into nothingness.

AURORA

WATER FLOWED OUT OF my lungs and I couldn't stop coughing. While my heart was rapidly pumping blood into my veins, my chest felt like it was about to burst into a thousand pieces. There was a lot of pain inside my chest and my breathing was far from calm.

The water dripped down from my hair and face, onto my body, and down to the floor like a waterfall. My gaze shifted to my surroundings, though all I could see was a never-ending whiteness. Although my clothing and hair were soaked, the bathtub was dry. When my gaze shifted down to my arms, I noticed how pale I was. Such paleness was not normal for a living, breathing human being. My body was shivering, fear paralyzed me, a type of fear that almost unmanned me. The room was way too cold for my liking.

Where was I?

The question remained unanswered inside my head. As I tried to stand up, my legs gave in and I flipped over, landing on my bottom inside the bathtub again.

That shit hurt.

With trembling legs, I stood up and fell over to the floor. As the bathtub mysteriously disappeared, it left me with a confused expression on my face.

"Where the hell am I?"

When my legs finally could carry the weight of my body, I stood up straight. A sudden warmness blew over me from the right, and as my eyes searched for its source, I realized it came from a bright and white light. Igniting the world anew with such safety, every inch of my soul was drawn toward it, making itself ready for the journey to the bright light. The oh-so-welcome warmth overwhelmed me and filled me with comfort at the same time. I looked back on the deceased people in my life before Grimhill Manor, causing tears threatening to spill from the corners of my eyes. A smile played on my lips as I saw every favorable moment of my childhood. A little girl playing in the park with her mother, the mother who later on hugged her daughter in such a loving gesture. I stepped forward one foot at a time and prepared myself to go to the light. The bright light made me remember things I had suppressed. For the first time in many years, I could finally feel peace.

Fairy tales, however, did not always end happily.

Darkness swept over half of the space I was in, spreading discomfort throughout my body and taking away the peace and tranquility I felt. Yet, I felt at home in the darkness, as if I belonged there. Upon approaching the bright light, my body heated.

How was this even real? Two different lights, making me feel both safe and unsafe?

Despite the dark light following behind me like a shadow, I became warmer as I approached the bright one.

"Help me get her out of the bathtub!"

I could hear faint voices coming from behind, coming from the dark light. The voice was too familiar, and when every puzzle piece fell into its place, I realized one thing. My home was in the dark light where Asher stood, but the bright light captivated me more than the dark light; it was my gateway to heaven.

I was torn between the two choices, and when I looked behind me in the dim light, a memory overwhelmed me, making me fall into a black hole.

"*Run, my beloved Rora, you have to run!*" *The woman's panicked voice grazed the young girl's ear when her small feet touched the gravelly ground. She prepared herself to sprint as far as her tiny legs could carry her.*

"*Mom! You have to follow me!*" *The little girl clung to the swing set, ready to run over to where her mother was. Her gaze stared upon her mother's widened eyes.*

In a worried voice, the girl said, "Don't cry, mom."

"*Mom isn't crying, darling, but you have to run now. You see those men over there?" asked the girl's mother with panic displayed in her tone.*

The little girl nodded in confusion, the men closing up behind the woman in front of her, and their guns were drawn.

"*Good, you have to run as far away from them as you can. Do not let them take you. Mom will find you very soon, okay?" The mother's gaze flickered everywhere.*

"*Okay," the little girl mumbled as she saw the tears stain her mother's cheeks.*

"*Run, my beloved Rora."*

But before the girl had time to run away, she was torn from the swing set. Screaming, she fought to get back to her mom. She distinctly heard her mother's heartbreaking scream. The little girl caught a last glimpse of her mother being pushed to the ground.

She knew it was the last time she would ever see her mom.

Chapter II
Her

A FAMILIAR COLDNESS AND silence washed over my wakefulness before the quiet was shattered by the roar of a storm outside the window. On the cold tile floor lay my body, clothes soaked in the icy water. My lungs struggled as my brain sent signals to take one deep breath in and one out. I could not absorb the air well enough, which made my lungs scream and hurt. Tendrils of coldness had their source in my frozen lungs, pressing and pushing. Water filled my mouth, automatically bringing tears to my eyes, and the liquid seeped out of my larynx. A burning sensation penetrated my entire body because of the coldness.

As my gaze flickered upward, I realized I was not alone. Above my head, there were three others, while two pairs of eyes stared at me nervously. Asher's gaze was blank, no emotion was shown in how he looked at me. I couldn't quite describe the feeling, but it felt like a kick in the gut.

The memories of him caring for me and whispering soothing things in my ear were still fresh in my mind. It hurt my pride that he acted as if nothing had happened. That side of him didn't care for me, and it made me wonder if he actually hated me that much. In waiting for my awakening, three people huddled close to me.

"Damn buddy, that was a tad too close," said Draven, who stood farthest away from me, beside Everlee. "I didn't think you would have her in there for that long! I never agreed on this, Asher."

My brain could not connect where I was, or how I had ended up on the cold floor with lungs fighting for air. Darkness surrounded me, the ceiling, the floor, and even the bathtub placed next to my body. The room was too gloomy, and the silence spread like a bullet through the drain. The storm outside roared and wooden branches knocked on the windows as the rain slammed against them.

"I told you to shut the fuck up, didn't I?" Anger flared at the tone of Asher's voice.

With his clenched fists, he was trying to maintain his cool around everyone in there. I wanted to open my mouth to ask where I was. Surely, now wasn't the right time, as Asher would get even more enraged than he already was. I could almost see the flames flaring up inside his veins. The way he stood there, his body so muscular, made me want to drag my hand along his torso. I felt as though my gaze fell all around me in confusion. Attempting to not irritate Asher, Draven paced back and forth as Everlee fiddled with her hands. He had kept his cool throughout his stay here, but even such a cold person as Draven would get unnerved by Asher's behavior.

Because of the cold spreading from the soaked clothes I was wearing, my body shook unconsciously.

I could see Draven's worry on his face when he glanced at me, throwing his hands at the same time as he spoke to Asher.

"She's freezing!" he exclaimed, his hands thrashing in the air. The arrogant façade he had displayed earlier was replaced with someone who cared.

"I will not tell you one more time," Asher snapped, his nostrils flaring. "Shut the fuck up!"

The scream from his voice ripped through the awkward silence in the room. Anger thrummed through Asher's veins, and I became scared for Draven's sake.

ASHER

RAGE RAN RED THROUGH my brain, clogging my every thought. It made me unable to see anything but the temptation to murder Draven on the spot. Never before had I felt such hatred for any of my friends before.

I needed to keep my cool.

He was my childhood best friend. I needed him in my life, even if he annoyed me. *He is my best friend.* I had grown up with him. It was us two throughout my childhood. He was there for me during those months when I had lived on the street after my mother died. He didn't feel mentally stable staying at home, so he ran away with me. And together we had climbed to the top. I had helped him financially when I inherited my parents' money after dad died from an alcohol overdose. *Suit yourself, fucker.*

Draven was like a brother to me and I knew that he knew I wasn't in the right headspace. He knew about the darkness inside of me, a secret no one but him and Josephine knew about. And I knew he had lived on the streets for much longer than I had, a time he never wanted to talk about. I would never tell his secret, and he would never tell mine. An unbroken bond of brotherhood in spirit.

I had never realized how much anger I had stored inside of me. Not until I felt that sort of rage flame up inside of me at the smallest thing Draven did. The sad part was that I couldn't find myself caring, not at that moment. The darkness devoured me, wishing death upon my friend. Wishing to see his lifeless, bloody body falling down. Draven had to leave the room straight away. Otherwise, his blood would smear all over the wall.

"Go," I mumbled through gritted teeth, but when nothing happened, anger rose inside me.

"LEAVE!" I shouted out loud, my hand aggressively pointing at the door out of the bathroom.

When the only thing I could hear was my own, and another girl's, breaths, I could finally calm my nerves. I was alone again with Aurora, the girl who was about to die.

The thought of being alone with her was like heating the body temperature in my body. I didn't intend to react like that, but the exhaustion of the day came crashing down. My gaze rested on the woman, still lying on the floor, as anger returned to me.

In resentment, I yelled, "Get up!"

When she was too slow, I pulled her up in my arms and stomped through the house up to her room. Her wet clothing soaked my sweater, and a loud sigh issued from my throat.

Her body jerked in fear as I shouted, "Nothing is going right today!"

She did not expect me to scream, and even through the darkness clouding my head, I felt my heart ache. Never did I want to hurt her or scare her, but the hollowness returned, wanting me to drown in my own despair.

Setting her down on the bed, I made my way to her closet to grab a towel and one of her many dresses. It was a simple one in a light green color that leaned more toward the white direction. The dress wasn't very long, and it had short arms. In a more careful manner, I extended my arms for her to grasp. I tried my hardest to be gentle with her. She deserved so much more, yet the anger bubbled up to the surface.

Aurora's arms were hugging her legs as she sat in a fetal position, silent drops of water rolling down her cheeks. My face became red with irritability. In an effort to ignore the constricting pain within my chest, I tried to breathe as I turned my gaze to her. It took me a moment to remember how I had arrived there. A light headache spread through me, making my head feel disconnected from my body.

What was I doing inside Aurora's room? And why was she crying?

The memories were like a blur, but I could not bear to see her cry. After I had waited a long time, I approached her small body. She was soaked from head to toe, both her hair and her body. My hand wanted to rest against her cheek. The feeling of comforting the adorable girl was overwhelming. There was something about her that made me feel drawn to her, pulling me into complete and utter ecstasy. I realized then that I would do anything for the girl who I had just met, for there was something special about her.

Then reality came over me like a hurricane, destroying everything in its path. The guilt came first, eating away at my heart inside. Then the nausea came.

What the fuck had I been thinking?

Theodore had confided in me and trusted me to save the girl, yet here she was, a crying mess inside her room. With the devil himself as her only protector.

For a second, I wanted to lean closer to her, take in her natural scent, and hold her close to me. My hand reached out to comfort her, but she jerked away immediately. In a way, it felt as if someone had stabbed me in the heart with a knife. She was afraid of me.

"Darling, please do not cry."

Her innocent eyes looked up into mine, and warmth spread through me. My desire to be close to her intensified. Tears ran down her cheeks, which I wiped away with my thumb. I needed to touch her, to feel her under my fingertips and realize that she was real. That she wasn't just a dream I was soon going to wake up from, only to return to my personal hell. Our eyes did not stop peering into each other, and the way she stared at me sent jolts of excitement down to my cock.

We sat there, staring into each other's eyes for a long while, and I could almost hear the way her heart pounded so hard inside her chest. By the way she looked at me, and bit her goddamn soft lips, I knew she wasn't afraid of me anymore. She had come to terms with the fact that I wouldn't hurt her, though the fresh memory of her flinching away made my stomach drop.

"I'm so sorry," I whispered into her ear, anxiety gnawing at my insides. The hurricane was still fresh in my head.

Chapter 12
Her

ASHER WAS LONG GONE. I had done nothing but stare at the beautiful doll on my desk since he left. Somewhere within me, there was a piece missing. It was as if my body wanted him close, as if it missed his presence, his intense eyes. I knew I wasn't healthy in my mind, for how could I want him near me when he had hurt me so much?

But my body craved him near, craved his touch like my brain craved freedom. There was something about him that made me want him, he brought me a sense of security even when he wasn't in his right headspace. I didn't know what it was, but a curse must've been placed on me for me to feel so much for the man.

Under the warmth of the blanket, I could finally stop shaking. The dream I'd had before waking up on the bathroom floor was one I never wanted to relive. It had been too terrible to experience again.

The thoughts rushed like a whirlwind inside my head. He had behaved in such an odd manner before. Dark wine pumped through my veins and sharpened my senses as fear pounded in my chest.

It had felt so comforting to have Asher's hand on my cheek while he wiped away my tears. Regardless of whether he took care of me afterward, he was the one who had caused them. When I had seen how dead-looking his eyes were when he screamed at Draven and later at me, my heart had sunk. In a way, it was as if I didn't recognize him, just as I knew he didn't recognize himself either. Losing yourself was the worst kind of pain, when you knew you had tried to fight to get out of the prison inside your head, yet it wasn't enough. When you could see yourself slowly slipping away, and there was nothing you could do about it.

Grimhill Manor had made me lose myself many times, and I had fought against myself for years. It wasn't easy to climb to the surface when people surrounding me always pulled me down like quicksand. I had tried to stay strong, but who could I be strong for when the only person in my life was me? I had lost the person I had tried to stay strong for, and after he left, I had never truly felt like myself.

In my head, I was constantly there with all the other children. I didn't know who I was anymore. Maybe I never had. I had grown up to act like an obedient doll, and those habits followed me, even here with Asher. In times when I was scared, I wanted to defend myself and hurt him. That wasn't how I had been raised, and sometimes it felt like I would always be his doll.

I felt the anxiety slowly creeping in under my skin, finding its way into my heart. I felt a churning feeling inside my stomach at the bare thought.

Who was I, if I wasn't his doll?

Frederick had scarred my brain for an eternity. I knew I would never heal from the scars of the things he made me go through. Every game he had played with me, every threat, every nasty gaze, it was all imprinted on my mind. And it troubled my sleep during the nights. Sometimes I woke up, sweating and panting while hearing whispers that weren't there. Every time it had felt as if Frederick was there in the room, ready to slice me open with his knife.

He was dead, yet the ghost of him haunted me.

My body arose from the position in which I was lying and I sat on the edge of the bed. The doll—Mary—was in my arms as I reached out and cradled her.

"You are so beautiful."

And then something bounced around my head, first in disbelief, and then in pure shock. I almost believed it myself when I saw the corner of her lips lifting, forming a tiny gesture.

A smile flashed across her face for a split second. After a blink, it vanished into thin air. Of course, she couldn't have moved a muscle. She was a doll. It didn't stop me from wishing she was real.

Real, and here with me.

With Mary close to me, I let out a soft sigh and lay beneath the warm sheets. The doll somehow gave me a feeling of comfort, and my eyes tired as the seconds passed.

"Goodnight, Mary," I murmured before my eyes closed.

A SLEEPY YAWN RUMBLED inside my chest, and my hand lifted to rub my tired eyes. In my ears, blood rushed down my spine as my heart pounded hard in my chest. For a moment, I had forgotten how to breathe properly.

Yet another nightmare. Even though they came frequently, I never became used to them. My mind was still occupied with the haunting memory of Frederick. That killer smile plastered on his lips as he screamed at me that he wanted his doll back.

He is dead.

Yet I couldn't grasp the reality of that fact. He was alive in my mind, he felt real in my mind. He hurt children, kidnapped them, and tortured them.

He is dead.

Yet it didn't feel like he was.

My hands were shaking from the stone in my heart that had become a daily part of me, anxiety at its finest. I sat at the edge of the bed, looking around for Mary.

She was nowhere in sight.

I was certain I had fallen asleep with her in my embrace, so where was she?

In an attempt to locate her, I scanned the room for evidence of her presence. She wasn't in the bed, nor under it. Beside the wardrobe that stood opposite the bed was a footstool. Its color had rusted, and something was sitting upon it.

The doll.

Mary was sitting on it, her face looking straight at me. My attention drew to the doll's eyes as they stared at me. Swallowing my nerves, I tried to reason with myself.

Someone had to have put her there while I was asleep.

Yes, that had to be the case. It was the only logical explanation for the unlogical event. It wasn't like she could have gone there herself. That would've been totally absurd. Though I could not help but feel an uneasiness fill every nook of me.

Getting up from the bed, my bare feet hit the cold floor as I made my way toward my wardrobe. It felt as though someone was watching me, but that wasn't possible. Grabbing a light-purple gown from its hanger, I dragged it over my head. The dress shaped my upper body, with lace covering the neckline. The arms on the dress were short, and the down part of the dress was fluffy and beautifully designed. It was one of the gowns I had brought with me from Grimhill Manor.

With easy steps, I made my way down the stairs and into the dining room. Asher was already seated in one chair with a plate of breakfast in front of him. What mood he was in now, I did not know. His actions last night did not diminish my fear of him.

There was something strange about his behavior and I didn't know how to respond. While the croissants were a surprise, the breakfast on the table contained the same things as the day before.

"Good morning, Dolly."

His lips were plastered with his infamous creepy smirk, with his eyes glued to mine. He motioned for me to sit down, which I did without sparing Asher a second glance. My stomach grumbled as my eyes scanned the appetizing food in front of me.

"My Dolly is hungry!" He exclaimed, then added in a soft tone, "Eat to your heart's content! Eat until you burst." His voice had an unpleasant tone, and he clapped his hands like a child.

While the entire atmosphere in the dining room made me uncomfortable, I couldn't help but blush in his presence. When he was near, his presence was so strong that I refused to admit to myself how much he affected me. Every move he made felt like it came from within me, as if I could feel them in my own veins. I felt every time he stared at me with those amber-colored eyes, giving me that intense look he always gave me, that heated my core even when it shouldn't.

His presence terrified me, though, and I did not know how to handle him. As I ate breakfast, I avoided small talk at all costs. The silence was enjoyable, as neither Asher nor I tried to communicate.

Once I had consumed the food, it was no longer possible to avoid conversing with him anymore. The awkwardness flew thick in the air, like small, irritating particles. My thoughts flew to the doll Mary and how she had moved without me touching her. I needed to ask Asher if he was the one who had repositioned her. It must've been him, for there was no other explanation.

"S-sir?" My nerves caused me to stammer, not wanting to say the wrong thing, the thing that would make him explode in anger.

"Yes, Dolly?"

"Did you move Mary while I was asleep?" I tried my hardest not to let my voice tremble as I spoke.

Asher's eyes shifted to mine, his head tilting slightly to one side. "No, why do you ask?"

It sounded as if my question had raised suspicion in him. He dropped his fork onto the platter and rested his jaw on his palm.

"I fell asleep with her in my embrace, but when I woke up, she was sitting in the chair."

His facial expression changed into something that I couldn't quite understand. He was acting strange. Nervously, his hand scratched the back of his head and his eyes darted around the room, looking everywhere but at me.

"You must have put her there when you slept." His explanation sounded surreal.

"No, Sir. I—" as I was speaking, he interrupted me in the middle of the sentence, not letting me finish what I was trying to get out. He stood up with such force that the chair fell backward with a clashing sound.

"You put her there when you were asleep. That is the only explanation. Understood?" there was a sense of seriousness in his tone.

His explanation wasn't logical at all. I had never sleepwalked nor talked. Something didn't seem right.

With rapid steps, Asher hurriedly made his way out of the dining room and slammed the door behind him. The sound made me flinch.

It had to be him who had moved her.

Mary wasn't haunted, was she?

God, I knew nothing anymore. Everything was swirling in my head, making no sense.

Standing up from where I had been eating breakfast moments ago, I walked towards the door he had slammed. Turning around, I scanned the area after Asher, but I could not find him anywhere. There was a weird feeling inside me of having to follow him and make sure he was okay. Because of his tense expression, I found myself wanting to talk to him. Somewhere inside him, there was a soft side that cared about me, a side that was attracted to me. I just hoped I was right, for he occupied my mind every day, making me feel like I had stumbled inside a bottomless well, with no way of escaping its high walls. With no way of swimming up to the surface.

I turned left and continued my search for him. He was nowhere to be seen, and I was about to give up on my search when something caught my eye.

A door.

The handle on the door was pressed down after I made sure there was no one nearby. It opened without a sound. Behind the door was a secretive and rather hidden hallway I had never seen before. I couldn't calm my nerves and swallowed the lump in my throat. Asher would be furious if he found me in here, a place I knew I wasn't allowed inside. Adrenaline pumped through my blood like wildfire. Paranoia filled me as I became scared of him finding me here. The door was closed behind me as I walked farther down the hallway.

To my right were windows a few centimeters apart, each with protruding frames. Between each window there was a pillar. The entire hall was painted in a warm beige color. On the opposite side were two benches made of dark wood. The window didn't let in much light, and the storm raged from the outside. Thunder reverberated through my ears, and the rain pattered against the windows. The only light came from the dark-gray clouds outside, and the few lit candles hanging on the wall. Grabbing a torch, I walked further into the hallway. Above the benches were many pictures. A few of them were black and white, as if they were pictures from a time before color even existed.

Setting one foot in front of the other, I inspected the pictures hanging on the walls. Some of them represented scenic landscapes, the sunsets caught at the appropriate moments as they shone on the water. Some pictures represented family portraits. Each picture was stunning. I was blown away by their beauty, which captured my heart.

Seeing another picture hanging inside a silver-colored frame, I stopped in front of it. That one was slightly larger than the others, and I couldn't help but observe it. Two adults were depicted in the photograph. There was one rather old woman—looking as if she could be a mother—and another man. In front of the adults were two children. From the look of it, it seemed as if the children were no older than fifteen years old. Both were boys, and appeared to be the two adults' sons. The man had his arms on one of the boys' shoulders and the mother had her hands on the other boy's. They all looked into the camera which was taking the picture. One of the boys seemed familiar to me. In some weird way, it somehow looked as if the boy was Asher.

Could it really be him as a child?

Beside that boy, there was another girl. Neither too old nor too young. Her clothes were vintage. She had a beautiful smile and her eyes lit up when she gazed at the camera in front of her.

An odd sense of familiarity washed over me. *Did I know her?*

With a shake of my head, I tried to convince myself it wasn't a familiar face. Although the girl looked much like someone I knew, they shared the same down-turned shape of their eyes and the same color.

Who could it be? Josephine?

But no, the photo had been taken a long time ago, making it impossible for it to be Josephine. She hadn't worked for the family for that many years.

My eyes stared at the adorable girl in front of me, her smile reminding me of one I had seen for a split second.

Mary.

The girl in the picture beside the boys looked precisely like Mary. Everything about her reminded me of the doll.

How the fuck was that even possible?

My nerves were eating me up inside, and my heart thumped so hard it felt like it was determined to destroy my ribcage.

The names of the people in the picture were written underneath, and my eyes scanned them. Among the five names written, three caught my attention. I stared at the letters with a headache that made me see double.

'Asher Thorington, Theodore Thorington, Mary Thorington.'

Chapter 13
Her

I'D NEVER ANTICIPATED THE day I would find out more about Asher.

It surprised me that the doll he showed me—Mary—looked exactly like the girl in the picture beside the teenagers. Though I knew I wasn't wrong, my brain did not play a joke on me. Mary was a miniature version of a girl with the same last name as Asher. It was difficult to process and absorb everything.

An add-on to my headache was a slamming door behind me and being yanked backward by haste.

There was a man behind me.

His eyes bulged from derangement, his face had turned a darker shade of red, and the veins in his neck throbbed. I watched as his eyes pierced through mine, but the shock of the sight in front of me seconds ago preponderated the fact that Asher had found me.

"What." His voice was stuck in his throat. I watched as his chest rose and fell, over and over again at a rapid speed.

"How?" There was another pause between his words.

I had known that it wasn't a very smart idea to step foot into the hallway, but curiosity had gotten the best of me. He clenched his teeth and stared at me. Rage was pouring out of him like rainfall in a storm.

"Who is that?" My hand lifted as I pointed toward the adorable girl in the picture, the one who looked exactly like Mary.

As soon as those words slipped from my tongue, I knew I shouldn't have uttered them.

He stepped closer to me, staring into my eyes with an intense gaze. The look he gave me was one I couldn't understand. I wanted to leave the corridor, knowing what would happen next. I was terrified of him, as he was furious with me. I had to get the fuck out of there. Without knowing whether it was the cold or if he was responsible, shivers spread down my spine. I was about to leave when his hand stopped me. Grasping my flesh tightly, it held me in place on my hip. He pulled me closer to him, and I could hear his heavy breathing, feel it as he pushed himself on me. In an attempt to escape, my body wiggled as I looked at him.

It did not work.

Fear pooled in my stomach, not knowing what would happen to me. He held me down with his gaze, causing something hot to run down my insides, from my chest down to the lower area of my belly. Putting his other hand on my other hip, he pressed his nails into my skin, drawing blood.

My body was on fire, flaming up from the insides as it craved his touch, needing his touch as if it was an oxygen tank below the sea. It was a traitor to my mind, turning into ice when it should've moved. My brain told me how idiotic I was for letting him come near me, for letting him affect me in that way. It thrashed to get away from its shell.

"Let go of me," I spat out, but all it caused was a low chuckle escaping his throat at the same time as he stared at me with amusement.

As his hands lifted under the dress I was wearing and neared my belly, I felt my breath rush out of my lungs. They were warm against my skin, making the outside of my body flame up, too. Embarrassment filled my body when he touched me so inappropriately. My arms hung limply against my sides, unsure of what to do with them. He held me with such a tight grip, making it impossible for me to try to escape. His mouth came closer to my ear, and the sensation caused something to stir inside, forcing me to swallow nervously. He harshly nibbled my ear, causing me to catch my breath. I couldn't see his face, but I knew he wore that smirk he always wore. My heart raced until it could beat no faster as I waited for his next movement, which seemed to take forever. His hand raised higher, touching the outside of my bra. Giving it a gentle squeeze, he touched my sensitive breast. The force made my legs tighten together, trying to release some pressure from my throbbing pussy.

It was wrong.

So fucking wrong.

But it felt so fucking right.

His hands stayed there, under my breast, and his eyes never left mine. My lips became dry, so I had to lick them to keep them moisturized. The motion caused his eyes to briefly look down at them, and then quickly up again. With such force, he grabbed my hips again, his eyes radiating anger and something else.

Lust.

"You should have something very clear in that pretty little mind of yours, Dolly." He gritted his teeth. "Don't ever fucking enter any room without my permission."

After that, he released me as if nothing had happened only seconds earlier. As if he hadn't touched me, making my underwear wet, anticipation filling my body. He clenched his jaw, and I felt embarrassment rise in my cheeks. It was the flames of hell that nurtured the monster within him. He was more devil than angel at that moment.

God, I was such an idiot.

Yes, I was pathetic for letting him touch me, for letting him make me react in such a way.

His heavy breathing caused his chest to rise and fall as anger took over his manners. He grabbed my wrist and began dragging me behind him, out of the corridor where something between us had changed.

I had a difficult time trying to keep up with his pace, but eventually, we arrived at my room. Using both hands, he pushed on my back, causing me to fall inside the room and land on my knees. The carpet in the room prevented the fall from scratching my knees and causing any major damage. My irritation was sparked by the loud bang I heard when the door slammed behind me. Brushing off the dirt from my bare feet, I stared at the door.

How dare he treat me like that?

In anger, I sneered as the space between my temples ached. *Fuck him.*

THE SOFT MATTRESS BENEATH me felt like how I imagined the clouds in heaven to feel. There was something comforting about laying in bed under the covers with a book in my hands, being transported into a fantasy world where everything was fine. It was that aspect of reading that I enjoyed most. By reading books that took me to faraway places, I could escape the harsh reality.

My body felt weak after lying in bed for such a long period, at least an hour or two. When my feet found the cold floor, I tipped over to the window for fresh air. The curtains were covering it, so I dragged them away and hung them inside the rope, forming a circle by the side of the windows. Rubbing my eyes, I yawned out loud. The sky outside was painted dark blue, the stars shining up in the sky. There was a sense of peace during the night, a sweet embrace of starry black. The dark blue color of the sky deepened over a broad and starlit sky.

Soft sighs escaped my lips, wishing I was outside. I'd dreamt of the moment in my life when I could stargaze under the midnight sky with the love of my life.

Dreams were just that: dreams.

There was no guarantee that they would become reality. People always said, 'Dream big, chase your dreams.' How could one dream if all hope had been lost?

As boredom filled my room, I walked to the door and pressed the handle. It didn't budge.

Had he locked me inside my own room?

Restlessness filled me, and I had no way of getting it out of my body. My legs began pacing the room. They took me over to the window as my eyes looked up at the peaceful moon, then back to the door again.

And so it continued until I felt my legs giving up on me. They were all wobbly and forced me to take a seat on the edge of the bed. Across the room, Mary sat on a footstool beside the wardrobe. As of yet, I hadn't moved her back to the desk.

Being too lost in my thoughts, I didn't hear the footsteps outside my room. Not until the door slammed open. A deep and loud voice was heard, its sound sending shivers down my spine in anticipation. I knew it was him and the bare thought of that made my palms sweat as I waited for him to enter.

"What the fuck do you think you're doing?" He asked, startling me with his facial expression.

When he stared at me, I could swear I felt a sudden surge of electricity run through my body. Trying to appear innocent, I fluttered my eyelashes.

"Nothing?" I asked him while putting my hands behind my back and holding a straight posture.

"You purposely want to get on my fucking nerves?" The insane amount of swearing from him did not disturb me; what disturbed me was the way his hands flew around aggressively as he spoke.

"No, I—Uhm," my voice stuttering was unbearable, and my eyes fell on the carpet I was standing on.

"Look me in the eye when you talk to me!" he demanded in a rumbling voice and once again, my eyes fell on his.

The hair on top of his head was tousled, giving me the impression that he had woken up minutes earlier.

"Come here," he gave me another demand, and I followed his orders.

The cut on my thigh didn't hurt as much anymore, and I could walk over to where Asher was standing without limping on my leg. Using my hands to support myself, I stood up from the bed and walked over to him. He stared into my eyes intently, which he did so often, and grabbed my shoulder. The look he gave me was deadly cold, as though there was nothing behind them. Shivers spread throughout my body as he gazed at me.

"Do you think it's okay to disturb others during the night? I can hear your loud ass footsteps from miles away!" The sound of his screaming voice made my body back away, flinching slightly at the unexpected sound level.

A temptation to speak up to him made me answer him. I had grown tired of the way he treated me. I deserved more. "I was bored! Is it that complicated to understand? I have nothing to do except read my books. Give me something to keep me occupied if you don't want me to fucking disturb you during the nighttime. It wasn't like you were sleeping, anyway." My voice matched the level of his and screaming back at him affected its tone.

I stared deep into his soulless eyes, waiting for his response, yet afraid of what he might do at my outburst.

"You're beautiful." The words he spoke rang in my head, swirling round and round in circles.

An endless tornado I couldn't escape from. My lips parted, forming a circle as confusion struck me. I must have heard him wrong. It couldn't be possible. A quietness swept across my brain for a moment. As if the emotions inside of me had changed gears, I felt a sudden change in my mood. My eyes closed, the letters appearing in the blackness behind my eyelids.

"Y" "O" "U," you?

"A" "R" "E," are?

"B" "E" "A" "U" "T" "I" "F" "U" "L," beautiful?

You, are, beautiful?

My eyes opened, the butterflies inside my stomach whirled around in the tornado as it spread to my whole body. When I opened my eyes, my eyelashes fluttered, and his dark amber eyes spread an unwanted warmth through me. Those eyes let me see the Asher that hid deep inside of him, the side he hadn't brought forward a lot of times.

It was under those dull eyes that I could catch a glimpse of the person who had cared for me. When our eyes locked together in that brief moment, it felt like space and time became the finest point imaginable. It was as if the world stopped rotating on its axis after I heard those words. My mind was playing tricks on me, or wasn't it? Maybe I was going insane?

I must be crazy.

I could only stutter when I asked, "W-what?" My words didn't flow smoothly like the ones in the books I regularly read.

"You are beautiful," the man in front of me repeated.

In his eyes there was no longer blankness, there was life. The same man, who seconds ago had screamed at me. The man who hours ago had slapped me across the cheek, was telling me I was beautiful?

It felt as if the surrounding room was spinning and the walls became unclear in my vision of sight.

"I–" my throat tried to muster up a sound, but it felt too dry. It was impossible to talk. I was driving myself crazy. There was no way he could have said those words.

You are going crazy, Aurora.

ASHER

I KNEW I HAD done something to scare her off. Seeing the way she looked at me like I had killed her puppy, I could tell the effect it had on her. And those terrified eyes, the gaze she gave me as my eyes locked with hers, were enough to hate myself even more. For I never wished to hurt anyone, especially not the adorable girl in front of me. Yet I had hurt her. And that thought made me want to crawl under a shell like a snail, only to never appear again.

Vague memories of my hand slapping her across her cheek made me want to jump out of my own body and escape everything. I wasn't aware of what was happening to me, and it terrified the living shit out of me. My mind couldn't comprehend what was going on. How the darkness sometimes took control of my soul, taking over everything that made me into *me*.

What was happening to me?

I felt like screaming out loud. It had become worse since she had arrived here. There was something about her that made me feel drawn to her. She lit something up inside of me, like sparkles lighting up the sky at night. With her, it seemed like I could keep my cool. I felt alive around her, with no understanding as to why that was. Looking at the girl made me want to run off with her somewhere.

I had not hurt her. It couldn't have been me. Who was it, if it wasn't me?

Because it was definitely me in the memories that became clearer with every second that passed. The urgent feeling of wanting to scream, cry, and throw a tantrum became overwhelming.

What was happening to me?

Then my eyes locked with hers again, and she looked so gorgeous. Her strawberry blonde hair with those purple tips lay perfectly on her shoulders, and her parted lips made me tempted to kiss her. I couldn't, not until I found out what the fuck was wrong with me.

Swallowing my words before I uttered them, my brain took in her steel-blue eyes. Those eyes, with splashes of dark purple, made me feel as if I could drown in them. As her body stiffened, I realized that those words of mine had already been spoken aloud.

"You are beautiful," I whispered, and it was only the truth.

She responded in a particular manner. Her posture became stiffer, her wide-opened eyes stared into mine, and her plump lips parted even more. I could tell she wasn't prepared for me to tell her that.

Getting more and more frustrated with myself, I repeated my sentence. She had dressed in a nightgown and she looked stunning. The gown was V-necked and made her breasts visible in front of my eyes. I felt a growing temptation to squeeze them. *You are such a pervert*. Rolling my eyes discreetly, I shook my head to eliminate those inappropriate thoughts. It felt as if I had no control over myself, over my own body.

As I looked at Aurora, I felt like she was the only thing that mattered. My desire to worship her made me want to throw everything away when she was near me. Both body and mind drew to her in a way I had never experienced before.

My mother's words flew to the front of my memory. *"If you one day feel drawn to a girl with no explanation, that means you met her in your previous life. She might be your soulmate, child. So keep your eyes open."*

She had been a psychic when she was alive, and she always used to tell me to keep my eyes open. Was that why Aurora drew me to her?

My eyes fell down onto her lips, but then returned to her eyes again. Of course, she noticed my brief glance, and she licked her lips with such sensuality it hardened the cock in my boxers.

I really was pathetic.

"I–" Her voice, my god, her voice sounded so angel-like it made me feel as if I was floating on the clouds in the sky.

"You are beautiful." It felt like I was repeating myself for the hundredth time. She was worth hearing it as many times as one could utter words.

Why did it feel like she belonged in my embrace?

The soft smile that formed on her lips could light up the whole sky. She had let down her guard around me and was comfortable with me, but I knew I didn't deserve her smile. Having difficulty knowing the reason behind my clouded mind pained me.

"We suspect you might be suffering from some kind of mental illness."

That same sentence had been replaying in my head for weeks. Still, I could not remember where or when I had heard those words.

What was happening to me?

The blood pounded in my ears and it felt like my feet tingled. My vision became a blur as if I was looking through a fisheye lens. The walls around me felt as if they were closing in on me, creating an even smaller space until I could not move at all. I banged on the walls as I screamed inside, hoping someone would hear me.

What was happening to me?

The screaming grew louder and louder, the walls came closer and closer. It felt like my heart stopped beating. Eventually, it stopped pumping blood to all the organs and blood vessels in the body and ceased to exist. The ringing in my ears disappeared, everything became silent, and not a single sound was heard. Clearly and distinctly, you could hear the drop of a needle. It was that quiet.

What was happening to me?

It hurt. The pain in my chest hurt when my lungs refused to receive air, refused to draw in air, to be able to keep me alive.

I am going to die, was the only sentence repeated in my head, behind my eyelids. Because it really felt like I was going to die.

What was happening to me? Why did darkness clog my mind every single time something felt off? Why couldn't I stop hurting Aurora continuously? Why couldn't I fucking stop wanting revenge?

All I ever wanted was to live without that darkness taking over. The beautiful girl.

Aurora.

The worried look in her eyes caught my attention. In her arms, she held my body, which felt like a dying one in contrast to hers, which was warm and vibrant.

Something stirred to life within me—a spark or something—when her eyes looked up at mine. The way she watched me with such worry made my heart ache. I didn't want to cause her any pain.

Our eyes locked together. At that moment, everything else ceased to exist. The only thing I could see was her beautiful, steel-blue eyes perfectly matching her strawberry-blonde hair.

When mine looked into hers, it suddenly didn't feel like I was dying anymore.

What's wrong with me?
I'm drowning inside my own head
When will it be enough?
What's happening to me?

I just want to be free from the pain in my head

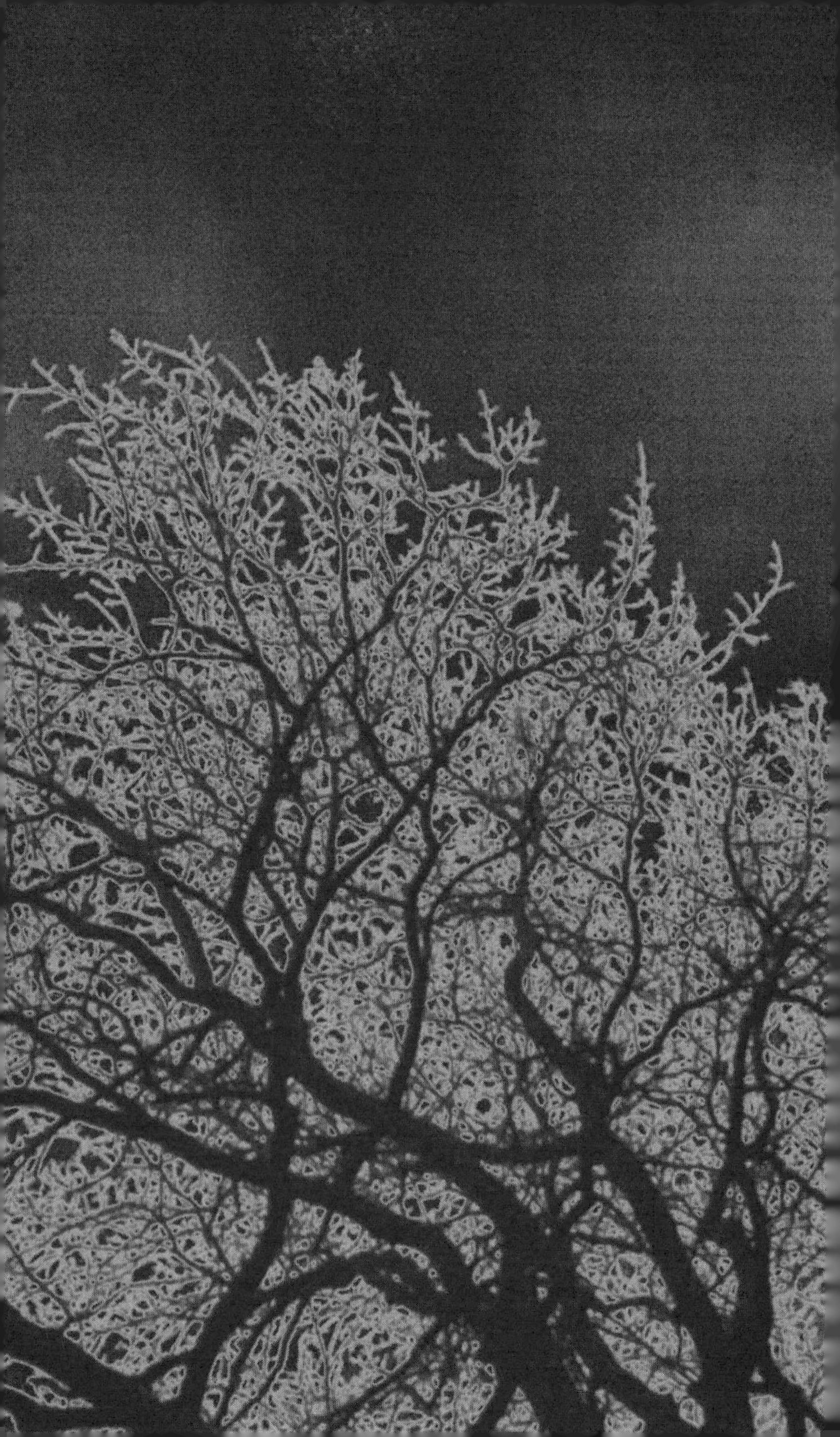

Part Two

Chapter 14
Her

THERE WAS SOMETHING PEACEFUL about looking out of the window and watching as the trees swayed from the wind that blew hard outside. Rain pattered against the glass, bringing a shroud of misery when the clouds spit it out. The storm's clap of thunder echoed inside my room, and when I watched the orange leaves swivel around, I found myself relating to them. All at once, the late summer collapsed into an abyss of autumn, taking away all the bright colors with it. As I sat there by the window, I longed to be like the leaves. They fell, but they also flew. Free with the wind as they spun around over the horizon and lived. They fell, but they always grew back when spring came.

Silent tears fell down my cheeks as I stared out at the leaves, remembering all the times I had spent like that at Grimhill Manor. Memories flashed in my mind, a turmoil inside my head. Memories of all the times I had stared at the leaves, wishing for freedom.

Freedom that never came.

Somehow, I could relate to the storm. The rain pouring from the outside was my tears rolling down. The wind gripping the trees was my heart clenching from the ache. The leaves falling were me plummeting down into a bottomless pit.

The memories from Grimhill Manor were slowly taking over, making them the only thing occupying my mind. Asher's warmth was what I needed. I had grown fond of the way he looked at me with curiosity, as if he wanted to know the real me. That night when he had let me rest my head on his shoulder, that time when he had held his hand on my skin—all of those tiny moments made me miss the way he felt against my skin. There could never be anything more than that, though. He didn't like me, that much I knew.

My life was not peaceful while I was in such pain. The feeling of my lungs about to explode was constant whenever I breathed. When I sneezed, it felt like my organs were tearing me apart. They restricted my lungs from breathing.

My bed was warm, at least. There was a stove on one side of the room that a few maids had brought in. With the help of a candle lighter, they had lit a fire on the stove, heating the room. The fire from the stove radiated warmth, and my body wasn't trembling anymore.

My energy levels had plummeted over the past week. Everything had been too exhausting and strenuous. Putting on a cute dress, brushing through my curly hair and making myself look decent would have drained my body of energy within minutes. Instead, I had worn a beige hoodie with matching puffy, soft pants that kept the cold away. Not my style of clothing, but they kept me warm. There was a whole roll of tissue paper on the bedside table next to the bed, and an entire bin full of used tissues below. My nose refused to stop running, my eyes red from the cold I had caught. Probably pneumonia on top of that.

As a result of the ice-cold bath, I'd spent the next few days bedridden. After a few nights, I had started feeling ill, feeling my energy dwindling. Asher had visited me only once after that night, the night when he had completely changed his personality.

That night when he had called me beautiful.

A wave of anticipation washed through my body and heated my cheeks. The thought of him calling me beautiful made the hair on my arms raise. My stomach had filled with butterflies as I heard those words and saw his tousled hair. He had called me beautiful, and those words competed with Grimhill Manor for the top spot on my mind.

Think about what he has done to you. My subconscious mind ruined the mood, and I had to cough. As the pain in my lungs increased, it became almost unbearable. It consumed my body and I felt like my chest had been stabbed a thousand times over.

"Here is your cough medicine." A female voice could be heard from somewhere in the room, and I tore my eyes away from the window to look at the one who entered.

With a tray in both hands, Josephine stepped into the room and laid it on the edge of the bed. Behind her came the man I had been thinking about for several days.

Asher.

Without saying a word, he sat on the footstool opposite the bed with a pleasant smile on his face. I knew it would get awkward after what had happened between us. He was a mystery to me, and I did not know what to say to him or how to act around him. That night it had felt like something was changing between us, as if all the stars lit up the sky and let their spotlights shine on just the two of us. Despite that, I could not avoid the thoughts racing through my mind.

Was everything a misunderstanding? Maybe he didn't mean that I was beautiful?

My brain may have played a prank on me that night when I felt he wanted to kiss me. His intentions remained a mystery, making it difficult to predict his behavior.

"This is Dr. Lawrence, Andrew Lawrence." Josephine's voice woke me from my thoughts, and my head was directed at a male doctor entering behind her.

He was wearing a white coat with light blue scrubs underneath. The man appeared to be in his thirties, with a freshly shaved face. Even though I felt like I was dying in my own bed, the smile he gave me made me smile back at him. From the opposite side of the room, Asher cleared his throat and stared at me intently.

God, I had missed those eyes.

The look on his face told me he disliked me smiling at the doctor.

Was he jealous?

The moment Asher stood up from the chair, he stretched his muscular body and glanced at me under the covers. My mouth dropped open when I saw the way his body looked so toned and stretched against the material of his white shirt.

"Doctor Lawrence was called here straight from the hospital to take care of you," Asher explained in his deep, raspy voice.

My nod of the head prompted me to cough. I closed my eyes from the pain, chewing on my lower lip with my teeth. When I let out a soft yelp from the pain, I could see the worried expression on Asher's face.

I could see his dull eyes hiding beneath the surface, ready to spring to life. I had a feeling that my Asher was going to slip between my fingers again.

"Alright, Miss?" The doctor looked at me calmly while he waited for me to tell him my last name.

My eyes fell on Asher, who was standing at the end of the bed, peering at me with such curiosity in his eyes. My gaze darted between the doctor and Asher, who both looked at me and waited for a reply I was unable to give. I swallowed hard and felt the agony fill my insides, making my heart beat faster and my palms sweat.

What was I going to do?

In an effort to think away the pain of their questions, I pushed my nails into my palm. The seconds passed and sweat formed on my forehead. My gaze flickered down to my hands, where I continued to press my nails down. Every part of me hurt as my blood pounded in my ears and my heart thudded in my chest.

Was I going to die?

It felt like I was when my entire body shut down, my eyes closing as dizziness took over my surroundings. My fingers pressed into my palms, drawing blood, and the pain was almost enough to distract me from the agony in my heart. It felt like cold, spider-like fingers crawled up my spine, whispering curses in my ears to make me unable to focus.

With a fuzzy mind, I looked down at my palms. A quartet of crescents formed, stinging, yet nothing hurt more than my heart breaking at the question. My hands shook like leaves in a hurricane, and I hid them under the sleeves of my arms.

My mouth felt dry, making me unable to speak. "I—I don't know," my voice was barely audible, only a whisper as I mumbled my answer. An overwhelming sense of dread settled over me.

"You don't know?" the doctor's voice mocked me. Through the way he looked at me, I could see how amused he had become by the situation. The blood in my body froze, making me sweat in a strange way.

"No."

Before I knew what was going on, loud footsteps were heard, and I saw Asher clenching his fists in front of the doctor. "If she says she doesn't know, she doesn't fucking know!" His voice showed no traces of judgment. My heart filled with deep affection as I heard his words and saw his gesture.

"Okay," said Dr. Lawrence, nodding his head. "I need you two to get out of the room while I take a look at Aurora."

The doctor looked at Asher and at Josephine, who was standing by my window as she dusted it off. When she heard what Lawrence said, she put the dustpan on the windowsill and left the room.

Asher remained.

"You need to go out too, Sir."

Asher's eyes darkened as he answered in a calm tone. "I am opting to stay here. I paid you to listen to my orders, not the other way around. You can work while I'm in the same room."

Lawrence nodded, "Very well."

Did Asher want to be here with me?

Was it to make sure Lawrence did not hurt his "plaything," or was it because Asher cared about me?

These thoughts swirled around my head, but I ultimately guessed that the second option was the correct one. Even though I wished for it to be the first and third option.

"Take off your shirt," ordered the doctor.

At the same time as I was about to lift my hoodie over my head, Asher growled disapprovingly.

"She shall not strip naked for you," he emphasized the word 'not' while clenching his fists. It felt like the hundredth time he'd done it since Dr. Lawrence showed up at the doorway.

"Sir, I'm not asking her to undress until she's naked. I'm asking her to take off her shirt so I can listen to the sound of her heart and lungs with my stethoscope. Nothing else."

The look on the doctor's face indicated that he was becoming increasingly annoyed with Asher.

"It's okay, nothing will happen," I whispered sweetly to Asher as he stared at the doctor with an expression that implied he wanted to kill him.

Asher nodded, and appeared to seem more at ease. I watched as he sat down on the chair opposite the bed, and kept a close eye on the doctor's movements. One could almost believe that he was protecting me.

I knew that was impossible.

The emotionally cold Asher he had shown me more times than I could count cared only for himself and no one else. And without wanting to admit it, the thought felt like a stab to my heart.

Even though my skin felt like it would catch on fire, I sat up cautiously on the bed. Following the removal of my hoodie, Doctor Lawrence pulled out his stethoscope.

"Take five deep breaths," which I did even though it felt like my lungs were giving up on me. During the examination, I saw Asher clench his fists, grip the sides of the chair tightly and stare at Lawrence with the same look he had given Frederick before he shot him.

No. Do not think of Frederick right now.

In the corners of my eyes, tears threatened to build. I pushed them away. I couldn't stop emptiness from filling me as I thought of the dead corpse that had laid before me.

If glances could kill, Lawrence would lie scattered all over the floor like a dead bird because of Asher.

"I suspect this to be a case of common pneumonia. Your fever is alarmingly high, so I will give you antipyretics along with cocillana for your coughing. You should take them twice a day, once for breakfast and once in the evening. I recommend you stay in bed until you get better again. Eat regularly and try not to move more than necessary." I nodded in understanding as he spoke.

"Call me if it gets worse." Dr. Lawrence turned his attention to Asher, who mumbled something inaudible. Then he nodded to the doctor and showed him the way out.

Once again, I was alone. I had been for the last few days, with only Josephine as a visitor who came with food three times a day.

ASHER

I HATED SEEING AURORA so vulnerable, but what I hated, even more, was the way the doctor looked at her as if she was his dessert. The last few days I had not been with Aurora, partly because I wanted to let her rest. However, I could not cope with the rigid silence I knew would arise if I was left alone with her again. A few days ago, Aurora had felt like the anchor holding me steady on the surface of the water, but I knew deep down I had tortured her.

And I couldn't bear the thought of that. I struggled to remember the memories of the past month, but only faint ones came to mind.

"*Please, don't do this.*" *The old man's voice broke as he spoke to me.*

His hair had a few gray spots on his originally black hair. The man had presented himself as I walked into the manor, though I had forgotten his boring name.

"*Beg,*" *I had commanded.*

"*W-what?*" *the old man stammered and looked me in the eye.*

"*Beg, for your life,*" *a grin spread across my lips as I enjoyed the moment. The terror I knew the old man felt.*

"*P-please, don't kill me,*" *he had whispered.* "*I beg you!*"

The old man lowered his gaze once again and gulped. The smirk on my lips grew wider and a deep, rough chuckle escaped my throat. Screams resounded all around us, as well as the cries from all the children and young ones. On observing the surroundings, I saw the kids running each other over as they tried to make their way to their rooms. A bullet flew from the gun I held in my hand and the sound ricocheted off my ears. The old man's lifeless body fell to the floor, and a puddle of blood formed around his corpse. A hole in his head had been created from where my bullet had hit him. I chuckled as I turned toward the beautiful girl who was now mine to protect.

As my eyes stared in front of me, I had no words to say. Something wet formed in the corners of my eyes, and when I blinked, drops of water fell down my cheeks.

I had killed someone.

The shock forced me to sit down in my office chair. I had killed someone. An innocent man. But he wasn't innocent. He had brutally killed children, kidnapped them, and tortured them. He had hurt *my* girl.

The glass of coffee tipped over after my fist struck the desk hard, and the liquid formed a puddle on the carpet below. A painful scream erupted from my throat as I opened my mouth. Around me, the walls seemed to come closer. My lungs felt like they were shrinking, and I wasn't getting any air. The second I fell onto the carpet next to the coffee puddle, I saw the photograph. It depicted me and Mary, the most beautiful woman I had known before I met Aurora. The small photo that stood on my desk brought tears to my eyes.

My life had moved on, yet it would never be the same without her.

The pain I felt was the kind of pain that etched onto your bones. A pain that forever bore a hole in your heart. Grief was the price I had to pay for ever loving her. Yet I did not regret a single moment. I knew the aching in my heart would never disappear. It would subside, but as I relapsed, the agony would come crashing down again. Almost like ebb and flow.

"Why? Why did you leave me, Mary?" I cried in pure pain, but no one heard me. "You were the one who was there for me, the one who understood me most of all. A piece of me died when you left. Why did you leave me?"

My vision became blurry as salty water drops fell down from my eyes onto the picture frame. My gaze lingered for a long time on the picture of Mary. The girl I had looked up to as a child, the one I had adored and wanted to grow up to be like.

The sister I had seen die in front of my own eyes.

My scream must have been heard from across the manor, because the door crept open a moment later.

"Please leave, Josephine." I forced out through gritted teeth, trying to keep my voice from breaking. A hiccup left my throat as wet drops fell down my cheeks.

As my hands pressed against my eyes, all they could see was darkness. Footsteps neared me, and a sigh escaped my lips.

"Josephine—" I tried again when my hands dropped onto my lap.

"Asher," a beautiful, young voice said my name, and it was a calling from an angel. The sound eased the knot in my throat, eased the tension in my shoulders, and made me able to lift my gaze.

Aurora stood there in front of me, her white nightgown perfectly fitting her curves. She was a real beauty, an angel I never knew I needed in my life. The sight of her made the corner of my lips lift.

Her eyes sparked with something vulnerable, and I realized it wasn't because she was feeling ill. No, it was because she felt for me. The purple in her eyes glistened as her eyes watched me closely, observing me as if I was an animal in a zoo. When she neared me, she stretched out her hands and tilted her head, waiting for me to lash out.

I didn't.

The anger was gone from my body, all I felt was hurt from the memories of Mary. My heart ached, and the pain felt like a serial killer was stabbing me hundreds of times over.

Aurora came closer to me, and she settled down on the carpet beside me. It had only been one day since Dr. Lawrence had visited, so it was a wonder she was up and walking. She needed rest, yet she came to me. That meant more than words could ever describe.

Her hand was placed upon my shaking ones, and seconds later, I felt the pressure of her head on my shoulder. She leaned closer to me, pressing herself onto me to bring me comfort. She was nervous, uncertain of how I would react based on the stiffness in her body. The breath of my lungs was a shaky one as I lay my head on top of hers.

"I heard you scream," she whispered into the comfortable silence surrounding us. "I needed to make sure—" she cleared her throat, and I nodded my head to her first word, unsure of how to reply. "Are you okay?" Her head lifted from my shoulder, her eyes looking into mine with that worried look in them.

"I don't know," I rasped out in a husky voice.

Aurora gave me a warm smile that made my insides heat. It was a smile meant to comfort me, and it did.

Her entire presence calmed me down and extinguished the flames running in my veins.

Her tiny arms wrapped around my large body in a hug, and I let her embrace me. I needed the comfort she gave me, for she was the only one who could make me feel that comfortable.

She was the only one who silenced the demons inside my head.

Chapter 15
Her

I N THE NEXT THREE days, I felt more alone than ever. My days were spent lying in bed, gazing at the trees outside my window, and reading books.

After our moment spent together in Asher's office, I hoped he would come to find me the day after.

He didn't.

I didn't know what I had expected. I realized Asher was unreliable. It would be wise to stay out of his way, not let him hurt me again, and not break any of his stupid rules. As long as I did those things, I knew I would be kept out of problems and heartache.

The ache in my heart felt deeper than the cut on my thigh. It felt as if a knife had been stabbed into me, constantly twitching and pulling, in and out in a painful rhythm as if it was trying to kill me. The cut on my thigh was more than a constant reminder that the person I had grown to care about had hurt me. It was a reminder that maybe my life was meant to be directed in a certain way, filled with cuts and scars, pain and aches.

He would do it again if I wasn't careful. But how could I stay away from someone who had made me feel alive when all I wanted to do was crumble?

It had been years since I'd had someone I cared about, someone who gave me closeness. And even though he had hurt me, it felt comforting to know he also had a heart. Deep down under those amber-colored eyes was the Asher who cared about me. That person was fighting his own demons as I was fighting mine. It was up to the both of us to arrive at the other side of the wall.

On the third day, Everlee and Draven paid a visit. Asher had called Draven to let them know I had become sick. The gesture was kind of sweet. I had missed Everlee, and I think Asher had noticed our friendship growing.

There was a knock at the door, and two people I had met over a week ago appeared in the doorway. Asher was nowhere to be seen, and I couldn't help feeling disappointed.

"Hello, Aurora," Everlee greeted me with a smile on her lips. She didn't seem as nervous as she had been earlier in the week, rather she seemed more relaxed around Draven.

"Hello," I replied in a weak tone. "Come in."

As Draven entered, he placed the helmet he had been holding earlier down, leading me to believe they had ridden motorcycles here. Everlee was wearing a pair of loose-fitting jeans and a simple white T-shirt, different from the dress she had worn when I first saw her. In her hands, she held a bouquet, which she handed over to me. There was a lovely scent coming from the yellow flowers, a simultaneously sweet and spicy scent that gave an ode to meadows and fruits.

"It's a bouquet of yellow roses," exclaimed Everlee, as she sat down on the edge of the bed after I scooted in.

Draven remained at the doorway, looking unfazed.

"Yellow roses represent friendship and happiness. Generally, yellow flowers are the quintessential friendship flower." Everlee continued as a smile spread across her lips.

Still sick, but not contagious, I sat up easier in bed. In my bare hands, I held the wonderful bouquet.

"Oh, thank you so much," I whispered and observed them.

It was the first time in my life that I had received flowers from someone, and my heart ached from the sweet gesture.

"Even though we don't know each other very well, you've become one of my closest friends. Not that I have that many, especially now, but it is what it is. I'm happy to be your friend, anyway!" As Everlee finished her sentence, she took a deep breath. Her shoulders were relaxed and not hunched forward as they had been the last time. It was clear she was comfortable around me, and she talked a lot.

Behind her, Draven was leaning against one of the walls. The black leather jacket made him look like a bad guy from movies, the ones who murdered people and played the villain.

"I'm glad to be your friend too," I said to Everlee, my gaze still on Draven. He was acting strangely where he stood, his expression looking serious as he observed me and Everlee.

"Anyway, we wanted to stop by and see that you were okay. Thank you for sacrificing yourself for me." Everlee hugged me as she spoke, and it sounded like she was close to tears.

Draven seemed to notice that, because when he heard Everlee's broken voice, his gaze softened and he turned his head to check on her. I was still looking at him with a thoughtful look. He had one leg crossed over the other and was still leaning against the wall.

"I don't think I would have survived what you survived. Thank you so much. You truly are a loyal friend."

"You are stronger than you think."

My words brought tears to her eyes, and I quickly wiped them off with the blanket I had wrapped around my body. Her arm was bare as she wiped away more tears with a light laugh. Draven's eyes narrowed as he noticed that, and he immediately dropped his tough façade, hugging Everlee tightly as he walked over to her. Shock filled my body at the sight before me, and my eyes fluttered open.

"We have to leave now, Everlee," Draven whispered in her ear as he spoke. She nodded her head and smiled at me.

"It was nice to see you again."

"Same," I replied as I kept my eyes on Draven and his body language.

He seemed to have completely dropped his tough façade, and nodded his head at me before saying, "Take care," with a stiff smile.

Everlee hugged me one last time and after that, they left. My body was still tingling from the shock.

What in the world had happened?

Draven had looked at Everlee with such concern in his eyes when he heard her cry. It must've been easier for him to drop his tough façade around people he felt comfortable with. He hadn't been that comfortable the last time he was here.

Knowing she was safe with Draven, I placed the flowers at my bedside with a smile on my face. The next time Josephine came, I would ask her to put them in a vase of water. Since I hadn't had company for a few days, that short visit left me exhausted. It was the first time in three days that I did not think about Asher when I went to sleep, but instead thought about my new friend.

THE HOWLING OF THE wind brought my eyes to open. For a moment, I didn't realize where I was. Darkness filled the room, but it wasn't the room at Asher's house.

Then it hit me.

I was in a room that was all too familiar, a room I never wanted to visit again.

It was familiar, yet it was not.

Dread pooled in my stomach, making me nauseous and ready to vomit.

In the room, there was a single, simple bed with flowery sheets and duvet covers in the same pattern. My body sat on the covers, with my feet tucked away behind me. A large bookcase covered one wall.

It was all too familiar.

That ghastly wind chilled my bones to splintering ice. Someone was in the room with me.

Several cracks were visible in the walls. There were wood chips covering the carpet, which had become dirty. If I put my feet down, I knew I would get deep wounds.

An icy wind blew from the open window, such a cold that made every cell in the body alert. The sound outside was from the howling of the wind, which screamed loudly in my ears. Terror gripped my body as if a monster was chasing my heartbeat as it pounded.

My gaze slowly swept across the room. The only source of light came from the moon. Even that cast an eerie glow.

In the corner of the room sat a doll on the floor. It stared at me with its deep, nasty eyes. Its hair was as black as the night, but glinted with silver from the moon, and its eyes were made of black buttons. The creature made sounds even though its mouth was sewn shut.

Scratch, scratch, scratch.

A humming.

The melody mommy and I shared.

Staring, the doll sang to me.

It came closer.

The menacing aura gripped me like a vice, paralyzing me to the spot. Anxiety came crawling through me like a rattlesnake, biting my leg and spreading its venom through my blood.

Drip, drip, drip.

The sounds came closer and closer, but when I tried to move, it was as if my body was glued in place. I could not get out of bed, no matter how much I tried.

The doll came closer.

My eyes landed on the walls, their colors stained red. They hadn't been red minutes ago. There was crimson red around the room, the color of blood, as there had been when all the children had died.

A cold wave embraced me as my mouth dried out, and the hair on my neck rose. Out of the corner of my eye, I saw movement, and the scream came from my throat as if from pain.

Killer smile.

The man had a killer smile.

"You were always going to be my doll," hissed the voice that belonged to the old man, Frederick, before sprinting towards me with that killer smile plastered on his lips.

IT WAS THE FOURTH day, and the flowers Everlee had given me stood in a vase on my nightstand. My palms were sweaty and my breaths hitched, the nightmare had felt too real and an overgrowing sense of sadness had settled over me.

I would never be free from that place.

Running my hand through my hair, I looked out at the trees outside of the window.

The autumn weather had taken a bad turn, no longer was the sun shining as brightly. The clouds cried out their agony through the rain, tapping against the windows. The sound calmed my senses. I had always loved the sound of rain. At Grimhill Manor, I used to sit by the window and look out on the dead garden while listening to the sound of rain. I remembered falling asleep easier with the sound in my ears, calming me, and washing away all of my anxiety.

Through the small opening of my window, I smelled the fresh rain lingering on the grass. The outside world was a combination of red, orange, and yellow. A beautiful sight for my eyes to behold.

Letting my hair lay down on my shoulders instead of tying it up, my eyes roamed around the room. They ended up falling upon the mirror, and I studied myself. I wore a dress around my body with lace that surrounded the bottom edge and the neckline. The sleeves were puffy but only reached down to the elbows. There were brown strings tied in bows on each side of the arms. They lay beautifully against the skin on my bare arms. A dirt-pink shade dominated the rest of the dress. It was the first day in weeks that I had had the energy to get dressed.

As a result of the medication working well, Doctor Lawrence informed Josephine that I no longer needed to stay in bed. Yet, I was told that I should avoid moving too much. My health would deteriorate if I overworked myself, he had told Josephine. As I was feeling better, I somehow managed to make myself look decent. Getting all the tangles out of my hair was a long and tedious process, but Josephine helped me out.

My heart was in my throat, and I could feel my nerves crawling under my skin as I stood outside the room Josephine had led me to. The living room.

He was in there, and I did not know in what mood I would find him.

ASHER

"COME IN, COME IN," one of the staff members called out to the person outside the living room. He had opened the door for the person, who shyly stepped in and looked down at the ground. Her hands were behind her back, her shoulders rolling back in a precise posture. The girl's dress was incredibly stylish and fit her perfectly.

"Good morning, Aurora," I said in my dark, morning voice.

It felt as if I had been eating my breakfast and dinner alone for weeks, accompanied by my books and games on my phone. I didn't mind that, but it always felt better to have another person to talk to other than my staff. The bags under my eyes were a clear sign to the outside world that I had not slept well enough. The nightmares kept me awake most nights. Dreaming of when I murdered a person with a gun in my bare hands.

Nightmares about what I did to Aurora.

Her scream pierced through my ears, a scream of terror and unbearable pain. The scissors she held in her hands dropped to the floor beside her, blood dripping down her leg. I let out a low, rumbling chuckle.

Shaking my head, I tried to shake off the memory of the nightmare that was one of my most common dreams. My brain knew that the dreams were real, flashbacks to situations from my past. It tortured my soul.

What was happening to me?

In the background, the TV was playing a movie on Netflix. It was just a random movie I had started out of boredom without knowing its name. I sat sprawled over the couch on one side of the room. It was soft and comfortable in a beige color that contrasted perfectly with the dark colors in the rest of the room. In front of me was the TV on a bench, its sound playing in the background with the volume turned down.

The room was the perfect living room and the windows were angled towards the forest, which meant no annoying sunlight could shine through and spoil the view of the screen.

Even though Aurora wasn't sure where to go, she still stood with such confidence, making me admire her. After everything she had been through, she was still standing there and managed to stick a smile on her pink lips.

"Are you hungry?" I asked her as I grabbed the remote and paused the movie, before standing up to meet her.

In response, I received a shy smile and nod, which was enough.

Together we entered the dining room, which was in the same corridor as the living room.

"Come and sit down," I said to Aurora instead, trying to put on the kindest smile I could.

I knew I had hurt her, that the wound on her thigh was my fault. That did not mean I couldn't try to be kind to her and make her feel safe.

If I could have a single wish fulfilled, it would be to take back all the damage and torture I caused her when I wasn't myself. The worst thing I ever did was hurt her. Though I knew she was strong, she had endured so much and yet she was still standing here with a confidence that shone on her surroundings. She didn't know it herself, but she had such an impact on everyone. Even my staff couldn't keep their eyes off her aura. With elegance, the girl walked from the door opening to a chair beside mine in a dress that complemented her body shape. I stood up to pull out the chair for her, and the smile she gave me beamed.

"Are you feeling better now?" I asked her, hoping to start a conversation.

The truth was, I had missed her company, despite occasionally checking on her through the gap in the door when she didn't notice me.

The only thing I looked forward to during the day was to see that beautiful individual. Her presence maintained my peace and sanity. Strangely enough, she had made me feel more like myself. The temptation to do unethical things had always been there in me, like a darkness lurking behind my personality. Whenever I caught a glimpse of Aurora, those impulses seemed easier to control. She had tamed the devil.

As if she was my savior, my heroine.

Yet, I knew I was the villain in her story. I knew I was the villain to her heroine.

"I feel better. Thank you very much." Her shy smile was adorable and the way it lifted the corners of her mouth made the birthmark on her cheek stand out.

She looked down at her plate while a maid came into the dining room and filled it. A sandwich with cheese, butter, cucumber, and bacon on the side was put on another plate. A glass of orange juice was placed in front of her, which she drank. I watched as her lips were set against the edge of the glass, and how she swallowed the liquid in it.

Blood rushed down to my hardened area as I watched those lips, wishing she had them wrapped around my cock. Wishing she was in my lap right now instead of on the chair beside me. I wanted her body against mine, but that was impossible.

Although I was aware I denied the truth and told myself I didn't like the girl, yet my body and heart reacted differently.

With no words to express my amazement, I swiftly shook my head and began eating my meal in silence. It was frightening to think about Aurora noticing what I was contemplating.

"The other day. I noticed you had a lot of books lying in your room."

She put the fork on the plate, chewed, and swallowed before answering my sudden question. Her head nodded in acknowledgment, and my eyes fell on her curly strawberry-blonde hair. When the purple tips faded over time, they became only a light purple color instead. It was a unique contrast to the dark purple in her eyes, which I adored too much.

"Yes," she mumbled before adding, "I love to read."

Her steel-blue eyes looked into my amber-colored ones, and it felt like I could drown by looking into them.

"What genre do you usually read?" I found myself asking her.

She took another bite of her bacon before she answered me. My attempt to initiate a conversation with her seemed to shock her. But what else was there to do? I had no memory of ever having spoken to Aurora about ordinary everyday things, and it was not too late to change that.

"Uhm, mostly books with romance, like suspenseful romance, gothic romance, and so on. But I can also read other genres, like crime and fantasy."

The way she talked about the different genres of books she liked to read made her eyes shine. She was so passionate about her books and talking about them, which made my heart flutter.

The more we discussed books, the more open she became. Within an hour of entering the dining room, Aurora was a completely different person. It was clear how comfortable she felt in my company. It wasn't long before we realized we shared a love for reading. I made a mental note about getting books for her sometime when I drove into town.

"How about getting out of here?" The words flew out of my mouth before my brain understood what it was saying, and now it was too late to take them back.

Aurora looked up at me, her lips parting while her eyebrows rose. My words shocked her almost as much as they did me.

"Wh-where are we going?" Her voice was too careful, as if she thought I was planning to hurt her, or take her somewhere she did not want to visit.

"It's a secret."

Her shoulders sank, and her tooth bit her lower lip–a habit she had when she was either worried or elated.

"I promise there's no danger. Nothing will happen to you. I just want to surprise you. Do you trust me?"

Waiting for her answer, which felt like the moment that would change everything based on what answer she gave, my heart pounded loudly inside my ribs.

"Yes," she answered. Her voice was barely audible and my gaze showed confusion. She looked me in the eye and nodded, then she repeated herself, "Yes, yes, I trust you."

AURORA

I COULD NOT BELIEVE I had uttered those words.

Did I even trust that man?

He had looked at me with such anticipation, and I saw how his chest rose and fell several times at a rapid pace. As nervous as he was, I was as well. My feelings had been precisely expressed at that moment. Instead of listening to my brain—which warned me about what he had done—I talked with my heart, which made decisions based on my emotions.

What could he do to me that hadn't already happened?

All my life I had lived in some kind of captivity, and to be able to do something that was possibly fun would be worth the risk.

"May I shower first?" I asked him, embarrassed.

Considering that I had been bedridden for several days, I hadn't had the energy to get out of bed and go to the bathroom. A shower was needed.

"Of course," Asher said before leading me out of the dining room and down the hallway of the house to a bathroom.

After thanking him, I headed into the room and locked the door behind me. I relaxed in the shower once the warm water washed over me. It was difficult to breathe because of the steam, but it was pleasant and relaxing.

Having rinsed my hair and body, I turned off the shower and was about to grab a towel when I realized there wasn't one visible.

Damn it!

My eyes cast over my surroundings in a desperate attempt to find a towel lying around somewhere, but I couldn't spot one. After getting out of the shower, I searched every cabinet and drawer I could find without finding a single towel. What kind of bathroom was that?

The water from my body and hair slowly dripped down and formed a pool on the floor. I needed to get hold of Josephine. My bare feet found their way to the door, careful not to slip on the water, and called for Josephine. She did not respond when I shouted at her.

What the hell was I supposed to do now?

"Has something happened?" asked a masculine, raspy voice on the other side of the door.

Oh shit.

"Uh, is Josephine there?" My eyes searched the bathroom once more after something to dry myself with, but there was nothing.

"No, I gave her the day off," Asher answered my question, and I silently swore to myself. "What happened?" he continued, and the concern in his voice could not be missed.

"I don't have a towel," I muttered, a pink tinge forming on my cheeks from the heat.

It was silent outside the room. There was no sound of breathing. Had he left?

In desperation, I swept my eyes around the room, but there was still no towel. I was an idiot for checking again for the third time, even though I knew there wasn't one in here. A knock at the door made me flinch.

A voice outside called out, "I have towels for you."

"Perfect, thank you!" I chirped out of happiness, almost making a fool out of myself.

After unlocking the door carelessly, I stuck my head out and was about to grab the towels Asher was holding when I noticed his gaze on me. At that moment, I realized my shoulder was visible, as was half my breast and my neck, too. They were wet and still dripping with water from the shower. The faint traces of hunger in his eyes could be seen as he scanned the visible part of my body. My cheeks heated when I realized he was staring at me.

"Damn it," he said under his breath, his neck reddening with embarrassment.

"Uh, thanks for the towels," I said before taking them from his hands and closing the door behind me. With my back against the door, I took a deep breath and tried to calm my pounding heart.

The way he looked at me.

A small smile played on my lips when I realized how he had actually checked me out. Like he wanted me.

Like I was pretty.

Wow.

MY SHOULDER WAS LEANING against the wall of the hallway, waiting for Asher, who said he would be there in five minutes. In a small shoulder bag, I had put one of my books, together with the doll Mary. If anything happened, I wanted to have her with me. It was the first time an object had attracted me in such a way.

My thoughts raced through my head as I thought about Mary Thorington, who was seen alongside Asher in the old photograph. All the features of the girl matched those of the doll that was in the bag hanging around my shoulder. Even the body structure of the doll resembled the form of the actual human being—the facial features, eye shape, and eye size were all the same. I knew better than to ask Asher about it, afraid of how his mood would be affected.

"Have you been waiting long?" The voice behind me made me jump, and my body straightened up into a better posture. Asher came down the stairs. A cooler bag hung over the elbow of one arm and the other hand combed through his chocolate-brown, tousled hair. He wore a T-shirt that fit around his muscular frame, and his arms displayed his muscularity well. It almost made me drool.

Almost.

The words stalled in my mouth. My tongue felt like it was stapled in place, so all I did was shake my head to say no. The coat around my body was of the same brown color as the bows on the dress's arms, and it created a beautiful contrast. Asher came up to me and threw on a blue jean jacket before heading out. I enjoyed breathing in the fresh air from the moderately warm day. The rain had been replaced by a warm October day and for the first time in over a week, I could breathe without pain in my lungs.

There was a black Mercedes parked outside the house. Lifting the long dress with my hands, I walked to the car door that Asher held open for me. A smile spread across my face at his thoughtfulness. A loud hum from the car greeted us shortly after we settled into our seats. It was a scenic landscape outside of his house. I would suppose it was normal for the countryside of England to be filled with moors, green grass and orange leaves on the trees. The landscape amazed me and my eyes opened wide as I examined the surroundings we passed.

"You're not planning to say where we're heading at all?" My gaze fell on Asher, one hand on the steering wheel and the other a few inches away from mine.

He looked so handsome as he sat behind the wheel. My nerves heightened when he looked at me instead of at the road.

"Keep your eyes on the road so we don't collide!" I shrieked.

He laughed a dark and sexy chuckle. "You said you trusted me."

"Not when you're not paying attention to where you're heading!"

Once again, he gave me that smile, a playful one that I had never seen before. It was so beautiful. As he put his gaze on the road again, his smile remained. It filled me with hope for the future. I never knew riding a car, gazing at the scenery, and spending time with a certain someone could have made me feel this free.

Chuckling at me, he said, "By the way, I said it was a surprise," and when my eyes fell on him as he was driving, I smiled too.

A genuine smile.

It had been many years since I had smiled with such sincerity.

Chapter 16
Her

THERE WAS A TANGIBLE beauty in the quietness of the side of the country we were in. In a place where few humans have stepped foot, there are no footprints to be found. A place full of personality, a habitat for nature's animals. An oasis that was better off without human influence. I had noticed our variety was prone to ruin things.

The fields were wrapped in a rich green color after the heavy rain that had lasted the past few days. Crossroads divided the fields into squares, it was a beautiful shade of green for the eyes to see. The wind galloped over the moors in a peaceful manner. The blades of grass swayed in the breeze, and the smell of previously wet grass found its way into my nostrils.

For the first time in several years, I felt somehow at ease.

We followed the paths through England's moors after we had parked the black Mercedes. In spite of the long journey required to walk there, the flat surroundings made it easier. There were several horses in a pasture on one of the fields, grazing on the grass below them as they stood stately. Their wailing and snorting could be heard, and everything felt like the scenes described in my books. To some extent, the moors had been preserved as they were during the nineteenth century.

There was a tree a few meters tall that was quite large. It stood in the distance, still graceful, but with strong roots that grew underground to find a way to survive. It stood there all alone, on one of the hills that surrounded the majestic landscape. As far as the eye could see, the moors stretched with no houses or people in sight. We were surrounded by grass that moved like waves in the sea. The branches of the trees had bloomed green leaves in harmonious contrast to the greenery of the grass blades. Given its immense size, the huge branches of the tree stretched out for several meters. Despite that, it was still a sight to behold.

Asher took out a large, white blanket from his cooler bag, which he insisted he'd carry all the way to the place where the tree lay on the hill. His hand motioned for me to sit on the blanket. I did it with lighter movements than necessary, careful not to get dirty from the grass outside of the blanket. Considering how much I loved the dress I wore, grass stains were the last thing I wanted to see on it. Having let my hair hang loose over my shoulders, I heard the wind swoop down on my hair and cool down my hot body with its breath as it blew out of the trees.

Somehow I had become rather sweaty after walking through the moors and had to take off my coat, which had been wrapped around me. After darkness fell and the night came with its shining stars, the sun shimmered over the horizon and brought new life to the landscape that had before been hidden.

When my eyes swept over Asher, I saw his handsome body more clearly than ever in the abundant sunlight. From the direct rays of the sun that illuminated him, he seemed to be surrounded by a halo of light. I wanted to drag my fingers through his tousled hair, just feel him close to me. Asher removed everything from inside the cooler bag, and arranged its content perfectly on the blanket.

It reminded me of the romantic picnics I had read about in some of my books, and it filled me with hope. While keeping my eyes on Asher, I sat down on the blanket. Between us stood two medium-sized bowls containing different kinds of berries. My mouth cracked open in a broad smile when I caught a glimpse of the raspberries.

"What are you smiling at?" I could hear the man laughing jokingly in front of me as he spoke.

There was a small tuft of hair on the forehead of the man, covering one of his eyes. With one hand, he ruffled his hair to put it in its right place. Something awoke inside me. Perhaps it was lust when I observed his toned and extremely muscular arms.

"The raspberries," examining the table setting in front of me, I replied. His laughter echoed in my ears as a ripple of pleasure passed through him.

"What about those small, pink berries?"

His finger adorned one of them, and when he put it in his mouth, he did so seductively. Was he teasing me?

"For me, raspberries aren't common. It is something I have eaten very few times, so few that I could count them by hand. Sometimes we had activities outside at Grimhill Manor." I cringed when I mentioned that place. "And when no one noticed, I and a few others used to run away from the house. There was this gap in the fence and a raspberry bush a few meters away outside of the fence. Berries hold a special place in my heart because I barely had the chance to eat any of them and actually risked my life to get some raspberries."

The chirping birds sang a harmonious melody that almost drowned out Asher's voice as he spoke.

"So eating raspberries for you feels like a luxury?" He asked as he swallowed a blueberry.

"Well, sort of." I fiddled with my hands, a habit I had probably gained from Everlee, who had more than once fiddled with her hands when she was nervous the first time I met her.

There were not only berries on the picnic tablecloth but also bread croquettes on a wooden plate neatly cut and laid out. A small mini bowl of melted chocolate was set up next to the croquettes. I couldn't wait until my taste buds could taste the food that looked so appetizing. The thought of it made me salivate.

Two mugs stood on a wooden tray, with a brown liquid inside each. I assumed they held coffee or chocolate. A beautiful floral bouquet lay next to everything, nicely tied together with a white ribbon and shaped with a small bow around. The flowers were a white Gerbera Daisy bouquet. I was moved to tears by the thoughtful gesture Asher had made, and I stared at everything he'd laid upon the blanket. No one had ever done that kind of thing for me before, especially not a man.

"Is this okay?" Asher's voice was darker than usual. His gaze lowered, as if to hide his shyness.

"Are you kidding? It's perfect!"

The croquettes I had dipped in the chocolate bowl tasted delectable. When I took a few bites, some of the chocolate spilled out and landed on my finger. Unconsciously, I sucked it off my thumb. He gave a groan from the opposite direction, and when I caught sight of him, his cheeks had taken on a pinkish hue. I pretended not to notice. Asher's eyes looked away out of shyness, and the groan he had made sounded like music to my ears, making the heat spread to my cheeks.

While I was reaching for the brown liquid-filled mug, I accidentally overturned my shoulder bag, which was standing next to my ballerina-shaped shoes. One of the books fell out of the bag, causing the doll Mary's hair to protrude beyond the opening of the bag, clearly noticeable for Asher to see. The anxiety grew inside me like a thundering tornado. The last time we discussed Mary, or rather when I had asked a question and received no answer, his entire mood had changed. My stomach turned when I saw the look in his eyes, and the intensity in them still made me feel uncomfortable. His tightening jaw let me know he was furious, and I knew I was doomed.

ASHER

"TAKE THE DOLL FROM her fucking bag! Break it apart into a million pieces, punch her hard somewhere, do something to make the girl in front of you cry out of pain!"

The impulse to do things to the beautiful girl in front of me grew stronger by the seconds. It felt impossible to fight back, impossible to ignore. Despite my best efforts, I couldn't control my emotions. The longer I spent staring at the doll in her bag, the louder the thoughts within me rose. It was like there was a second part of myself that told me what to do and how to feel. Every corner of my brain felt as though I was about to fall into oblivion. In an effort to avoid harming her, I had no choice but to take control of my body. The simple sight of that doll beside Aurora brought anger to life somewhere deep inside me. The rage flared up inside my veins. A fury I had never experienced before. Or had I?

I could not fucking remember. Why couldn't I remember?

"Take the fork and push it into her hand."

Frustrated, I pulled my hand through my tousled hair, groaning in irritation at the loud voice inside my head that tried to crawl to the surface. A small part of me awoke when I saw how the girl in front of me jerked when she saw me raise my arm. Did she actually think I would hit her? Harm her in any way?

I tried to find her gaze through my blurry vision, and I quickly found it. Her fear covered the shimmer I used to detect in her eyes, and her mesmerizing steel-blue eyes almost made me drown in them. The calmness settled over me like the end of a rainstorm did after its fiercest part, the brutal part that had destroyed everything in its way. Silent and with nothing to fear anymore. The anger inside of me was completely extinguished. It had disappeared as if by some kind of magic. All I felt when my gaze fell on Aurora was the calm she gave me, which now radiated throughout my entire body.

"Sorry." Whispering, I added, "I didn't have the intention to hit you."

A nervous laugh fell out of her throat, and her head shook.

My explanation was met with the response, "It's an old habit I have, uh, to flinch. Since I have been hit a lot in the past." Her mouth formed a tight line at the thought of her past.

"I'm sorry for what they did to you, darling."

It physically hurt my heart at the bare thought of all the torture she had gone through. Both of us had experienced more pain than an average human, and I would never wish that upon my greatest enemy. I knew Aurora was strong. She had those fighter eyes, lingering behind the steel-blue cover with purple splashes. Theodore had been right. Her eyes were unique. And I felt myself falling for those eyes every time I looked into them.

"It's not your fault."

"I know, but it doesn't make it any more wrong." Upon hearing my sentence, she gave me a faint smile.

"Did you take Mary with you?" I asked her in an attempt to change the sensitive subject.

The only difference was that I didn't feel angry when I gazed at Aurora's doll this time. That part of me was gone, at least for the moment.

"Yes," she chewed on her inner cheek as she spoke to me.

"May I?" I asked, and she nodded her head.

My body leaned over the blanket filled with food and grabbed the doll. I looked at her splendid face, the face I missed most of all. My hands found the doll's hair, and I gently stroked it as if she were alive. In my memories and mind, she was. To me, she was a very special person.

"What do you think of her?" My voice was low and husky as I spoke to Aurora.

"She's adorable, extraordinary even. Not like any other doll I have seen before." She was, of course, right in that aspect.

"Mary is really not like other dolls," I whispered.

"Pardon me?"

She stopped chewing on her inner cheek and looked at me when I asked her, "Do you want to know one thing?"

Holding Mary in my embrace, I was careful not to damage or break her. There was no denying that I was in a pathetic state.

"Okay?" Aurora asked in a low voice that was barely audible at all.

With a deep breath, I told my story. "After my sister passed away, I ordered this doll handmade. She was the most wonderful person I knew, and seeing her die in front of me—" I had to pause before I could continue. "It's something I wish I had never experienced. It was traumatizing. I traveled to France and stayed there for two months to get this special handmade doll from a doll maker in Paris."

She was looking at me with compassion in her eyes, as if she had been suffering with me. That was something no one had ever done, except for Mary when she was alive.

"That is beautiful. You're honoring her in ways no one else could. I'm sure she would be so proud of you."

The pang in my heart felt like a hundred stabs. Mary would never meet Aurora, never spend time with her or get to know her. Mary would never see me at the altar getting married to someone, if that ever happened. She would never be an aunt, never experience her own wedding. Life was so fucking unfair, and she was the one who had died instead of that motherfucker. My heart felt like it was bleeding an ocean, and my eyes stared unseeingly.

"When did she pass away?" Aurora broke me from my grieving trance. From her way of speaking, I knew she was worried about how I would respond to that question.

With a sad smile on my face, I said, "Ten years ago."

"Asher—" but I interrupted her before she had time to finish the sentence. "I have something I need to tell you."

"What?" Her face filled with a look of surprise as I nodded my head in acknowledgment. Aurora's questioning look made me realize there were plenty of things I needed to explain to her before she could relax.

I just did not know how to explain it without the darkness fighting its way up to the surface, taking control of my body once again.

The darkness was always there, turning me into someone else.

Chapter 17
Her

LEANING MY BACK AGAINST the trunk of the huge tree with a deep, dark brown color, I spotted the birds sitting in their nest a few meters away. The nest was built by the birds themselves, using branches and pine cones as materials. Their chirping sang in my ears and the late afternoon sun laid low in the sky. More clouds than before had formed above us and surrounded the sun as some kind of protection.

Asher sat in front of me with his focus anywhere but on me. His legs were pulled into a tailor's position and the T-shirt hung tightly over his shoulders. A gray hoodie was placed over his upper body as the afternoon had brought cold to the relatively warm October day. The only thing he needed was a little space, but as time passed, my impatience escalated. His gaze fluttered over the surrounding landscape, but mine stopped at him as I noted his behavior. There was something he did not tell me. My discomfort was caused by the straight lines formed by the corners of his mouth.

Was he in a foul mood now?

Having experienced such a mood in the past, I felt apprehensive about experiencing it again. It was an expression Frederick had had. My face contorted as though I was struggling not to cry.

Killer smile. That was the word to describe his face. His lips were in a tight line, yet they were stretched too far, as if cut open by a knife. It was unnatural and made every cell in my body crouch, fearing for their lives. Frederick stood in front of me, his eyes dark and murderous, his smile huge and scary. In his hands, he held a knife. A bloodied knife. Blood dripped down from the blade.

Drip, drip, drip.

A metallic smell settled around us. We were alone. Everyone else was asleep, and he had me cornered in the parlor room. The only light came from the torches on the walls, casting unnerving shadows over us. It flickered behind my eyelids, and an immense pressure came from the left side of my arm. As if someone was holding me down for Frederick's advantage. Whispers were heard inside the walls, but it wasn't the children.

No, it was something else.

Frederick just stood there, staring at me, walking closer to me. I took a step back, and we continued as if in a dance. My back hit the wall, and his smile widened, his eyes narrowed. The knife was inches from my upper arm. His breathing rang like bells in my head, and I thought, 'this is where I will die.'

"My little Aurora. You have been a very obedient doll. I thought Theo had taught you better than that." He tsked in disappointment when he saw the tears roll down my cheeks.

My entire body was trembling, and every sound coming from the outside made me flinch. The wind gripped the trees, causing them to tap on the windows. A sound that echoed along with Frederick's voice. His smile came closer to my face, the knife pressing against my arm.

"Remember that you are mine," he hissed.

I thought back to the moment the guy a few years older than me had helped me hide last week when the hatch to the attic had stuck. He had helped me find a better place to hide, and Frederick had seen us together. I was his, he said. But I didn't want to be his. He only caused me pain.

His smile was etched into my memory, a killer smile I would never forget. And as he put pressure on the knife, blood dropped from my arm. A gripping scream escaped my throat, but no one could save me. Normally, no one survived his wrath, but I was his favorite doll. I didn't like it. He would have never allowed me to leave, nor would he have allowed me to die. I was bound to that life forever.

I miss my mom.

There was no denying my misery from the haunted look in my eyes. I had been twelve years old at that time, and he had already, years before, claimed me as his doll. Dread twisted in my gut and I could feel nothing but pure terror inside my veins.

Frederick wanted me.

I would suffocate if I didn't breathe, yet my lungs didn't accept any air. My hands shook as if they were aspen leaves, and my heart beat so hard in my chest it hurt.

He wanted me.

I opened my mouth to scream, but no sounds came out. Something pressed against my throat, against the most sensitive part, preventing me from taking a deep breath. Someone tried to kill me. Someone was holding my neck.

But it was just in my head. No one pressed against my neck.

He would come after me.

I wanted to scream, run away, fight, do something to get rid of the feeling inside me. I was in a bottomless well filled with water that would soon pull me under the surface and drown me. A well that would show Frederick where I was.

He wanted me.

And he wouldn't stop until he received what he wanted. He never gave up, he didn't care. As I opened my mouth, I found even words had deserted me, and I couldn't scream. I wanted to scream, scream away the pain inside me. Yell at Frederick to leave me alone.

Scream, scream, scream.

"Aurora!" A loud voice made me shift my gaze to the person next to me.

I saw nothing through my blurry vision, only a silhouette of a man with broad shoulders. His muscles strained against his clothes and those eyes of his were a mesmerizing color.

Was that angel going to help me out of my nightmare? Was he going to take me away from it?

A hand was placed on my shoulder and gently squeezed it.

"Look at me," the dark, masculine voice of the silhouette demanded, and I obeyed. "Breathe with me, yeah?"

I saw Asher beside me. Those amber-colored eyes looked at me with the same safety and intensity as always. Insisting that I follow him, he started taking deep breaths. The pain inside of me was fierce. My lungs were burning and my throat was parched.

I felt him grab my hand and place it over his heart as he whispered, "Breathe, darling."

His chest heaved up and down as I felt his heart beat beneath my palm. Following his example, I felt his heart thump and knew he was real.

He wasn't an illusion. He was here, and he was breathing with me. My hand was still pressed above his heart while he held it in his. The feeling of comfort and safety finally allowed me to calm down. Tears brimmed in the corner of my eyes at the relief of finally being able to breathe.

"Thank God you're okay. You were unresponsive for a good minute."

His eyes glowed with worry. While his eyebrows were slightly raised, his fearful and wild eyes stared at me.

Frederick was dead. He wouldn't get to me. Asher had saved me from my worst nightmare. Relief made me want to cry.

As he softened his eyes, I must have mumbled my words out loud.

"He will never get you again, darling. You are safe."

I merely nodded my head, staring at the houses from afar. They lived so peacefully.

I felt the sparkles in me come alive as Asher grabbed my hand, heated it, and instilled a feeling of warmth in me.

"You said you had something to tell me." I remembered Asher's words from before.

His body froze, and he stared at the horses along with me. There was something else I needed to think about than the memory, and what Asher told me might provide that distraction. He said nothing for a few minutes, and I wanted to give him more space, but my patience was wearing thin.

Tired, I stood up and put on my light pink ballerina shoes that matched the dirt pink dress I was wearing. Getting up from the ground, I grabbed my shoulder bag and began walking away from Asher and the tree.

As my mood was ruined by his secretive nature, I muttered, "See you in the car."

With arduous steps, I climbed down the hill. Just when everything seemed to go so well, it was ruined in an instant. As fast as possible, I moved toward the car to escape him. My eyebrows furrowed with irritation, and the bag was flung back and forth against my shoulder as I walked with determined steps. It annoyed me how he left me hanging like that, without giving me a reply. At that moment, I couldn't bear to stay with him, not until he was back to his normal self again.

My wrist was grabbed by an unknown hand before I knew what was happening. It was someone else's hand that pulled me to a muscular body whose owner I recognized immediately.

"What do you want?" I leveled a glare at him.

"If I told you about the darkness inside of me, would you still look at me the same way? Will you still stay with me?" His question shocked me and made me pause. The pain in my heart was excruciating.

"Come back, I promise to tell you. You said you trusted me." He pleaded.

Without giving me the chance to reply, he walked back up the hill while still holding my hand. He took me to where the picnic blanket was still lying by the tree, and I was dragged behind him. Because I was filled with irritation, I couldn't resist rolling my eyes.

Mary was sitting next to the bowls of raspberries and blueberries when I sat down again on the blanket. In that moment, I was too annoyed to care if it became patched with grass. My gaze shifted to my hands as Asher sat in his former seat across from me. There was no point in looking up and meeting his eyes, not until he explained himself, at least. Even so, I was still irritated with him for letting me leave.

"Talk," is what I demanded from him with a tone that was clear enough to get interpreted as annoyance.

"I have never told this to anyone." As soon as he mentioned it, I was overcome with pity.

The weight of my conscience felt like a heavy rock pressing down on me. I had acted harshly toward him, and his voice now sounded so broken it made me feel guilty. From a plastic bag that had been in the cooler bag, Asher pulled out a book. The book was old, with tattered pages and broken edges. It looked like something antique, certainly not like it was made in the current decade. With a puzzled look in my eyes, I received the book he had handed me.

"What is this?" I asked with a bewildered expression.

His Adam's apple moved as he swallowed and nodded at me. "Read it."

Initially, I was in a state of confusion, which made it impossible to flip it open and read it. To be honest, I feared what I would find in it.

With the book in my hands, I leaned against the tree and sat with my back against it. Asher lay down on the blanket next to me with his hands supporting his chin so that his head was raised. In his eyes, it was clear he was struggling to cope, and I became more apprehensive about what I would read next. Taking a deep breath, I opened the first page with shaky hands.

"20th February 1790,

My dearest diary, the house is ready. Thorington Manor is now open to the public for viewing. My wife, Catherine Thorington, is pregnant with our third son! There is no doubt in my mind that it is a son; I do not wish for another daughter. We are looking forward to building our own lives in Thorington Manor, and may our children inherit the house and stay forever. Should that not be the case, I will personally shoot them with my hunting rifle. I sincerely hate my children. It is Catherine who is the only person I need in my life. I wish they all would pass away.

Signed by Edmund Thorington."

"19th July 1820,

Dear Diary, I am writing this entry in this unsightly book on behalf of my parents. May they rest in peace. Although my father was not the kind of father a child would choose, he was aware of this awful thing. When my mother found my father inside the cowshell, there were several buckets filled with white milk from the animals. My father was dead, if that wasn't apparent already. His death was caused by suffocation from hanging himself inside their stable. My father was, as I mentioned previously, not an exemplary parent. He cursed excessively, which my mother did not appreciate, and drank lots of jugs of whiskey. Furthermore, he had a strong dislike for children. Precisely like his father, my grandfather, used to have. I am not aware of the reason for his having five children with my mother. Then again, there was nothing ordinary about my father. I am relieved to learn of his passing, but may he still rest in peace.

From your Mr. Grantham Thorington."

"No date signed,

I am delighted to inform you that my beloved wife Rosemary gave birth to our youngest son today. We are naming him Asher. It is likely that he will be my favorite son out of the two. There is an aura surrounding this baby. We pray God will show him the light in the world and that he will live a long and prosperous life. There is a lot more I like about this baby than I do about my other son, Theodore. As much as Rosemary wishes for more children, I do not wish to have any more. There is no need for more than three of those incompetent things. It was only my intention to have one son who would inherit

Thorington Manor, but now I have two and one daughter. However, I do still love my children. I AM a good father, unlike my own.

Yours, Charles Thorington."

As I read, more thoughts swirled inside my head, but it became clear that not every man in Asher's family had been friendly towards children. Conversely, every generation had hated its offspring and every father had been sick in the head. In front of me I held the diary with shock reflected in my expression, but Asher's was blank. My heart ached at the thought that his father had favored one of his two sons. It was not in my power to imagine that horrible feeling.

"Ash, what is this?" My throat tightened as I swallowed the lump.

He watched me skimming through the start of the next entry book. His head was still raised like before. He demanded with a stern expression, "Continue reading," to which I did.

"Dear diary, this book has been around for several generations, and now it's my turn to take care of it. If you read the previous pages, it should be clear to you that my ancestors were idiots all over the place, and they were sick too. Sometimes I wonder if I have inherited their diseases. The diseases that drove them crazy. It's been two years. Two freaking years and I still have not talked to anyone about how I feel. Honestly, I don't even know how I feel, or how to feel. An emptiness has filled me, a feeling that has become standard for me. When asking people how they feel, their standard answer is 'I am good,' even if it's a lie, but I cannot find the energy to lie to people anymore or pretend that I'm fine. 'I am empty,' is the answer everyone receives from me, but no further explanation. I know I need to somehow let my feelings out if I am going to be able to survive in the future. Because I don't trust anyone, this diary has to be my therapist.

That night, two years ago, I saw her die in my arms. No one helped. I made the mistake of putting my trust in people, especially him.

Her boyfriend.

But look how that went. A man, choking her until her eyes turned red. The red covered her white eyeballs, coloring them until they were bloodshot. When he noticed she was still alive after his choke, he became angry. His fingers stuffed into her nose to make her unable to breathe through it, to make her stop from breathing at all. There was blood everywhere. She was covered in blood.

Blood.

Every.

Where.

I will never forget that day. The day she died in my arms. The day we escaped from the apartment he lived in so that we could find a neighbor who could save us from the psychopath who was chasing us. No one saved us. I lost confidence in humanity that day, two years ago. He came out after us, a knife in his bare hands, blood dripping down his arms. That day two years ago was the day I held her in my arms as she took her last breaths. As tears streamed down her cheeks, she whispered she loved me. The only thing I wished I could have done was switch places with her. I wanted to be the one who died instead of her. That day two years ago, I lost her. My beloved sister.

Written by Asher Thorington."

The page ended with no more handwritten text. My hands shook even more. With a shaky breath, I let the book lay open in my lap as I felt the tears fall down my cheeks. They fell into my mouth and tasted salty on my tongue. They were silent tears, no sobs or sniffles, only quiet droplets running down my face and blurring my vision.

Even though I couldn't see clearly, my eyes were fixed on the book and I tried not to hyperventilate.

My heart broke for Asher, for the horrible experience he had been through. The desire to know more about him was lost, and I did not feel able to continue reading. All I wanted now was to put the book down and stop torturing myself with the images of his dead sister in my imagination. My nose stung from crying as I wiped my tears away with my coat sleeve. Looking at Asher, my eyes drew away from the book. His eyes were as blank as before.

"Go on," he said to me and I shook my head.

I did not want to read more, could not read more. Still, I knew I had to keep on reading. I had to do it for his sake, not for mine.

I grabbed the book with a deep breath and started reading again, trying to stop the tears from flowing.

"Dear Diary,

Whenever I feel something, I can't find the words to express it. He hit me again. Using his belt, father whipped me on the back until blood was dripping down my legs. He blames the death on me, as if I could have saved her when I was just entering my teenage years. A psychotic murderer cannot be stopped by someone who is that young. There was no action taken by my mother to stop the abuse. The only thing she did was watch from the corner of the room. But I couldn't blame her. My sister's death affected everyone. I miss her more than anything."

My tears kept flowing down my cheeks, and I forced my next words while hiccupping, "Please Ash, I can't continue reading."

He just stared at me with an emotionless expression. It was all becoming too much for my psyche to handle. I discovered so much about his childhood for the first time, and what I learned was shocking. My eyes had begun to sting from all the tears that had gathered.

"Continue," he said with his lips pursed and his teeth grit together.

It was for that reason that I turned several pages and continued to read, just so Asher would have a chance to be heard once and for all.

"Dear Diary,

Ever since my sister died just over ten years ago, I have felt darkness kindling within me. I felt some relief when my father passed away and my mother hung herself from the pain of his passing, but I sometimes wake up from the pain inside of me. Agony so suffocating that my heart could stop. Sometimes the only thing I see is darkness and I am unable to think properly. Far too many times have I felt like hurting people. The darkness devouring me, tearing me into pieces, exceeds every rational thought. I'm trying to survive as best as I can, but I just feel so lonely. The pain of Mary's death is too heavy of a burden to bear alone, and even worse, being blamed for her death by my father is excruciating. I once tried to talk to someone about my feelings, about the darkness, but that person did not listen to me. Since then, I have never uttered a word about it. I lost faith in humanity ten years ago when she died.

A month ago, a girl came here. She lives in the room upstairs, which was previously an unused guest room. The girl is a beauty with strawberry-blonde hair and light purple tips. Her smile is the most beautiful I have ever laid eyes on. And her eyes are of the most unique color. She is almost as beautiful as my beloved sister. The girl's name is Aurora. I do not want her to leave me. Looking at her gives me peace of mind. She calms the flames itching inside my skin. She absorbs the darkness only to turn it into light. She is the angel I never knew I needed. She keeps the pain away, but I know it will come. It always comes back. The darkness arises in situations where it feels like I have lost control of my own life. Sometimes it's like looking at my own life, my own actions, in the third person. It's like I'm aware of what's going on, but I cannot control my own actions. It feels as if the darkness within me is living a life of its own, and when the evil version of me fights his way to the surface, it feels as if I am completely losing control. It feels like the darkness within is impersonating me. Like it lives my life pretending to be me. The darkness made me murder someone in cold blood, and that nightmare has been following me ever since. It's becoming too much to handle. But no one listens to me. I miss you so, my beloved sister, Mary."

Chapter 18
Her

As I closed the worn-out book with a loud thud, my heart hammered hard inside my chest. It was as if my heart skipped a beat. Silence spread around us and I couldn't find words. It even felt like the birds stopped chirping, like the horses stopped neighing and snorting, and like the wind stopped howling. Silence fell everywhere.

As I was fumbling for words, I realized I couldn't express my feelings at the moment. My tongue was stuck, refusing to utter a single syllable. There was no point in even trying.

Asher had changed position, so he was leaning against the tree, too. We sat side by side for several minutes without saying anything. The silence was inwardly rigid, as it sometimes was when it fell upon the surroundings. Despite not being able to articulate my thoughts, I was able to show all my unspoken understanding through my eyes. Both our heads angled inward, and our eyes gazed into each other. The depth in his eyes made me understand the pain he was living through. His lopsided attempt at a smile made the butterflies in my stomach flutter.

Despite not speaking to him verbally, my eyes said a lot. With a single look, I told him all my feelings. They poured out of me like a flowing waterfall. My eyes said *I'm here for you, I believe you, I hear you, be brave enough to trust me.* I wanted to be the person he could rely on. More than ten years with no closeness or love. There was no greater pain than losing something you once had, when you remembered how it felt to have it. To know that you once had something worthwhile, but it was now gone forever.

It was late afternoon, and clouds were forming all around the sun. The sun no longer stood high in the sky like when we had first arrived at the tree. The evening air was warm, but the clouds were darkening far away in the sky.

I placed the book between me and Asher, the book that contained all his feelings and secrets. The book he entrusted me to read. I could feel my heart beating faster and his fingers brushed against mine. My hand was still holding the diary when I felt his hand approach. Even though I tried to appear unruffled by his actions, my stomach fluttered as I stared beyond the horizon. Throughout the waiting process, I felt a sense of anticipation.

And then it was there.

That warm feeling of someone else's skin against yours. His touch felt like magic, lighting up my insides as if in a fairy tale. His little finger rested against mine on the white blanket. As his fingers slid closer to mine, I felt the smoothness of his skin. The air made me shaky as I inhaled and kept my gaze pointed downward, out of shyness. For never had I held someone's hand with such intimacy, and never had I felt so many stars light up inside of me. In my head, it felt as if fireworks had been set off in a dark blue sky inside me. I had experienced more pain than words could ever describe, more loss than any normal person with a normal childhood had. That place was the reason for all of it.

Grimhill Manor.

For yes, allowing the man beside me to hold my hand was a huge step to take. To allow him to touch me became my way of showing my support.

In some cases, there was no need for words at all. Not when there was a spark between two human beings, and certainly not when these two had something in common that no one would ever understand.

For it was me and Asher, two souls shaped by fucked up childhoods.

"Say something," he asked rather than demanded, breaking the silence between us.

"I–I don't…" Swallowing, I continued. "I don't know what to say," my voice came out as a stutter. There were so many feelings inside of me.

"What do you feel, darling?" At his last word, my heart fluttered once more.

"Ash, thank you for letting me read this. I have no words."

There truly were no words to describe my emotions. At that moment, I was unsure of how to react or how to feel. The shock of what I had read was lingering like a thick fog above my head. What did you say to someone who had just shared their traumatic childhood?

I did not know.

Damn, I wish there was a handbook for reacting in social situations. Asher's smile was soft as he looked at me, his eyes showing relief, but also pain from reliving the memories. We stared into each other's eyes for a long time, just looking at each other. In the end, the expressions on our faces spoke louder than any words we could ever say. His mesmerizing amber-colored eyes fixed on mine, only to drop to my lips for a brief second, and then up again. A blush crept up my cheeks as I cast a glance over England's moors. I was too shy to look him in the eye again.

"Look at me," he whispered in the softest voice I had ever heard.

Something stirred to life within me upon hearing this sentence. I couldn't help but stare at his lips as I turned my head toward him again. With everything I had, I tried desperately not to kiss him, not to give in. It felt impossible.

In a whirlwind, butterflies flew through my stomach, making it tickle and feel wonderful. Not once did he break eye contact with me as he leaned his head closer. In a silent gasp, I bit my lower lip out of habit. The moment he saw me, his eyes fell on mine and he was filled with desire. It felt like my heart would melt when his face was so close to mine that I could feel his breath fanning my mouth.

The tip of our noses bumped into each other for a second. Not only did his hand grab one of my own, but his other one pulled my body closer to him as well. With my free hand, I placed it on his chest and felt his heart beat rapidly inside.

"If you want me to stop, say it now because I don't think I'd be able to once I've had a taste of you," he whispered, sending shivers down my body.

During the few seconds that followed, I said nothing to him, only stared at him in anticipation and waited. A slight movement forward caused his lips to brush in a gentle act against mine. It was as if all the worries in the world had vanished at that moment. He kissed me carefully, slowly, and gently, his hand still holding mine. I had never experienced a kiss like that before, and I was blown away by it. One that was like a warm blanket on a cold winter's day.

For a brief second, he stopped kissing me, leaving me surprised and hungry for more. But as fast as he left off, he pressed his lips on mine once again. I felt my heart swelling as our tongues tingled together and the passion of the kiss surged through me. It was something both of us needed—a hungry kiss after all the stares and tension between the two of us. Something that needed to be explored between us. His hand gripped the back of my head to pull it even closer to his and the pressure of his body against mine also made me feel his erection through his pants. There was a sensation of heat between my legs, causing my cheeks to assume a redder hue. We both needed each other.

Eventually, we had to break away from the kiss, both being too breathless and having too much to talk about.

"Damn, how do you do that?" he muttered with a smile on his face. On those lips that I wanted to kiss again. For that man in front of me was the man I had come to care about a lot.

"Do what?" I asked him, completely unaware of what he meant.

With one hand, he took hold of my other hand and pressed it against his pounding heart. "Make my heart beat even faster every time I look at you," he said as his voice faded to a whisper against my mouth. I could feel how close our faces were.

"I wasn't meant to feel this way about you," he said, more to himself than to me.

Even though I heard his sentence, I pretended I didn't. There was something about the man in front of me that drew me to him.

After reading his diary, I understood it had not been his intention to hurt me the first time I saw him.

He was the one who showed me tenderness in my weakest moments, and now I showed him affection. And it was at that moment that I felt brave enough to share my story with him.

"When I was younger," I took a deep breath before continuing, feeling his gaze on me. "I was ripped out of my mom's arms. There were men coming for me. I was too young to understand what was happening back then. They kidnapped me, and took me to Grimhill Manor. The place where they dress the kids as dolls, preparing them to become dolls for future doll masters." Tears glistened in my eyes as I spoke.

"The games they played with us there are worse than the ones you played with me. We became their pawns, their dolls with which they could do whatever they pleased. Each doll had a room, but there were strict routines to follow, such as when to eat all meals and when it was time for activities. It sounds like an orphanage, and it sort of was, except they kidnapped young children to bring them there. The games weren't harmless child games. They were horror games. I didn't realize it at first, not until everyone tried to escape after you took me. Everyone had been brainwashed, thinking 'this is how life is supposed to be.' Child activities such as hopscotch, hide-and-seek, tag, and jumping on trampolines all became games of horror. Death, torture. We were all brainwashed. Those who refused to play the games broke the rules and were taken to a room, never to be seen again. Or, in the worst-case scenario, they were killed in front of our eyes."

I felt a burning sensation pressed against my chest as I spoke about those terrifying years of my life. Silent tears fell down my cheeks, tears of all the pain both of us had experienced. It was tears of agony, a type that broke your heart from the inside.

His hand came up to my face and grazed my tears only to wipe them away from my skin as they fell. He touched me and something in me came to life.

I looked at him as he spoke, "Aurora, you are safe now. No one at Grimhill Manor will ever touch you again. Okay?" He made a pause only to look me in the eye as he continued, his eyes shining so brightly it made me want to believe him. "I am going to help you find a way to heal from those moments. Do you trust me?"

"Yes," I whispered.

At that moment, I had forgotten how he had made me play the same games as they had done at Grimhill Manor. The Asher in front of me now outweighed the things he did before. He had his past, and I had mine. I knew that together, we could help each other heal.

"I will be here for you too, whenever you need me," I promised him.

The smile he gave me was sad, with a glimmer of relief at having told his story and heard mine.

As we looked into each other's eyes, I could see the desperation for closure in his. A particular feeling filled me, a tingling that could not be ignored. I wanted him as much as his eyes told me he wanted me. He put his arms around my shoulders and pulled me closer to him. My head leaned against his chest as I listened to the sound of his breathing and the peaceful beating of his heart. It told me he was alive, that he wasn't a fairy tale I'd made up in my dreams. It said he was here, and that he was holding me.

When my eyes met him once again, I saw his head come closer to mine. Before I knew it, he had planted a soft kiss on my lips. My lips were dry at first, but when he moistened them with his, they softened, allowing me to kiss him back. A soft kiss was what it was. A kiss we both needed, both longed for. After everything we had been through, I could find peace in his arms.

Our kiss soon became something much better, something I could never imagine happening between two human beings. When our lips met in damp, sloppy kisses, his hand made sure to grab mine. With his other hand, he pressed me closer to his muscular body. It was almost as if he needed me closer. As if he needed to make sure I was truly there.

"Aurora," his dark voice whispered into my ears.

The sound of it, the sensation, made my entire body fill with anticipation. While waiting for him to devour me, I sensed the desire before I felt it. As his tongue slowly made its way into my mouth, it met mine in a gorgeous moment. During that time, I was able to feel everything, especially the tingles of excitement that shot through my core. Having his hand around me sent electricity coursing through me, making me feel too much—an overload of emotions whirling around. There was something about the way his muscular body pressed against mine that made me feel so aware of him. My desire to touch his body had been deep since I encountered him for the first time, but it was even deeper at that moment. A feeling much more intense.

As he broke away from the kiss, my eyes spotted the heat in his eyes, as if I were the sole of his existence. My hand grasped the back of his head, pulling his lips to mine again as the desperation grew stronger. When our lips met, our hands clasped together and the feeling of him had my core tightening. It was a sensation so strong, yet not enough. It was never enough.

Asher's hand let go of mine, and our fingers detangled much to my disappointment. My body already missed the proximity of him, and although that could be a good thing, it scared my brain that had never been committed to someone. Within a few seconds, I could feel his hand wandering over my body, and the scent of him filled me with a voracious craving. His hand caressed my neck in a gentle manner, down to my shoulder, letting me feel the texture of his much bigger palm compared to mine. He was huge, over six feet as I was five-foot-four, and somehow the size difference made it so much better. The sensation of his touch on me stirred something to life in my stomach as I realized what was happening, and anticipation filled me with nerves. His caresses sent chills down my spine, making me gasp softly. At the sound of me, a smirk tugged at the corner of his lips—a motion he tried to hide by looking away, but failed.

"So beautiful," he murmured as his hand found its way down to my leg.

Starting from my knee, he dragged the hand upwards toward my thigh, lifting my dress. While I waited, my gaze locked into his. No words were spoken when he had his moment with me, everything we wanted to say transferred through the tensing emotions in our gazes. It felt like minutes before he reached my thigh, a period of time that made me greedy for more. Giving me a light kiss on my lips, his fingers traveled until they reached the edge of my panties.

Inside my chest, my heart was beating like a madman, nervous but at the same time excited for what I knew would come. As his fingers brushed above my underwear, on my most sensitive spot, I could feel every emotion inside of me heighten. The pure pleasure he gave me by only gently tapping my clit, made my panties soak, something that should have made me embarrassed but did not. I had never been that soaked before. The look he gave me told me he loved what he was seeing, his eyes never waved from my body and they shimmered with reverence.

"This is the most beautiful sight I've ever seen," he whispered in my ear.

His words brought a smile to my lips, and a low chuckle escaped from deep within me. I swatted at him, embarrassed, and tried to hide my face in my hands. His larger hands gripped mine, holding me as if they were handcuffs.

"Kinky."

At my word he began to laugh, such a dark and beautiful sound that it vibrated through me like a melody to my ears. When I smiled at him, my gums showed, and his eyes sparkled with delight.

His hands still held mine as he said, "Never hide your face from me," causing my cheeks to heat up, and the feeling of wanting to hide returned.

Under me, I could feel him adjusting his pants, and it was at that moment when he moved that my body felt the hardness inside his boxers. A smile spread over my lips once again as I shifted position, and he released my hands as he put them at the edge of my panties, causing me to squirm under his touch.

The desire to feel him so intimately against mine motioned me to put my hands over his pants as I tugged at them, urging him to remove them. The heat in our eyes was something I had never experienced, it made me dizzy with want. Taking a moment to take his pants off, he removed his hand from my clit and my body immediately missed his touch once again. It craved more, longed for more.

When he had pulled down his pants, after making sure no one was around us, he pulled me closer to him. I found his stiff erection as my hand brushed over his boxers, it felt unusual but still so right. His face rested in the curve of my shoulder, and his breath fanned against my skin in a tantalizing manner. A wave of lust roiled through my womb, ensnaring me in a vortex of heat inching outward and spinning me into oblivion.

Even though I was so intoxicated by want and need, the uncertainty still resolved again. Never before had another man touched me in this way and the thought of it made my cheeks heat up.

I swallowed hard in an attempt to clear the lump in my throat, a lump that wanted to take over and make me stop my movements before panic took hold. But I couldn't stop, I wanted this as much as he did, and I couldn't let my insecurities ruin the moment.

"I—I have no idea," I paused before my eyes found his. "I do not know how to touch another man."

My gaze shifted downward, trying to ignore him because of the embarrassment I felt. He knew how to touch another girl, but I had no idea how to please a man. It was evident that he knew these motions in the way his fingers moved with so much certainty, as if he had done this a thousand times over. Even though I knew this moment meant as much to him as it did to me.

"Don't worry, darling. I will show you," he smiled before grabbing my hand.

Using his hand, he placed mine on his hard dick inside his boxers. He removed them, pulling them down to his knees. My eyes bulged at the sight of his length, and I gulped nervously.

He was huge.

A certain warmth spread through my body, a heat that almost made me drip from the wetness in my pussy. He chuckled as he saw my expression, a quirky smirk plastered on his lips.

"You do it like this," he whispered in his dark, sexy voice before showing me how to stroke his dick.

When my hand landed upon it, doing as he showed me, a deep groan slipped from his throat.

"A-am I doing this right?" I carefully asked, not daring to look into his eyes. I was too scared to do it wrong.

His fingers brushed against my chin and he lifted it up, forcing me to look into his eyes. "Yes, baby," he said before he planted a soft kiss on my lips.

My hand continued to do as he showed me, stroking his cock in a manner he found pleasurable. The low moans coming from him sounded like heaven, and I knew I had given him pleasure. Never before had I given pleasure to another man. The moment felt both unique and beautiful. His hand found its way to my panties, pulling them down, and revealing my wet folds. As my hand continued pumping his dick, his fingers touched my pussy.

"So wet for me," he whispered before pushing a finger inside of me in slow motion.

The sensation felt weird, but his gaze locked with mine made me feel completely and utterly safe. And as he slowly pulled back, and pushed in his fingers at a slow pace, I found pleasure in the act. Moans spilled from my lips. Both of our sounds of pleasure combined with a beautiful sound, almost as if it were melodic.

"Fuck, darling," Asher rasped as he continued to finger me, causing my eyes to roll back.

With a puff of air, I inhaled around him as my inner walls fluttered rhythmically. My back arched against him, my hips rocking in the same tempo as his against my hand. I focused on the sensation of his skin against mine, a gesture so small yet so special in my heart.

My hand quickened up the pace, stroking his dick and he let out grunts of pleasure. In response to the wet sounds, I bucked my hips faster in a desperate attempt to fight the feverish passion burning in my veins.

"You love how you make me feel, don't you?" He growled in my ear as he worked his fingers faster, and all I could do was whimper from the pleasure.

I never imagined something could feel that good. In his quest to make me reach the climax, he ravaged my body, taking and feeling everything he wanted from me. The sensation had me rolling my eyes as I desperately tried to continue stroking his erection.

Our moans filled the moors as the wind blew against our bodies, creating more friction against my clit. It was so peaceful out there, which made the moment even more special. In the heat of the moment, I wasn't even scared of being caught, even though I knew nobody would be nearby.

"Please," I whined against him as his lips devoured mine in frantic and poisonous kisses.

It was a kiss of poison masked as sugar, making you savor death's taste. A taste I never would get enough of.

When I felt him tense under me, I could feel my own body clench around his fingers inside of me.

"A-Ash, I'm—" I said, trying to let him know I was close. No more words came out of my mouth, the pleasure was too intense for me to function.

The moment was too beautiful.

"I know, darling. Me too," he rasped out as his chest heaved.

In a matter of seconds, our moans grew louder as we chased each other's releases. Before I knew it, a pleasure so strong it caused tears to form in the corner of my eyes filled my body. As if I were being sucked down under the surface of the ocean, the pleasure burst inside me like explosions of stars.

His dick jerked as I watched his cum pour out of him, onto my hand. My body shook, him still fingering me until I screamed out from the pleasure and came on his fingers. The aftermath of my orgasm forced me to suck in lungfuls of air.

We were both drenched in sweat. My eyes closed as my body leaned against Asher's chest, enjoying the moment. He planted soft kisses on my forehead before embracing me, and the safety I felt in his arms was overwhelming.

"You are so beautiful," he whispered.

"You are so handsome," I said in sincerity with a smile, causing him to chuckle.

My head was leaning against his chest, hearing the beating of his heart. As we sat there, his hand was held in mine and his fingers intertwined with mine. Our hands remained firmly clasped while we gazed at the surrounding landscape in comfortable silence. On the horses, the birds, the moors. And I wished I could freeze the moment. To always have it within reach and finally, at last, get to live a life with only love surrounding me.

To finally be free from the pain my childhood caused me.

Chapter 19
Her

THE END OF OCTOBER was approaching. Winds settled over the weather in breezes that forced you to pull your coat tighter. The beauty of the season had been astounding. It was the season of harvest, when the country people reaped the pumpkins they had grown for three months, when the kitchen people made jam out of the fruit from their gardens and the cafes made drinks flavored with apple pie.

The scent filling my nostrils was that of fresh apple crisp intermingled with warm and mouthwatering spices.

"Two apple pie caramel lattes are ready," said a middle-aged woman in a singsong from behind the counter.

With a smile on his face, Asher walked over to the woman and grabbed the mugs. He set both of them down on the table we were seated at, with a perfect view of the outside world. The leaves were piling up on the streets, making it slippery for people as they walked. A combination of orange, red and yellow colored the landscape, making it a wonder to look at. Leaves fell from the trees like snow fell during winter, and the mug in my hands permeated me with its heat.

It had been a week since Asher had taken me to the picnic by the tree, and we had stayed inside ever since. Day in and day out, the rain had poured down outside, the thunder had roared and the flash had taken out the electricity in the manor. Candles were what we had used to see anything, and Josephine had cooked food based on how they did centuries ago. With no electricity or light, Asher and I had spent the days wandering around the house, reading together, and playing card games along with Josephine. A blush crept over my cheeks as I thought back to the time Asher and I had read together.

"Aurora, come here. I'm bored." Asher shouted for me from the floor below.

My feet touched the cold floor as I scurried over to the stairs with a one-piece covering my body. I used a torch to walk down the dark stairs, and Asher waited for me at the end of them. He reached out his hand for me and I took it as he led me to another room we had visited earlier in the week. The room was a kind of library, with a huge couch at one of its ends. Bookshelves covered another wall, and closest to the door was a stove.

He led me over to the couch and I settled down, watching him light up a fire on the stove. Heat radiated throughout the room, warming up my cold body. When the couch's cushion tipped to one side as Asher sat down, I made myself comfortable under the soft blanket. In Asher's hand was the 'Wuthering Heights,' by Emily Brontë, a historical and gothic romance. He laid down under the blanket with me before opening the book. My head automatically placed on his chest as he pulled me closer. The musky scent of him calmed me down, drowning out the thunder from outside. He planted a kiss on my forehead with a faint smile on his lips. A gesture so innocent, yet it melted my heart. For I did not know where I had him, but the time we had spent together made me wish we could stay like that forever.

246

I could get used to that.

He made me feel safe.

"'I'm tired of being enclosed here,'" read Asher out loud, his voice making his chest vibrate. "'I'm wearying to escape into that glorious world, and to be always there: not seeing it dimly through tears, and yearning for it through the walls of an aching heart: but really with it, and in it.'"

"I can relate to Catherine," I whispered and snuggled closer to Asher.

"How so?"

"She feels imprisoned. She wishes to always be in the glorious world, without seeing it dimly through tears. That was how I felt at Grimhill."

Asher put a bookmark on the page we had read and laid the book on the shelf beside us. His warm body lay against mine and he dragged in the scent of my shampoo. Eyes lingering on mine, his presence made the butterflies tingle inside my stomach. I wanted to take advantage of the time with him, for I knew he may not feel the same. His warm eyes told me he did, but I feared the dullness would return.

His lips met mine in a wondrous kiss, melting away all my worries.

"Not now?" he asked after my statement, and I shook my head.

"Not now."

"Good, I never want you to feel like a prisoner in here." A worried expression etched across his face.

"I don't."

With Asher, I felt more free than I ever had. Although I was scarred from my past, I knew he was too, and together we would make it. He would fight for me, that I knew, and I would fight for him.

If it took fighting forever, then so be it.

"What are you thinking about, darling?" Asher's voice broke me from my flashback and I gave him a smile.

"That time we read Wuthering Heights together."

He chuckled and drank from his coffee. We were in a town called Millvale. It was a two-hour ride from Thorington Manor. Since I had recovered from my pneumonia, I was allowed to go out, and Asher wanted to take me to the town he used to visit as a child. Apparently, his parents had been in some kind of committee for the founding families. The town was a rather small town, but had everything the citizens could possibly need. Millvale was also the town closest to where Asher lived. We were in a coffee shop at one end of the town. Sunlight shone through the clouds, despite the wind blowing.

When I looked at him, I saw something weighing on his heart like a mine ready to explode in anguish any moment. As I tilted my head, I watched as his lips opened slightly.

"I am truly sorry for ever hurting you," he paused. "That's one of the things I regret the most in my life."

Remorse was visible in his eyes, and my heart ached for the man who had been through so much.

"Ash, you have already apologized."

I felt the glistening behind my eyes at the thought he needed to apologize more times than he already had. I had forgiven him, that was all in the past. I had never been the one to hold a grudge against anyone. Yet, he couldn't seem to let it go, and that remorse, guilt, and compassion were something I admired about him.

I took a sip of the coffee, and the taste melted on my tongue. "This is really good," I said to Asher, to which he nodded.

"Yeah, I rarely drink coffee, but this was tasty."

He was dressed in a black coat draped over his body, and his arms were placed on the table. Those eyes I loved were looking at me with his chin resting on his hands.

"What do you usually drink?"

"Tea. There's a shop on the other end of town called Tea N Me. I usually get my tea there."

His voice sent tingles down my core. It was so dark and raspy as he spoke about the drink. Who knew talking about tea could be so sensual?

I remembered our intimate moment at the picnic, and my cheeks immediately turned a rosy, red color.

"You have to take me there," I stated, and he nodded his head.

Asher stood up from his chair and helped me up from mine before he led me out of the shop. The street we were on sloped upwards, with shops lining the sides. Hand in hand, we walked towards the main square of the city and my eyes took in everything. Years had passed since I had been in a city, and all of it seemed unreal.

With eager steps, I dragged Asher with me as we walked to the central part of the city. On one part of the main square, there was a patch of grass, with several hay bales and pumpkins surrounding it.

"Look, look!" I exclaimed with too much eagerness.

Asher's chuckle found its way into my tympanic membrane and warmed my frozen body, as if the sound of his laughter could make me stop freezing.

"Wait here," he said with a mysterious smile, and I raised an eyebrow at him.

While he walked off to a couple a few yards away, I ran up to the hay bales and touched the straws. Never before had I touched something that felt so prickly. It smelled fresh and was a completely different feeling than what I was used to.

It smelled like freedom.

Within just a minute, Asher returned, his arm encircling my shoulder and pulling me closer.

"I asked them to take pictures of us."

I tilted my head, but nodded. Everything felt so unreal, like I was living in a book I was about to wake up from. Having sat down on a hay bale, he placed me on his lap. I felt everything inside me come to life when he kissed my lips with a smile. All the organs began to function, the butterflies swirled in my stomach as if in a whirlwind, and happiness filled every cell of my body. The sound of a picture being taken was heard, and the couple approached us with Asher's camera. He thanked them and together we looked at the pictures.

"You're so beautiful here," he whispered in my ear as he pointed to a picture where my hair was blowing in the wind and a smile was on my face as I looked at Asher.

Feeling happiness had seemed impossible to me. Frederick had always made me feel the opposite. He said I didn't deserve happiness, but Asher contradicted everything he said. Maybe I could be freed from the demons inside me, after all.

I wanted to seize that moment. It was as precious as all the others with him. There was something in his manner, the way his amber-colored eyes brought warmth to my life, the way he looked at me as if he wanted to protect me from all evil. Asher just made me feel safe, and sometimes everything felt like a dream. A dream I would wake up from in my old room at Grimhill Manor. A dream where none of it was true, and I was still living in Frederick's hell.

"You make me feel safe," I whispered to Asher as I leaned my head against his shoulder.

"You make me feel like myself," he said back to me and I could feel his smile grow.

It was so strange. Feeling that way for another man was something I never thought I would experience. My hope for a future had been destroyed by Grimhill, and I knew Asher's faith in humanity had been destroyed by the death of Mary and his parents. Two broken souls who found refuge in each other.

It was everything I had ever dreamed of, and more.

We sat on the hay bales together; I remained on his lap as we looked at the pictures together. Our first photographs with each other.

My gaze was fixed on a crowd forming further away—where the forest began—and the shouts of the people filled the stillness of the town. Asher's body stiffened and his grip on me tightened.

"What's happening?" my voice shook as I spoke.

Screaming was something I hated, especially after Grimhill.

"I don't know. Stay behind me; if anything happens, I want you safe." Asher helped me to my feet and grabbed my hand before we headed toward the crowd that had formed. His touch calmed my nerves and stopped the panic attack I felt was coming.

Several people had pale facial expressions, upset voices could be heard, and someone called an emergency number. Together we pushed our way to the front of the crowd and the sight before me made my stomach turn inside out. Tears formed in my eyes, and memories all too clear took over behind my closed eyelids.

She, with hair shimmering like copper, screamed a terrifying scream, and her forest green eyes filled with so much dread as she watched the man point a gun at Frederick.

There was a girl in front of my eyes. Blood was dripping from her feet from dozens of wounds.

Her hair clung to the skin of her face, where she lay with her eyes closed. I immediately pushed my way to the girl, not caring if I happened to bump into someone in the crowd. My only focus was on the girl. Crouching down next to her, I placed two of my fingers on her neck. There it was, the faint throbbing of her heart.

"Hurry!" I shouted at no one and everyone at the same time, "Get the ambulance!"

A hand was placed on my shoulder and with panicked eyes, I looked into the person's eyes.

"She has a weak pulse, but I don't know how much longer she'll be fine," I muttered in horror.

I had seen too many children in harm's way over the years and I couldn't bear to witness another. Asher nodded and removed his coat, which he placed over the girl's body to warm it up. My hands were trembling, the event clogging my mind, making me want to black out.

"Can you hear me?" I asked the girl, but her eyes were closed. "Damn it!" I muttered to myself and took off my own coat to put it over her.

While her eyes fluttered open, sirens could be heard in the background.

Forest green eyes.

The same eyes as the girl at Grimhill.

The tips of her hair were colored lime-green.

The same way Grimhill Manor forced the girls to have their hair.

"Aurora?" mumbled the girl sleepily, her eyes about to close again and her body limp where it lay on the ground.

My heart started beating faster as I stared at her.

"Aurora, is that you?" her voice was smooth when she murmured, which made me gasp.

"How, how do you know my name?" My eyes were wide open as the shock settled over me.

"Everyone knows who you are," her eyes slowly closed, and I yelled at her to wake up.

"I'm so tired. I've been walking and walking, living on whatever wasted food I could find, walking through forests. I am so tired."

Panic hit me once again. The sirens of the ambulance came closer and closer. Asher's hand held mine as I yelled at the ambulance men to hurry. In their hands, they held a stretcher and medicine bag. Her eyes were closed again. Inwardly, I hoped she hadn't passed away, because I didn't know how to handle another loss.

The paramedics put a breathing mask over her mouth and lifted her to the stretcher. Her body hung limply over it. She had lost consciousness. They quickly rushed to the ambulance and turned on the blue lights. I witnessed the girl being taken away.

"Darling, what was that?" Asher's worried eyes looked into my terrified ones.

I felt my body give way, and all I wanted to do was collapse, but Asher held up my body weight.

"Cassia," I mumbled, not sure if he could even hear me.

"Cassia?"

"She came from Grimhill."

My emotions were overwhelmed when I discovered she was one of those who had survived. Although she survived, she had not lived the life I thought the children would live after escaping.

"I'm taking you to the hospital," Asher said, without needing any further explanation from me.

He knew I needed to talk to Cassia, that I had to.

As we walked to the car, I felt my entire body give up on me and I wrapped my arms around myself. We followed the ambulance to the hospital, and I sincerely hoped that Cassia had made it.

Opening the hospital door, I walked into a room where the girl in front of me was connected to an IV drop. Her smile was faint as she saw me enter. Her eyes had dark circles underneath them and her entire body was wrapped up in bandages and plaster from all the wounds she had received. Asher had let me go inside her room by myself, understanding that I needed the time alone with Cassia. He was waiting for me outside in the waiting area.

"Hello," I said with a smile and made my way over to a chair next to her.

"Hi," she weakly replied.

The awkwardness settled over the room, and I did not know what to say. What were the odds that I would meet a girl from Grimhill Manor here?

It just didn't make any sense.

She looked so vulnerable, and all I wanted was to wrap my arms around her and protect her from the cruel world. She was sixteen years old, only a few years younger than me, yet she looked like she could've been twelve. Her body was so broken, lying in the bed with old scars from Grimhill and new wounds from her journey away from the place. Tears of relief glistened in her eyes as she stared at me, and I grabbed her hand gently.

"You must have been through hell." I wanted no one to experience the things I had experienced, but she had. She had been one of Frederick's dolls and my heart broke for her.

"I have," she whispered before continuing, tears slipping down her cheeks. "It was so terrifying, the woods at night, the howling of wolves from afar. I never knew when my next meal would be. I am free now. He promised me freedom."

Her last words had my head spinning and my face pale, the blood roared in my ears, as if they would never stop howling.

"What do you mean?" I asked with a quivering voice, trying not to sound too afraid but failing miserably.

"Frederick promised me freedom once he died, if I fulfilled his last wish. And I did." A smile etched on her lips as she looked at me, it was a smile that meant no comfort. One that promised evil and the pain hell caused.

His name caused memories to pile up in my mind, and I felt a stomach liquid creep up from my throat and fill my mouth. It was like an acid regurgitation that I wanted to throw up, but couldn't.

"I finally found you."

Her voice played in my mind and, stumbling backward, I fell to the floor with a loud thump. Panic gripped every cell of my being as I desperately tried to escape from her, but my limbs were frozen in fear. The laughter that came from her echoed inside the room, one of a true maniac. On her lips were that same killer smile that Frederick used to wear. It was the same unnerving smile, one that made my mind black out.

"I found you, I found you. I FOUND YOU." She screamed over and over, and I crawled backward until my back hit the wall behind me.

She continued to smile at me, and dread filled every corner of my soul. A being inside of me that scratched at my insides, causing pain in every organ of my body. Desperately, I tried to open the door, but it didn't budge. My mind wanted to freeze, but I fought against every nerve as I banged on the door, trying to signal to someone–anyone–outside that I needed help. No one came, and I heard nothing from outside. It was as if I was caught in a nightmare, a night terror where the dangers got closer but I could not move a single muscle.

"He promised me freedom if I killed you. He said he would haunt me otherwise. I don't want to be haunted, Aurora. I want my freedom. I don't want to be reminded of him every single day. I have to kill you." Guilt filled her eyes, but quickly dissolved.

A heart-aching scream rippled from my throat as she rose from the bed, coming closer to me with every breath I took. She yanked the IV drip from her hand, dislodging the tubing as she moved closer with it.

She would strangle me.

She came towards me at such a speed that I didn't have time to perceive it. With the tube around my neck, she screamed until her voice went hoarse, pushing with all her might. Black circles dotted my vision from the lack of oxygen, and my chest heaved as it fought for air. A strangled and weird sound released from me, something I had never heard before and hopefully never would–if I even survived the attack.

Panic piled up in my throat, and with all my strength of will, I managed to throw her off me. There was a burning sensation in my lungs as the air pushed into them, and my eyes were wide open as I stared at her in horror.

She was on me again quickly after that, and we rolled away from the door. The oxygen disappeared from my lungs, and I did not know how long one could survive strangling. I tried with everything I had, but damn, she was strong. Much stronger than I was, and she was determined to kill me—a thought that made the panic grow. In another attempt, she pulled the tube around my neck and tightened it once more, but it was a harder grip than before. The air left me, my eyes rolled back until the whites were the only thing that could be seen, and my vision disappeared for a second as her grip on the tube tightened, strangling me with no possibility to breathe at all.

While I tried with everything I had to pull free from her, she had a grip that was too tight. My head spun as I tried to gasp for air to no avail. She just wouldn't budge.

I could not fucking breathe.

With my elbow, I somehow managed to push her back, causing her to loosen the grip. I gasped for air, using my last strength to scream with all that I had.

The moment I was about to give up, accepting that I wouldn't survive the attack, the door opened. Drawing their weapons, two guards entered the room.

"Release her, or we will shoot." One of them threatened the girl, and to my luck, she let go of the tube.

The door opened wider with the two guards running inside, and tears rolled down my cheeks. Warm arms embraced me, a familiar muscular chest pressing me closer to him. The only embrace I felt safe in.

"I found you!" the girl screamed as the guards injected her with something, and her body fell to the floor. The killer smile was still etched on her expression.

My face was pale, the room was spinning, and saliva filled my mouth as I felt like I was going under. My body was frozen, my mind was blank, and my muscles sore.

The warm embrace held me, and a sense of calm settled over me when I looked into amber-colored eyes.

"I've got you. Shh darling, I've always got you."

The angelic creature before me must have been my imagination, for in an instance I was back at Grimhill Manor in my head. I relived every moment of torture I had been through, remembered Cassia's horrifying scream as she saw Frederick being killed, and relived the pain he had caused me both mentally and physically.

A strong grip tried to shake me awake, but my mind was elsewhere. Frederick touching me, him killing another guy for touching me, him promising I would forever be his, that no one wanted me. Frederick promised me I was his doll, in this life and all to come.

I didn't know I had screamed until someone lifted me up into his embrace, walking me out of the room, which caused my mind to disappear from reality. I was set down on something soft, and the material calmed me. The muscular chest I was pressed against made me feel safe, and I could finally see who it was. Asher was sitting with me on his lap, caressing my cheeks as he wiped away the tears. I didn't know how long I had spaced out, but we were in another room. Two police officers sat on the other end of the small room as they observed me. Asher pressed a kiss on my forehead.

"Could you tell me what happened?" The woman in uniform asked.

Could I? What had actually happened? Everything was a blur, a distant memory it felt.

"I–uh," my voice was stuttering, and the officers waited patiently for me. "She just started screaming that she had found me, I've never met her before."

A lie. Both Asher and I knew it was a lie, but I couldn't tell them about Grimhill manor. There was a reason the manor was so secret, struck off every record with no proof of ever existing. Children disappeared, but no one knew where they had gone. Assuming they had died somewhere or been kidnapped ,they stopped searching. The police wouldn't believe me if I told them about a house that treated children as real human dolls.

"Why were you visiting her room?" The masculine officer spoke with one eyebrow raised.

His gaze on me made me nervous. It was as if he was suspecting me of something. Could he see through my lie?

"I–uh," my eyes were wide open, but when Asher's hand landed on mine in a gentle touch, my nerves eased. "I was one of those who helped her into the ambulance, I just wanted to see how she was doing."

The masculine officer still looked at me with suspicion, but the woman looked sternly at him. She smiled at me and nodded, "We have everything we need. Thank you for your time, we will take care of the patient from here on and make sure she receives the best medical help she can get."

Then they stood up and went out of the room.

"How are you, darling?" Asher asked as he caressed my thigh.

"Shit?"

He chuckled at my statement, although sadness was lingering in his eyes. "You are safe, I promise."

I nodded my head and wiped away a tear that escaped my eye. "She said she had to kill me to get freedom."

"People who go through traumatic experiences can often develop some kind of mental condition. I know I have, and you probably have too. We're all fucked up in our minds, but it's up to ourselves to make sure we can go on."

I hugged Asher and felt his familiar scent in my nostrils.

"It's just, I thought I was finally free from that place. And then she appears, searching for me, wanting to *kill* me because Frederick told her to when he was still alive."

He shushed me and held me tighter against his chest. "Shh darling, she will be taken care of. No one will ever hurt you again. Do you trust me?"

"Yes."

"Then don't you worry," he pecked my nose and gave me a warm smile. "Let's go get you tea from Tea N Me and head home."

I wanted to forget about that day, forget about Cassia. The words she had whispered, "*I have found you.*" I thought I was free from Grimhill Manor, but it seemed as if the house haunted me even in the daylight.

Chapter 20
Him

"THANK YOU, OFFICER," I said before hanging up and putting the phone in my back pocket.

Aurora's wandering gaze looked at me with interest, causing a smile to spread across my face. Getting to know her had been such an honor, the way she always lit up my days when the emotions inside of me became too much. She didn't know about my more frequent breakdowns lately, breakdowns where the anxiety became a punch in my stomach and sucking out all oxygen. I never told her because I didn't want her to worry, she had enough on her plate. What she didn't know either was that she always made me feel better, making me want to become a better man for her. How could I have been so fortunate?

"Who was it?" Her voice sang into my ears like a beautiful song.

"The police. They announced that Cassia was admitted to Rosewood psychiatry not far from Millvale. They suspect hallucinations, but they can't comment on anything else."

She nodded, putting down 'Wuthering Heights,' the book we had been reading before we were interrupted by my call.

The mention of Cassia's name made horrible memories form in my head. The heartbreaking scream that come from Aurora that day in the hospital had cut into my ears, as horrible as nails on a chalkboard. Immediately, I had flown out of the sofa I had been sitting on, running hastily to the hospital room she was in. Behind me, two guards had joined in, and together we pushed open the door. Seeing Aurora so terrified sitting on the floor, completely white in her face, had broken my heart into a thousand pieces, while the anger against Cassia grew. Aurora's cheeks had been tear-stained, her mascara running down her cheeks, forming black streaks. Even though she looked like a wreck, she was still the most beautiful person I had ever seen.

I remembered lifting her in my arms, taking her to a bathroom to help her wash her face. As we had stood there, I'd known Aurora was unaware of her surrounding, her gaze blank and expressionless. It had been like staring a dead human in the face.

A few days had passed since the incident, and Aurora had slowly recovered from the traumatic experience. I adored the strength of her mind, the way she had gone through everything she had yet was still standing strong. Cassia had wanted to kill her because of Frederick, and I knew that feeling haunted Aurora. She woke up in cold sweats at night, screaming. Every night I held her until she calmed down, sat with her until she fell asleep, and stayed awake myself to make sure she didn't wake up again. We decided she would sleep in my bedroom from now on; that way I could be present when she woke up.

Aurora was the light of my life, and for the past week, she had kept the darkness at bay. I knew Aurora felt I was the one who saved her and helped her with her demons, but rather she was the one who saved me. Without her being aware of it, she had become my anchor. The first person in ten years who trusted me, and believed my story.

That day when I had told Aurora my story, a feeling of relief had filled me. The stone in my chest was no longer there. Sharing my story was like throwing away a heavy backpack. My heart could pump blood more easily, my lungs could breathe more easily, and everything just seemed easier. I still had a long way to go, and I knew it wouldn't be an easy path to walk. But deep inside, I knew I would make it with her in my life.

An idea came to me as I thought back to all of her nightmares, and I knew what I had to do for her. She had her own demons, and I had mine, but I wanted to be the one to help her find herself after all the years of torture. My brother had told me to save the girl from Grimhill Manor, and that was exactly what I was planning to do. I had to save her, not only for Theodore's sake, but for mine. That girl, who had come to mean more to me than I had anticipated, deserved so much.

"Come, I'll take you somewhere," I told her.

Aurora was sitting cross-legged on the couch, with Mary on her lap. "Where are we going?"

"Do you trust me?" I asked as I leaned against the door frame and looked at the beautiful girl in front of me.

Compared to the first time she saw me, she did not look scared of me anymore, which was a huge fucking relief.

"Yes," her lips broke into an even broader smile, causing something inside me to come to life.

She grabbed my hand as I extended it to her and said, "Come on."

Together, we stepped outside into my black Mercedes. In the shining sun, the bright red hues of her strawberry blonde hair were accentuated. Her dress was white and short-sleeved. At the top was a white corset with black buttons that made her breasts look fuller. Our trip to the car was taken in the midst of a lovely view of the landscape, and she looked around, so enamored with what was nature. That was something I adored about her. I opened the car door for her and held it open while I waited for her to sit down.

"What a gentleman," she said, and the giggle she let out melted my heart.

It took a while to drive to where I had planned to take us, but the music from the speaker kept us company throughout the ride. Aurora looked peaceful as she sat in the passenger seat, her foot tapping the floor of the car in time to the music pouring out of the speakers. It was a totally different feeling to feel so at peace and happy.

I only wished for it to last.

AURORA

ASHER DROVE ME SOMEWHERE, but I didn't know where he was taking me. In response to his previous question, I trusted him. The music my ears heard made me hum along to the songs, even though I didn't know how the lyrics went.

During the long car ride, my eyes were glued to the window in order to see the outside world. England's moors surrounded us, the reflective greens of the landscape glowed brighter in the sun's shining light than they had done on previous days. There were no clouds in the autumn sky, nothing to prevent the sun's rays from shining on the landscape and its inhabitants.

When we first sat down in the car and started driving, it was early morning. Now the sun was at the top of the sky. A feeling of heat and electricity spread through my body, sending signals to my brain. I felt one of Ash's hands on my thigh, the other remaining on the steering wheel as he kept his eyes on the road. My lips twitched with a smile.

"Knock knock," I said through the music.

"Who's there?"

My gaze shifted to Asher as his attention was half on me and half on the road. "Boo."

I tried not to pay attention to his hand on my thigh.

Asher focused on steering the car towards a road that led inside the forest before he talked. "Boo who?"

"Hey, don't cry!" My eyes saw a tug playing on his lips.

"That was a really terrible knock-knock joke, darling." He chuckled and his hand was still resting on my thigh.

"I know, I just felt the need to tell it."

"Oh really?" He cocked an eyebrow and a smark plastered on his lips.

If it weren't for the fact that every muscle in my body was in full tension, and my heart was beating so hard near him, I would never have noticed that small squeeze on my thigh. The road we drove on was deserted, with no signs telling us about the maximum speed, no cars, and no animals. The grass grew wild in the middle of the road. The path had a familiar feel to it, but what was it?

A dark green forest surrounded the car on both sides. In some way, it was beautiful and charming. All the leaves that belonged to the trees were still hanging from the branches. Not a single one had fallen to the ground. The dense growth of the forest made it impossible to see into it. There was nothing too visible in the forest except trees and bushes. Gravel from the bumpy and uneven road flew off the tires as we drove forward at full speed.

My face began to fade in color. My stomach fell to the floor of the car with a wave of nausea that caused saliva to form in my mouth. The feeling was like a heavy stone pressing against my chest, preventing me from breathing. Despite my lungs' efforts, I could not draw in enough air. That was the first panic attack I had experienced in a long time. I clenched my fists so tightly that my nails dug into my palms.

In my head, I was screaming in an agonizing manner. Why was he bringing me here? To this place? Would he send me back?

Panic struck as I fumbled with the car's door handle to open it. It was locked.

When the world began to spin, it felt like all the air had been sucked out of me at once. *Breathe, breathe Aurora!*

Even talking to myself didn't help. When my hands started shaking as they pushed on the car door, I knew I had reached the limit of my body's endurance.

"Aurora!"

It sounded like a male voice in the car, but I couldn't figure out where it came from. In the swirling environment, my breaths sounded strained.

"Look at me!" I was grabbed by the arm and panic seized me again.

Let me go, please let me go! No one seemed to hear my thoughts.

"Look at me," the voice sounded calmer, and I tried to find where the voice was coming from.

My eyes landed on Asher who was sitting there in the driver's seat, studying me. He ran his hands up and down my upper arms in a soothing gesture.

"There you go, breathe with me?" He asked me, and I nodded.

Then he took a deep breath, waiting for me to follow his lead. His gesture slowly melted my heart, as if he was heating a candle to let its wax melt down.

He cared about me.

Somehow, that feeling was the most valuable thing I had ever felt. He cared about me, he looked out for me. I realized I had a protector born of pure love, and he was my home.

His warm eyes looked into mine, and I could see his humanity in them. From behind his dull eyes, the warmth had risen to the surface. As he looked into my eyes, he saw my fear, the anxiety I felt. It was as if he could see right through me, feel everything I felt, and share my burden to lessen mine.

"Breathe in, breathe out," he motioned for me to continue breathing in the same way he did.

When the color finally returned to my face, and my cheeks were rosy again, my breathing became softer. As his pensive look eased into a soft smile, his lips parted. The car was stationary on the side of the road, although I hadn't noticed that we had stopped driving. Asher's worried gaze locked on mine.

Astonished and shocked, he asked, "What happened?"

My eyes were wide open as I stared at Asher and my surroundings. I murmured, "The road."

We were on the same road we traveled when he first drove me to his house after picking me up at Grimhill Manor.

"Nothing will happen, I promise." Even though he sounded so convincing, I still felt pressure on my chest.

"Do you trust me?" he asked again, and I nodded in response.

To be honest, I was uncertain about trusting him at that moment.

Would he take me back there? Dump me because he was tired of me?

Against my will, the pain in my chest returned, pressing against my lungs in an attempt to make me stop breathing.

You are just his doll.

He turned on the car and pressed the pedal to start driving.

"Good," he smiled, his lips forming that comforting smile. That smile made the anxiety inside of me fade away.

At that moment, as he glanced at me, I saw something I would never find in anyone else's eyes. He gave me that loving look he only gave me, no one else. It was as if at that moment, our souls made a bridge.

Within only a few minutes, we arrived at a large gate that separated the manor from the rest of the outside world. It was impossible for me not to stare out at the house. Asher was holding the door open for me, as he had just parked and stepped out of the car without me noticing. His hand extended to assist me and I exited the vehicle.

The wrought-iron gate was wide open, the grass had grown wild as if no one had cut it for weeks. Compared to the last time I visited, the house looked so different. After seeing many accidents throughout my childhood, I examined the manor in a heightened state of anxiety and with a pounding heart. We walked through the gate with Asher holding my hand.

"What are we doing here?" I asked, worrying my lip.

"I said I would help you get over your past." His answer to my question only raised even more questions within me, but for now, I took in my surroundings asking no more questions.

Among the trees in the yard was a swing set surrounded by a fence. It was a set of eight swings lined up on the same stand, one of the swings being a bird's nest made of sturdy rope. The kind of rope that could hold an entire ship in place. It was a brisk breeze that blew over the swings and caused them to sway. Across from the swing set was a large climbing frame where the older kids used to hang out. Someone had painted hopscotch using real, white paint on the asphalt that led up to the front door. My stomach turned when I saw the uncut grass, the untrimmed bushes, and the abandoned appearance of the yard. Shovels and buckets made of plastic, almost buried in the grass that had grown over them, lay everywhere on the lawn.

"Do you want to check out the house?" asked the man who was waiting for me, and I nodded.

With Asher's hand in mine, I dared to take the steps toward the house, and soon we were at the front door. I tried pushing down on the handle and the door slid open with a light push. As soon as we entered the parlor room, I thought I saw something white and black flicker in my peripheral view, making my heart race.

Not now, why now?

It was here, the presence I had felt as a child was still here, waiting for me as if trying to say hello again. Although I tried to ignore it, my eyes fell over the room, where furniture was everywhere, crisscrossed, not neatly arranged. It looked as if someone had run away from a panicked situation.

Which was exactly what had happened.

While my heart raced in the pit of my throat, I squeezed Asher's hand. He pressed back and angled me towards him so we were face to face.

"You can handle this," he whispered to me with a reassuring smile.

Seeing the place I grew up in so empty and abandoned was strange to me. There were still breadcrumbs on the tables and coffee mugs that had been spilled out. Across the carpet were shards of glass strewn under the table.

I released Asher's hand and walked toward the piano near the stairs leading to the second floor. The piano felt cold under my fingertips, the dust stained them gray and most of the piano keys had dislodged from their original places. My eyes closed as I remembered what it had been like to play the piano when I was young, and all of a sudden, a memory filled me.

The melody sounded lovely to my ears. The melody my mother had taught me. My hands flowed naturally over the piano keys, and I felt the melody in every corner of my body. Mother would have been proud of me for learning our melody on the piano.

"You play very well," I opened my eyes and looked at the boy standing next to me.

"Thanks?"

"Theodore. But you can call me Theo, all my friends call me that."

"Okay, Theo. I'm Aurora." He smiled at me and darted away. Once again, I was engulfed by the calmness of the melody that washed over me.

A memory from when I was seven years old. It was such a long time ago. There were footsteps behind me and a hand placed on my shoulder.

"Are you okay?" His gaze was wide with uneasiness.

"Yeah, it was only a flashback."

He took my hand again, and we moved on. As soon as we entered the room, my eyes drew to where Frederick had been shot. Although it had only been months, it seemed like it had been years. The house was so dilapidated and abandoned that the windows had cracks in them from the trees outside that hadn't been trimmed. As we ascended the stairs, we remained silent.

"You can't catch me," teased the boy, running up the stairs.

My legs couldn't catch up with the boy who was three years older.

"Run, Aurora." He laughed and rounded the corner, disappearing towards the bedrooms as my legs ran with everything they had to grab Theo. His laughter echoed in the corridors and at the far end, he stood with a playful smile on his face.

"You're too slow," he teased me.

"No! Not at all." My brows furrowed in an attempt to look angry, but it only made him laugh, which resulted in me laughing with him.

"Children, do not run in the corridors. You know that."

"Sorry, Mrs. Johnson," Theo and I shouted at the same time.

The corridor we reached looked almost exactly as I remembered it. With all the dirt that had accumulated, the former red carpet had turned a slightly darker shade. Some doors leading into the children's rooms were closed, while others were wide open. I could feel my heart beating fast inside me. Opening one of the doors, I brought Asher into a room. A single window was in the center of the room. Next to the window on one side was a single bed with an old-fashioned and gold-colored headboard. The bed was made with flowery sheets and duvet covers in the same pattern as one of the walls had been wallpapered in. There was a large bookshelf on the other side of the window filled with many books collected over the years. In front of the bed was a large chest where clothes had been stored. The room did not contain any paintings or photographs. There was something very impersonal about it. Between the bed and the bookcase was a pink but oblong carpet for the sake of decoration.

With Asher's hand in mine, we stepped into the room. I walked over to the bed and sat down. The material felt uncomfortable, and the bed was too stiff, not as soft as I had become used to at

Thorington Manor. Another memory filled me as soon as I touched the bed.

I was lying in bed reading one of my books. Deeply immersed in the events of the book, I flinched when I saw Theo standing next to the bed. I tore my eyes away from the books as I laid eyes on the suitcases standing outside the door to my room. Tears glistened in the boy's eyes.

"I came to say goodbye."

I felt the color drain from my face. My heart stopped beating and the headache hit.

"Wh-what are you saying?" I stuttered.

But then I saw the woman and the man in the doorway. I had never seen them before and they stood impatiently waiting for the boy who was now holding my hand.

"I am sorry," he whispered.

Tears began to roll down my cheeks, and I threw my arms around Theo. I hugged him as hard as I could because I wasn't ready to let him go. We had promised each other that we would escape from here together.

"We can do it now," I whispered in response in his ears, careful so the couple waiting for him wouldn't hear. Theo shook his head, his cheeks puffy from all the tears.

"I cannot. I am so sorry Aurora. I'm sorry."

I frantically shook my head. "No, no, no! Don't leave me!" I screamed in pure panic.

He put his hand on my cheek, "You are strong Aurora," and something was placed in my hand. "Take this, remember me forever. Happy twelfth birthday. I will miss you." Then he let go of me and walked out of my room.

It was the last time I saw my best friend.

With the memory of what he gave me fresh in my mind, I recalled what he had given me. The bookshelf was within reach, so I practically rushed over and pulled all the books out. The blood was ringing in my ears and adrenaline filled my body. Asher's gaze burned into my back, and I knew right then that he was shocked.

That was the moment I discovered it.

The item in my hand was one that my best friend had given me all those years ago. The necklace was a beautiful piece of jewelry. A chain, just like the sterling silver chain of the necklace, supported a flat circular pendant. I had missed that necklace, the necklace that meant so much to me. When had Asher picked me up to take me to Thorington Manor, I had forgotten to pack down the necklace.

Air entered my lungs, and then I blew away the dust that had formed upon the dainty piece of jewelry. Even today, there was still a shimmer in the circle. My heart pounded in my chest when I saw it, making me lightheaded. It was engraved onto a necklace I had received from my very best friend.

That name.

Thorington.

Chapter 21
Her

THERE WERE A LOT of thoughts swirling around in my head. It was impossible for me not to stare at the necklace with wide eyes. Around me, it seemed as if everything was about to crumble. All the muscles in my body felt paralyzed.

Thorington.

The necklace I had received from Theodore all those years ago was engraved with the name 'Thorington.' His last name and… my heart stopped beating.

Asher's last name.

Asher Thorington.

Without realizing it, I dropped the necklace on the floor at my feet. With my eyes glued to the bookshelf beside me, I couldn't organize one single thought.

How could that be possible?

"Aurora," a voice somewhere in the room called after me. I couldn't tear my eyes away from the bookshelf.

"What is this?" Asher's hands on my shoulders snapped my body out of a trance. As he stared at me in horror, he held the necklace in his hands.

"What is this, Aurora?" The volume of his voice increased, and I saw how his eyes reflected how desperate he was. Looking at him with my lips parted was all I could do.

"Aurora!" He roared loudly, and as I lifted my gaze to meet his, tears began to stream down my cheeks. "How do you have this?" When I didn't reply, he added, "Answer me, Aurora!"

Frustrated, he ran his hand through his tousled chocolate-colored hair. Same hair color as Theo.

How was that possible?

My body trembled as Asher's arms shook mine, and I was unsure of how to respond. Why did he appear to be angry at me? What was happening?

"My best friend gave it to me seven years ago." I could feel the lump in my throat, making it harder to breathe and swallow.

The color drained from Asher's face, and he stumbled backward as if he had lost his balance. "What?" he asked, but had to swallow his saliva. "What was his name?"

The shock in his voice was obvious. I had to swallow several times before I could utter a word. "Theo. Theodore."

If anyone could have appeared whiter in the face, it would have been Asher at that very moment. As I stared at him, I kept my mouth open in the shape of a circle. A cloud of dust appeared in Asher's vision as he looked down at the necklace he was holding.

"Ash, explain," I stuttered out in shock.

He nodded and licked his lips before sitting down on the edge of the bed. There was no doubt that he needed support from the bed so as not to fall down. The color of his face was too pale, and he rooted in place. For a second I wondered if he was going to puke or faint. He was that pale.

"I was nine years old when my older brother, Theo, was sent to the United States for unacceptable behavior. Dad told me and Mary that he and Mom sent him to a reformatory school. As long as Dad kept us updated on Theo's condition, we didn't think much of it."

When his hands started shaking, I sat next to him on the edge of the bed, putting my hands on his shoulders. It was my attempt to give him some kind of comfort, to tell him I was here. As a matter of fact, I needed to touch his shoulder for my own comfort. My organs were being twisted by this new information.

"This necklace, I gave it to Theodore before he left. It's a family heirloom with our surname on it." Asher continued while staring at the necklace.

All the puzzle pieces fit together perfectly.

How was it possible?

It was possible because instead of sending Theo to a reformatory school in the United States, he had been sent here to Grimhill Manor.

Where I met him.

According to Everlee's story, children were sometimes sent there for money. The parents sold their children.

"There is a lot more I like about this baby than I do about my other son, Theodore." I thought of the writing I had read in Asher's diary, the one his father had written about his newborn and his distaste for children.

Everything made sense.

The thought of what must've happened made me lose my breath. At the realization that my best friend had been sold off for money, only because his father was incapable of loving all his children equally, I felt as if my heart had been stabbed hundreds of times. He was one of the most loving and humble people I had ever met. A big brother to me.

"This necklace has been there for me for seven years, helping me through the times here when I felt most alone. It was my anchor, my savior," I said in a broken voice as tears dripped down my cheeks, creating wet spots on my white dress. "Whenever I felt alone, I used to touch it, remembering Theodore didn't want me to feel sorrow."

Because the necklace was Asher's from the beginning, he had been there for me all these years without me knowing it. A sad smile spread across his face. His nose was stained red from tears.

"Darling, I have something I need to tell you, but please do not freak out." The tone of his voice made me panic, my eyes refusing to close as I stared at him.

Nodding my head to make him keep on talking, he swallowed harshly before reaching for something in his pocket. My heart thundered inside my chest, in muse with the thunder from outside the manor. With shaking hands, I grabbed the letter he handed me.

"Dear Asher.

You are receiving this letter as I have something extremely important I want you to have knowledge about. I am alive, little brother. You and Mary must have been told I was sent to a reformatory school all those years ago, which is not the truth. Father is not the man you thought he was. He was a man of honor, a man who only cared about his properties and money, and he sold me off to a secluded house far away from society, a place no one knows about except the inner circles. This must sound surreal to you, I know. It came as a shock to me too. That place, it's a place you never want to visit. I do not have much time left. The man and woman who took me away from the manor will be back soon. I am dying, Asher. And I am so sorry for not being able to deliver this letter to you personally. I wish I could, but I live in the States at the moment. This man and woman, they are going to kill me. It has been their goal ever since getting hold of me. They are truly sick in their heads. But, little brother, I have found peace in this refuge. I was never supposed to survive the manor, and I have accepted my fate. I hope you will too. It will be hard for you, but I do not want you to mourn me, for I was never supposed to survive. Live your life to the fullest, for me.

They are going to kill me, and therefore, this letter is sent in a rush. You need to receive it before I die, for I don't know how to move on in the afterlife if you don't help me. When this letter is sent, I understand that you will do as I ask. Only then can I find peace in life after this. The house I was sold to, it's a hell house. A place where they dress the children and force them to behave like real dolls. It's really creepy. It's a secret organization, one which kidnaps and buys children as if they were toys. You need to put a stop to this trafficking ring, please, little brother. I cannot stand any more children getting hurt.

In the house, there's a girl. Her name is Aurora, and she has the most unique eyes I have ever seen. You will know who she is by looking into her eyes. This girl has been my best friend since arriving at the house. She helped me survive all those years and made the place better. With her there, it wasn't a burning hell house for me anymore. Then I was taken away from her, and the look in her eyes told me that she would not be okay. The house is the devil's house, I can assure you of that. Please save her, Asher. Please save my best friend from all the pain that the house causes her, save her from her traumatic childhood. This is the last thing I wish for on earth, only this. Go to Grimhill Manor and save the girl who saved me. Please save my best friend. Only then will I be able to rest in peace.

Yours sincerely, Theodore."

I felt dizziness take hold of my consciousness, my hands shaking as much as an ash leaf. Wet spots smeared the ink from the pen and the letter fell in slow motion from my hands to land on the floor. Outside the room, creaking floorboards could be heard, but we were alone in the house. The air squeezed out of my lungs as I realized what the letter meant, and what I had meant to Theodore.

My best friend.

He had asked Asher to save me, and he did. In more ways than expected from someone who was set out to have a soul as dark as the devil. And if that was true, then I was his fallen angel.

Tears blurred my vision and a warmth spread over my hands as the man next to me held them. Theodore had saved me, and now he was dead. The thought made my heart shatter into a thousand pieces, and a loud cry escaped my throat. A heartbreaking, hoarse scream of pain and love for the boy who had been my best friend. Theodore was gone, and I felt myself slowly but surely suffocating from the news.

Asher's hand stroked my head, scratching my scalp to calm my nerves. "He loved you like a sister," he murmured against my hair, inhaling the scent of me.

I closed my eyes to momentarily calm myself down, and slowly piece together my heart. "He was my best friend," I whispered in a quiet voice, but loud enough for Asher to hear.

Taking comfort in each other's arms, we sat on the edge of the bed. A sense of comfort for the losses we both had suffered. We could find comfort in our past, which bonded us together. He had lost his big brother, and I had lost my best friend.

Soulmates were never something I believed in. Not in the kind I used to read in classic romance novels where soulmates existed, and certainly not in falling in love immediately with the person you just met. Destiny was hard for me to believe in. No one truly deserved a bad life, it was our actions that shaped us into who we were. Our actions defined if we were good people or bad people. No one was born evil, and if a person became a villain, it was because of how life had shaped them into one. Destiny wasn't something I believed in. Certainly not when it came to 'meant-to-be' destinies.

I never believed in destiny until that time. I didn't realize it was fate until that day when I was sitting in my old room with Asher holding my–our–necklace. Every spark that lit up inside of me, every electrifying tension between us whenever we touched was a sign of faith.

We were meant to meet, there was no doubt in my mind.

After several minutes of sitting in my old room, Asher decided we should pack all the books that were in my room into a bag. Together, we loaded two bags of books down into the trunk. Asher was loading one bag into the car, so I quickly removed the sheets and mattress and found what I needed. In its usual hiding place, where I used to hide it from the staff and especially from Frederick, I had managed to get a hold of my computer. In a hurry, I stuffed the computer among the books in another bag.

When Asher came back, he said, "We have two things left to do, come along," and he grabbed my hand.

In silence, we walked downstairs, through the parlor room and the dining room into the spacious corridor. A corridor I had never seen before. We stepped into a room that resembled an office.

"This is where Frederick kept all the files," Asher muttered as he began rummaging through drawers.

He put two stacks of papers on the desk after a long time. I leaned closer to get a better look. *Aurora* read one of the bundles. In an effort to grab the stack of papers, I felt my heart race. While I flipped through the papers, I sat down on one of the chairs. There were pictures of me from the time before I was taken away. Pictures from when my mother and I were playing in the park together that day when I had been kidnapped.

My mother. She was so beautiful.

She had the same blonde hair and eye shape as I remembered. The smile she gave the little me was comforting, and it was apparent that she was happy. My breath caught in my throat when I thought of the mother I'd been dying to meet for over ten years.

My time at Grimhill Manor had been documented in pictures. March of the same year was the last time a picture had been taken, two months before Asher took me away from there. The photograph pictured me sitting at a table while I was deeply engrossed in a book. There was also a page with information about me on it.

Name: Aurora
Surname: Madison
Age: 5
Height: 3'6 feet

As I read through my profile, I stumbled upon my name. My surname.

Madison.

"Found anything interesting, maybe where your mother is?" Asher's voice sounded curious and I found myself getting excited to share my last name.

Never in my life—perhaps except when I was six years old—had anyone told me my surname. At Grimhill Manor I was just Aurora. Plain, simple, boring Aurora.

"Yes," I breathed out and turned to face Asher. "Aurora Madison."

"What?" he asked, pulling up his eyebrows in contrast with his forehead.

"My name is Aurora Madison," I repeated.

"Madison." Asher tasted my name on his tongue. "I like it, it's beautiful."

While blushing, I turned my attention back to the bundle of papers before I did anything stupid, like kissing him.

<u>Legal guardians:</u>
The child previously lived with her mother.
Father is unknown, one-night stand.
<u>Mother's name:</u> Jane
<u>Surname:</u> Madison
<u>Age of death:</u> 30

And on the same page was a picture of my mother.

Tears filled my eyes once more, and I screamed at the top of my lungs. My stomach turned like a wave of nausea, so I ran out of the office and threw up immediately on the carpet outside. The weight above the heart felt like a gunshot.

My mom had passed away.

She was gone.

Screaming and kicking everything around me, I cried out in pain. The walls were covered with paintings, which I tore down.

Screamed, tore, kicked.

Over and over again.

Nausea filled my mouth with saliva and I threw up again on the carpet. Screamed again, kicked more furniture, and tore more paintings.

My mom was dead.

The mom I had hoped to someday meet. She was dead. I continued to scream through the pain, punched the wall in front of me, and screamed again. All those years of hope came crashing down like a bomb. My hopes had been dashed when I learned that someone I had hoped to meet ever since I was a kid had died the same year I was kidnapped.

It took a while for the energy to drain from my body as I slid the wall and landed on the floor. I sobbed uncontrollably.

A hand touched mine as he encircled me with his arms.

"Stay with me, Aurora. Don't lose your grip. Shhh, I'm here darling." Asher's voice calmed my hunching body.

I nodded and cried into his shoulder. His hand drew soothing circles on my back and finally, I fell into his arms from exhaustion.

"Had I known your mother had passed away I would never have brought you here to Grimhill Manor. All I wanted to do was help you heal. I wanted to give you a chance to find out what happened to your mother when you were kidnapped." His voice filled with sadness that could not be forgotten. He sounded completely and utterly devastated at what I had found out.

A void filled me. It was a bottomless pit with no way out. When my eyes locked with his, the stars began to shine, and despite the devastation, there was a feeling of *aliveness* in his presence.

"I know," I whispered to him and he nodded his head, the pain in his eyes as visible as mine.

He felt what I was feeling, he was sad because *I* was sad. And that was something I loved about him. His compassion.

My brain sent signals to my heart that I could not ignore. His face was so close to mine as we sat in the ruined hallway. Inside, I could feel how hard my heart was beating and how the blood was roaring in my ears with anticipation. Asher's hand tilted my head upwards to meet his face at eye level. I leaned closer to his touch. Our lips were only a millimeter apart. His eyes shone, waiting for me, and he lifted my chin up even closer.

Before either of us knew what was happening, my lips were against his. Suddenly it felt like everything went oddly quiet, almost like the silence in the sky after the lightning and before the thunder. Asher placed his hand on my cheek as he kissed me. At first, his lips were stiff against mine, but soon they softened and the kiss made everything else in the room disappear. For a moment it felt like it was only the two of us, no horrible pasts, no dead people, just happiness. The sparks that were brought to life inside me made my stomach flutter.

I clung to Asher as we sat on the floor. For at that moment, it felt like he was the only stable thing in a world full of evil. His lips evoked sensations within me and made me feel alive. I knew I wanted more than just that kiss. His hand roamed over my body as if he wanted to feel every inch of me. His eyes filled with such hunger and desire. For me.

I made him feel like that.

My lips pressed against his as one hand found its way to his tousled hair. He planted kisses on my mouth, my cheek, my chin, and further down to my neck. Tilting my head, I gave him more access. He held my waist with one of his arms as he continued to kiss my neck, giving me shivers. An almost inaudible moan made its way from my throat, and I could feel my cheeks heating. A low chuckle released from him. My gaze met his, and automatically my tongue licked my bottom lip. I could see Ash's pupils dilate at the sight. The sound of our sloppy kisses was the only thing that could be heard in the otherwise deserted corridor. Two souls linked by that moment in an environment of such destruction.

My hands found their way to his T-shirt, and slowly and seductively I took it off. Never once breaking eye contact. His hard chest muscles met my gaze and with my hand, I traced the lines of his abs.

"Such perfection," I murmured, more to myself than to him.

Because at that moment I could allow myself to let go of the terrible thing that had happened. It was about me and Ash, about how we would manage to move forward together and become strong together.

As his hands found their way in under my shirt and kneaded my breasts in a tender gesture, I couldn't stop thinking about him. In his eyes, I could see the change. His beautiful amber-colored eyes had such warmth and love in them that words were not even needed.

A moan escaped my mouth as he touched my nipple under the bra, cupping my breasts. He continued to kiss my lips, his tongue searching my mouth. I let it.

We were both breathless after a few seconds, our foreheads leaning against each other, our noses touching. I tried to press myself as close to him as possible, feeling the heat radiating from his skin. I kissed him from his lips to his stomach. Beneath me, I could feel his erection. The feeling spread warmth through me which Asher noticed and let out a smirk.

"Not here, baby," he said. "I do not want to have sex with you here, in this hell house."

A pang of embarrassment filled me and a red hue crept up my cheeks, forcing me to turn away my head. "Oh, okay," I whispered against his lips as he pecked mine with a soft smile.

"Patience, my love." He scooped me up in his arms.

At that moment, I wished I could sink underground and never be seen again, the embarrassment was too much to handle. He had rejected me, and that was humiliating.

Asher took me out of the house while still carrying me, and I felt eyes on me. As if someone was watching me from behind, in the left corner of the room.

The same corner as when I was a child.

A chill spread across my spine. Carefully, he put me down on the ground. The humiliation of the rejection was still fresh in my mind. I was staring at the manor with such hatred in my eyes. A huge black hole filled my heart at the bare thought of my dead mom, and I knew I could never heal from that. That place had caused my mother's death, for had I not been kidnapped by them I was sure she would still be alive today. Those burning eyes of mine filled with rage.

"You said we had two things left to do," I murmured against Asher's neck. The feel of my warm breath against his skin gave him goosebumps.

"We have one more thing," he told me, and I glanced up to look at him. An unmistakable grin spread across his lips as he stood there.

"What?" Curiosity took over me while I tried my hardest not to think about my mom, dead.

Gently, he held my face in between his hands and planted a small kiss on my forehead. Then he went to the car parked outside the gate to the manor. Looking around one last time, I took in the place where I grew up.

There was only one purpose with that place: to cause pain.

Having Asher there was such a relief for me. That place turned children into obedient and submissive human dolls, only to sell them off as slaves for doll masters.

Asher came back and handed me something.

It was a petrol can.

"What is this?" I asked as my eyebrows raised in confusion, my teeth tugging at my bottom lip.

"We will remove all the horrible memories from your childhood," Asher promised as he walked towards the house with his own gas can in his hands.

I was shocked to see him pour gasoline on the couch in the parlor room as I followed him.

"What are you doing?" He ignored me and grinned reassuringly.

Confused, I opened the petrol tank and started pouring gasoline as well. Seeing the lighter in his pocket made me understand what we were doing. No way was I going to miss out on that opportunity. Together, we helped pour the liquid all over the house. Downstairs, upstairs, and finally the hall, and out onto the balcony that was by the front door.

"Will it not be linked to us?" The concern was clear in my voice.

"No. It is an old house made of wood, and it is abandoned. The fire department and police will assume that it is a fire of natural causes."

Hand in hand, we walked back towards the house after putting the gas canisters in the trunk. Taking a deep breath, I grabbed the lighter Asher handed me. My hands shook as I leaned the flame towards the gasoline trail we had left inside the house.

It spread like wildfire.

Within just a few minutes, the whole house was engulfed in flames and burning down.

We stood in front of the house that had been my nightmare for so many years while Asher held me. It was a feeling of relief that washed over me. After all these years, I was free. Freed from the cause of all my nightmares. At that moment, as I watched the house crumble in front of me, I was able to breathe again.

The house's walls, roofs, windows, everything was on fire. As if a dragon were breathing fire inside the house, vicariously puffing away. The crackling of the wood collapsing was a peaceful sound. My nose scrunched as the acrid and unpleasant smell of the fire searched its way into my nostrils. We stood there looking at Grimhill Manor forever disappearing from my life as the dark-gray smoke surrounded the burning building like a blanket.

"Thank you," I whispered to Asher.

Despite the house burning down in the background, he kissed me softly for the second time that night. Having that, I knew I could finally begin my healing journey. It was finally time to let go of all the worries the house had caused me. I could finally restart my life, a life after Grimhill Manor.

A life in which I was free.

Chapter 22
Her

WE REACHED THORINGTON MANOR after being in the car for what felt like hours. After all that time, I still couldn't help but feel embarrassed about the rejection.

With one arm under the folds of my knees and the other around my waist, he lifted me in a sort of bridal style. Laughing at the shock, I tried to figure out what was going on. The eerie silence greeted us as we entered the hall, and the gargoyles standing to the side felt as if they were alive. They seemed to be watching us.

In the manor, a frightening echo reverberated from the front door. In a gentle movement, he set my body down on the floor. The stone floor felt chilly under my bare feet, but anticipation took over all emotions. He stared deeply into my eyes, and a blanket of cold and fierceness spread over my body with the look he gave me. The intensity of my gaze fell on him just as deeply, and my teeth bit my lower lip in a sensual manner. That was his cue because in the next second I could feel his soft, lovely lips against my own, taking over me, devouring me, making me realize he was the only one I needed. The heat he brought me made me feel feverish as he kissed me. His hands found their way up to my neck, pulling me closer to deepen the kiss, making sure I cherished and enjoyed every second.

"I want to slowly explore your body and see what you taste and feel like," he whispered in my ear, breaking the kiss and taking my hand in his.

Within seconds, we reached a bathroom, and I could feel the liquid heat inside of me. Tingles spread all over, nervousness and excitement for what was to come.

"Is this what you want, Aurora? You want me to taste you?"

His words made the color of my cheeks deepen, those dirty words filling up my heart and body with need, yet with unfamiliarity. I nodded my head while my eyes stared into his. He released a deep chuckle from the bottom of his throat.

"Use your voice," he smirked that familiar smirk I had seen far too many times. As he turned on the shower behind him, the water began to flow.

"Y-yes," I stuttered when I felt his hand touching my body, slowly undressing me in a sensual way.

Once he had removed every piece of clothing from my body, I helped him off with his before he pressed his lips against mine once more. Our naked bodies collided in a beautiful wonder. The warm water washed over our bodies, blurring my vision for a second before I felt his hard abs pressed against my stomach. His mouth was so close to mine, our noses were touching.

"Mmm," I murmured as his hands roamed over my body, touching me everywhere. Just like he had promised me.

The feel of his hands along with the warm water washed away all nerves, all tense muscles softened, and I allowed myself to live in the moment. Asher's hands slowly, teasingly, worked their way from the top of my stomach to the bottom of my inner thighs, as I leaned against the wall. Before I knew what was happening, he was on his knees in front of me, planting small kisses on my thighs.

"Oh, Asher."

My wet hair stuck to my back, and I inspected Asher closely. His gaze met mine before falling back to my thighs.

"You wanted this, didn't you, darling?"

The corner of his lips twitched, and I knew he enjoyed teasing me. In some way, I found comfort in grasping his damp hair, and felt the significance of the moment. His lips approached my clit, his fingers touching me everywhere except where I needed his touch the most.

"Please," I begged, trying to push myself closer to him, the desire growing stronger with every second he did nothing.

"Please what?"

At that moment, I hated him for embarrassing me like that, but at the same time, I loved the way he was making me feel, all flushed and filled with ecstasy.

"Please," I murmured as I let the water run down my body. My cheeks heated with the humiliation of having to use my words, but I was too desperate. Too needy for him. "Please touch me." And as soon as I uttered those words, his index finger stroked my clit, slowly approaching my inner labia and feeling how wet I was.

Against my thigh, I could feel his lips form a smile. His finger pushed inside me, curling it to feel my G-spot. With each repetition, I felt as if I was about to unravel within seconds. He stopped. Whimpers escaped my lips, and I looked at him with pleading eyes. He shook his head and adjusted his position. My eyes cast a glimpse at his hard erection. He kissed my clit before beginning to lick and suck on it, sending butterflies all inside of me. The sensation made loud moans escape my throat, my eyes rolling to the back of my head. The feeling was too extreme, too erotic as he licked me like I was his goddess. He worked his tongue like magic.

The fallen angel licking his girl.

"Ash," I moaned in desperation.

Two of his fingers entered me as he continued to lick and suck on my clit. Soon, he would send me over the edge, send me above the clouds to the kingdom of heaven. Within a few seconds, my stomach clenched, and I felt myself orgasming in his face. My initial embarrassment soon turned into delight when he licked it, making me feel so much more than I ever had before.

This fallen angel of mine.

He rose to his feet, his cock harder than before. His lips kissed mine and made me taste myself before he wrapped a towel around my body, turned off the shower, and scooped me up in his arms. My legs straddled his waist, and his lips never left mine. I didn't even notice which room he took me to. Not until he lowered me onto the bed and his gaze swept across my body.

"You are so, so beautiful, Aurora," he whispered against my mouth. Removing my towel, he looked at me with adornment in his eyes. He took his time placing himself between my legs. "Are you sure?" He asked, his eyes soft with tenderness, motioning what he meant.

It made my heart melt.

He cared.

My smile was a good enough response for him. I had waited far too long for this moment. All the electrifying stares, all the tension built up between us, were all worth the wait for that precise moment.

"Damn, you're still so wet," he smiled and touched my clit with his hand. I shook from the shivers. "Have you ever been touched like this before me?" he asked me, continuing to rub my sensitive abdomen. I shook my head. "Shit, no guy before?"

"No." After hearing my confession, I feared he would stop, as some guys did in the novels I had read.

However, Asher had already proven that he was nothing like them. He was my fallen angel, and even if he had hurt me, I also realized that was a totally different side of him. Everyone deserved a second chance if they proved they would make it right. I saw it in his eyes, he regretted his actions. The remorse under his surface was stronger, shining through like the sun on a warm summer day. He hadn't been himself before he met me.

With me, he found himself.

With him, I found myself.

"That means I'm your first." His eyes shone with excitement and pride at being my very first. "That you're only mine, no one has ever had you before." The smile he gave me was the widest I had ever seen him give.

"And you are mine," I said through a giggle.

"Are you really sure you want this?"

As I looked into his eyes, I could see a glimpse of desire, but also a sense of concern and worry. It made my heart swell at the thought of how much he actually cared about my well-being. Especially in such a vulnerable state as that.

"Ash, I want this. Hell, I have never wanted anything more in my life. If you decide to stop, however, I won't push you."

A grin appeared as he whispered, "I want you," making me smile even wider.

He positioned his erection against my wet pussy. My clit was throbbing in anticipation. "This will hurt, but I will take it slow. You trust me, right?"

"I do," I whispered. He kissed me again, parting my lips with his tongue.

Then I felt it, his cock thrusting inside of me.

There was a burning pain inside of me, and he didn't push further. Adjusting to his size, I took a deep breath and nodded. This time he pushed further, and the pleasure he gave me was exhilarating. Soon enough, the burning pain disappeared and was replaced mainly by pleasure.

Some say losing your virginity hurts like hell, but for me, that wasn't true. The pain was bearable, the pleasure was something out of this world.

The feeling of having this man—who had come to mean extremely much to me—inside me was indescribable. It felt like this was it.

This was the meaning, my destiny.

He pushed his cock in before pulling it out, continuing in a pattern, hitting my G-spot every single time. Never once did his eyes break contact with mine. It was the most erotic thing I had ever experienced in my entire life. He made love to me at a slow pace, making sure I enjoyed every second. Making sure I saw in his eyes how much the moment meant to him.

Keeping my gaze locked on his, I started grinding against him, meeting his every push inside of me. The gathering slickness between my thighs made it possible for him to slide in and out with ease, and the heat extending from his eyes spread like a wildfire inside of me. My body turned into an inferno, burning and flaming with no end in sight. Asher pushed into me, harder with each time, and as he put his finger on my clit, he started circling it. The sounds of our flesh slapping filled the room, echoed through the walls, and I would have been embarrassed had it not been for the pleasure he was giving me.

"Fuck, Ash," I cussed out through a moan, my eyes struggling to stay open.

Pleasure exuded from my clit as his finger circled it, and I couldn't help myself but grind more against his cock.

Our grunts and moans filled the room.

"That's a good girl," he murmured in my ear, causing goosebumps to spread down my spine. "You're taking me so well," and from his words, I nearly came undone.

I cried out as my hips rocked relentlessly against him, desperation filled every cell in my blood, craving for everything he had to give. When I felt a growl vibrating against my mouth, I spurred into action.

When he brought his hand up to knead my breasts, his lips were just a mere inch from mine. The room was filled with the scent of sweat and the minty breath coming from his mouth. It was as if he devoured me completely, wrecked every inch of me inside, devouring me until I was at his mercy. The thought terrified me, yet it excited me at the same time. He leaned down and softly sucked on my skin, the action causing me both immense pain and pleasure. It would leave a mark, that I knew. The mark he planted in the grope of my neck was licked clean by him.

"This is to claim you as mine," he whispered in that husky voice of his.

As I frantically and erratically moved my hips to get him to fuck me harder, I replied, "You already know I am."

No longer was there any pain, only pleasure. His hand on my clit, circling, nibbling, sent delicious shivers straight to my core, making me even more wet.

"That's it, darling. You're doing so well."

Asher's praises made me feel as if I was in heaven.

His lips kissed mine, and it felt like they belonged together. Our eyes said all the words our mouths could not.

As he continued to make love to me, I made sure to remember the moment forever. He was there, he was with me. And he made love to me there with such tenderness and love. He had saved me from Grimhill Manor, saved me from the house which had been my prison for over ten years, and helped me burn it to the ground. It was he who took my virginity, my innocence, and I would never forget that moment.

A memory forever imprinted in my heart.

I would never forget the time when Asher made me feel again. When he brought the spark inside of me back to life.

When he eased the demons inside my head.

Chapter 23
Her

A SOUND CAME FROM the TV the next day. Moving slowly towards the living room, I heard creaking from the floor. The thought of Asher being in there made my stomach flip with butterflies. As I stepped into the room, my eyes fell on him sitting on the beige sofa with his feet placed on the coffee table in a comfortable position. His shirt hung loosely over his chest, making my cheeks heat. There was no denying how attracted I was to him, but I wasn't just attracted to his looks. He was perfect from head to toe in every way on the inside.

The scowl on his face told me he was deeply engrossed in the news playing on the TV. Walking over to him, I sat on his lap, and he pulled me into his chest, placing his large hands around my waist. I felt the heat of his kiss spread through my blood as it landed on the grope of my neck.

"What are you watching?" I asked him as I leaned closer, my back against his stomach.

He pointed toward the screen with his head and I couldn't stop my heart from racing. It was a feeling that almost unmanned me, one that turned my face ashen. Every breath of wind was as loud as a blood-curdling scream in my terrified mind. Asher's grip around my waist tightened, and he rested his chin against my shoulder. I felt his breath against my neck, and feeling his closeness calmed me down.

Breathe, Aurora.

On the TV screen, there was a house in flames, its orange colors spreading and finding their way into my eyes, a bright light even though I wasn't there.

The house was all too familiar.

"The fire brigade have been working all night to put out the fire, which has no clear cause. They are still working feverishly to extinguish the heavy flames. The house was previously owned by Frederick Grimhill who earlier this year was murdered, and the killer has not yet been confirmed. The house was previously used to store kidnapped children, the kind that the police had been trying to locate for several years. It is with the murder of Frederick Grimhill that this trafficking ring has been stopped, as he was the leader. Surviving victims have reached out to the police and received the help needed."

With a gasp, I grabbed Asher's hand and held it in mine. Warmth washed over me as though a brick had been lifted from my shoulders. I could feel and breathe again, knowing that those children had survived Grimhill Manor. They wouldn't have to suffer from the torture anymore, they would only go forward from there and heal their scars.

There were some children who had suffered through more torture than others, some who had been physically abused and some who had been mentally abused. I had a few scars on my body, but nothing that was too visible. They were still there, and it was a constant reminder of what had happened. The mental abuse I had suffered through from Frederick was terrible, but knowing that those children were finally saved made me feel lighter than air.

One after another, the inner parts of my mind danced with joy, and the gloominess that used to settle upon me was replaced with a brighter shade of gray.

They had found their freedom in this wicked world, and I had found mine with Asher.

He looked me into the eyes, and the security I felt through them meant everything. The love he had for me may not have been expressed through words, but it was revealed through his eyes, as mine had done for him. None of us were good with words, but sometimes eyes said more than words ever could.

We would move slowly forward, but I knew we would fight together, and we would be warriors. He would fight my demons just as I would fight his, and we would make it.

For Asher was the only security I had left.

DARKNESS FELL OVER THE horizon in front of the road where we were driving. The branches of the trees, set in motion by the wind, resembled monsters that seemed to be reaching for the limousine, but it was no less beautiful for that.

My head was leaning against Asher's, and I was still tired from my nearly three-hour nap. Everlee who sat across from me was just as tired. Her sleepy eyes blinked open and the smile Draven gave her felt like a rush of happiness inside me.

Asher's hand was wrapped around my shoulders, his matching three-piece suit fitting his muscular body perfectly, making my mouth water. His hair was tousled and in a lazy gesture, I ran my hand through it out of habit.

The four of us were heading to the town beyond Millvale, a place neither I nor Everlee had visited before. Asher had hired a limousine driver, and together we had all gone for a night out. Something Everlee and I had never experienced before.

Four hours ago at Thorington Manor, we had both been in my room giggling as we made ourselves ready. As we matched eyeshadow colors to each other's dresses, we did each other's makeup together. Unlike what I was used to, the dress draped around my body was short. It reached until just above my knees and was black with long sleeves and a slight V-neckline. Being dressed in such a way was unusual to me, but I felt appreciated when Asher glanced at me from time to time. Heat radiated from his eyes, and lust took over his thoughts as his tongue licked his lips. I loved seeing the effect I had on him, knowing that I was the one who made him act like that.

I wore a dress that matched Asher's suit, and we both wore black outfits. The thought of us looking like a classy couple made butterflies fly around in my stomach. Everlee had a similar dress, only that hers was short-sleeved and red, protruding her brown hair. She looked amazing.

"Slept well?" Asher asked me, his breath brushing my ear and sending shivers down my spine from the sensation.

I murmured a 'yes' before yawning. Once inside the limousine, I had fallen asleep as tiredness had taken over. As the car journey was three hours long, I'd had plenty of time to rest. Considering how newly awake Everlee looked, I could only assume that she, too, had fallen asleep.

The limousine pulled up in a parking lot, and Draven stepped out as he held out his hand for Everlee to take. The anticipation filled my body with nerves, but I was eager to see what the night would bring.

"Ready?" Asher exited the car and helped me out, before hooking his arm with mine.

"I think so," I replied in an unsure voice, to which he chuckled.

The four of us entered a narrower street together. The sidewalks were filled with shops, and many people were talking to one another or dancing at the bars that lined the street. There was something strange about seeing people acting so freely. They existed without a care in the world, something I envied.

The buildings where the bars and shops were located had been built in old architectural styles. They were made of brick and had few windows. It was a beautiful sight to see plants hanging in drifts along the walls of the houses. Nearby, there was a tree with green leaves despite it being autumn. Several couples took pictures by the tree and smiled at the camera. When I thought about how free people acted, warmth spread through my body.

There had been many people who seemed envious of others being better off than themselves, but I felt the warm glow spreading through me, heating me up from the inside. Those lucky people had not suffered through the same horrible thing I had. Knowing that not all people on earth were evil relieved me.

It was Asher's worried expression that caught my attention as soon as my eyes landed on him. There was a slight raise in his eyebrows and a parting of his lips when he observed me. He had noticed the change in my behavior. With a reassuring smile, I was able to ease his concern.

We entered a bar together. In the room where several people mingled, there was a kitchen in which tables were arranged. A large stone staircase leading downstairs was in the corner, and Draven showed the way. He and Asher had been there before.

Below the stairs was a large dance floor in the middle where people crowded and danced to the music playing from the speakers. Lights shifting between red, blue, and purple circulated in the room, making it possible to see all around. We sat down on one of the white sofas in the corner. There were already drinks prepared at our tables when we arrived.

When Asher had booked the limousine, he had also reserved a table at the city's most prestigious nightclub. From the music pouring out, I could already sense that the night was going to be enjoyable. The first thing we did was sit down at our table and talk together about everything. Upon swallowing my first drink of alcohol, I felt a burning sensation. The liquid took over and a feeling of lightness filled me, as if I had nothing to worry about.

"Come, let's go dance, Everlee," I sang out loud and stood up on wobbly legs as I grabbed her arms.

Asher sat slouched in his seat, his legs spread in a comfortable position. The veins in his arms stood out more when he was relaxed, and the heat in his eyes felt like fireballs hurtling toward me.

Everlee and I walked onto the dance floor, but stayed close enough for Asher and Draven to see us.

"How are things going with Draven?" I asked Everlee as my body moved to the music. The alcohol had started to spread through my body.

A pink color appeared on her cheeks as they heated. "He kissed me last week for the first time."

My eyes widened at her confession. "Oh my God!" I squealed, earning a giggle from Everlee. "I need all the details!" My voice was drowned out by the music.

We both danced to the sounds booming out from the stereos, and I felt how intoxicated it made me. Feeling so much freedom due to just alcohol and music. I had never had so much fun in my life as I did that night.

"We were at his house, and I teased him for spilling food on the floor. Before I knew it, he had me up against the wall and was kissing me." Happiness sparkled in her hazel eyes, and a wide smile formed on my lips.

As we danced, I hugged her and kissed her cheek. "I'm happy for you."

The music moved around us as we danced, making me move automatically as if I were a puppet on strings. Because of the high temperature, sweat formed on my cheeks, which made my hair stick to my skin.

"And you?" Everlee asked as our hands were in the air like everyone else's.

The music was like a drug I voluntarily took, pumping through my veins and making my body float on clouds. The alcohol made the room spin and made me feel like I was on a boat in rough waters. That didn't stop us from dancing. There was love and happiness in the air, and everyone was there to have the best night of their lives.

I was dancing as if I was one with the music, one with every crazy person in there. For a moment, I felt an adrenaline rush running straight through my body.

I fucking loved it.

"He fucked me." I blurted out before I could think of the words, and Everlee's wide eyes showed she was even more shocked than I was when I had found out about her and Draven.

The look on her face made me laugh as I moved my body as if my life depended on it. No more words were said between us as we moved through the crowd and felt the music pumping through us. Everyone on the dance floor screamed with happiness. Drinking alcohol was like being connected to an IV drip together with everyone else in the room. Rainbow lights and soul-stirring beats filled the nightclub.

A calm but sensual song began to play, and I felt my hips swing as if it was natural to me. While I stood and moved my body while dancing, every cell in my body was firing at full capacity. My eyes fell on Asher who was staring at me with his intense eyes. The look he gave me made me braver, and I let my body loosen up even more. All I felt was freedom as my hips swayed to the music. My eyes were fixed on him the entire time, and I noticed the bulge in his pants as he looked at me with those eyes. He stared at me and with his eyes, he stripped me of all my clothes, devoured me, fucked me.

Slowly, I started lifting the dress up higher, teasing him with a smug smile on my lips. The music, the alcohol, the entire atmosphere made me a different person. It might have been who I was at my core, but Grimhill Manor had made me feel like I lived in a prison. My senses were heightened, I felt every inch of myself and enjoyed dancing, feeling drunk for a moment.

Asher and I were the only ones left in the room when everyone disappeared for a second. I danced for him, and he loved the sight of me. His eyes were filled with clarity.

After adjusting his pants, he stood up, his gaze darkening as he studied me. The butterflies flew in my stomach as if they had been thrown into a whirlwind that was impossible to escape from. Anticipation filled me as he came closer and closer. His breath reeked of vodka as his mouth pressed against mine in a dominant gesture.

Without really understanding what was happening, he grabbed my hand and led me out, away from the dance floor. He pushed me up against the wall in an empty hallway and brushed his lips against mine. The kiss he gave me was full of passion, a million loving thoughts condensed into one moment.

"He was staring at you," Asher whispered in my ear, and the hair on my arms rose at the sensation.

"Who?" my breath hitched.

"The guy you danced next to."

A blush spread across my cheeks, "I didn't notice."

Asher planted wet kisses on my neck and I felt the nature of his soul through them.

He lifted me up, my legs wrapped around his waist, and kissed me as he pushed me into an empty bathroom. He locked the door with accustomed hands, before pushing me against the wall again while still lifting me. Before I could catch my breath, his lips were on mine in a desperate manner.

Our lips tangled in unison, his tongue seeking acceptance from mine, devouring me until I no longer felt my legs. If he hadn't still been carrying me, I would have fallen from the intense feeling the kiss instilled in me. Our lips were ignited by the inferno in my body that erupted from me, lighting us up, making us shine in the spotlight.

While kissing me, Asher's hands grabbed my ass and squeezed it. My eyes closed, and the sound of our wet kisses reflected as if they were coming from speakers inside the bathroom.

Normally, I would have been embarrassed to do something so reckless in a public place; there were probably several people waiting to use the toilet. At that moment, I couldn't care less.

I was free, free to do what I wanted, free to kiss Asher the way we both wanted.

I was no longer someone's puppet, and alcohol made me forget everything from my past. Only happiness and ease flowed through my body, and I transferred those feelings to Asher with my answering kiss. My hands found their way up into his hair, gripping it like it was my lifeline. Sounds were released from my throat, sounds that made my cheeks flush. Asher's look said it all, he loved what he did to me. Carefully, he sat me down on the edge of the sink, my legs wrapped around his waist to hold him closer. The room smelled of Asher, a musky scent and the vodka from the drinks we had had. And then there was the strong scent from the soap.

His hands roamed my body, finding their way down to the V-neck in my dress. For a second, he stopped, our lips no longer connected. His gaze was on me for a moment too long, and all the emotions he felt burned behind his irises. The tip of my tongue darted out to lick my lips that had become too dry, and his gaze landed on them with that intensity that made me squirm in my seat.

"I haven't been able to stop thinking about taking this dress off you all night," he whispered, his breath fanning over my mouth.

Quickly, I grabbed his neck and pulled his head closer to mine, our lips meeting again in frantic kisses. I was desperate, and from his body language, I knew he was too.

A heated liquid pooled in my core and my pussy responded to his touch on my chest by beginning to throb. His hands kneaded my nipples, and moans were released from me at the sensation.

Asher was everywhere, on my body, in my head, in my soul. And I couldn't have wished for anything else.

The alcohol made me desperate, but it also made me admit things to myself that I previously did not dare to. Like how much I actually longed for Asher.

My gaze dropped to his waist, and the bulge was clearly visible. A big grin spread across his lips when he saw my reaction. My hands were placed on the edge of the sink, and gently I rubbed my sex against his hard bulge that brushed against his suit's pants. I felt an incomparable rush of feelings when I was stimulated by that stimulation, an incredible feeling that took me to heaven.

"My beautiful, good girl," he whispered in my ear before planting a kiss there.

A burning sensation arose as he nibbled on my flesh, sucking and repeating the motions. In a way, it hurt, yet at the same time it was nice to feel that way.

"You're mine, and this hickey shows it, darling."

A smile spread across my lips as he claimed me as his. I had always wanted to belong to someone, to have someone who cared about me. Asher was just that person.

"Don't forget you're mine, too," I said loudly for him to hear. That familiar smile appeared on his lips from the relief at my words.

"Never, love."

With clumsy fingers, I tried to remove the belt from around his waist, and when I succeeded, I threw it to the ground. The sound echoed against the tiles, and if there was anyone outside the bathroom, they would hear it.

"Whoa, whoa, someone's feisty."

"Shut up," I replied teasingly.

Before I could remove his pants, he stepped back and inspected me. Feeling brave, I lifted my black dress above my head in a teasingly slow motion, never once breaking eye contact with the man in front of me. An animal-like growl released from him.

When the dress was off, I sat on the sink in only a black bra and panties. Asher approached me, his jacket long gone, and his fingers traced from my neckline, down to my stomach. The motion sent shivers down my spine. I squirmed under his touch, waiting for his next move. His fingers were so close to my entrance, where my wetness was visible. When he ran his hand over my panties and clit, he noticed the way they were soaked. My hips pushed closer to him, hoping he would touch me, desperately needing it.

"Don't be so greedy, darling."

He slowly removed his pants as he forced me to watch, his cock even harder against his boxers. We were both in our underwear, and anticipation filled the bathroom. There was a release that made me feel like heaven when his fingers found their way in under my underwear. He pulled them away, and ran his fingers between my labia, smearing out the liquid from my pussy.

"I don't even think you know how much I want you, crave you," he murmured. "I would have fingered you, but I'm selfish, darling. And we both know you want me right away, just like I do."

My head lifted to meet his lips before nodding. I stripped him of his boxers in record time, his cock bursting free from its captivity. Before I could process it, his cock was pressing against my opening and my wetness spread over his cock, making it easier for him to enter me.

"Are you sure?" he asked me for a quick second, and my nod was all he needed.

He pushed into me, and the loud moans from both of us filled the bathroom. The sounds bounced off the walls, making it echo along with the sounds of his body pressing against mine every time he pulled out and back in. The position we were in gave him direct access to my most sensitive areas—my clit and G-spot. He lifted me again, my legs wrapped around his waist and his cock buried deep inside of me. His hands supported my body by holding my ass. Slowly, he took us towards the wall, and he pressed my back against it. The cold from the wall would otherwise have bothered me, but in the heat of the moment, it didn't.

"Fuck, Ash." I moaned out, my eyes rolling back from the ecstasy and turmoil of emotions inside of me.

He kept pushing into me, getting deeper and deeper each time.

"I'm the only man allowed to stare at you," he rasped out as moans escaped his throat, too.

We were too loud not to be discovered, and it was just a matter of minutes before someone would realize what we were doing.

His possession of me made me even more desperate to have him, the feeling of belonging to him was something that could not be described in words.

"Fuck, darling."

He kept pushing into me, kept hitting my G-spot, faster and harder each time.

The knocking on the door outside didn't stop us, we were too deep in our lovemaking.

Within just a few minutes, I was close to cumming.

"Fuck, keep squeezing my cock, darling," and I did, the whites of my eyes the only thing visible.

"I'm coming," I moaned out and once I came, my whole body shook from the sensations. Asher came soon after, planting loads of kisses on my neck and lips as he did so.

"I-I think I love you," he whispered against my ear.

A moment of hesitation appeared, shocked at his words. I wondered if I had heard him wrong, but the shy smile he gave me told me otherwise. Those words melted my heart.

What had I done to deserve that kind of happiness?

"I think I love you too," I said with a smile.

When he sat me down on the floor, my legs were sore, and his cum trickled down my legs. By wetting a napkin, he helped me wash it up. Before we walked out of the bathroom, he helped me with the dress as well, and when he took my hand, he smiled.

Outside stood two young women, and they stared at us knowingly. Had I not been so affected by the alcohol, I would have been embarrassed.

Draven and Everlee sat at the coffee table, and I saw Everlee's wide eyes as we sat down. Confused, I looked at her, but was interrupted by Asher's mouth against my ear.

"My mark on you is sexy, darling."

To that, it was my turn to open my eyes. Everlee looked at me with a meaningful look. After staring at each other for a few seconds, we laughed like immature teenagers.

My life had changed so much in just a few months, but only now did I suddenly realize how good it had become. Having such amazing friends in my life like Draven and Everlee was something I never thought would happen after losing Theodore. Having Asher was like being in heaven.

    I just wished it would last.

Chapter 24
Him

THE VOICE OF A beautiful girl rang out from inside the hall. "Can I come with you?" she asked. The dress had been replaced with a dressing gown wrapped around her body.

"I thought it would be a good idea to stay home today and rest, and Josephine wants to bake cookies with you."

Her lower lip protruded as she began to pout. With poppy-like enthusiasm, she looked at me with hope in her eyes, but I wasn't willing to let Josephine down because of that.

"Pleeease," she practically jumped towards me, where I was leaning against the edge of the door with my jacket wrapped around me, and the car key in my jeans pocket.

"Aurora, I'll be back before dark. You trust me, right?"

To that, she merely nodded her head. "Fine. Josephine, what cookies do you want to make?" She shouted through the house and walked away into the kitchen.

When the hum of my Mercedes was heard, I saw her face push up against the windowpane where she stood. She waved at me as I drove away from the house.

Something inside me was brought to life when I was around her. Never before had I felt such feelings for anyone else. It was as if every time she smiled at me, she melted my heart. Every time she talked to me in that soft voice of hers, her eyes so engaged in her words, she stole my heart.

And fuck, I wanted her to keep it.

Though I knew it was both a blessing and a curse to feel this way about her, so very deeply. I had lost everyone I cared about, and it felt dangerous to have someone in my life worth losing. She was too tangled up with me for me to let her go. She consumed my every thought, yet I knew she needed someone better than me.

For there was darkness inside of me, something I had no control over. Something that came unexpectedly, devouring me entirely. And I couldn't love the girl with only half of my heart.

One day I knew I'd lose her. I would either fuck things up and she would leave, or I would completely shut her out. I didn't want to let go of her. I didn't want to be without those beautiful steel-blue eyes as she met my gaze. I didn't want to lose those soft lips kissing mine, didn't want to lose our small talk.

I simply did not want to lose her.

Aurora was the one for me, why hadn't I realized it before? That feeling inside of me felt strange, a feeling I couldn't describe in words. A feeling of hope inside of me, tingling. I wanted her with all that I was.

But could I keep her?

The drive into the city took me two hours. Crooked roads and gravel characterized the ride through the English countryside.

Once I drove onto the paved main trail, I was able to accelerate and approached Millvale town, far northeast of Yorkshire. Throughout the trip, I couldn't stop thinking about Aurora, despite the music blasting in my ears. She was stuck in my memory like a photograph in a camera.

The small town was the closest to Thorington Manor. That was the town I had taken Aurora to a while ago, and it had everything one could want. It wasn't a metropolitan city like London, but it was good enough. There was one bookstore that offered a large selection of books and literature. Besides the bookstore, there was a grocery store owned by a private couple, who ran it together. To the right of the grocery store was a shoe store and next to it was a dry cleaner. In the center of it all was a small square, with a fountain into which I used to throw coins when I was a small child. Aurora had thrown a coin in it when we had visited the town. That day she had been so happy until the event with Cassia.

The town was quaint and small, a place where everyone knew each other and greeted each other. A friendly place for those who did not enjoy the bustle of city life.

Shopping for groceries was something I had to do in town every month, and that was where I was heading. Residents of the town had only one store where they could buy groceries. Apart from that, there were only small kiosks where you could buy produce and other items for a much more expensive price. However, those kiosks didn't have everything a human could possibly need.

The shop was large with a wide selection of groceries which made it the perfect store to shop at. The next nearest store was an hour's drive away from here, three from Thorington Manor, and I didn't feel like driving that far. Upon arriving at the store, I took out my shopping list and a basket into which I could load all of my purchases. In some ways, shopping was peaceful. Being around other people allowed me to observe how they spent their time. Partly why I didn't let the maids do the grocery shopping.

I put more bacon, eggs, and flour to make pancakes into the basket, which was filling up. Aurora loved the breakfast that was served every morning, and I wanted to do things for her that would put a smile on her face.

I fucking loved her smile.

I needed to buy one thing for Aurora there, but I didn't know where I could find it in the store . Red cheeks accompanied the thought of what she needed. My attention drew to a woman in work clothes ahead of me in the aisle, and I asked her for assistance.

"Excuse me?" I asked, embarrassment creeping up my spine.

The woman stopped what she was doing and turned her attention to me. "Yes, Sir?"

Her hair was black, the color of the sky during the night. Looking into her eyes, I noticed a long scar that stretched from her left eye down to the corner of her mouth. It was horrifying, and I couldn't help but feel uncomfortable under her gaze, even though I knew it was wrong to feel that way. I swallowed and avoided her gaze as best as I could, without seeming too rude. There was something about her scar that made me think of *him*.

The man who had raised me and abused me.

Quickly, I closed my eyes and shook my head to get rid of the anxiety rising to the surface.

"Where are—" I began, running my hand through my hair before forcing myself to continue, "Where are the pads and tampons?"

When the words were out of my mouth, I shifted my body weight onto one leg. She smiled at me—a reassuring smile—and asked me to follow her.

"What kind do you need?" the woman asked as she led me to another aisle where multiple supplies were lined up.

The question she asked me caught me off guard. What kind did I need? How the hell was I supposed to know what kind Aurora needed?

When she replied, "Well, I can pick something, if you want," she said it with another smile, as if she had noticed how uncomfortable I became.

The motion made her scar crinkle, causing it to pucker and create bubbles in the skin on her cheek. It wasn't a pleasant sight and made me feel rather uneasy. Guilt filled me as I thought about the ugly scar.

"Yeah, thanks." I laughed nervously as I watched the woman begin to pick something up.

She handed over three articles. "These are pads with wings if she prefers," she pointed to a pink package with the word 'wings' on it. "These are without wings," she continued, holding up the package next to the ones with them. "These are tampons. I think your girlfriend can probably find one she likes amongst these three."

The sentence she uttered made me stop, my eyes narrowed, and I looked at the woman in shock.

"Girl-girlfriend?" I managed, as all I did was stand there, staring at her, obviously making her uncomfortable.

Her body stiffened and my eyes fell on her throat as she swallowed hard. "Sorry, I thought it was for your girlfriend," she replied in an apology before walking away without further comment.

I stared in front of me, at the spot where she had been standing a second earlier.

Girlfriend? Did she think I was shopping for my girlfriend? The questions were spinning in my head, but I couldn't understand why I had reacted like that.

Aurora was not my girlfriend. Was she? Or was she a close friend of mine?

No, she felt so much closer to me than a friend. She was my lover, someone I would do everything for. The word 'girlfriend' was an odd term, for our relationship was something more intense. Putting a label on us felt wrong.

We just were.

We existed in the present, finding each other more every day, loving each other more with each passing day.

The relationship between me and her was complicated, but I so wished that the beautiful girl sitting at home now, most likely reading, could stay with me forever.

Even though I knew it was impossible.

For I was not the type of person someone could fall in love with. I was the villain in her story, and eventually she'd realize it. And when that day came I would be prepared to say my last goodbye.

Until that day arrived, I would make sure she enjoyed her time with me so that she would leave with only happy memories. All I wanted for that girl I adored oh-too-much, was for her to be freed from her childhood demons.

THE BAGS OF GROCERIES were in the back of the vehicle, waiting for me to drive them home for another two hours. However, it had to wait a while longer. After closing the trunk and locking the car, I put the keys back in my jeans pocket and put one foot in front of the other as I walked to the right.

The weather was as good as the day before, with the cool wind blowing pleasantly. I wasn't surprised when the wind caught my hair and tore it into a tangle, as it did so often. My gaze fell on my surroundings, the town where I'd grown up. Millvale looked almost the same as it had when I was a child–hardly anything had changed. Shops surrounded the center square, and behind them were parks that people often visited. Just a few minutes away on foot, there were apartment buildings where people lived, and on the other side of town were houses.

I approached the venue I was walking toward, and my eyes landed upon a woman and a man sitting on a bench. The man had his arms around her in what resembled a hug. She had the brightest smile on her lips, and I could tell they were a couple. I couldn't help but think about Aurora when I saw those two.

Fuck! Why did I always think of her?

As I stepped into the venue, I was greeted with a friendly smile by the receptionist. Her hair had grown gray over the years, her previously blonde hair long gone. Her brown-colored square glasses sat on the tip of her nose, and she pushed them back into place. She was absorbed in something. Observing her, I noticed she was reading a seemingly ancient book, lying on the desk in front of her. The chime of the bell made a sound as the next customer stepped in and the lady's gaze broke from the book. It landed on me.

"Oh Asher!" With open arms, she walked over to me after getting up from her chair. Involuntarily, I hugged her back as she embraced me, kissing me on each cheek. "You've grown so much!" She inspected me from head to toe, her glasses falling back to the tip of her nose.

"Barbara, we met a year ago," I laughed as I looked at her petite figure.

Her skin had begun to wrinkle and her back bent too far forward. It felt like she had shrunk. Her age was showing, and it gave me a lump in my stomach to think about how few years she had left.

"Whatever," she replied, waving her hand as if to dismiss me. "Looking for books?" she asked me after shaking hands with the customer who had been behind me all that time.

"Yeah, I'll buy some new ones," my hand ran through my hair as my eyes scanned my surroundings.

"Then I won't disturb." Her petite body settled back into her seat behind the table, where she yet again became engrossed in the story of the book she was reading.

All around me, every single shelf was filled head to toe with books, neatly organized by letter and genre. I knew exactly what I was looking for. There were so many titles on each bookshelf, yet they were all so similar, and each book had a unique cover.

The books in my hands felt heavy as I brought them to Barbara who sat at the desk at the reception.

"I did not know you enjoyed classics," she stated.

I nodded at her with an awkward smile and paid for the books, then I accepted them in a bag before rushing out of the bookstore. Not before I had said goodbye to the old lady, though.

I hadn't realized how late it had become until I saw the sun begin to set behind the clouds that obscured it. Its rays cast long shadows across the ground and tinted the sky with an orange hue.

My thoughts couldn't help but wander to Aurora. How her beautiful strawberry-blonde hair shaped her face so perfectly, how she had hugged me whilst we leaned against the large tree by England moors that day a few weeks ago, or how we had made love. I couldn't help but remember the day when we had burned down the house. That house was the reason for all her inner demons. The smile that had formed on her lips, the gloomy fog that had disappeared from her eyes only to be replaced with a look of relief. In my observation, she had appeared to feel more relaxed afterward, as if the heavy rock had lifted from the pit of her stomach. I wanted to be the one to help her heal, the one to help her overcome her worst fears.

The problem was that I was a damned soul with too many scars for her to be able to stay with me. All I had to do was ensure she was able to continue on her own, and then I planned on leaving her to live her life, free from pain. For I knew I would never be freed from the demons inside me, and she deserved so much better.

Before I headed home, I had one more stop to make. Across the street from where I was standing was the place I was heading toward. The glass door opened inward as the clock above me jingled. The shop was one of the town's most popular cafés in the afternoons when all residents craved tea at the city's only—and finest—tea shop called "Tea N Me." Aurora had loved their tea.

The owner was an old lady who had taken over the shop after inheriting it, and her daughter and granddaughter worked there during the days. The shop had been passed down for several generations, making it a special place for the family and the inhabitants of the town. The tea shop had a special place in everyone's hearts and no one could imagine anyone else taking over the shop except for the family that founded it. It was crowded inside the shop, the line stretching all the way to the door as I walked inside. Individuals conversed with each other, couples enjoyed their tea, and some even studied.

It wasn't until I stood in the line that I heard it. The voice I hadn't heard in ten years, not since Mary had died. And my heart began racing, my environment getting blurry. The blood rushed in my ears, making me unable to hear anything else, yet I still heard it.

That voice.

Her voice.

"Asher? Asher Thorington?"

Chapter 25
Him

THE VOICE WAS ALL too familiar, freezing my blood. A voice that belonged to a girl I hadn't seen in ten years. She wore black high-heeled shoes and a beige coat, looking grown up and mature in the tea shop's doorway. She was the same, but looked as if she had aged thirty years when it had only been ten.

The moment my eyes fell on her, I felt as though my brain had stuttered. No words came out, no thoughts occupied my mind. It was all blank inside. My hair stuck to my forehead where cold sweat had broken out as if it had been glued to a piece of paper.

Because right there, in front of me, stood the girl I hadn't seen in ten years. The girl who had left Millvale with a promise to never come back. Someone who thought it was too painful to live in a city full of memories from her childhood. The city where we had grown up together, the place where we had played as children. The girl I never thought I would see again. And she was so similar, with the same hairstyle and the same style of clothing, yet she wasn't the same. Her eyes were not as lively as they had been back then; they were filled with a gloominess that seemed to be there constantly, as if the years had darkened her soul.

My throat suddenly became dry, and my eyes could do nothing but stare at her. I swallowed without saliva, and it felt like my tonsils were on fire.

"Juliette?" I stammered, my eyes wide open and my mouth forming a circle, the kind that Aurora used to do.

The woman in front of me nodded her head way too fast. She scrunched her nose as if to stop the tears that were rolling down her cheeks, but they fell uncontrollably. Her arms flung around me as she threw herself at me and her scent found its way into my nostrils. She smelled as good as she had done ten years ago. I felt the same feeling of closeness as I had back then, when Mary had still been alive.

HAVING GUESTS OVER AT my house was something I hardly ever did, and now that I thought about it, I wasn't even sure why. After meeting Juliette Farrel at 'Tea N Me,' I knew I had to invite her over. Ten years ago was the last time I had seen her, ten years ago she vowed to never return to this hideous place.

So what would she be doing there?

We stepped out of my black Mercedes that I had parked outside the manor's gates. They screeched when I opened them, rusty and untended to. It wouldn't be long until I needed to call someone there to fix them.

With Juliette behind me, we walked across the gravel road that crunched under our shoes, and on towards the front door. The late afternoon sun shone over the manor, creating an orange light, a beautiful sight over the dark building.

Juliette emitted a gasp behind me, and when I turned, I saw her staring at the manor with wide eyes. Her hands were shaking slightly when she beheld the overwhelming scene, and I knew it must have been difficult for her. She hadn't been there for years.

The house was the same as it had been, with the same type of gothic architecture and unsettling feeling. It had been tended to well over the years, and was much fresher.

Juliette helped me carry my groceries into the kitchen and Josephine met us in the hall to help me with the bags.

"Let me take them, Sir." I cringed when I heard the formal word she used to summon me. I had tried to get her to call me Asher, but she kept addressing me as 'Sir.'

"Do you want me to put the teakettle on?" came Josephine's voice from the kitchen, a simple shout as I showed Julie where she could put her shoes and hang up her coat. With the heels off, she was even shorter than me. About three inches, at least.

"Yes, thank you."

I guided Julie through the corridor into the kitchen with an effortless hand movement. She had never been the one to create awkward silence. Even until that day, that woman was a real chatterbox.

"What a beautiful kitchen!" With her hands in the air, she swept her eyes around the room. "It looks so different to how it did back then." She leaned forward on the kitchen island.

Back then, the kitchen flooring had been tiled, but I preferred a wooden floor. White wood covered the floor, but almost everything else in the kitchen was dark. In the middle was a kitchen island surrounded by bar stools where I had spent a lot of time with Draven.

"I renovated it a few years ago."

There was nothing more to our conversation than cold talk. We avoided talking about the most important subject, which I didn't feel ready to discuss. Not yet.

The different styling of her hair caught my attention as I took in her beauty. "You have dyed your hair," I pointed out, noticing how her eyes rolled discreetly.

"A woman can never go ten years without changing her hair!"

The pride on her face made me laugh. When Josephine left the kitchen and handed each of us a cup of tea, the cheerful mood was quickly ruined. There was only a ticking clock and our breaths that could be heard in the room. It was late afternoon.

As the clock ticked, we knew that time was passing, and that we were not using it sparingly. Because soon Julie would have to head out if she was going to get to her place on time before it went too dark outside.

"What are you doing here?" I asked her, as if to break the silence.

When she replied, "I am drinking tea with you," her smile did not reach her eyes. It was obvious that she was attempting to avoid my question.

"Julie, I'm serious. What are you doing here?"

And the sigh she gave me was a clear sign that nothing was right. "It's mom, she's passed away." Her answer was given with a short smile, an emotionless one.

"It's okay to feel down," I tried to reassure her, but it didn't quite work.

She nodded her head before replying, "I know. I know I should feel down, sad or angry, but I just feel relieved." A deep sigh escaped her.

Juliette's parents had been as shitty as mine had been. When she was young, her mother had remarried a man who was an alcoholic—like mine—which resulted in her mother eventually becoming one as well. Physical abuse, mental abuse, and horrible things like that became normal in Juliette's everyday life.

That was when she had found Mary. They had just started school and ended up in the same class. Ever since the very first year at school, they had been best friends, simply inseparable. They did everything together and had sleepovers every weekend at our house. I had tailed them like the pathetic little brother I was who had a crush on his older sister's gorgeous-looking best friend.

Mind you, I was ten when I fell in love with my fifteen-year-old sister's best friend. Those feelings quickly disappeared when I realized I was just that, Juliette's best friend's little brother.

And the day Mary passed away, was the day I thought I'd never see her best friend again. During the time I had needed someone who understood me as well as Mary had, she'd disappeared.

Just like that.

I couldn't blame her. Everyone was deeply affected by Mary's death since she was loved by so many—even those who barely knew her. I couldn't even remember how many 'I'm sorry for your loss' cards we received at our address in the first few months, or the number of flowers and candles outside our house. The town was small, everyone knew everyone. Rumors spread like wildfire, and I was glad that Thorington Manor was a two-hour drive from the city. My family had been lucky on that front.

Although Edmund Thorington had been one of the founding families that had built Millvale, he had bought a house outside the town in the countryside. In those days, it had taken four hours to travel into the town by horse and carriage. Juliette's ancestors were also among the founding families, which was why her mother—Anne Farell—had been on the Millvale Committee. It was a group of people that ruled over the town, making sure the town worked and that everything was in order. In some towns, there were mayors. In Millvale, there was a committee of several mayors.

"I'm sorry for your loss," I said to Juliette, and she laughed it off with a shrug.

"You don't need to be sorry for my loss, we all know she was a lousy mother and citizen." Yet another deep sigh was released from her.

"I sense a 'but' here," I remarked.

Juliette swallowed and moistened her lips before nodding. "But, I have to take her place on the committee. That is the reason I am back, even though I vowed I would never return."

"Shit." I took a sip of the tea from the mug in front of me.

"Yeah, shit." Julie followed my example and took a sip of the tea. "This was really good," she murmured into her cup of Earl Grey tea, the sound almost echoing off it.

"Where did you leave off to?" I suddenly blurted out, completely unannounced.

"I—" Holding the mug to her lips, she slowly set it down on the kitchen island with a loud thud. She swallowed several times before answering, eyes as wide as a startled deer on the highway. "You know, a little here and there."

An all too familiar sigh came from her as she tapped her fingers on the mug. Her well-maintained nails were long and beige-colored. The ticking of the clock continued, several minutes of silence in which neither of us uttered a word. I was waiting for her to provide me with a more comprehensive response.

"I moved to New York, couldn't stand being in the same country with all my childhood memories. So I moved my entire life there, and didn't have any contact with my mother until I received a phone call saying she was dead."

She looked down at her nails, inspecting them. That's when I saw it, the ring on her finger. The emerald was dark green with a sparkling appearance. My realization that she had found a rich man was sparked by the value of the ring. Julie had never lived in wealth, and now that I thought about it, the old version of her would never have walked around with designer bags as she had done when she arrived here earlier. It was still a good thing that she'd found someone she could love, however.

"You are married?"

Her gaze shifted to her ring finger, and she smiled at me, "Yup, but he's still in our suite in New York. He doesn't like small-town life, but we'll make it work. We always do. What about you, do you have a girl in your life now?"

"Mhm." I took a sip of my tea.

It was complicated between me and Aurora, a difficult situation that was challenging to explain. We felt for each other, but there was no label to what we had.

"What happened to you after, you know, she died?" Juliette leaned forward and supported her chin with her palm.

Her elbows were against the kitchen island as she looked at me and asked the question I suspected would come eventually.

"I don't really know." *Think about what you say, don't come across as crazy.* "Everything is rather indistinct, a blur." *Good job, now you come across as a freak instead.*

"Alcohol?" she asked me, not a single trace of judgment in her voice.

"Something like that," but what I said was far from the truth, I did not drink.

After the death of my sister, my father's addiction brought out his aggressive side, which exacerbated my aversion to alcohol. I couldn't tell Juliette about the darkness that had been living inside of me since Mary had died, resurfacing every time something triggered it. I would appear crazy, and so far I had managed to keep that side of me under control. At least during the past weeks.

We spent several hours sitting in the kitchen chatting. During our conversation, we discussed everything that had happened since we last saw each other. It was a warm feeling to meet and talk to someone who had been so close to Mary, who had known her as well as I had. Someone who could relate to me, just like Mary had. We talked about everything between heaven and earth, and by the time darkness fell over the sky, we had drunk several cups of Earl Grey tea.

"I should get going." Juliette pulled the bag that she had left hanging over the barstool after she put her hair up in a bun over her shoulder.

"Would you like a ride to Millvale town square?"

With a smile, she shook her head, "No thanks, I ordered a taxi. It should arrive in…" she paused and directed her gaze toward the ticking clock hanging on the kitchen wall. "In five minutes."

"Okay," I stood up from the bar stool and walked over to Juliette.

She threw her arms around me and embraced me with a big hug. A hug that made me feel at home, the kind of hug I had received when I was eight years old and a little boy.

"Take care," I muttered as my head directed inwards towards her hair.

"You too, I've missed you so much."

She was still hugging me, and I let her. Because I knew this hug of a reunion was something we both needed. After ten years of sadness and heartbreak, hugging the girl who had been my sister's best friend brought me great comfort.

When I heard a soft gasp coming from the kitchen doorway, I noticed that the mood in the room had switched to something else. Immediately, I let go of the hug and saw Aurora. The beautiful dress she had worn earlier that day was replaced by a pink nightgown, which perfectly shaped her figure and made the contrast of her hair come forth. She looked amazing.

The sun had completely set by that point, and the moon was casting its dark light over England. Through the window, moonlight spilled into the doorway, lighting her up as if she was in a fairy tale. The moment I saw her red-rimmed eyes, I immediately wondered why she was crying.

"I should go," Juliette said to break the stiff silence that had ensued, then she made her way out of the kitchen and into the hall.

A few seconds later, I heard the front door close, and Aurora remained in the same place as before. Her gaze drew to Juliette's silhouette as she exited the house. When I reached Aurora, she was shaking her head frantically, tears streaming down her cheeks.

"Go to your girl," she spat out. The hostile glare she gave me was something that didn't suit her beautiful face.

"Aurora—" I tried to get out, but she cut me off, "No! Was that why I wasn't allowed to come with you to town? Is that why you were gone all day? To be with her? You have spent weeks with me, taking me on dates, reading with me, you fucking saw me in my most vulnerable state, Ash! You took my virginity. And now you are with a new girl? Was I not enough?" she shouted and my heart broke more with every second that passed.

She didn't let me answer her questions, she didn't even let me explain what had happened. She just ran away.

Away from me.

The front door swung open, and my heart pounded a thousand beats per second, making me unable to move a single muscle. She had run out of the manor.

Shit! I had really fucked up.

Chapter 26
Her

AS FAR AS MY legs could handle, I ran and ran. With no clear goal in sight and no place to go, I was lost. Darkness was overtaking the landscape, and I was unsure of how to avoid tripping over a root.

Tears ran down my cheeks but quickly dried from the wind that blew harder and more intensely as night fell. The surrounding trees were many, and the path I followed was small. There wasn't much to see in the forest during the night. It appeared as though everything became more unpleasant and unnerving during the darkest hours of the day. The owl that howled up in the tree sounded like it was following me. With every step I took farther away from it, the closer the sound seemed to come to me from behind. Branches and bushes tore at my clothes and bare arms.

My fingers were stiff, unable to work the blood circulating inside. A crisp and chilly wind grabbed hold of my hair and tangled it, only to make my ears hurt from losing their warm protector. The cold air stung my cheeks as the strong wind whipped them. While I ran, I could only hear the wind whining and my bare feet crunching the branches covering the ground. Every cell in my body trickled into ice at the sound, as if someone was weeping.

Unlike a few weeks ago, I no longer wanted to run away from Thorington Manor. The security that Asher exuded was comforting, and his presence eased the demons inside of me. He put them at bay, taming them. He understood me in ways no one had before. The feeling of intimacy that came from having someone who understood you and what you were feeling was something I never knew I needed. With Asher, I felt like I belonged in a way that I had never known before. He made me feel at home. A euphoric feeling always settled over me once he came near.

When I had watched him hug another girl, I had been overcome with pain. Someone was running on my heart, crunching it, breaking it, throwing it away. As if all of our memories, my happiness, my soul, had been sucked into a black hole, only to never return.

I thought we'd had a connection, and that he had considered me important to him. Seeing him with another woman—who was a hundred times prettier than I was—had given me the instinct to run away as fast as my legs could.

For how could I stay with a man who made me *feel* when he was with another girl, too?

These past four months, his home had become my home. I did not know where to go. My feet were aching, the gravel was pressing under the soles of my feet and I wouldn't be surprised if my feet started bleeding after that. The hole that was growing inside me became wider with every step I took. A caving of my heart.

Where the hell was I supposed to go?

In front of me was an opening between two trees with extremely thick trunks, surrounded by several trees with thinner trunks. The treetops swayed from the night wind. It was like something out of a horror movie. My feet took me towards the opening and when I emerged from it, I was panting more than ever. In front of me was a large open field, behind me was nothing but trees and a large forest. Thorington Manor was nowhere in sight. Not that my eyesight was very sharp given the darkness. Sweat ran down my forehead and down between my breasts, my lungs struggling to get air. The feeling made the tears fall faster as I felt them burning inside my chest.

It seemed as if my legs were running across the open field for miles. My ears were pricked up by a scream coming from the forest behind me. When I heard the heartbreaking cry, my spine tingled with shivers. I sincerely hoped it came from an animal.

My heart was aching, my lungs, my soul, but most of all, I felt a numbness creeping up, ready to spread over me like thick fog on a rainy and cold day. A severe impact on my foot caused me to fall over. The adrenaline that had compelled me to run as far away from the house as I could started to wear off. My foot began to ache and a symphony of pain sounded from all over my body. I couldn't stop the scream that fell from my lips. Intense pain radiated throughout my body, and I couldn't move.

Where could I even go?

Because of the humid air that had risen, the grass around my body had become damp. The energy I needed wasn't there, so I couldn't stand up or run away. I couldn't because I had nowhere to run to. The tears began to flow as I realized I had no one to turn to, no home to call my own. It hit me that Grimhill Manor had taken everything from me, and Asher had instilled hope in me only to let it crash down.

Or were my feelings only one-sided?

I was lying on the grass with my head resting against the freshly cut grass that smelled as fresh as it would've had if it had been a summer day. The moon lit up the field I was lying on. There was a liquid running down my toes as my foot ached and stung. After falling on something, I was left with a bleeding wound on the bottom of my foot. The only thing I could focus on was my chest rising and falling.

Inhale, exhale and focus on breathing.

Although I was in pain, I coughed from time to time as my lungs burned. There was a cold wind blowing over the moors that night, and I wished I had my brown coat with me. All I had on was underwear and my pink nightgown. In the same way that I had been drained of adrenaline, all my energy had left me as well. My gaze was directed up to the sky. There was a sense of peace in the woods, and if the screams I heard inside had not been there, it would have seemed even more peaceful. Screams from foxes or deer, I hoped.

There was no way I could lift a muscle. I began to regret running away from the house. Instead of running away from the kitchen, I wished I had stayed inside. A thousand daggers were being stabbed into my stomach and chest. The pain in my soul was too much for me to bear.

But what would I be doing at the house of a man who had a girlfriend? It hurt so fucking much to know he had another.

APPARENTLY, I HAD FALLEN asleep during the night, because when I opened my eyes the next morning, the sun was already making its way through the cloudy sky. The sound of voices had surrounded me in the dream I'd had. I had dreamed about living a normal and happy life with my mother somewhere far away, and that everything was fine again. Life was anything but normal. In the dream, I had been free from pain, free from responsibility, and free from everything.

The burning sensation in my lungs caused me to groan out of pain, and I wished I could go back to my dream. During that moment, I wished I could cease to exist. In my blurry vision, I saw the sky.

Child-like giggles were heard nearby, but no one was there. A chill skittered across my skin like ice-cold snow on a winter day.

"S-stay a-awake," a whisper sounded in my ears. The same one I had heard the first night at Thorington Manor.

As something rustled in the grass behind me, my heart skipped a beat. There was an ache in my body, in every part of me. Nearby, I heard some indistinct voices as I blinked several times to clear my vision.

"Y-you h-have to s-stay awake."

Behind my eyelid on my left eye, I could feel the flicker of something being there with me. Telling me—begging me—to stay awake. But I was so tired.

The world appeared to be groggy, and in my eyes, the clouds clumped together and became one big mass. My eyelids felt heavy above the eyes, and fatigue took over. As I lay on the damp grass, the world around me began to spin.

Sometime between dawn and when the sun reached its highest point in the sky, I felt someone lift me into their arms. My body bobbed up and down as the human carried me somewhere. My eyes were too heavy to remain open, so I just let the person carry me. I was too exhausted and decrepit to care who carried me or where they took me. What did it matter where anyone brought me if I had nothing left to lose?

Deep down, I wished it was Asher, but he had consumed my trust. If it had even been there, to begin with. There was a dull ache in my whole body, and my stomach was rumbling for food.

"Thank you so much for calling."

The voice that spoke sounded so close, yet so far away. My head rested against a muscular chest that vibrated as the person in question spoke.

"You're welcome."

An unknown voice whose owner I had never—I supposed—met. Who were those voices around me? Slowly, I forced my eyelids open, and was greeted by a concerned look from a pair of amber-colored eyes. The person's eyes gave me love and warmth, security, and a home, but when the memories hit me of who he actually was, I immediately squeezed my eyes shut.

"Aurora, I know you're awake." His dark and raspy voice sounded next to my ear, a sensual voice. The voice of the person who had made love to me. The voice that had brushed against my clit, making me feel pleasure. But also one that had someone else other than me.

After hearing a car door open, I was seated in something comfortable. A car seat. My head hung low, and someone fastened a seat belt around my waist. When the car door closed again, I was alone in the vehicle, and my head rested against the windowpane. There was a sigh of relief. My thoughts of what he had done or the way he had made me believe in him were no longer worthwhile. I was just relieved to finally have a roof over my head.

"D-don't f-fall asleep," a young girl's voice drifted nearby. "Y-you h-have to fight, to s-survive this."

Nothing the voice whispered made any sense to me, my head was pounding.

"H-he needs you, s-stay a-awake." The same shivering voice I had heard that first night. Mary's voice.

Even though I tried to stay awake, the pain was too unbearable. Exhaustion overtook my body as I let my heavy eyelids close.

ASHER, EARLIER

THE CAR'S TIRES SKIDDED across the ground, sending gravel flying through the air. As I flew over the asphalt road I had driven out onto, I turned the steering wheel in the direction I wanted to travel. My foot pressed the gas pedal to the floor. With the brakes pressed down, I swerved to the right. The forest road in front of me was not suitable for my Mercedes, the holes in the gravelly ground caused me to hit the roof of the car several times. The clock on the screen showed eight a.m.

"Turn right at the next exit, then drive a hundred meters straight ahead," came from the car's speaker, and I pressed down harder on the gas pedal. *"You have reached your destination."*

With my foot on the brake pedal, I pushed it, stopped my Mercedes, and threw the door open with the car keys still in the ignition.

Panic was all I felt, worried over what state I would find her in. She could be hurt, and I hadn't been there to protect her. Still, I was furious. She had run from me without letting me explain anything, and that fury ran through my veins like fireworks. Impulsive thoughts ran through my mind, thinking about what I would do to her as soon as I knew she was okay. I wanted to fucking bend her over my knee and spank her until her ass turned red, hear her whimpers as she found the act painful yet pleasurable. The urge was so strong, wanting me to do it right there in my car, but that would mean Draven could see us.

No, she was mine. Only mine, and I didn't share what belonged to me.

My hands shook from the adrenaline filling my blood, causing me to pant, and my hands gripped the steering wheel tightly.

I would punish my naughty girl, spank her until she moaned. She would learn not to disobey me again.

One thing I had learned about Aurora throughout the months was that she enjoyed being dominated. She needed me to guide her through the days, help her overcome her darkness. I knew she secretly liked my dominant ways of taking her by the way her pussy became wetter by the seconds.

In front of me was a large open field, and my car headlights illuminated the road ahead. Two large tree trunks created an opening to the field, and Draven Brax was walking toward me. Without closing the car door, I jogged up to him. He wore a military-style outfit as if to camouflage himself in the forest, his cargo pants hanging loosely over his waist. In his arms, he carried the girl I had been looking for for hours. Seven hours had passed since she left my house. A whole night without sleep, because how could I sleep when she was missing? I had walked round after round in the forest for several hours, hearing the screams of the foxes somewhere far away.

She had been nowhere to be found.

Finally, I had returned to the house to check if she was home. According to Josephine, she had not been near the house. Josephine had sent several of the staff members out to look for Aurora on the farm and near Thorington Manor, but without success. After searching the entire house, in case she was somehow in there, I had received a call from Draven. He had found her in an open field and I had immediately stepped into the car and driven there at full speed.

The girl in his arms was Aurora, *my* Aurora. She hung limply in Draven's arms as he lifted her over to my embrace. Her eyes were closed, her hair was stuck to her forehead from the sweat that had formed, and her clothes were torn. I noticed that one of her feet had bled, and a lot of dried blood had coagulated over the large gash.

"Thank you for calling me," I thanked him as I exhaled. He handed over her sleeping body to my embrace.

Draven nodded, "Don't worry about it."

His hair was combed back by a black beanie and his brown-green eyes appeared calmer than usual.

"Where was she?" I asked, while looking down at my girl's beautiful face.

"She was lying on the open field. I found her like that. She must have laid there for hours before I found her," his voice almost shook and it made me surprised.

Draven barely ever cared about anyone, yet he seemed to care about Aurora and Everlee. I'd never thought I'd see Draven get concerned about another woman in his life. Something had changed since he met Everlee, and it appeared that he was actually happy. Though he would kill me if I told him that.

I brushed away a few hair strands from her face and watched her intently. I could almost feel Draven's curious eyes on me.

"Shit man, you're whipped for her," a smirk tugged at the corner of his lips as he watched me observe Aurora when she slept.

"Yeah, I so fucking am," I mumbled loud enough for him to hear. He walked over to where I stood, patting me on the back in a brotherly gesture.

"Take care of her."

That was the moment I realized he cared about someone else than me. It warmed my heart, somehow.

"How is everything going?" Draven surprised me by asking.

"What do you mean?"

"You think I don't know my best friend? I have known you forever, I can tell when something is wrong." He made a pause as he insecurely scraped the back of his neck. "I know you have darkness within you."

At his words, my mouth dropped open and I couldn't seem to comprehend what he had said. Every thought in my mind was silenced, and every sound around me became quiet. All I could hear was the blood rushing in my ears when I stared at Draven as if he was a stranger.

"There is nothing to be ashamed of. Call me if you need anything, alright mate? You know you can always talk to me. I'm here for you, brother." A small smile formed on his lips.

His sentence completely and utterly shocked me. I had not seen that coming. As hard as it was for me to accept his words, to admit that something was *wrong* with me, I couldn't feel more grateful to have him in my life. I had never expected Draven to realize those details about me, nor for him to pay attention to me in that way.

My mouth couldn't form any words, but I knew it wasn't necessary. With Draven, words simply weren't needed. A single smile and nod were enough words for us both, and he saw the 'thank you' in my eyes.

I returned the smile he gave me, and with a final nod from him, he put on his tough facade again. He was never one to show his soft side for a long time, but I knew it was always there under the surface.

On his back hung a hunting rifle. I couldn't imagine what would have happened to Aurora if Draven hadn't been out on one of his weekly hunting trips.

My eyes couldn't break away from her, *my* Aurora. That thought made my heart leap in my chest, making me smile like a fool to myself in the woods in the middle of the night. I tentatively placed Aurora inside the car and sat in the driver's seat. The car's headlights lit up the road ahead, and at that time I would drive more carefully. By dodging all the potholes in the ground, I managed to avoid hitting my head on the roof of the car. Out of the corner of my eye, I saw Aurora's eyelids flutter, but her head remained against the window.

When we pulled into my lot, I parked in front of the house and scooped her up in my arms. It was Josephine that met me in the hall when I carried her in.

"Oh my God! What happened?" The sound of her concern echoed throughout the hall.

"Draven found her on one of the moors where he hunts."

Josephine's eyes widened, and she hurried up the stairs and into Aurora's room. With her sleeping body in my arms, I carried her up to her room. The soft mattress of the bed cushioned her body. Her beauty remained intact despite all the injuries she suffered.

"I'll wash her and change her dress, Sir."

"That will be great, thanks, Josephine."

My heart filled with relief since I knew Aurora was in good hands with Josephine. After a brief moment of silence, she smiled, and I walked out. I had not slept for over twenty-four hours and exhaustion started to take over my fogged mind.

At one point, I had thought I would never see Aurora again, that she had run away forever and that she would never be found. I cursed myself for caring so deeply about her.

I hadn't intended to fall for her, yet it had still happened.

Taking a deep breath, I made my way toward my room. A few hours of sleep wouldn't hurt, and after that, it was time for me and Aurora to have a talk about everything. For I had to earn her trust again, I needed her to stay with me and by my side. But it was nearly impossible because of the darkness lurking just beneath the surface of my being, waiting for the right moment to ruin everything I had built up.

For *it* didn't find us worthy of love.

Chapter 27
Him

"YOU DON'T KNOW HOW worried I was!" I shouted, my voice clear and loud in the dining room.

After sleeping until the next morning, Aurora was in the chair next to me as I ate breakfast.

"You lied to me." Her voice came out as a whisper. Fork in hand, she took a bite of the bacon on her plate. I let out a deep sigh of annoyance.

"You have to trust me!"

Her throat bulged as she swallowed her bacon. Her plate of food had almost been consumed when she looked down at it. "I did, at first."

"Juliette and I have nothing intimate between us. I met her yesterday in town and invited her here for a cup of tea. I haven't seen her in ten years!" Frustrated, I ran my hand through my tousled hair. "Do you remember what I showed you that time on our picnic? The diary?"

She nodded her head and her eyes lifted to meet mine.

"Julie was Mary's best friend," I observed as Aurora's eyebrows raised, clearly shocked, and then furrowed. She opened her mouth several times without being able to say anything. With her tongue, she moistened her lips and stared into my eyes.

"I didn't realize—"

"No, because you assumed the worst and fled!"

The worry that made me frustrated persisted within me. What would have happened if she hadn't been found? My anger was sparked by the fact that she put both of us through that.

"I'm sorry."

In response, I nodded curtly and stood up, the haste causing the chair to tip over backwards. I ignored it and quickly left the dining room.

"Asher—" Her voice was heard behind me, but I pushed faster forward, not having the energy to fight with her.

"Asher!"

A hand grabbed my wrist, and before my mind could comprehend what my body was doing, I had Aurora pressed against the wall. I captured her there, my two arms on each side of her head, making her unable to escape the confinement. My chest was heaving from the adrenaline pumping through my veins. Her eyes fluttered open after having them closed, and she looked at me with an apologetic gaze.

"I'm sorry," she whispered in a low tone.

It was nearly impossible to hear her voice, my mind was elsewhere. Her hair lay perfectly on her shoulders, framing her face shape. Her lips were plump and her enticing eyes drew me in with the adoring gaze one might expect from a puppy. When my eyes lowered, taking a deep breath, they landed on Aurora's upper chest. The dress she was wearing made her breasts appear fuller, and desire filled every inch of my body. Desire made me want to put my hand on top of them, to feel them on my skin. I wanted to take her, fuck her, and make love to her in the corridor we stood in. The thoughts made my cock jerk in my pants, blood filling it as my erection grew.

Fuck, she was perfect.

Every inch of her body as well as her personality was sculpted as if she had been made for me.

Hunger was visible in my eyes, and although I was still mad at her, she calmed the rage. I lifted her dress, dragging my hand along her thigh and up to her panties. A gasp released from her and the heated look she gave me was my cue to put my hand above her panties. Rubbing them, I teased her clit, which was longing for my touch.

"Never fucking run away from me again, darling," I growled in her ear, which caused a blush to spread upon her cheeks.

She tried turning away her gaze to my displeasure. "Eyes on me."

They immediately turned to me, and I smirked knowingly. She loved me dominating her, loved it when I told her what to do. A soft gasp released from her when I continued to rub her sore pussy, and I couldn't help but press my cock closer to her panties. My cock was begging for her as much as her clit was begging for me.

"Are you going to run away from me again, darling?"

At first she didn't reply, and only stared at me with wide eyes, secretly liking my filthy words. She wanted me, needed me, and it was clear from her body language. Her eyes were gleaming with desire, but she still hadn't replied to my question. A moan escaped her pretty, plump lips, but as I noticed how she came closer to orgasm, I removed my finger from her clit. Aurora whined like a child, and pouted like one too, as one would do if they didn't receive their candy. I chuckled in response, finding amusement in her displeasure. My eyebrow cocked as I waited for her, and her hips came closer to my finger, desperately needing release. I stepped back, leaving her all flustered and red, needy for me.

"Please," she begged.

"Are you," I made a pause to emphasize my words, letting her hear them loud and clear. "Going to run away from me again?" She made me growl out my last words, anger and lust flaring inside of me.

"God! No. Just, please, Ash."

Her neediness caused a chuckle to escape from me, and I smirked at her attempt to form a sentence. "Good girl."

With both of my hands, I ripped off her dress, leaving her in only her bra and panties. Then I removed her underwear and touched her pussy with my fingers, feeling how wet she was. My cock jerked in reaction, and it took all my self-control not to fuck her right away. She needed to learn not to disobey me again, needed to learn to trust me as she said she did.

I rubbed her clit with my fingers, and she nearly collapsed from the sensation. Moans escaped her lips, and her body shivered from the pleasure I gave her. As I pushed a finger inside of her, she whimpered and her legs budged under her. I caught her with my other hand, holding her up as I pushed against her most sensitive spot–her G-spot.

"Oh fuck, Asher."

I continued to fuck her with my fingers, and eventually, her body started shaking as her orgasm built up. The sound of her moans filled the corridor in which we were standing, and I was sure she would be heard by my staff as well. If they said even one word about it, I would fire them. No one should mess with my girl, especially not make her embarrassed.

I fingered her until she came, and once she did, her entire body was shaking from the orgasm and I was supporting her body with my arms. Although she was panting heavily and her eyes were half closed, I wasn't done with her yet.

I unzipped my pants, removing them and my boxers as I leaned her body against the wall. I grabbed a condom from my pocket and slid it on before I positioned myself against her pussy. I looked into her eyes to make sure she was okay, and from the look she gave me, and from the loud moans, I knew she was loving what I did to her. A knowing smirk graced my lips as I continued to fuck her. Both of us were panting, moaning, seeking pleasure in each other. My hands rubbed her clit, which caused her to almost lose her balance and fall down to the floor, but I managed to catch her.

Just as I noticed she was close to cumming for the second time, I pulled out of her, leaving her a whimpering mess. Her eyes glistened from the release she so desperately needed, but wouldn't get.

At least not yet.

"Asher, please," she whined, but I didn't intervene.

After a few seconds, I pushed myself inside her again as my hips worked hard and fast, much to her liking. She started moaning loudly again, almost on the verge of cumming.

But as I noticed her being close, I once again pulled out.

I was torturing myself, but most of all, I was torturing my girl. The whimpering intensified, and she became more desperate to get her sweet release.

"Will you run away from me again, darling?"

"I won't. Please, Asher. Please let me cum," she desperately begged me.

"Hmm, we will see about that."

I gave her a wink before I entered her once again, teasing her pussy, fucking her harder and harder against the wall. Moaning and whimpering, she was a wretched mess.

She was all mine. All of that for me.

Continuing to tease her, pulling out of her, I repeated the process over and over again.

"You are such a good girl, darling," I whispered in her ear after denying her pleasure for the fifth time by pulling out of her.

Her eyes were tear-streaked, the desperation for pleasure making the tears fall down her cheeks. I kissed them away, brushing away hair that had glued itself to her sweaty forehead.

When I decided she'd had enough of orgasm denial, I pushed into her for the last time for the day. My hips picked up the pace once again, and I slammed into her over and over. Our moans filled the corridor and her pussy clamped around my cock as it tightened, and I knew she was cumming. Thrusting inside her harder and faster, I made her cum over my cock, her body shaking against the wall. I came quickly after, spilling into the condom, releasing an animal-like growl. As her legs trembled, I lifted her in my arms and carried her to her room after having removed the condom and tossed it in the trash can.

"My good, beautiful girl," I murmured in her ear as I tucked her into her bed, letting her rest from the session that made her exhausted.

I lay beside her on the bed, holding her close to me as I gently patted her head. Her eyes fluttered to a close as sleep took over, and I smiled to myself at how lucky I was. She gave me a small smile before snuggling closer to me.

I ENTERED AURORA'S ROOM the day after she had been in the dining room. With my hands behind my back, I hid something, and my smug smile told her it was a surprise.

I remained standing in the doorway and asked her, "May I come in?" to which she merely lifted her head to nod.

Before I sat down on the footstool next to the wardrobe, I handed her a gift wrapped in pink paper.

"Asher," she looked into my eyes, "You didn't need to get me anything."

"Open it," my eyes sparkled with excitement over giving her the gift I had bought for her when I was in Millvale.

Aurora tore open the fine paper. Upon examining her facial expression, I noticed that her eyes glistened as she opened the package containing three books.

"Really? For me?" Her tone sounded more shocked than questioning, and to reassure her, I replied, "Yes, for you."

When she grabbed the books, her eyes landed on the nicely designed covers. A smile tugged at the corner of my lips at the happiness on her face.

"I-I haven't received my own set of books in years," and she couldn't help the tears falling down her cheeks.

Having made my way toward Aurora on the bed, I asked, "Don't you like them?"

There was a side inside of me that worried she wouldn't appreciate my gift.

"Are you kidding me? I love them!"

My relief shone through my eyes and I exhaled, "I thought I had hurt you. With the books, that is."

A laugh erupted from her, and the smile she gave me warmed my heart. While shaking her head, she said, "No, it's perfect."

From the floor below us came a muffled sound. The walls were isolated, but it was still audible. A drop of something like glass would never have bothered me if it weren't for the voices afterward.

People made mistakes, and Josephine must have dropped something because that voice belonged to her. When she dropped it, she screamed, as if she was filled with fear and shock. My cheeks felt drained of color after a torrent of profanity followed.

"You worthless piece of shit!" The man towering over me was my father, the one standing in front of me holding a leather belt in his hands. "Fucking come here!" he shouted aggressively, and my little body jerked.

The pain that spread across my back as the leather whipped me, created a huge burning sensation. His profanity along with the pain was a toxic mixture of alcohol, the kind that could kill people in minutes if too much was ingested.

"Stop crying, you damn kid," his voice rang in my ears, like the rattle of a rattlesnake.

He was a rattlesnake, slithering around and hurting anyone he thought had done anything to him. The whips continued, the pain continued, and the poison spread and would soon paralyze my body.

Everything hurt.

"It's your fault Mary died," the man spat out.

That pain was the worst.

Then suddenly it hit me. The feeling of numbness. The feeling that I was worthless, like he had told me year after year. The feeling that she needed someone better, that she didn't need me.

She deserved someone better than me. And I knew I would ruin the mood, yet I couldn't help myself. The darkness was slowly taking over my body.

"I am a monster. Can't you see that, Aurora?"

The shock on her face told me everything. I had ruined it.

"W-what? Where is this coming from?" Her eyebrows pulled up in confusion.

I couldn't help myself, feeling myself slowly but surely losing grip on reality. "I am the villain in your fucking story." The words poured out of me like a water flow.

Realization dawned on her face, her beautiful eyes filling with concern and precious tears. The realization that I was slipping away from her.

"You are not!" she exclaimed loudly while tears ran down her face.

I had to turn away my face, not being able to stand the sight of her crying. Her hands found my cheek, turning my face to meet hers and her steel-blue eyes looked into mine. Those dark purple splashes in them, the most unique pair of eyes I had ever seen.

"You are not bad, Ash. You cannot see your condition as being a villain. Do not let it define who you are, my love. You are so much more than that."

You cannot see your condition as being a villain.

She knew.

She knew that something was wrong with me, that something was terribly wrong with me. And yet, the bare thought of that did not terrify me. Rather, it lifted a weight from my chest. And yet she hadn't run away from me.

"I see what you are thinking, Ash. You are not like any other I have ever met, but that does not matter. Your condition does not define who you are. You are not the villain in my story, you are my hero. You saved me in more ways than I ever thought possible. Why can't you see that?"

When she was done talking, she was breathless. The pain in my chest decreased. I had found my remedy in her.

"Really?" I asked her, almost on the verge of crying too.

"Really," she confirmed.

My hand touched her cheek to wipe away the tears that had escaped her eyes.

"God damn, you're so beautiful," I blurted out, leaving her completely shocked.

A hair strand happened to be in front of her eyes, and with my fingers, I placed it behind her ears. Her cheeks heated as she witnessed that completely innocent gesture. At that moment, I felt something stir to life in my stomach. She couldn't stop her head from leaning closer to my hand as our eyes looked into each other. Seeing my gaze directed at her lips, she naturally moved even closer. The way she looked at me was so erotic. Our lips were only a few millimeters apart.

For the first time, I wanted to be kissed. I craved to feel her and have her lips against mine. A devilish smile was on my lips. The fact that I knew I would devour her didn't deter me. My hand brushed against her jawline, lifting it upwards. As I was much taller than her, I had to bend down my head to be able to brush my lips against hers. Connecting my mouth to hers ignited the spark inside me.

I loved the feeling of it, loved the way she made me feel.

Our lips tangled together in union, none of us seeking acceptance, only closeness. She parted her lips for mine, letting me push out my tongue to meet hers. There was not a single second of hesitation. Holding on to my neck with her hand, she clutched me tightly towards her. My eyes closed during those few moments in order to feel more, and I could only hear the sound of our lips kissing. There was something so sexy and erotic about the sound.

As she rested her head on the pillow, I laid on top of her. With my elbows, I propped myself up so that she would not get injured.

After checking that she was comfortable, I broke the kiss briefly to say, "God damn, Aurora."

Her cheeks turned a redder hue at the sound of my voice. I could feel her craving my touch as much as I was craving hers. I smashed my lips against hers, no longer as softly as I had a second earlier. She kissed me back like no one had ever done, our tongues colliding in a determined and delicious manner. The taste of her silenced all my worries, her presence made me want more.

So much more.

Shuddering, Aurora let out a kind of groan from the back of her throat. By sliding her tongue to meet mine, she deepened the kiss as her hand trailed over my body, under my shirt to feel my abs. That moment when our bodies collided would come to be one of my favorite memories with Aurora. Having sex with her was making me crave her insanely.

More than the first time.

It was almost as if the act itself became a necessity for both my body and soul. My hands were caressing her breasts over her bra as I leaned my waist and hips against her pussy, which was still covered in clothes.

"You are the most beautiful human I've ever laid eyes on," I said.

"I love you," she whispered almost too low to be heard.

Her confession made my heart thump so hard in my chest that I felt like I was going to collapse.

"I love you," and I kissed her again.

She could feel my hard erection pressing against her, rubbing against her clit, making her even more needy for me. My hand traveled down her body.

"You okay with this?" I asked, breaking the kiss, and she nodded.

She was a panting mess when she replied, "Yes."

A gasp was released from her throat when she felt me pushing away her beige sweatpants. I trailed my hand over her panties, right above her pussy. The sensation of touching her made the fire inside of me flare up. It was a delightful feeling.

My hard erection pushed against her panties, and without breaking eye contact with me, she undid my buckle with desperate fingers. The chuckle I let out made her look away from shyness. She helped me take off my pants as I pushed them down on the floor, and they landed beside her sweatpants.

"You are so fucking gorgeous, and you are mine," I whispered.

A smile tugged at the corner of her lips when she replied, "I'm yours, Ash. And you are mine."

"Yours," I murmured in response.

My stomach fluttered in anticipation. Grabbing my hair, she pushed my head closer to her and pressed her lips against mine. The sparkles were stirring inside of me. With the help of my hands, she pushed the beige hoodie she was wearing over her head. Her white lace bra was the only thing left covering her breasts. I looked at her, studied her, and I knew she had never felt so utterly exposed before. Yet she liked the feeling of being adored by me. She liked the way I looked at her, as if she was the only girl I had ever wanted.

And she was the only girl. Her gaze told me all of her emotions.

Shoving her panties to one side, my finger brushed against her clit. With circular movements, I touched her and devoured her. Our eyes locked as I gave her pleasure, a feeling so intense it nearly made her cum immediately.

"My girl," I whispered in her ears, making a blush creep up on her cheeks.

My heart was pounding inside my chest as I traced kisses from her neckline, down to her breasts. With my other hand, I caressed her breasts while continuing to draw circles on her most sensitive spot. She could practically feel my cock getting stiffer by the second as my lips traced down her stomach, making her shiver.

"Are you sure?" I asked her and she smiled in reply. "Fuck," I breathed and withdrew my hand to remove my underwear.

Uncertainly, she grabbed my hard cock and stroked it. My gaze fixed on her, and a smirk appeared on her face. Leaning forward, she stuck out her tongue to lick it, her gaze still on mine in a sensual manner. I pushed her backward as I groaned, making it impossible for her to touch me. While kissing her right below her ear, my head shook, causing the girl underneath me to squeeze her thighs to relieve some of the tension.

"If you touch me, you're going to make me cum before I've even been inside of you." When I whispered, my breath was warm against her ear.

A red heat spread over her cheeks. My eyes caught her attention as I yanked a condom from her nightstand, the sound of the wrapper ripping making my heart skip a beat. Pulling it over my cock, her mouth watered. Her pussy lips got spread by my two fingers as I saw how wet she was. She couldn't help but bite her lip, earning another groan from me above her.

"Are you sure you want this?" I asked, the same glimpse of concern in my eyes that had been visible the time I took her virginity.

"I am sure." She gave me a reassuring smile, and that was the cue for me to place myself between her legs.

She could feel my cock teasing her clit. My hands cupped her breasts as my cock continued to tease the most sensitive part of her body.

"Please," Aurora begged me when I didn't enter her.

A low and sexy chuckle was heard from me before I gently and slowly pushed myself inside of her pussy. The sensation of me inside of her once again, made her eyes roll back. Both she and I moaned in unison.

"Fuck, you're so tight, darling," I growled.

I pushed out my cock before inserting myself again between her pussy lips. When I slammed myself inside of her, she moaned out loud. Her pussy gripped my cock as it squeezed it with every thrust. Our moans echoed inside her room, bouncing on the walls. That feeling, that intimacy I had never felt before I met her, was the most lovely feeling. The pleasure it brought me to share that special moment with Aurora felt as if I was walking on clouds.

I continued to thrust inside of her, chasing both of our releases. With one hand, I continued to touch her sensitive clitoral area. The look in her eyes was so intense, she had this crazed look in her as I gave both myself and her pleasure. With each thrust, the sound of our skin slapping against the other's filled the room.

"I am close," she moaned out, feeling breathless, but also like she was in heaven.

"Me too."

And at that, I thrusted even faster, hitting her G-spot. In seconds, I could feel her body shaking, the pleasure of my cock inside of her making her orgasm. I moaned as I came inside the condom. My nose was filled with the scent of her perfume and the smell of sweet sex inside her room as I inhaled. The smile that played on her lips was enough to make me feel like the most handsome man on the entire planet. With my hand, I stroked away a few hair strands from her forehead and she leaned into my touch. My lips brushed against hers in a soft manner.

"Thank you for giving me the finest gift ever."

She couldn't stop the giggle from escaping from her.

AURORA

I HAD NEVER INTENDED to fall in love with anyone. Then I met him. It wasn't my intention to fall in love with Asher. But then there was the way he smiled, the way he looked at me like I was worth something, and the way he made me feel.

Holy shit.

I knew I had fallen deeply, madly in love with Asher Thorington. And there was no turning back, not now and not ever.

Chapter 28
Her

LIFE WAS GREAT. WITH him, it was. It never crossed my mind that living would feel so good. Especially in his presence.

Asher Thorington helped me ease my demons, he helped me burn them, he made them suffer and dragged them to hell for me. He moved heaven and earth to save me from myself. Just as I was there for him. Together, we fought every day.

Together, we would make it.

There were days when life felt unbearable; the demons still lived inside of me. They crawled under my skin during the night and when I woke up from nightmares, he was always there for me. I spent days crying, remembering my mother's death, which left me feeling hopeless. There would always be a carved out hole in my heart, a hole that wouldn't increase in size, but it would still be there. In the end, it would always be there, no matter what anyone did. I had been through too much for it to heal, but I had Asher. And he helped me forget the hole.

Piece by piece, he covered it with soil.

I knew I would have to live with the pain. Grief was a part of the process of life. A living proof that you loved someone dearly. It was truly beautiful to have love in my life—something one should not take for granted. Asher's love for me was what made me feel alive, it was what made me survive the hard days. Every time he read for me when I felt down, it was an expression of his affection towards me.

The dullness was gone from his eyes, and he seemed happier. There was only warmth behind those amber-colored eyes I cherished so much. We had made it, we had survived the hardest days and could only move forward from that point. Despite facing our own demons every day, we were warriors.

I would always fight for him as he had done for me.

"Asher?" I called out to the man who was somewhere in the house.

"I'm here, darling."

Following his voice, I walked into the kitchen where he was making food. As I walked up to him, my arms wrapped around his waist from behind in a hug. The musky scent of him filled my nostrils, calming me down and easing the pain caused by the memories of my mother. He turned around to face me, the bacon in the frypan making sizzling sounds.

"Is something wrong?" His eyes were filled with worry.

"Everything's alright."

After giving me a suspicious look, he hugged me and kissed my forehead. I rested my head against his chest, feeling his heart beat hard against my ear.

Something was up. I did not know what.

He gave me a smile, but it didn't quite reach his eyes. It wasn't the genuine smile he had given me the past months. Dread gripped my stomach.

The food was once again the focus of his attention, and he resumed preparing it. "I will tell you when the food is ready."

"Alright," I whispered and walked into the dining room to wait for him with a book in my hands.

There was a heavy feeling inside me, an instinct in my gut telling me something wasn't right. I didn't know what it was, and the future terrified me.

Asher came with the food, and we ate in silence. He said nothing to me, just occasionally cast me a smile that didn't feel genuine. Everything seemed so unusual, he wasn't himself. The Asher I knew talked with a smile on his lips during every meal we shared, the smile glimmering in his eyes, making him even more handsome. The Asher I knew was happier, light-hearted, a fighter.

My fighter.

The past few months he had been alright, he had been happier. Could it all have been a façade?

My stomach dropped to the floor at the thought, and panic made the food come up in my mouth again. I forced it down, swallowing, and drank from the orange juice.

There had to be a reasonable explanation.

"Is something wrong, Ash?"

He stopped eating midway, just stared at me in disbelief. "Everything's alright, darling."

He used my own words against me.

There was something in his eyes. An aura I could not describe, they were gloomier than usual, darker than normal.

Seeing that my hands were shaking, I brought them under the table and glanced at Asher as he ate. Not a single word was said to me after that.

Something was definitely wrong.

In his eyes there was dullness, no longer were they shining bright with vividness. No longer did they warm me like a comfortable blanket on a cold winter's day. No longer was there life behind his eyes.

What had happened?

I walked up to Asher and wrapped my arms around him in a hug. "Love, please tell me what's wrong. I know something is wrong." I begged him, as I couldn't stand the silence he created, couldn't stand that he shut me out after months of letting me in.

"Nothing is wrong," his voice was monotone.

I saw the agony in his eyes, the pain. In that instant, I felt all the sounds around me getting numb, swirling, and swirling until only crust remained. A havoc of feelings crumbled until nothing was left of me, as if my essence had disappeared. Nothing was left but dread.

Horrifying, breath-stealing dread.

The realization made me numb, a turmoil inside my own head. He had hidden everything from me. He had hidden his feelings from me, wanting me to be happy, not wanting me to worry.

How could I have been so stupid for not realizing he was feeling down too? How the fuck could I have assumed everything was alright, when it clearly wasn't?

Tears trickled down my cheeks, and I gave him another hug. Guilt pressed down on me, making me desire to fall down a deep hole, and be buried alive so that I wouldn't feel this pain anymore.

I thought I had helped him with his demons, as he had helped me. All along he had pretended to be fine, all of that to see me happy. The happiest people were sometimes the ones who hid their pain well, so no one knew they were suffering.

"I am so sorry," I whispered against his chest, my voice quivering.

His body trembled as he held me. When my eyes landed on him, I saw his tears. Red-rimmed eyes adorned his face.

"I am so sorry for not realizing."

"It's not your fault, darling." He rasped, hugging me tighter, holding me against his warm embrace.

I wiped away his tears, looked him straight in his eyes. "I am here, okay? Please tell me when things are off. I will be here for you the same way you were here for me. I will help you fight, okay? We will fight together. I will walk down the battle line for you."

His body trembled against mine, holding me as if he never wanted to let go.

And the guilt draped over me even more.

ASHER

SILENCE PENETRATED MY EARS. The past few months, I had been happy. Happy with Aurora. She made me feel things no one had ever made me feel, she eased the pain inside of me. Aurora had become my anchor, the only reason I made it through the days. Partly why I made sure she had everything she ever wanted– she deserved the world.

There were still things inside of me that needed to disappear for me to be truly happy. Seeing her care for me so deeply had made me cry out in agony, to know she was there for me was something so beautiful. Aurora was my everything, but I couldn't give her more than my heart if I only had half a heart.

Some days, it felt like I would never heal from the pain, from the trauma my childhood had caused me. Then I looked at Aurora and saw how she stood strong and confident. She had survived hell, and yet she was still alive. I adored her, but not everyone had the strength to survive.

After sharing a passionate kiss, I had told her I needed some space, which was why I was in my office.

The picture before me was one I never wanted to see again.

Breathe in, breathe out, my brain tried to tell my lungs. But it was too late.

The feeling was there, taking over every part of my body. All I focused on was the photograph of the horrible person holding a little boy. The boy had chocolate brown hair and a cute smile on his lips. While staring at the picture, I clenched my fists and tightened my jaw. If only looks could kill.

Breathe in, breathe out.

Though it didn't work, because the feeling only intensified. A feeling so strong, so overwhelming that it could take over my entire body. My hands tightly held the photograph, which was framed in a brown—and so damn ugly—frame. Glass surrounded it, and I knew that soon the glass would be on the floor in a thousand pieces. And there was nothing I could do to stop it, to stop the feeling that took over.

The darkness.

I knew deep down that everything I had built with the girl I had fallen in love with would disappear. And there was nothing I could do about it.

It was like seeing myself through the third person. In my head, I could see myself sitting on the chair in my office with that damn photo in my hands. The knuckles stained white from my forceful grip. *Breathe!* I tried to shout to myself, but it was in vain.

My feelings completely took over, and before I knew it, the frame of the picture was broken. Glass shattered on the carpet, my hands soaked in blood, and with them, I ripped up the happy picture of the family that had ended in pure fucking tragedy. My feet planted themselves on the floor next to the shards of glass and with everything I had, I screamed out loud. My emotions burst forth in a roar.

I needed to fucking get rid of the anger!

In third-person view, I saw myself kicking the chair I had been sitting on just a few seconds earlier. My hand dragged over everything on the desk, sending the objects flying to the floor just like the frame of the photograph.

That damn photograph.

"Fuck you, dad!" I spat out.

The books on my bookshelves were torn to the ground. All my energy was spent on hitting the wall, which resulted in more bloody knuckles. Somewhere behind me, a door opened, and a gasp from a woman was heard.

Aurora.

"Ash?" Her voice was way too squeaky, howling in my ears.

The bookshelves in my room shook as my hands hit them. That fucking photograph. *Get the image out of my head!*

A warm and soft hand was placed on my bare arm, and with a quick movement, I lunged around Aurora. She tumbled backward, a harsh thud was heard as her bottom hit the wooden floor.

I didn't want to hurt her, but I couldn't stop the darkness that was taking over. *I don't fucking want to make her suffer.*

"Do not touch me!" I yelled at her.

The anger grew faster and faster, the rage surging through my veins. Somewhere deep within me was a voice, one that said *"Help her, don't you dare hurt her."* I didn't want to hurt her. I didn't want darkness to control me. I didn't want flames to surge under my skin.

"Ash!" cried the woman on the floor, and my gaze directed at her.

I noticed the tears forming in the corners of her eyes, and deep down within me, I felt such shame and guilt for hurting her. Yet I couldn't control my body.

That fucking image.

"Get out!" I screamed at her with everything I had, needing her to get as far away as possible from me. She couldn't stay, there was no way she could survive my wrath if she did. I needed her to stay alive, and I couldn't control the darkness.

All of my actions were because of that picture. Dad, the one person who had been supposed to be there for me when Mary had been murdered in front of my eyes. Yet he had been the one who'd blamed me for her death. And the darkness made me take out my revenge on everyone in my path.

What is happening to me?

"What are you even doing here?" I roared as I clenched my jaw. "Stay away from me."

"After what happened, I thought—" She stopped mid-sentence, her eyes glistening.

"For god's sake Aurora, leave!"

Screaming and thrashing my hands around, I tried to control my emotions. But the darkness drew me in closer by the second. I couldn't stand still, the anger only grew inside me. It grew stronger every second. The woman still sitting on the floor irritated me.

Her voice filled with shock when she said, "You're my only home."

And inside of me, my heart broke. Because she was my only home, a home I had to move away from. A home I had to abandon. It was a type of pain you felt when your only home had burned down, with all its personal belongings in it.

"Get. Out," I spat out in a desperate attempt to get her to leave me alone.

Why couldn't she see she needed to leave me? How could she be so fucking stupid?

"Ash, what are you saying?"

I clicked my tongue as I stared at her, who was at the moment trying to get up from the floor.

"For fuck's sake, just get out!" My hands threw down the lamp from the table, it broke into a thousand of pieces on the carpet.

Why didn't she fucking leave? Why couldn't she see I was the villain in her story?

Everyone in my staff probably heard everything going on in my office at the moment and to be honest, I didn't care one bit. Something clicked in her eyes, a type of realization of what I had been saying.

"Let me be here for you," she yelled in desperation, making me even more irritated.

"Why don't you see it? You know what I am capable of doing. I wouldn't be able to live with myself if I were to do something to you again."

Aurora stood up from the floor, all too cautiously. "Ash—" she started, holding up her hands in front of her, "Fight through it. Fight through the darkness."

She didn't realize. The constriction inside my ribcage made it impossible to breathe regularly.

"Don't you think I have tried? I have lived with this darkness inside of me for over ten years!"

Tears streamed down her face, and sympathy showed on her face. I didn't want any sympathy.

"LEAVE!" I screamed at her for the last time, turning my attention to the empty desk. I threw the chair across the room. It landed only a foot away from her.

I could see the fright in her expression—she feared me, something I never wanted her to feel, but there was darkness inside.

She turned around, looking all heartbroken and like a lost puppy. She didn't look like herself, and I despised that. My feelings echoed hers as I realized I had crushed her.

The darkness was eating me up alive.

Chapter 29
Her

SOBBING UNCONTROLLABLY, I SOMEHOW managed to get into my room. Both my hands and knees were shaking. As I plummeted to the ground, my body curled up into a ball. Never before had I felt as defeated as I did then.

Everything we had built together, our relationship, our trust in each other, everything had been broken into a million pieces and crumbled in front of me. My heart had to follow suit. I couldn't understand what had happened, what had gone wrong.

After he had told me he needed space, I had gone to my room to read. While searching for Asher, I had heard him scream from the top of his lungs. I had wanted to be there for him, to help him through the pain. But some people were too far gone to be saved. And that hurt me more than anything.

I knew I had to fight for him, as he had fought for me.

After all the time we had spent together, I never imagined a day would come when he would hurt me again. Tears streamed down my cheeks as I closed my eyes. I let them fall free, feeling as if I deserved them.

"Who are you?" The older man in front of me asked my mother.

"I'm your sister!" said Mother to the man, whom I now recognized to be my uncle.

"I don't have a sister. Who are you?" My brain couldn't comprehend why my uncle didn't know who my mother was.

"What is your name?" asked my mother instead of answering his question.

"I am Leonard." Recognition ignited in her eyes as she slowly nodded her head in acknowledgment.

"Hello, Leonard. This is my child, Aurora."

Why did my uncle say his name was Leonard when it clearly wasn't?

"Nice to meet you, Aurora." My uncle bent down to his knees so that he was on the same level as me. He reached out his hand and took mine. Confusion struck me. Why didn't my uncle know who I was? And why didn't my mother tell him I was his niece?

Later that evening, I had overheard my mother talking on the phone with someone and mentioning something about a mental disorder. My small brain hadn't known what that was. And before my mother had been able to get my uncle any professional help, it had been too late. My uncle had been found a few days later, dead in the bathtub.

A loud gasp released from my throat as I fought for air, my heart feeling as if I was dying. The tears tasted salty on my tongue. *A mental disorder.*

As if caught in a whirlwind, my thoughts swirled around in my head. At that point, I was determined to learn more about it. I quickly grabbed the computer I had packed inside the bag of books we brought from Grimhill Manor. When I opened the screen, a notification came up, telling me I had to connect to Wi-Fi. Luckily, no password was required to join it. It took me a while to find what I wanted as I hadn't used a computer before–I had only seen Frederick use one. Eventually, I found the search bar and tried to google the disorder. However, I couldn't remember what my uncle's disorder had been.

Keep an eye on the behavior of anyone you suspect may be suffering from a mental illness. In all cases, it's important to keep yourself, those around you, as well as the person in question, safe. No risks should be taken, and professional help shall be sought immediately if the situation is urgent.

Mental illness can present with different signs and symptoms, depending on the disorder, circumstances, and other factors. There can be a range of effects on emotions, thoughts, and behaviors as a result of mental illness. Some symptoms you might need to look out for are:

- *Excessive senses of guilt, worry, or fear*
- *Mood swings with extremes of highs and lows*
- *Feelings of excessive anger, hostility, or violence*

My brain stuttered for a second. Sunlight shone into the room through the curtains and unexpectedly, my surroundings became much brighter than previously. I needed to run to the toilet in the corridor outside my room. Upon entering the bathroom, the first thing I did was turn on the cold water on the faucet. Using my hands, I splashed water over my face. The cold subsided, allowing me to breathe properly again.

Some days, cold water helped me cool down, and extinguished the fire threatening to burn me up from the inside.

"Mood changes." My voice echoed as a memory emerged from behind my eyelids.

"I'm sorry, Sir," Frederick replied and lowered his gaze to the floor, avoiding the man's stare.

"Oh dear, an apology will solve nothing." The creepy man's mood changed in the blink of an eye.

As I shifted my weight to the other leg, I glanced down at the floor, attempting to block out everything around me.

The moment I realized the man had grabbed something from his jacket's inner pocket, I heard a scream. The item the man held in his hand was black and familiar to me. Something Frederick used every single month. The man was holding a revolver and pointed it at Frederick's forehead.

"P-please, don't kill me," he whispered. "I beg you!" Frederick lowered his gaze to the floor, and I watched as his throat gulped.

The man's smirk grew wider and a deep, rough chuckle escaped his throat before he killed the man in front of him.

"Excessive anger," my voice whispered when I thought of what was written on Google.

"For God's sake Aurora, leave!" he screamed and thrashed his hands around.

My voice filled with shock when I said, "You're my only home."

"Get. Out," he spat out in a cold tone.

"Ash, what are you saying?"

He couldn't be telling me to leave him, could he?

He stared at me as I was trying to get up from the ground, and he clicked his tongue.

"For fuck's sake, just get out!" His hands threw down the lamp from the table, causing it to break into a thousand of pieces on the carpet.

Tears streamed down my face, but I refused to leave him alone. I knew that he, deep inside, needed me to stay with him. Under the fucked up part of him, he wanted me. I just knew it, but Asher was far too gone in his headspace.

"LEAVE!" He screamed at me for the last time, turning his attention to the empty desk.

He threw the chair across the room, it landed only a foot away from me. The fright filled me, and I became scared of what he would do to me. His anger was so strong, nothing seemed to get through to him.

The more flashbacks I had, the more certain I became. The man who hurt me was not the Asher I had fallen for. The man who played horror games with me was not the same person who made love to me, cared for me, made me feel safe.

No, the man who made me breakfast earlier was hurt, and he could only express anger as the dullness and agony took over. The Asher I knew, the Asher who loved me, was not a man who expressed his anger so destructively. The Asher I knew was kind-hearted and cared for everyone.

He was the man I had fallen for. The man I loved more than life itself.

He, who was in his office at that moment, had darkness surrounding him. The darkness that had grown within him after everyone in his life either had failed him, blamed him for the death of his sister's murder, or left him when he'd needed them the most.

My heart broke for the little boy he had been before, the one who had lost everything. It bled for the man he had grown up to be. Nothing I did would ever be enough to heal him. I had eased his demons as he had eased mine, but one could only fully heal from professional help.

And then my blood ran cold.

I broke out in a cold sweat as my eyes stared at the bathroom door I had left slightly open. His voice could be heard downstairs as he yelled at someone. There was a clear sense of anger and frustration in his voice. If I had to guess, I would say that it was me he was shouting for. I strained my ears, and it felt like my blood would freeze to ice when I heard the stairs leading upstairs creak. Someone hurried up the stairs in silence.

Everything happened so fast after that.

I threw the bathroom door open as I rushed over to my room. Running over to a chair—which was next to the bed—I slid it back under the handle, making it impossible for anyone to open the door. In the midst of my heart rupturing, I felt a burning sensation in my chest. My room and its door were approached by footsteps outside. Upon hearing someone breathing outside my door, I felt my heart skip a beat. My hand flew to my mouth to stifle a scream that threatened to escape from me.

"Open the door, Dolly," hissed the voice outside, and I felt tears spill from the corners of my eyes.

That old nickname made my heart break into a thousand pieces, as if it was made of fragile glass. He had not called me that for months, and now everything we had was slowly falling apart. The walls I had torn down around him had regrown by themself like ivies. An object scraped against the door.

"We're going to play one last game."

It didn't take me long to understand what the man was trying to say outside my door.

He wanted to kill me.

Yet he didn't, for deep inside, I knew he loved me.

Tears ran down my cheeks in a rush and I realized that my heart was breaking more and more with every second that passed. Because the man outside was not *my* Asher. The man outside was a man who was fueled by anger and only anger. A man who hated everyone for what had happened after his sister died. Something had gone wrong.

Earlier when I had stepped a foot into his office, I had spotted a photograph of an older man, and the frame was lying broken on the floor, surrounded by shards of glass.

That must've been what triggered his emotions, for I did not know what else it could've been.

Everything had been so good, for months everything had been perfect. It had been too good to be true.

You need to stay strong for him, Aurora.

Yes, he was the one for me. I would not give up.

We'd had so many good moments, created memories together, and it hurt so fucking much to lose that. While I had thought he was fine, I now realized the slightest trigger from his past could make him lapse into oblivion. Slip away from me.

And he had slipped away from me.

I had lost the love of my life to a deep, evil and spiraling black hole, and I did not know how to drag him out of there.

"You are my doll and you are behaving very rudely right now." His voice was too calm.

With tears still falling down my cheeks, my hand began to become soaked with tears as I covered my mouth. He couldn't hear my raspy breaths, nor could he hear the way I inhaled sharply to breathe in air. Neither of us said anything, but the breathing outside could still be heard.

The pain I felt over that Asher—the darkness living inside *my* Asher—wanted to kill me, felt like falling into a cactus. Like my heart had been punctured a million times, over and over again by the thorns of a plant that grew in the deserts. As if my body was stuffed with a thousand needles. The pain felt unbearable.

The more seconds that passed, the more the stinging pain faded and was replaced with numbness. An overwhelming feeling of numbness filled me as I realized what needed to be done.

The man out there had saved me, first by saving me and taking me away from Grimhill Manor, and then he had released me from the shackles of that house forever when we had burned it down together. My mind had been at peace ever since then, when I realized Frederick would never return to torture me again.

That none of them would.

The only one who could, and had, hurt me now was the man outside my door. Even so, I knew he could be saved because somewhere beneath those dull, amber-colored eyes were the warm eyes I had fallen in love with. He was not a lost cause.

And it was my turn to help him.

Asher had saved me when I didn't know I needed to be saved. He had given me a place to stay, a place to call home, and he had helped me rebuild my ability to trust. He had loved me when no one else did. He had made me feel *alive* and as if I mattered. It was my turn to help him overcome his past so that we—in the future—could have our happily ever after, like in the books.

Asher's breathing outside faded, along with the footsteps, and I knew I only had a few minutes to do the thing that needed to be done. The chair was secured under the door handle and I opened the computer that I brought with me. Since I didn't own a phone, I searched on the computer for a phone number, my heart pounded hard in my chest. There was something jabbing at my skin, perhaps it was an insect or just my crippling fear. All I knew was that a brusque jolt of something spread through me, like a poison ready to take my heart and squeeze it apart. The feeling made my hands shake, and my throat constrict.

When I searched on Google, I couldn't find anything.

Then it dawned on me. During my trips to the bathroom, I had noticed Asher's landline was in the hallway some distance from my room. Again, I listened to see if anyone was outside, but neither a person nor a sound could be heard.

I slipped out into the corridor slowly and silently, removing the chair from the door. With ease, I reached the landline on tiptoes. It was about being quick and not attracting his attention.

With every second that passed, I felt my heart shrinking even more. I made the call I should have made a long time ago, using the number I had found a few weeks ago in Asher's office. For no matter how much I tried, I couldn't help him when the demons had engraved themselves on his soul. If only I had called that number earlier, maybe he wouldn't be so broken. My life had been one full of torture, just like his had been. I hadn't even realized my life had been hell until he had made me live in heaven.

The man with the chocolate brown hair that was always tousled and his mesmerizing amber-colored eyes.

The man who stole my breath away.

"Auroraaa," sang a voice from the stairs, and I headed to meet him.

This is something I have to do, I reminded myself. Inhaling deeply, I approached him.

With a smile so as not to seem rude, I asked, "Yes, what is it?"

"We're going to play one last game," Asher repeated the sentence he had previously uttered.

Answering him, I nodded my head. "How fun!" I exclaimed with far too much enthusiasm.

Asher cocked his eyebrows and looked suspiciously at me before purring.

"What do you want to play?" With all the will I could find within me, I answered without a tremor in my voice.

"You'll see, come with me."

He grabbed my hand and pulled me down the stairs. The stairs I probably never would walk down again, through the hallways with the lit candles and the ancestors looking down at me. It all felt surreal, and my brain switched to its fight-or-flight mode.

You have to fight.

We walked out of the manor we were in. It felt as if the gargoyles standing in the hallway stared at me as I left, their gazes following my movement in a suspicious manner. The tall trees creating the dense forest stood side by side, like an army preventing me from running away.

My hair, which covered parts of my face, helped to conceal my fear. By keeping my face down, I tried not to show how pale I was. After having heard an object scrape against my door earlier, I knew Asher had a sharp object with him.

Please, please hurry, I silently prayed.

He led me to a part of the yard outside that was paved. From there, you could see the forest more clearly, and the cold wind blew more strongly. The house was still visible. It cast shadows over us, like a monster waiting to drag us into its lair and kill us. The ground consisted of cobblestones in a fine pattern, and I wondered how I had never been over there before. Maybe it was because it was located by the scarier part of the forest. The darkness of it made me feel unsafe, like anyone could jump out and scare me.

When my eyes landed on the cobblestoned area, my blood froze to something colder than ice. What I saw was terrifying. An intersection of white squares and black lines marked the middle of the road. There was something all too familiar with it, and I was overcome with dread.

A hopscotch area.

It was a fucking hopscotch area.

My eyelids were visibly swollen as I recalled memories I thought I had forgotten. My eyeballs were itching, craving to force away the memories. My mind didn't want to remember what had happened at Grimhill Manor.

"We're going to play here." There was a creepy smirk on his face again, the one I hadn't seen for many months. His hands clenched and clapped like a small child.

Just like all those months ago.

"You are going to jump, and if you make the slightest mistake, you will be punished with this." He pulled something out of his jacket pocket.

A sharp kitchen knife.

My heart flew up to the pit of my throat, and my mouth became dry. *Hurry, hurry,* I prayed inwardly.

"Let the game begin, Dolly."

A hint of déjà vu filled me, almost causing me to lose my breath and fall backward. It was the exact same sentence he had said to me the first day I had arrived here, before the first game he had played with me.

Slowly, I walked up to the hopscotch squares. Any time I could gain at the moment would be heaven for me. My attention was drawn to the surroundings as I approached the start of the area. The branches of the trees swayed around us and the birds chirped as if it were an ordinary day. For them, the day was like any other.

With darting eyes, I tried to see if anyone was approaching Thorington Manor, but so far I could see no one.

Come on, where are you?

"Begin the game, Dolly," Asher's voice sounded irritated, as if he was impatient.

I swallowed hard and hopped a square. When I was in the middle of the square, I took a deep breath and hopped on one leg to the next and then the next. My time at Grimhill Manor had taught me something about jumping, and my survival instinct told me I could never fail.

On the fourth hop, I lost my balance and put my foot on the line, my heel was inside the box and my toes outside of it. A chuckle came from the man guarding me, and I heard his footsteps approaching. Concentrating on breathing, I closed my eyes.

Fuck, fuck, fuck! I wanted to scream, but my throat was too dry from anxiety.

Just like the first time I had seen Asher at Grimhill Manor.

"You have such bad luck, Dolly," he laughed and dangled the knife in front of me. My neck was grabbed, and the knife was thrust against my flesh.

One last game.

He knew I would lose the game. It had come to the point where he'd had enough of me, and now he was going to kill me as a punishment. The tears ran down my cheeks for what seemed like the hundredth time that day. I knew that somewhere deep inside those dull eyes was the man I loved, the man who was *mine*. Though it wasn't the man standing before me at that moment. No, that man was about to cut my throat. And *my* Asher would never do that, he would never hurt a fly.

"You've been an absolutely perfect plaything, a perfect doll to play with," he whispered in my ear.

I knew that if that was *my* Asher, I'd have goosebumps all over my body. If that was *my* Asher, I would have enjoyed the feeling of his breath against my skin. I would have felt the need in my body.

But it wasn't *my* Asher.

It was a man who felt nothing but rage toward everyone he saw and knew. Darkness had devoured him.

"Why are you doing this?" I asked with as much steadiness as I could muster.

"Why? Isn't that obvious?" He laughed a humorless laugh without emotion before adding, "This is my way of making up for all the years I've been beaten for my sister's death! This is my way of getting revenge!" he shouted, and I felt somehow sympathetic towards him.

This man was one who knew nothing but that—his revenge. He took out his anger on someone who didn't deserve it, someone who had never hurt anyone before.

Just like his father had done to him.

Because I knew Asher was innocent. He hadn't killed his sister. Yet he had been blamed for her death. It was always easier to blame someone else.

"Asher, I know you think you need to do this, but please think this through." I put up my hands in the air as if to show him I wasn't a threat.

He pointed the knife toward me and screamed, "I am not the only one who should suffer! He took everything from me."

I watched as his eyes darkened, and I could no longer see the warmth behind them. I could no longer sense the Asher I loved. He was slowly slipping further away from me.

Where the hell are they? Hurry! I screamed inside my head.

When I felt the sharp blade of the knife against my throat, I realized I would never survive this. The man I loved was about to kill me, to slit my throat while blinded by rage and darkness.

The man I loved held a knife to my throat, ready to push it into my skin any second and feel the rip of my flesh under his touch. Even so, it wasn't the man I loved who controlled the actions of the body.

It was the darkness.

The sirens could be heard nearby, and as several cars approached the house, I blinked away my tears.

"Drop the knife before we shoot you," a feminine voice shouted whose face I couldn't see.

"What the hell?" Asher let go of me and looked around confused.

I fell to the ground as he removed the grip and soon two men in uniform were behind Asher, holding him in a tight grip.

The familiar smell of flowers helped me get up to standing position.

"Everlee," I whispered as tears ran down my face, my knees trembled and my face became pale with nausea and fear. It was difficult to stand steadily, but Everlee held me tight in her embrace.

"Come here," said a man's voice that could only belong to one person.

"Draven."

He helped support my body along with Everlee, and the relief of having both of them there made the pain inside my chest ease. Two men in uniforms held Asher in a firm grip.

"Are you okay?" the woman who had called out to Asher earlier asked me.

'Eliza' read the name tag pinned to her blue uniform. My head nodded despite the fact that I wasn't feeling well. The pain inside my heart broke it into a thousand pieces, as if cut by a knife, leaving shards of glass cutting through my insides. They made my organs bleed, causing my heart to ache even more.

During his screams and growls, Asher kicked his legs around and cursed. His dark eyes were filled with rage as he stared at me, as if he hated me. I felt like screaming at the knife twisting inside of me, causing my already broken heart to crumble more. He watched me as if he hated me.

He hated me.

The man I loved fucking *hated* me.

It hurt more than anything could ever describe, but I needed to stay strong for him, the Asher who loved me. I needed to make it through everything, to fight through the pain, to stay strong. I had to do it for him, because that was what I was best at; taking care of the people I loved. In order to save the man consumed by darkness, I had to keep my head above water.

He couldn't get me anymore.

After letting go of Everlee and Draven, I took four steps in Asher's direction, something that left my whole body shaking. Most of all, I wanted to sink under the surface, never to appear again. The officers were behind him and it took me several swallows before I dared to speak out loud, the knot in my throat tightening.

"I love you, I truly do. I fell in love with you when we had that picnic by the tree, and I fell even deeper when we were at Grimhill Manor. I started loving you the time we first kissed each other and I've loved you even more after each time you've made love to me, several times." My voice was croaky from suppressed sobs.

"I know you are overtaken by darkness. You are Asher, a man who is broken because of his awful and heartbreaking past. A man who was abused by his father, a man whose mother wasn't there for him when he needed her the most. A man who lost both his sister and his brother. I know you are a man filled with only rage and hatred for everyone around you. Someone who wants revenge for what happened to him when he was just an innocent child. But I also know that there is another side to you, Asher," I took a shaky breath before I continued talking.

"You can do this Asher, I know you are strong. Do not let the darkness define who you are, for you are not the villain in my story. You are my hero, and now I will be your heroine. I love you, I truly do, though I can't live like this. I can't trip on my toes around you, in fear that the darkness will come forth when I'm with you. I am so sorry. I have no doubt that with proper professional help, you will be able to get rid of the darkness. I know you will. Because you are strong, the strongest person I have ever met. I love you so much. There will come a time when you won't be filled with rage all the time. I am so sorry for this."

I bled the salt of my soul through my stinging eyes, it poured and raced down my cheeks. It was like a river escaping its dam, and my hand wiped away the wetness on my skin. When I finished talking, my bottom lip quivered in an agonizing manner.

How could he be there, but not there at the same time? It fucking hurt.

"I hate you! I will fucking murder you! I hate you. I hate you. I hate you. Fuck you!" the man in front of me shouted as he was dragged away by the police behind him.

Everlee embraced me, like the sister I never had. She stroked my head, whispering soothing things in my ear, making sure I was okay. Draven embraced us two in his huge arms, ensuring me I would survive, that the man I loved would survive. They let me be their shoulders to cry on as I watched the man that had stolen my heart being pulled away from me.

"And I love you," I whispered through the sobs, watching Asher disappear in the police car.

Epilogue
Her

I HAD NEVER INTENDED to fall in love with anyone, but then I met you. Falling in love with you wasn't my intention. Then there was the way you smiled at me and the way you looked at me like I was worth something. There was the way you made me feel, and the way you eased the pain in my chest.

I never intended to fall in love with you, but I did–I fell deeply and madly in love with you. And I knew there was no turning back. Once I had fallen down the well, there was no way to climb up. Still, I didn't want to escape the well. The well kept me close to you.

There would never be a time in my life when I forgot the day they took you from me. The sunlight cast a dim light on your eyes, eyes that were void of life. There was nothing behind them when I told you I loved you. My heart broke into a thousand pieces and my surroundings whirled as if I was in a spiral.

The worst thing wasn't the way I still held onto the hope of getting you back. It wasn't the way the tears stained my puffy cheeks. It wasn't even the way I saw them drag you away from me while I screamed that I loved you more than life itself.

No.

It was the way your eyes looked so dim in the sunlight, the way your eyes didn't radiate the same love and warmth as they had hours before. The worst thing of it all was that while I tried to hold onto the feeling of still loving you, you looked at me with those dim eyes and uttered those words I never wanted to hear.

The worst thing was the way you said it, the way you spat those words out as if they were poisonous. It was the way you screamed with such rage that you hated me, and at that moment, I believed you. Your eyes said everything. You were gone from me, you had slipped away from me. And I knew I had lost you. You had been the one to save me, but I couldn't do the same for you.

The worst thing was the way you threatened to murder me, to rip my skin apart under your touch.

And yet, I still held on.

Two years have passed since that day...

My heart was pounding as I stood outside Rosewood psychiatry. Nerves filled my body and almost made me bend forward to throw up. The lump in my stomach felt like a heavy stone being pushed down inside me, causing my lungs to give way. It wasn't that I didn't want to be there, because I did. It was just that the mere sight of the place made the hair on my arms stand. It was because I was going to meet him.

The man I never gave up hope for.

Taking a deep breath, I took the first step closer to the gates. My white tank top tightened around my stomach and breasts, making them appear fuller. The skirt matched the shirt I wore and was pleated to give more volume. The outfit was perfect for the day. An outfit that was so different from what I used to wear two years ago.

The glorious summer sun shone down on me where I walked. The sound of my heels clicking on the ground echoed.

"Remember to breathe and take it easy. Count to ten if you get overwhelmed by anxiety or nervousness," I replayed the sentence my psychologist had told me before I'd headed out to Rosewood.

Two years ago, he had left me, taking a part of my heart with him. He had left me feeling completely and utterly lonely, defeated. It had been then that I'd decided I had to make this work, to give us a future. With the money he had given me access to and the help of Josephine, I'd hired a company. The money was something I had never had a use for, not until he'd left.

The manor could not be a place he would recognize, for I knew his trauma would return if he saw the house again. It would make his memory relapse, and the staff at Rosewood psychiatry had told me to avoid that at all costs. They had also forbidden me from having any contact with him.

I knew how much the place meant to him, and the fact that the manor was old gave me another reason to renovate it. It was the same place, the same house, but looked entirely different.

All so that he would have a home to come back to, a place to build our future.

It had been a year ago since I had decided to take control of my life and consulted a psychologist. Losing him had been too much for my psyche to handle, and the nightmares had appeared every night. My life had been miserable, and I had not known what to do. The feeling of giving up filled me every single day, every waking hour.

Then I remembered *him*.

My psychologist, Maya, had been instrumental in helping me cope over the past year. Through her help, I had been able to handle my anxiety and begin the process of recovering from my horrible past.

Deep inside, I knew that what Asher did for me was the major part of my recovery. Burning down the house with him had killed a part of those demons inside of me. During the past year, Maya had given me the tools I needed to process and cope with what had happened at Grimhill Manor. Sessions twice a week had been needed, and every day I had done some practices. She had been like the mother I had never had.

I took another deep breath and counted to ten with my eyes closed, like she had advised me to do. As I swallowed forcefully, my throat bobbed, and the knot eased. When my eyes opened again, I made the last few steps to the gates. There was a large fence surrounding the building, making the gates the only entry and exit points.

My name and the purpose of my visit were given to the guards before they permitted me to enter the property. There were several processes I had to pass through before I could meet with the case manager.

After I got through the gates, I had to go through security, sign lots of paperwork, and restate my purpose of being there. The entire process made me realize the place was highly secure. Then, I sat in the waiting room with several other people, many of whom were relatives of other enrolled patients there.

"Ms. Aurora?" a female voice called out and when I looked up, a heavily built woman with a floral patterned short dress and jet black hair met me.

My skirt straightened in a flash as I stood up and followed Mrs. Dalton. Upon entering, we found ourselves in a cramped, small room. There was only one desk in the middle of the room, as well as a laptop. The desk was accompanied by a chair on each side.

"Sit down," the woman instructed, and I obeyed.

There was an air of trustworthiness about her that made you not want to argue with her. A stack of papers piled upside down on the desk in front of her, which she picked up.

"We're about to go over some details before you're ready to move on," she said, and I could hear the American accent in her English pronunciation.

While feeling uncertain, I nodded my head, which she did not notice. With her hands, she picked up the papers and checked the first one. It was impossible to tell whether or not she was kind. A sour expression covered her face most of the time, as if she hated the world and everyone in it.

"The patient has made a lot of progress over the past year. The patient's psychologists had a hard time identifying the underlying disorder. It is still hard to tell. However, we do know the patient has been, and is, suffering from heavy depression. An investigation regarding bipolar disorder has been going on during the patient's time here. There is no diagnosis of that disorder yet. The patient has undergone something called psychotherapy, a type of therapy that includes talk therapy and counseling. Together with his psychologist, the patient has worked through the reasons for various triggers of his rage episodes and talked about what these mean. They have talked about what may have caused the disorder in the first place."

Although Mrs. Dalton read the papers in a monotonous and dull tone in her voice, the information was important for me to listen to. She flipped through papers and continued reading.

"The patient has undergone hypnotherapy, which is another form of therapy. Hypnosis can help bring out repressed memories. The patient and psychologist have decided together which medication the patient should take to get the most beneficial results. Together, they have talked about how the patient should handle situations when rage overtakes and how to get pulled out of the darkness. For the first few months, the patient was unable to interact with other patients, as more aggressive sides developed. Now the patient is on the road to recovery and can handle his disorder more easily, and he is no longer as violent."

After adjusting her round glasses, Mrs. Dalton put away the papers she had already reviewed before moving on to the next pile. "This is a booklet that comes from the patient's own psychologist who has written a personal message to you."

The papers were handed over to me and I accepted them with shaking hands.

Dear Ms. Aurora. Below is essential information that should be read as soon as possible.

"The patient is diagnosed with depression. He has been going through an investigation regarding bipolar disorder, which is a mental health condition marked by extreme mood swings that include emotional highs and lows. I am together with the patient, still investigating if this disorder applies to the patient.

The patient's diagnosis arose from trauma as a child. Something you and the patient should talk about in privacy as I am bound by confidentiality.

The violent episodes the patient has suffered can be a type of coping mechanism. This means that the person in question shuts down emotions and more or distances himself from events that are considered too traumatic. Together with the patient, I have worked through what triggers the patient's outbursts. You, Ms. Aurora, should avoid knowingly talking about the patient's childhood or showing pictures from the patient's childhood unless the patient asks for it. The patient has been prescribed antidepressants and anti-anxiety medicine to be taken every day at the same time. Henceforth, the patient needs to come in once a week for a therapy session. Please find my contact information attached below in case you ever need to contact me.

Sincerely, Camila Wilson."

Nodding in agreement, I thought about all the therapy I had to undergo in the past year to cope with everything that had happened during my childhood. The fact that both he and I had improved in two years comforted me and made the time apart worthwhile. When he had left me, two years ago, I had been completely devastated and had not known where to go. Over the course of a month, I had suffered anxiety and panic attacks as a result of the overwhelming emotions. When I had reached that point in my life, I'd realized I had to take control of it. In the course of the year, I had received several tips and advice from a psychologist who helped me.

It was a huge improvement to be able to remember my childhood and Grimhill Manor without shrieking out loud in agony. During the past year, I'd realized how much I had changed. The girl I had been when I first got to know him was no longer the scared one I used to be. My self-confidence had improved. My smile spread across my face as I thought about it.

"Take these papers home," announced Mrs. Dalton and handed over the papers, which I folded to put in my purse.

After that, she gave me jars of medicine and a prescription that was meant for him. A faster heartbeat accompanied the passing of time. My fears and nervousness were growing as time approached, and I was both excited and terrified simultaneously.

Two entire years had passed.

Mrs. Dalton stood up and led me out of the cramped office we were in a second ago. In front of us stretched a long corridor with several doors on the sides leading into rooms. I heard my heels echo as we walked along the corridor, which was almost empty of people.

A girl and an older male in uniform talked as they came closer to us. The girl's hair reminded me of someone, and my heart leaped. She had copper shimmer hair, and when her gaze lifted, the forest green was visible. She stopped dead in her tracks, staring at me with a gaping mouth. I stopped too, leaving the male in uniform and Mrs. Dalton confused as to what was happening.

"A-Aurora?" she stuttered, her eyes calmer than I remembered, and her expression full of surprise.

I didn't know how to react, my body rooted in place. It was if someone had glued my feet to the floor, refusing to let me go. My brain told me to run as far away from there as possible, to stay rational. *She had tried to kill you.*

My heart wanted something else. Although dread seeped through me, filling every blood vessel with poison, making it impossible to focus on anything else than the human in front of me. She tried to come closer to me, but the man stopped her by holding out his hand.

"It's best we get you checked out now," he said as he cast a glance at me.

"I need to say something first." She spoke in a low tone, her gaze flickering nervously back and forth.

My eyebrow raised, and I stared at her skeptically. With my arms crossed, I awaited her response. She had tried to kill me, yet my heart wanted to listen to her. It wanted to give her a second chance.

"Cassia," I nodded my head to her, showing that she should speak before it was too late.

Seeing Cassia there surprised me, but then I remembered the day they told us she had been confined to Rosewood two years ago.

"I wasn't in the right mind. I'm sorry Aurora. I was fucked up by Frederick." Her gaze lowered in shame, her eyes glistening.

After hearing his name, I expected the pain in my heart to appear, but it didn't. Relief filled me as I nodded my head. "It's okay."

I had forgiven her, but I would never forget. He used people to manipulate them into being his obedient little dolls. And someone as young and naïve as Cassia would immediately fall for his act. She couldn't be blamed, and all I felt was peace, knowing she was fine. That she would be okay.

"We have to go now, Cassia," the male in uniform said and before they walked away, Cassia threw her arms around me in an attempt to a hug. My body stiffened, but I accepted the hug, not wanting to be seen as rude. A tight smile formed on my lips as I watched them walk away.

Social interactions were still something I hated, and a touch from any other than *him*, too. To say her hug made me uncomfortable was an understatement, but I was glad she got that off her chest.

I and Mrs. Dalton continued through the corridor and stood in front of a door at the far end.

"So, here's the patient's room. I will be back in ten minutes and help you discharge the patient," she announced, turned on her heel, and then walked away from me.

Standing in front of the door that led to a room for several seconds, I found myself frozen and paralyzed. To avoid collapsing from nerves, I took a deep breath to keep my legs from giving way under me. With shaky hands, I knocked on the door, heard a voice from inside, and gently pushed the door open.

That was the second I saw him again.

Standing before me was the man I loved.

The tears formed in my eyes, and for the first time in two years, I finally felt able to breathe again. Seeing his shy smile, I jumped into his arms and he embraced me. His scent found its way into my nostrils, a scent I hadn't felt in two years.

Therapy could not heal the hole in my heart that I'd had for a year. There was only one thing that could, and that was *him*.

He was the one who made me feel whole. He was the one who had taken my heart. For the first time in two years, I felt at home. And that was because of *him*.

Only ever him.

"Hey there, darling," he said in his dark and raspy voice. That voice I had missed more than anything else. The voice who made my skin tingle in anticipation, and made me relax in his arms. There had been a small part of me worrying about him not wanting me anymore, but as soon as I felt him against me, skin against skin, the feeling dissipated. *This was where I belonged.*

It was amazing to feel my body pressing against his, as if I were floating on top of the clouds. He still had his imposing muscles, and he was the same Asher as he had been before. Now his eyes were always warm, lingering around my soul like a shield of protection with a promise never to let go.

"Hi," I murmured against his chest with a soft smile on my lips.

Inhaling his scent through my nostrils, I closed my eyes. He smelled the same as he had two years ago. A masculine and musky fragrance. It was a scent that caught my breath and made me tingle.

Slowly, his fingers lifted my chin, allowing me to look at him. The feel of his skin against mine rekindled the sparks inside me. They had been dormant for two years. The love Asher showed me was unlike anything I had ever experienced before. He looked at me with the same intense look he always used to give me, but that one was full of love and warmth. His eyes were no longer clogged with dullness.

My heart skipped a beat as his head bent down to approach me. His breath felt lovely against my mouth and I enjoyed the minty smell of the toothpaste he used in the morning.

"My Aurora," he whispered, making my cheeks heat, turning a rosy color.

"My Asher," I whispered back before he finally lowered his lips to mine and caressed my mouth in a lingering kiss.

At that moment, it felt as if my world exploded into shards of molten light. It was the sweetness of the passion that ignited. His lips felt soft against mine, and they moved slowly in a romantic kiss. The taste of salt on my lips made me realize Asher was crying at that moment. Our tears mixed together in a perfect blend as our lips met each other in a long kiss. One that both needed. Taking a moment to look into my eyes, Asher broke the kiss.

"I have missed you so fucking much, darling."

I couldn't find my voice as I hiccuped from the tears, my chest aching at his words. The only thing I could do was nod frantically, letting him know I had missed him as well.

He grabbed my hand and laid it on the chest above his heart. "This is what you do to me, Aurora."

The tears continued to stream down my cheeks as I felt his heart beating faster and faster under my fingertips. The way he said it made my heart melt. More than he would ever understand. For hearing those words reminded me of our picnic by the tree. That day, I had felt even more connected to him. And his words and actions caused a memory to play in my mind.

"Damn, how do you do that?" he muttered with a smile on his face. Those lips I wanted to kiss again. For this man in front of me was the man I had come to care about a lot.

"Do what?" I asked him, completely unaware of what he meant.

With one hand, he took hold of my other hand and pressed it against his pounding heart. "Make my heart beat even faster every time I look at you," he said as his voice was a whisper against my mouth. I could feel the closeness of our faces.

It was the same action as then, with my hand placed upon his beating heart. My other hand grasped his hand, and I placed it upon my heart. "And this is what you do to me," I said, noticing a genuine smile form on his lips.

His lips brushed gently against mine before deepening into a passionate act.

My lips against his.

Lips against lips.

We were bound to each other, there was no doubt about it. The years of solitude had been worth every moment. For being there with Asher, reuniting with him, made me feel alive again.

"I'm sorry for everything I've done," Asher said, to my surprise.

His eyebrows lowered, and I could sense the regret in his eyes. I quickly shook my head and answered him, before he started to worry even more.

"You shouldn't apologize for anything. These past two years have been filled with healing for both of us. We needed these years apart to become even stronger together. You shouldn't apologize for actions you couldn't control. What you did to me was not okay, but I also know it was done because of your demons. You helped me help myself. Two years ago, it had been my turn to help you help yourself. We both have healed, that's the main thing. We can both start over now. And I know I won't want to start over without you by my side. Because you gave me life, Ash. Before you, I had nothing but the hope that my mother was still alive. After you, I had more than hope. I felt alive, I felt whole. After I met you, it felt like my heart was made whole again."

I witnessed his tears fall down his lips and wiped them away from his cheeks.

Asher opened his mouth to say something. "I love you, Aurora. You have no idea how much you mean to me. No idea what you have truly done for me. I am so grateful that I met you. I'm so lucky that Theodore wrote me that letter three years ago. Thank you for giving me a chance to get better for you. For all I ever wanted was for you to be safe, for you to feel loved by me. Because I love you so much. So fucking much," he said with all the tenderness and emotion he could muster.

I always knew he had a hard time expressing what he felt, but in his eyes, I saw it all. I was able to look into the depths of his soul as he stared into my eyes, seeing the way he felt. In his eyes, I saw the same love for me I felt for him. It was clear in his eyes that he regretted what he had done to me at first encounter. In his eyes, I could tell how much meeting me at Grimhill Manor for the first time meant to him. In his eyes, I could see how much he loved me.

In essence, that was all that mattered.

"And I love you, Ash."

As our lips met once again, I knew kissing him was not something I ever would tire of doing. The feeling brought life within me. He was the only person who could accomplish such a feat.

"Now we're going home, my love. Josephine has missed you, Draven, and Everlee, too. We are all here for you, caring about you. You are not alone in this anymore. Everything will be fine now."

As I gazed into his amber-colored eyes, I felt mesmerized. Those eyes had been on my mind ever since that day. Those eyes imprinted on my memory had given me comfort when all I felt was giving up.

"Everything will be fine now," Asher repeated.

And our hands collided with each other as if by habit. There was something so perfect about the fit between his hand and mine. The two of us looked into each other's eyes. We held hands in the way that made our pasts fade away, in the way the pasts shaped us into those strong people, and in the way it brought us to that unwavering sense of security and love.

The moment we walked out of the psychiatric institution hand in hand, I tilted my head to look into his eyes. As the sun shone down on us, both of us became the main characters. It was as if we were the only people close by, and all I could see in front of me was him. It was obvious from his eyes that he was relieved. I blinked to take his eyes into my soul, forever remembering them.

There was something about the way Asher looked at me that made my heart race. Before he spoke the words that would mean everything to me, he kissed me again. Because despite our past, together we had found a way to move forward, and with each other, we would become stronger.

For it was him and me. Asher and Aurora.

The only thing that meant something, and having him by my side was the cure I never knew I needed. It meant everything to me, to him, and to us when he spoke those words.

"We are finally free, my love. At last."

His Love For Her

Him

A few months later…

SHE HAD DONE IT. She had actually, truly done it. *For him, for her, for them.*

The darkness I had felt more times than I could count was still within me, but it was controllable. I had healed, just as she had. The things she had done for me would always remain in my memory, and I would always be grateful. Not only did she help me become better, she also saved me from myself.

The time at Rosewood Psychiatry had been hell, especially the first few months. A certain pain came with losing something so good, and I wasn't able to do anything about it. Because I had been out of memory, something I would always be ashamed of even though Aurora never let me feel bad about it. The time at the psychiatry had been good for me, for my headspace had been somewhere completely else that last day. It was a guilt that would always gnaw at me, a feeling that always told me what a bad person I was.

"How are you, my love?"

Aurora was sitting across from me in the reading room, with her legs prodded on mine. My thoughts were elsewhere, and I wasn't as present as I had wished. It was during moments like these that I wished I could go under the surface, disappear so I wouldn't have to feel all the guilt from that day. Avoid feeling the darkness within me, the darkness that consumed me. Things had gotten better since Rosewood but the tension was always there, and it was in moments like these that the anxiety became too much, to the point where I didn't know what to do with myself. Aurora always noticed when something was wrong with me, no matter how hard I tried to hide it. It was like a secret signal inside her was telling her to be extra attentive.

She got up from the chair she was sitting in and put away the book that was on her lap before walking over to me. Carefully she sat on my lap, straddling me with her legs around my waist. The look she gave me was one full of love, one that radiated everything she felt for me. One that made me remember I wasn't alone.

I had never been good with words, but Aurora knew me better than I knew myself, and she always knew what to do to make me feel better. Together we had battled our mental illnesses, and while there was still a long journey to travel ahead of us, we had come more than halfway there.

Just because we had each other.

Within seconds her soft lips were on mine, and for a moment I was able to forget all the feelings of anxiety within me. The kisses became more hectic, filled with feverish and passionate love.

It was with her that I belonged.

The time in Rosewood Psychiatry had been hell, but over the months I had become accustomed to it. I had known it was necessary for me to be there, and the therapy had helped me a lot.

She had actually done it.

The day I was discharged, I had been nervous. All the thoughts had been swirling in my head, all my insecurities had rose to the surface. Two years had lapsed with no contact between the two of us.

What if she didn't show up? What if she had given up on us? Abandoned me?

Thoughts had been racing through my mind, and paranoia had taken over. I had known that I couldn't expect her to show up since I had said some bad things to her in my fucked-up state of mind. The psychiatry didn't allow us any contact with the outside world, so it had been impossible to know if she still counted on me. If she still loved me as I loved her. Everyday was spent worrying about her not wanting me anymore, longing to feel her touch against mine, to feel the heat of her body.

Then she had appeared in the doorway, and all my worries flew out the window.

I still remembered the sense of relief I had felt when she was near, the wonderful smell of her rosy perfume finding its way into my nostrils. I still remembered how her soft lips had felt against mine, and at that moment, everything had felt perfect.

She had taken me home, but the place had been far from how I remembered it. And for that, I would be eternally grateful. She had taken the time to renovate the place, to make it as unlike my memories as possible. She had done it for me, for she wanted me to be happy.

And she made me so damn happy.

The taxi we had gone home with had taken us all the way to the gates, which were no longer there. When we had exited the car, she had grabbed my hand and given it a gentle squeeze to show her support.

The feeling had left me teary-eyed.

The house walls were no longer dark, but they were made of white stone. The shape of the house had changed during the renovation, and the windows had been replaced. It had been greener than I'd remembered it, and beautiful flowers of all colors had been lined up, creating a pathway to the door that had also been replaced.

I was so lucky to have that woman in my life. I had made it, I had fulfilled Theodore's last wish, and I had made her mine.

She had led us into my bedroom which had been transformed into our bedroom. The walls had been painted a darker beige color, a color that suited the room perfectly.

"I chose the color myself," Aurora had said and the smile on her face had been so big it had made me smile.

My old, uncomfortable bed had been replaced with a larger bed and the headboard was velvet like something a royal might have. Above the bed hung a white four-poster that surrounded the bed perfectly, and I'd smiled because it felt so Aurora-esque. That was her dream room, which instantly made it become mine, too. Because her room was my room, and I couldn't ask for anything better.

The moment she'd closed the door behind us, my lips had been on hers. It had been too long since I had held her in my arms, felt her touch on me, and I was desperate.

She'd looked like a goddess I wanted to worship.

My tongue had parted her lips, and I'd poured every drop of the tension I had felt during the two years that had passed into the kisses, bleeding them into her mouth which she lapped up as if she liked the flavor. Aurora had grabbed my hand, and put it above her heart just like I had done in those times before Rosewood. I'd felt her touch, the fast beating of her heart that had told me she had missed me. My teeth had nibbled against her lip, gracing down to bite, earning a low vibration from deep within her. Like a cat purring from pleasure.

We'd continued to kiss each other as we walked closer to the bed, and I had pushed her down on the soft mattress.

"What are you doing?" She had giggled out of surprise.

"Inaugurating *our* new bed," I'd said with a wink.

I had propped myself on my elbows and looked into her eyes filled with warmth before I had pressed my torso against her as I'd settled myself between her thighs.

"The skirt you're wearing today hasn't left my mind. You look absolutely gorgeous."

Lifting her skirt up with my hands, my fingers had skimmed up her thighs as I had planted kisses along her neck, causing her to shiver.

"Too bad I will have to rip it off," I had said before forcefully tugging it down, causing the hem to give off a ripping sound. "Damn, no panties?" I'd smirked at her, feeling myself growing harder by the second.

She had said nothing as I'd removed the belt from my pants, stepped out of them and lain above her again. While I had bucked my hips against her, she had opened her legs wider without me saying anything.

"Good girl," and her cheeks had reddened more, as if she was ashamed.

"It's been too long," she had whispered in my ear to which I had nodded. "I'm on birth control," she'd added with a shy smile.

Her words had made my heart beat way too fast, because I had known that moment would be more special knowing that I would get to feel her—all of her—around me without the risk of her getting pregnant.

"Never again will I be away from you."

At my words her limbs had wrapped around me as my cock had pressed against her swollen clit. I had lost myself to the moment as the turmoil inside of me had become a frantic whirlwind of emotions.

My fingers had dipped between our bodies, and I had worked my way to feel between her folds. Her wetness had become evident on my fingers, and a gasp had released from her as I had circled her clit. My heart had pumped erratically inside my rib cage while she'd bucked her hips against mine in a desperate manner to have me.

"Please, Asher," she'd begged and whimpered against my lips, and I had done the only thing that would ease her mind.

I had positioned myself against her folds, and her eyes had rolled back as the top of my cock had pressed against her. It had slid between her and the reward was the loud sounds of her moans, the most beautiful sound to ever come from her.

For two years I had been waiting for that moment, a moment I feared would never come. As long as I lived, I would savor the moment in my memory.

Words had never been something I had been good at, not words that mattered anyway, but words simply hadn't been necessary between the two of us.

We both had moaned simultaneously as I had continued to thrust into her, hitting her most sensitive spot and causing her moans to escalate. Every muscle in my body had been a thread ready to break as we'd worked each other towards release.

The sweet sound of her moan had drenched my ears as if in a sweet dream, and I had groaned when my stomach had tightened from excitement as her juices had soaked my cock with every withdrawal. Aurora had dug her nails into my back, as she'd arched her own from the pleasure I was giving her.

"Fuck," she had gritted out.

I'd worked my hips faster, driving deeper inside of her until she had been a whimpering and shaking mess underneath me, her eyes glistening with love and lust. The sound of her long and tortured moans had been enough to send me over the edge of ecstasy. Her inside had clenched around my cock, grabbed hold of it until bullets of pleasure shot through my every cell. We had both been panting messes when we had come down from our highs, and she had never looked more beautiful.

"Never again will I be away from you," I had whispered in her ear after I'd pulled out of her and placed her next to me, her eyes closing in pure wonder and safety.

WE SAT ON THE porch outside the house, overlooking the pond in the garden that was rearranged to be as unlike my childhood memories as possible. Aurora sat on my lap, head leaning against my neck, planting small kisses on my neck. The feeling made my cock harden, and her cheeks flushed when she noticed.

Her beautiful steel-blue eyes with those dark purple splashes in them looked at me with curiosity, but also intense emotion. She was happier, just like I was. She loved me, just like I loved her.

She had renovated the house for me, and no room looked the same. The walls had been repainted, the furniture had been replaced, and the rooms had been rearranged.

All that for my sake.

Because she loved me, just like I loved her.

If someone had told my teenage self that I would find the love of my life, he would have laughed and slapped that person. But it had happened.

Aurora had eased the demons inside of me and saved me from myself, as I had for her.

"Someday I will marry you," I whispered in her ear and her cheeks heated to a pink shade, one that made her all warm inside.

"With you, I'm finally free," she stated before she pressed her lips against mine.

And fuck if I wasn't free with her, too.

She was my everything, and so I uttered the words I had told her all those months ago, seeing her eyes glistening from the emotions.

"We are finally free, my love. At last."

The End

Did you like His Doll?

I would truly appreciate it if you could leave a review on both Amazon and Goodreads. As an independent author, your support is invaluable, not only because it makes more people aware of our work, but also because it provides the feedback we need to improve.

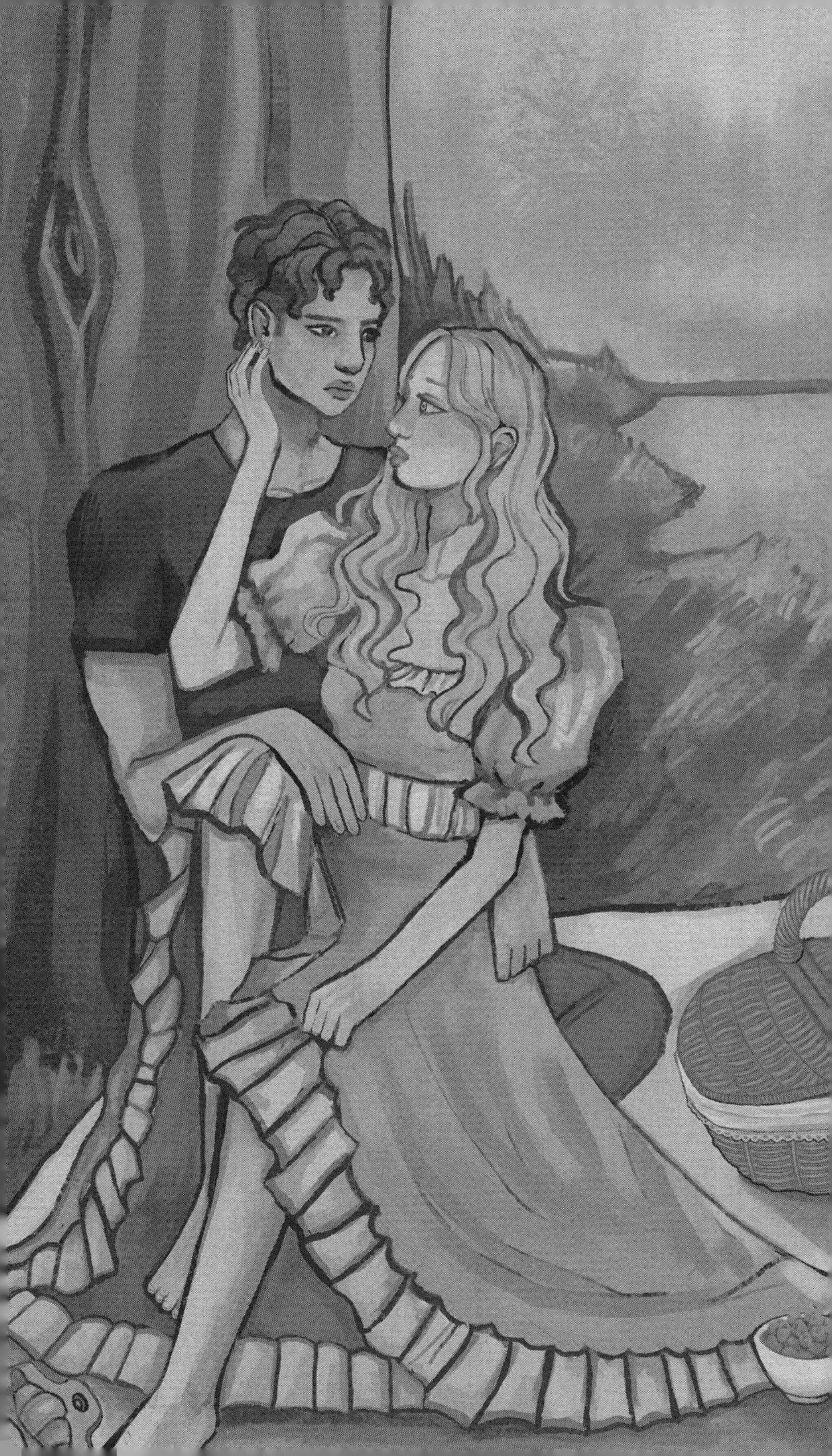

Acknowledgements

His Doll was written for the very first time back in 2019, and published as a fanfiction. Throughout the years and until July 2022, the story grew on me, a kind of craving that made me feel that the story deserved to be improved, polished, and changed. His Doll is the book that is truest to my heart because it became my distraction from reality during the most difficult and circumstantial months of my life.

There are many people I want to thank. First of all, I would like to give my thanks to my very first readers. Thank you for giving His Doll a chance and giving me the motivation to keep writing.

Thanks to all my readers for choosing to read this book. You are the light of my life and I will forever be grateful. If you have the time, please let me know, I love hearing from you.

To my mother who raised me into the person I am today. Thank you for everything you do for me and my sisters. You are the anchor of my life and I will forever love you.

To Sebastian, the love of my life. You've been there for me through it all, and even though you hate books and tease me about my obsession, your support has helped me a lot. Thank you for your patience with me and my many 'ignore everything and only focus on writing' nights. Even if you don't understand what I mean when I talk about my books, you still look at me with love in your eyes. Thank you for being here.

A huge thank you to Luísa who has been my alpha and beta reader and has read all versions of His Doll from the first drafts. Without you, this would not have happened. Thank you for becoming one of my closest friends even if you live hundreds of miles away. Thank you for supporting me with new ideas for the book, pushing me to keep writing, and giving me the motivation I didn't know I needed.

Thank you to my other beta reader, Natalia, for your support throughout the book and for the motivation you provided.

To Ebba who offered to proofread my book and made the art. Your help has been tremendous and I am so grateful.

Thank you to Wafiyah who supported me and gave me tips to calm my nerves. Publishing your first book is a big step but I always had you I could count on. I am so grateful.

Thank you to 3Crows Author Services for the wonderful cover and the patience you had with me. You truly are amazing.

ABOUT THE AUTHOR

Rainelyn is a dark romance writer and the author of the debut romance novel His Doll. She is an independently published author who is always striving to make her readers' hearts swell, and their love to grow for characters who straddle the line between good and bad. When she's not writing, she enjoys cuddling with her dog and partner, aka her real-life book boyfriend. She is a sucker for gaming, listening to music, and creating new book adventures.

Want to stalk her on social media?

Instagram: @authorrainelyn
Facebook: @authorrainelyn

To find all of my links including Newsletter, Website:

Printed in Great Britain
by Amazon

18439720R00239